sixth covenant

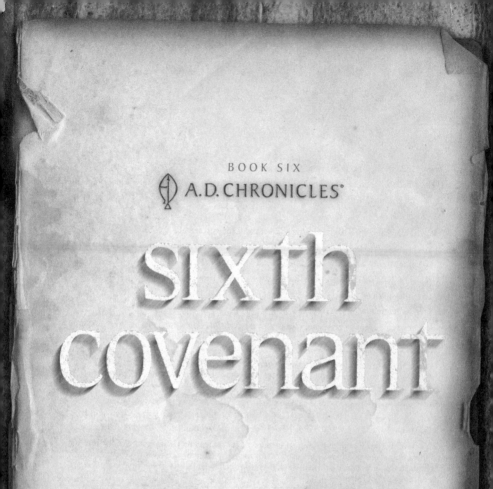

BOOK SIX

A.D. CHRONICLES®

sixth
covenant

Tyndale House Publishers, Inc.
Carol Stream, Illinois

BODIE & BROCK
THOENE

Visit Tyndale's exciting Web site at www.tyndale.com

TYNDALE and Tyndale's quill logo are registered trademarks of Tyndale House Publishers, Inc.

A.D. Chronicles and the fish design are registered trademarks of Bodie Thoene.

Sixth Covenant

A.D. Chronicles series designed by Rule 29, www.rule29.com

Interior designed by Dean H. Renninger

Edited by Ramona Cramer Tucker

This novel is a work of fiction. Names, characters, places, and incidents either are the product of the authors' imaginations or are used fictitiously. Any resemblance to actual events, locales, organizations, or persons, living or dead, is entirely coincidental and beyond the intent of either the authors or publisher.

Library of Congress Cataloging-in-Publication Data

Thoene, Bodie, date.
   Sixth covenant / Bodie & Brock Thoene.
      p. cm. — (A.D. chronicles ; bk. 6)
   ISBN-13: 978-0-8423-7521-4 (hc : alk. paper)
   ISBN-10: 0-8423-7521-X (hc : alk. paper)
   ISBN-13: 978-0-8423-7522-1 (pbk. : alk. paper)
   ISBN-10: 0-8423-7522-8 (pbk. : alk. paper)
   1. Jesus Christ—Fiction.   2. Bible. N.T.—History of Biblical events—Fiction.
3. Herod I, King of Judea, 73-4 B.C.—Fiction.   I. Thoene, Brock, date-   II. Title.
III. Title: 6th covenant.

   PS3570.H46S59 2007
   813'.54—dc22   2006035035

Printed in the United States of America

13 12 11 10 09 08 07

 7   6   5   4   3   2   1

With thanks to our dear friend,
copy editor Jan Pigott
Psalm 91

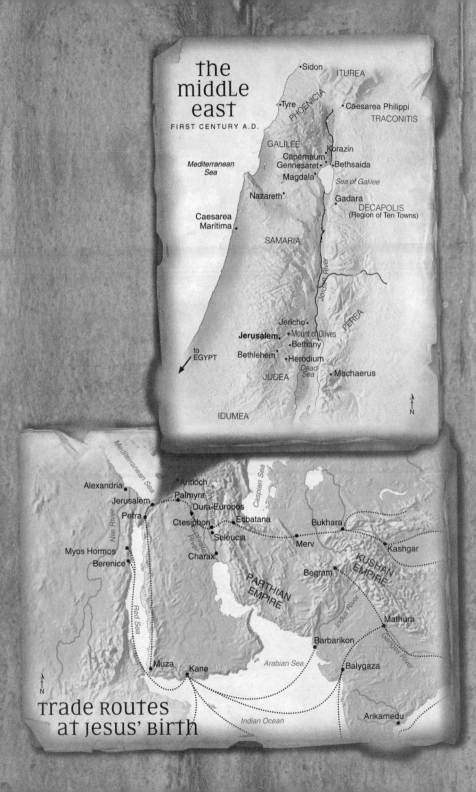

the middle east

FIRST CENTURY A.D.

Sidon
ITUREA
Tyre
Caesarea Philippi
PHOENICIA
TRACONITIS
GALILEE
Korazin
Capernaum
Gennesaret
Bethsaida
Magdala
Sea of Galilee
Mediterranean
Sea
Nazareth
Gadara
DECAPOLIS
(Region of Ten Towns)
Caesarea
Maritima
SAMARIA
Jordan River
PEREA
Jericho
Jerusalem
Mount of Olives
Bethany
to
EGYPT
Bethlehem
Herodium
Dead
Sea
Machaerus
JUDEA
IDUMEA
N

trade routes at jesus' birth

Mediterranean Sea
Caspian Sea
Alexandria
Antioch
Palmyra
Jerusalem
Dura-Europos
Petra
Ctesiphon
Ecbatana
Bukhara
Seleucia
Merv
Kashgar
Nile River
Myos Hormos
Charax
KUSHAN
EMPIRE
Berenice
Begram
PARTHIAN
EMPIRE
Indus River
Mathura
Red Sea
Ganges River
Barbarikon
Muza
Kane
Arabian Sea
Balygaza
Indian Ocean
Arikamedu
N

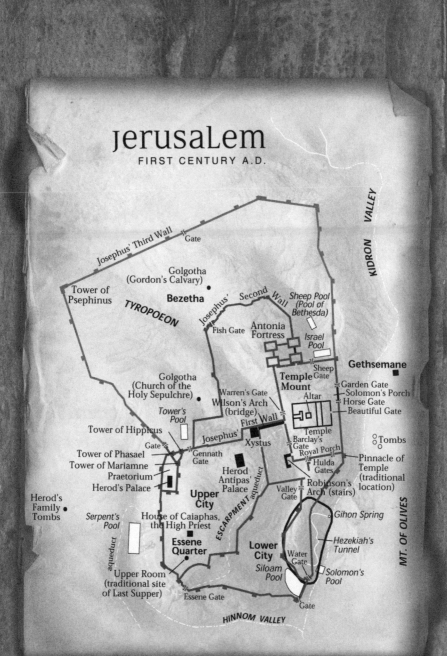

Jerusalem
FIRST CENTURY A.D.

KIDRON VALLEY

Josephus' Third Wall

Gate

Golgotha
(Gordon's Calvary)

Tower of
Psephinus

TYROPOEON

Bezetha

Josephus' Second Wall

Sheep Pool
(Pool of
Bethesda)

Fish Gate

Antonia
Fortress

Israel
Pool

Gethsemane

Golgotha
(Church of the
Holy Sepulchre)

Warren's Gate
Wilson's Arch
(bridge)

Tower's
Pool

Tower of Hippicus

Josephus' First Wall

Temple
Mount

Sheep
Gate

Altar

Garden Gate
Solomon's Porch
Horse Gate
Beautiful Gate

Gate

Xystus

Temple

Tombs

Tower of Phasael
Tower of Mariamne
Praetorium
Herod's Palace

Gennath
Gate

Barclay's
Gate
Royal Porch

Hulda
Gates

Pinnacle of
Temple
(traditional
location)

Herod's
Family
Tombs

Serpent's
Pool

Upper
City

Herod
Antipas'
Palace

ESCARPMENT

aqueduct

Valley
Gate

Robinson's
Arch (stairs)

Gihon Spring

House of Caiaphas,
the High Priest

aqueduct

Essene
Quarter

Lower
City

Water
Gate

Hezekiah's
Tunnel

MT. OF OLIVES

Upper Room
(traditional site
of Last Supper)

Siloam
Pool

Solomon's
Pool

Essene Gate

Gate

HINNOM VALLEY

PART I

On the eighth day, when it was time to circumcise Him,
He was named Yeshua, the name the angel had given
Him before He had been conceived.

LUKE 2:21

1

The newborn was wide-eyed and quiet in the manger of the lambing cave. He raised His right arm, stretching tiny fingers toward the face of Yosef.

Such a calm, serious baby! The midwives marveled.

Mary, His mother, rested in fresh straw beside the makeshift crib. Yosef, earthly guardian of the Messiah, lovingly studied the infant's features.

Let us make man in our own image.[1]

Nearby an ox and a donkey munched fodder. Lambs and ewes slept in pens, unperturbed by momentous events. The elapsed time since The Eternal Son of God first drew breath as a Son of Man on earth could be counted by a single hour and a handful of minutes. Yet His true age was beyond time—everlasting—and thus beyond human comprehension.

Israel had sought the Messiah like men search for gold in the heart of a great mountain. Stone by stone the earth was overturned, yet the Eternal Treasure remained locked away. So many generations had longed to see His face that now most suspected the Messiah was only a legend.

But on this last night of Hanukkah the final candle had been lit. *For unto us a son is given.*[2]

A single gold nugget, washed from the heavenly mountain by the will of God, glinted in the flickering light. Hope was reborn. Redemption, for which the suffering world longed, was fulfilled in the cry of a newborn. By design of Yahweh, The Eternal, this babe was the guarantee that Eternal Treasure awaited all who called upon His name!

Could it really be true, the shepherds wondered, that the Lord Almighty chose to express His love for Israel through the birth of a baby? Upon reflection it was decided that the best stories in Torah almost always began with the birth of a long-awaited son.

Yet tonight everything had seemed so ordinary: A young woman in labor urgently seeking shelter in a village packed with travelers. A baby boy born in the warmth of Beth-lehem's lambing cave. It was hard to see the miracle in that.

Yet it was a miracle. The Son of God reached out to the world from the womb of a virgin as the prophets foretold. The first bleating cry of His voice was heard from the midst of firstborn male lambs destined for Temple sacrifice. Perhaps one day it would all make sense, but tonight the meaning remained a puzzle to the participants in the drama.

The brilliant transitory star that shone as first herald of the birth of the true King of Israel faded and vanished. The sign of two bright planets, which had been dancing within the constellation of Israel for months, was now concealed behind a layer of clouds that closed in over the territory of Ephratha.

The chill of a coming snowstorm was in the air. Shepherds stamped their feet and stretched out hands to the watch fires in an effort to stay warm. The rhythm of life in Beth-lehem resumed. There were things to do. Tasks to accomplish.

After the birth, Rachel, midwife of Beth-lehem who tended Mary and her child, had called for more water to be drawn from the ancient well of David. It had been heated to bathe the Son of David. But Rachel had not considered God's covenant with King David as she'd washed the film of Mary's blood from the newborn's ruddy skin. The baby had simply been in need of washing, like all newborn babies.

Those shepherds who had seen and heard the angels from the pastures of Migdal Eder scanned the skies and hoped for more heavenly proclamations to resound from the hills of the terraced amphitheater of Beth-lehem.

Had anyone ever witnessed such glory before this night? What could it mean?

But instead of angel voices, the soft song of the infant's young mother drifted out to a dozen rough shepherds. "Hush, my babe, lie still and slumber. . . ."

So young, Mary was. Why was she chosen by Yahweh to give birth to the one the angels called Immanu'el, "God-with-us"?[3] Could it be?

It had not happened in the way anyone had imagined it. Mary of Nazareth. Betrothed wife of Yosef of Nazareth. Not much more than a girl and so . . . ordinary. Yet the angels had declared that this was the birth of the Son of David! This baby boy was the fulfillment of every prophecy in Torah. The hope of all generations in Israel!

Some herdsmen returned to the flocks. Others coalesced into small groups to discuss in awed whispers what they had witnessed.

Zadok, tall, rawboned shepherd of the Temple flocks of Beth-lehem, turned his back to the flame and looked heavenward. The supernatural glory that he and the others had witnessed tonight burned in his mind.

Would the angel armies come back? Zadok wondered. Would they appear in the Temple of Jerusalem at dawn during the morning sacrifice? Would the Most High God cast fire down from heaven to devour Boethus, King Herod's high priest? Would sulfur and brimstone consume the imposters who wrongly wore the priestly robes of Levites?

On this last night of Hanukkah, would the Temple at last be cleansed by Yahweh's final judgment? Would all the earth be purified by fire and made ready for the rule of the infant King, the long-awaited Son of David?

Zadok's brother-in-law, Rabbi Eliyahu, blinked at the embers. "Someone will have to write it down. Aye. Put the words down in a scroll just as we heard them."

Rabbi Eliyahu's pregnant wife, Havila, arms heaped with blankets and supplies, trekked up the path toward the limestone cave. Havila, broad-shouldered like her brother Zadok, smiled at her husband and brother but did not pause to chat. Her expression told them all was well.

"Women," Eliyahu remarked. "Called to deal with practical matters. They see to the needs of mother and child while we men are left out in the cold to ponder the meaning of it. I almost envy them."

"My sister, Havila, is enjoyin' herself." Zadok stamped his feet in an effort to warm them.

Lem, the red-haired father of five sons, rubbed his palms together. "Cold night, eh? You should write how cold it were, Eliyahu. The night Messiah was born? Standin' out here. Messiah picked the coldest, darkest night of the year to be born."

Zadok glanced upwards. "Havila will write a song about it. Mark my words. By mornin' we'll have a song about this night. Angels and flocks of sheep in the fields."

"And snow by mornin'." Lem wiped his nose on his sleeve.

Eliyahu nodded and nodded again as he stared into the cave. His voice broke as he groped for words. "One day we'll be old, and they'll ask us to tell the story of this night. 'Where were you?' they'll ask. 'When did you see the angels? What did they look like?'"

Zadok's lower lip jutted out. "Have you ever seen such skin as angel faces? All aglow, like . . . like the luster of pearls on the crown of a prince!"

Eliyahu agreed. "And people will ask us what they said, word for word. What did we hear? Were we afraid?"

Zadok's eyes widened. "Afraid? Aye, I was afraid. We'll none of us forget where we stood or sat when they came. Or what we first thought when the light began to grow."

Lem added, "Or the sound of it."

Eliyahu glanced again at the entrance to the stable. "Angel voices. The rumble of earth and sky. And I! There by chance, standing watch with you in the fields because Noah was sick and asked me to stand his watch for him. Think what I might have missed!"

Zadok pulled his cloak close around his ears. "I'd sleep on the hard ground the rest of my life to see such a sight again! And hear their singin' again! Aye! Nothin' like it in all the earth. Not ever. It's not a moment any of us will forget!"

Eliyahu warmed to the conversation. "Your Rachel delivered the baby. Think of it! My Havila came along to help."

"Our wives, Eliyahu. The long-desired babe not born in a palace. Not as we imagined Messiah would come. Our women washin' him in water drawn from David's Well and in Beth-lehem's wine. Just as our own sons were washed. Our women, rubbin' the royal Prince of God with salt . . . with their own hands. Anointin' the Messiah with olive oil from our scruffy olive trees. 'Tis an honor." Would such a role in the birth of the King of Israel one day result in a position in the King's court? Zadok wondered.

"Aye," Zadok continued. "When he's rulin' in Yerushalayim and David's throne is restored . . . all of us who live in Beth-lehem will have a story t' tell about the night he was born, I'll warrant. Our sons, our little boys—all of them close in age t' him—maybe they'll serve the King. Who can say?"

Lem huffed, "And write about Mordechai at the inn. How he turned them away. Denied a room for the birth of the King. Sent them instead to a lambin' cave!"

Zadok prodded the coals of the fire. "Aye. Stinkin' publican. When he sobers up, we'll have t' tell him. His unkindness may be long remembered. A disgrace the rest of his days."

For a time the men lapsed into silence. They searched the skies, wishing the angels might return. The clouds crowded in, covering the last of the stars. Zadok remembered the crowds at Mordechai's inn. Rough fellows some of them. Roman officials, political spies, and Herodian tax collectors.

The newborn cried from within the cave.

Eliyahu whispered hoarsely, "I'm glad it wasn't just me alone who saw it. And heard . . . what we all heard. They'd think we were crazy, except that there were twelve of us in the pastures who saw them."

Zadok craned his neck back and searched the underbelly of the clouds. "Not a star in sight now. Aye. Who'd believe our report if there weren't so many of us?"

"So . . . ordinary seeming," Eliyahu mused. "I mean the mother. Sixteen years old, I'd guess. And the father. A carpenter. Of the House of David. Here for the registration. It isn't at all the way I thought it would happen. If it wasn't for what we all saw . . ."

"A fine, handsome baby. Listen to that lusty voice. Strong, he is." Zadok tugged his inky black beard. "Big hands. Did y' see the hands on him?"

"Big." Lem spread his fingers wide.

The wind shifted, blowing smoke in Eliyahu's face. "He'll grow up to match the size."

"Hands such as the hands of the lad will grow big enough to grip old David's sword!" Lem imitated the swipe of a blade across his throat. "And you know whose dissipated head will be stuck on the pike above the Dung Gate? The Butcher King himself, if he should live so long!"

Eliyahu coughed. "They say Messiah will bring peace to Yerushalayim."

Lem replied, "Peace always follows war."

"The peace of death." Zadok noticed other shepherds within earshot. They raised their heads at Lem's jubilation like deer sensing danger.

Zadok nudged Lem hard and drew him aside. He lowered his voice to a gruff whisper. "Watch your tongue, Lem, if you want t' live. Don't speak of rebellion on such a holy night as this! You come close t' speakin' true treason in a world where even the birds may be employed as Herod's spies."

Lem's defiant grin faded. "I only meant to say . . ."

"No matter what you meant. You've got five sons and a good wife in Sharona. Don't be a fool. Remember my own brother Onias, crucified on the side of his house."

"Sure. Sure, Zadok. I was thinkin' our worries'll soon be over. The angels—"

"It'll be some years before this little one is big enough t' lead an army into Yerushalayim. When that day comes, the men of Beth-lehem will march, swords drawn, beneath his banner. Meanwhile there is a ruler in Israel who murdered his own sons. Like Ahab of old, he is. Do you think such a creature would stop at anythin' to hold power? Lem! There are twelve men here by the fire. And boys, too. What if they speak about what you said? The head of the king on a spike above Dung Gate? We're no more to Herod than a beetle creepin' across the floor. He would crush us and never bother t' wipe our guts from his shoe."

Lem blanched and tucked his head. "Who would repeat what I said?"

"It only takes one t' say the wrong thing in Yerushalayim. A slip of the tongue." Zadok clapped him on his shoulder. "Here's the way of it, Lem. There's no keepin' the news that a flock of angels appeared among us shepherds. We'll break if we can't speak of such a sight. And the birth of this babe. But mind what you say about present politics, eh? There is a certain danger t' all of us in this. And especially t' the baby, I'm thinkin'."

A dim oil lamp hung from a metal hook driven into the rock wall of the stable. The smell of livestock lingered, warm in the gloom.

Rachel, weary from the long and desperate struggle to stem the hemorrhage of the young mother, sat on an upturned box and leaned her back against the gate. Wrapping her woolen cloak tightly around her shoulders, she closed her eyes and sighed with relief.

Havila, cheeks chapped from the wind, entered the stall carrying a bowl of stones that had been heated in boiling water over the watch fire. Almost as tall as her brother Zadok, Havila was big-boned and broad-hipped, strong as a man. A hawklike nose between piercing brown eyes was her most prominent feature. Havila shifted the stones easily from one arm to the other as she towered over Rachel.

Rachel raised a finger to her lips, motioned toward Mary and the baby, and mouthed the word *asleep*.

"Brisk out there," Havila whispered in a surprisingly childlike voice that belied her appearance. "Most everyone gone home to bed. They say it will snow."

"These will keep the chill off." Rachel wrapped the stones in cloth and placed each beneath the thick fleeces that covered her patient and the newborn. Neither stirred.

"Cozy in here, eh?" Havila rubbed a hand over her obviously pregnant stomach. "It must be quite a shock for a baby to enter the cold, cruel world."

"A cold, dark night to be born," Rachel agreed, clucking her tongue. "And also a cold, dark night for a woman seven months pregnant to be out, eh? So, Havila, go home. Go back to bed."

"Grandmother's with the boys. I don't want to miss anything. Eliyahu says . . . such a night! What if angels come back and I sleep through it?"

"Angels have better sense than to go out a second time on such a night. So the baby is born. He looks like other babies. Eats like other babies. Needs washed and changed like other babies. I think heaven has said all it has to say about the wee King of Israel until he grows up."

"I'm not tired."

"Tell your husband that *Rachel* says he should walk you home, eh?"

"Eliyahu wants to stay. He and Zadok. Frozen on the back side and toasted on the front by the bonfire. Almost the only ones still here." Havila gazed down at the mound of fleeces that all but concealed Mary and the baby. "What a night."

"A few hours in bed will do wonders for you. Look, even Yosef, her husband, is asleep. Everyone asleep but you and I. The sheep have more sense than us. And I'll need your help tomorrow. Please, Havila. Be sensible."

Havila frowned. "You can manage?"

"I can manage if you'll stop thinking of things to do. I'll sleep here if you'll just go home. There'll be plenty of work come morning when we bring them to the house. You're not near enough to full term to take chances with early labor. How many trips have you made back and forth from the house and the well and carrying the warming stones?"

"Before I go to bed, I'll tend the fire in the birthing room."

"Fine. You do that."

"It will be nice and warm by morning. And I'll have breakfast ready. Dawn?"

"Yes. Just before sunrise, which is not so long. We'll be ready. Send Lem and Yoachim down in the morning. Tell them to bring the stretcher. We'll need their help to carry her to the house."

With a cheerful glance at the new mother, Havila departed.

Rachel resumed her perch on the box and nodded off. In her half slumber, she considered the palace of King Herod and the birthing of Herodian princes upon jewel-encrusted beds. The Eternal must have a sense of humor to bring forth His Son in a sheep pen!

King Herod awoke from another nightmare. His bedclothes were drenched with sweat despite the chilly air. His thin, stringy hair was plastered against his skull. His lips moved in an apparent attempt to cry out, but all that emerged was a hoarse rasp. One set of the king's gnarled fingers plucked convulsively at his sleeping silks while the other went round his uncooperative throat.

There were no servants in attendance, and the Caesarea Maritima bedchamber was almost pitch-black. Herod's rheumy eyes darted fearfully about the room but found no physical counterparts to the accusing figures of his dreams.

"Do not torture me, Mariamne!" he croaked. "Alex. Ari."

The cry of a distant watchman announcing the watch echoed into the tall, south-facing window. A few stars glimmered in the narrow, arched opening. Herod's frantic breathing slowed at last. The king relaxed as his grip on reality returned.

The king's palace on the seacoast of the Roman province of Judea was favorably sited to enjoy the Mediterranean breezes. But tonight, a few days before the Roman New Year, in the twentieth year of Roman emperor Caesar Augustus, there was no breeze. An especially low tide had caused the sea to desert the harbor. The stench of rotting fish and seaweed, mingled with the rank odor of the city's sewage, assaulted Herod's nostrils.

It was the smell of death.

The king had recently abandoned his capital, Jerusalem, in order to escape the Holy City's winter. But here in Caesarea, it seemed, not only did chills creep into Herod's bones, they lay alongside him as he slept.

Even now a feathery mist crept in at the window like a plumed serpent. Fog clung to the walls and draperies.

Near the top of Herod's window, The Guardian, blue-white Sirius, peered in.

Herod stared at it. The rising vapors first hid, next displayed, then encircled the gleaming star. A second spiral of fog followed the first, then a third. Branching, recombining, forking once more, floating mist hesitated over the foot of the king's bed before swooping into the corners of the room. Herod, terrified again, gave a convulsive cry. "No! Leave me alone!"

From beneath a cushion he produced a dagger. With it he slashed at the air and bellowed for his guards. "I am the king! I am the *only* king of the Jews," he snarled to the empty room. "Me! I am the king. No one can have my throne! Guards! Guards!"

Herod again babbled the names of the wife he had executed twenty years earlier and of her sons, only lately dispatched. He shrank from the encircling mist as if real arms reached toward him. "Leave me alone. Leave me," he sobbed, crouching beside the bed and feebly waving the knife.

It was there Hermes, his chief bodyguard, found him.

CHAPTER 2

The town of Tadmor marked the border crossing between Roman-controlled Syria and the lands of Parthia. From here Parthia stretched eastward for two thousand miles. The area had been fought over repeatedly for several millennia past, but at present an uneasy truce prevailed. Trade was, for the moment, more profitable than warfare. Tadmor's caravansary boasted silk and spice merchants going westward. The Roman Empire's traders spoke silver and ivory in reply.

Melchior of Ecbatana was not a merchant of any kind; nevertheless he was part of a caravan bound toward the Mediterranean. Standing on a hilltop south of the city, he saw its torches but could not see into the inky blackness of the nearby canyon. Even so, the aroma of rotten eggs told him he was near the town's spring of precious but sulfurous water. The stream belching out of the volcanic peaks had founded Tadmor's existence eons earlier and explained its importance still.

Not that the creek mattered this year. There had been almost continuous rain for the past week until tonight, when the heavens cleared.

Judging by the sky, it was a few hours before dawn, on this date just after the winter solstice. The figure of Orion the Hunter already reached into the western horizon with one arm. Orion's head, belt, and sword would soon follow.

Twenty-six-year-old Melchior was court astronomer to King Phraates of Parthia. For the better part of a year Melchior and his mentor, Old Balthasar, had observed a series of celestial events never before recorded.

Turning about to face the place where the sun would eventually rise, Melchior studied the constellation of The Virgin. None of the so-called stars were visible now. Nine months previously though, Mars—called by the Jews Ma'Adim, or The Adam—had nestled close to the heart of The Virgin, next to Porrima, The Star of Atonement.

It was a sign, Old Balthasar had said. It was a reminder that the One True God, Yahweh, had not forgotten His covenants with His people.

And that had been only the beginning of the wonders.

Since then Jupiter—which the Jews named Tzadik, The Righteous— had carried on a complex dance with Saturn—Shabbatai, The Lord of the Sabbath. The two planets had combined and recombined three times between May and December. What was more, those two bright lights spent all three seasons preceding this winter enmeshed in the sign of The Two Fish. The Two Fish, Old Balthasar instructed, was where events related to the Jews were written in the sky.

Nor was the triple conjunction of Jupiter and Saturn the sum of all the remarkable occurrences. Indeed, sign had followed sign, including an eclipse of The Lord of the Sabbath by the Holy Spirit, the moon.

To Old Balthasar, himself a Jew, and Melchior, a Gentile follower of Yahweh, God of the Jews, the parade of sights in the heavens fore-told a momentous event. "A Messiah, a Deliverer, will be born to the Jews, and his coming will bless all the nations," Balthasar had taught his protégé.

Which is what had brought Melchior and Old Balthasar and others to this place and this night. Believing that the prophecy "The star that will arise out of Jacob"[4] was linked to Isaiah's words about the com-ing of Immanu'el,[5] Old Balthasar had set out on a quest to meet the heaven-sent King.

They had already traversed the Zagros Mountains and the Plains of Mesopotamia. Then here, just before midnight, as The Righteous and The Lord of the Sabbath were setting, a miraculous vision, surpassing all previous ones, occurred. Low in the west a third evanescent star had appeared between the two planets—a star brighter than either, bright as a flame of fire. Old Balthasar likened the vision to the fire of Yahweh appearing between the cherubim atop the Ark of the Covenant.

"Messiah has been born. He's alive *now*," asserted the older man.

Their traveling companion, a magoi of the Zoroastrian faith from the Far East, Gaspar by name, concurred.

Melchior did not know enough Jewish Scripture to vouch for that claim himself, but he did not need to. The golden light in tonight's sky had been the culmination of the year's revelations. It must be true. The predictions of Mosheh the Lawgiver and those of the prophets Dani'el, Isaias, and others aligned with the signs in the heavens.

It had to be so!

Reviewing all the occurrences of the last nine months kept Melchior atop the hill instead of inside his tent, asleep. What would happen now to their quest to find and worship the newborn King of the Jews? If this night's display had been the last, how would they find Him?

Old Balthasar spoke with assurance that by the time the caravan reached Jerusalem, everyone would know of Messiah's birth. They had only to go there and ask.

Melchior wanted to believe it to be true. But when he finally headed toward his bed, doubts and worries refused to obey his command for them to sink into the west like Orion.

Walking quietly so as not to disturb the slumbering encampment, Melchior descended from the hill. As he entered the shadowed lane between his tent and another, he was startled to hear someone whisper his name. "Who's there?" he hissed, grasping the hilt of a short dagger at his belt.

"Esther."

A figure emerged from the deeper gloom beneath the canvas awning at the entry to Old Balthasar's lodging. It was the old man's eighteen-year-old granddaughter.

"What's wrong? Has he gotten worse?" Melchior asked.

Balthasar had contracted a lung ailment during the damp trek. Because of Balthasar's age, Esther fretted over his illness, even though he now rested in a luxurious tent belonging to their comrade Prince Aretas of Parthia. Gaspar, the magoi, had provided costly, sweet-smelling frankincense that Esther used in steam to ease her grandfather's coughing and tightness of chest.

Had tonight's midnight excursion to view the miraculous star harmed the old man?

"No," Esther assured Melchior, "he's resting well. He was very excited, and it was hard for him to drop off. But now his breath doesn't rasp, and he smiles in his sleep."

Melchior could not prevent a grin of his own. The mental picture of Old Balthasar being so secure in his belief in Messiah's arrival pleased Melchior. "But why are you awake? It's not safe for you to walk around the camp unaccompanied."

"I haven't been away. Prince Aretas told me you were off watching the stars and I . . . I waited for you to return."

Melchior's heart began pounding again, but it was from fear of a different kind. For a long time he had watched Esther mature into young womanhood. But it was only within the last year that he had fallen deeply in love with the raven-haired beauty with the tawny skin.

But he—not a Jew by birth and pale of skin, hair, and eyes—had been afraid to ask her grandfather for her hand. And she . . . how did she feel about him? Was he still just a companion with whom she had grown up?

"Are there more signs in the sky?" Esther asked.

Melchior reached for her arm. "Are you bundled up? It's freezing out here." The brief touch told him she was wreathed in fleece over a heavy cloak. Then, "Come with me."

Without reascending the slope, Melchior led Esther a short distance to a lane with a clear view south and east. Facing her away from the torchlight, he instructed, "Wait a moment. Your eyes will adjust to the dark."

"It's beautiful!" she exclaimed after a minute. "The night is like crystal! The stars seem so close!"

Standing behind Esther, Melchior pointed upward. "Do you see where that one curving set of stars connects to others that make a straight line?"

"Like a sickle and its handle? Yes, I see it."

"Just so. That's the head of Aryeh, The Lion of Judah. And that bright star at the base of the handle? The Romans call it Regulus, The Little King. Your grandfather says it relates to a prophecy about the Messiah sitting at the right hand of the Almighty until all his enemies are under his feet."

"But not tonight," Esther returned. "Tonight he's just a baby. Tonight he's sleeping beside his mother."

It was a surprising thought. All along Melchior had studied the signs in the heavens in their grandeur and majesty. His thoughts had related to giving proper homage to a heavenly ruler, a figure of power and glory. But Esther was right. All those portents about the coming King pointed to . . . a child?

"A baby," Esther repeated, as if reading Melchior's thoughts. "Do you suppose those who are caring for him are looking at the stars, just as we are, and wondering what his future holds? How will he go from The Little King to 'his enemies under his feet'? What can it all mean?"

Esther leaned back against Melchior's chest. "And we are going to see him," she murmured.

They stood that way for a long time. Finally Melchior put his hands on her shoulders and turned her to face him. "Together," he said.

When Esther tilted her chin upward, the starlight sparkled in her eyes. Melchior felt her warmth against his cheek . . . inhaled the sweetness of frankincense in her hair. "I . . . ," he said. "We . . ."

Stretching up on tiptoe, Esther kissed him on the lips. Then, ducking under his arm, she darted back toward her grandfather's tent.

Melchior stood, unmoving, staring after her, thoughts and emotions all jumbled together. Finally entering his own shelter, he lay down.

But he did not go to sleep until the stars had fled from the sky. Until the glow of the first dawn of a new era climbed round the corner of the world.

Obi, the adopted infant of Rachel and Zadok, slumbered in his crib. Though the sun was not up, the ebony-skinned baby was the only one in the house who was not wide-awake. Two-and-a-half-year-old Enoch, one-year-old Samu'el, and their one-and-a-half-year-old cousin, Dan, played noisily on the sheepskin rug. Grandmother had awakened them an hour earlier to ask which of them had swallowed the Hanukkah prize.

None of the three could provide her with an answer.

Grandmother, who was half the size of Havila, leaned on the broom and surveyed the small pyramid of dirt and ash on the stone floor. She shook her head slowly from side to side and sucked her gums in consternation.

Havila was out of ideas.

The old woman screwed up her face at the piercing squeal of little boys playing on the rug. "Half deaf I may be, but I hear them all the same. And I tell ye one of them has et it. Either your boy, Dan . . . see him creep like a beetle. Eighteen months old and already with an eye for gold! I suspect him in this! At that age they eat anythin' they find on the ground. Makes no difference what they find. Put it in their mouths, loll it about, and down it goes. If not your boy, Dan, then Enoch or Samu'el has done it. There's no place else it could be but swallowed down the gullet of a kid."

Fists planted on wide hips, Havila studied the clean-swept pavers. "A gold coin, you say? An old Hasmonean twenty drachma?"

"Minted in the days of the true kings of Israel descended from the Maccabees! Before the slime of Rome oozed in and brought Herod with it," Grandmother proclaimed. "Minted when Herod's father was still slave to a priest in the Temple of Apollo. Last of my old, old dowry coins. And I thought, being so old as I am, this may well be my last Hanukkah and I should bestow it. And there being only one coin and there being two of you girls? Rachel and Havila. How could I choose? I thought I would give it to whichever one of the two of you found it after Hanukkah supper. But then supper came and went and Sharona's eldest boy arrived at the door. . . . What's his name?"

"Jesse," Havila replied.

"Aye. Jesse! Sharona and Lem's oldest boy. Five of them, all boys! Who can remember a name? A good boy. Looks like his father, Lem. They all five look like Lem. None look like poor Sharona. Wild red hair like a cock's comb. Every woman needs at least one daughter . . . but where was I?"

Grandmother waved her bony hand as if to swat down the swarm of thoughts that were flying from her. "Oh yes! Then the boy, Lem's oldest, comes to the door . . . the excitement . . . all that goin' on in the lambin' barn. Rachel rushin' out the door to tend to the birth . . . to deliver the babe. You boilin' water and the like. Well, I forgot to have the contest. I forgot to have you search for the coin. Fifty-seven years I've kept it safe, and now it's gone!"

Enoch let out a shriek as Samu'el reached for his wooden cow.

"Grandmother, maybe you've forgotten where you hid it, eh?" Havila consoled.

"Enoch has et it, I tell ye! Or Samu'el." Grandmother cocked a disapproving eye at Dan, who crawled eagerly toward the heap of dust as if it were honey on porridge. "Or your own little Dan? We can hope we'll find it in a day or so when it passes out t'other end of one of these boys. Unless it gets stuck forever. We'll have to be on our watch. The only one we know for a certain is not guilty is little Obi. Still too young to eat things of value."

Havila inhaled and asked patiently, "Again. How was the coin lost, Grandmother?"

"As I said, it was hid—not lost. For Hanukkah!"

"Where did you hide it?"

Grandmother appeared insulted by the question. "How am I to remember such things, eh? It was hid—that's all."

"Well hid." Havila scanned the room that had been swept a dozen times. Every stick of sparse furniture had been moved. Every crack and crevice had been scrutinized. The rafters, hung with dried lavender, had been searched.

"Aye. And now there's a Prince and his mother in Beth-lehem! A Prince! Here! A once-in-a-lifetime event, if you ask me. Or less than once in a lifetime. Never again in my lifetime. A Prince of David comin' to stay. The honor of it! Though why a Prince would come here to stay, I can't say. All the same, he's here, and I have no gift. Think of it! Last of my gold dowry coins, devoured by a child!"

Havila patted the old woman. "Almost sunup. They'll be bringing the mother and baby soon. We'd best finish tidying up."

"The floor is clean enough." Grandmother propped the broom in the corner.

"The birthing room cozy and warm. Bread is baked. Eggs boiled."

"A twenty-drachma gold piece! Hasmonean. A fitting gift for David's Son." Grandmother turned slowly around. She stared resentfully at the boys. "And one of them has et it for breakfast."

The sun rose as tendrils of mist uncurled like living vines up the ravines from the valley floor.

Yosef slept on a mound of hay outside the birthing pen where Mary and the baby rested. The stirring of animals mingled with pleasant whispers. He thought he heard Mary singing softly, as if she were very near. Was he dreaming?

Someone tapped his shoulder. "Yosef?"

Opening his eyes in the dim light of the cave, he could make out the features of Rachel stooping over him. His sword was at his side. The details of the long night returned in a flood. *The baby!* How strange it seemed that the miracle of birth, like death, brought with it a sense of disbelief for those who witnessed it.

Rachel was smiling. "Yosef? Almost morning."

The First Morning!

"Is . . . everything all right? Is Mary . . . the baby . . . are they well?" He sat up and rubbed his eyes with the back of his hand.

"Shalom, Yosef. All is well."

"Praise be to The Eternal. Shalom." Straw clung to hair and beard. Outside, in the gray light of predawn, a group of four hearty men waited, stamping their feet with the cold. They had brought a stretcher to carry Mary and her child like those priests of old who had carried the Holy Ark in the days of Mosheh.[6]

Yosef studied the curtain of tattered blankets that sequestered the Living Presence of God's Anointed and His mother within.

Morning prayers flowed silently through Yosef's mind with words he had recited every morning of his conscious life. *How goodly, Jacob, are your tents. Israel, your abodes. O Adonai! I love your dwelling place, whereupon your glory rests. There I humbly bow the knee before the Lord, my Maker. I offer prayer in time of grace, Eternal! Unto you, O Yahweh! Ever merciful, respond with true salvation!*

At the rising of the sun this very day, the rising prayers of every righteous Jew since Father Abraham had been answered!

The merciful God of Jacob has responded at last. True Salvation, Yeshua, is born to be King in Israel!

Yosef found his voice and asked Rachel, "Mary will be well again now?"

"Soon. Recovered enough to be moved from the stable, praise be to The Eternal. Her bleeding has slowed. But she's not strong enough to walk the distance on her own. We'll carry her and the baby to the house. Everyone's gone home but a few. Breakfast is waiting at the house."

With a crook of her finger Rachel motioned for the men to enter but not to advance farther than the low overhang of the entrance. Yosef recognized Zadok the Shepherd and Eliyahu the Rabbi among them. Shepherds of the Temple flock were of the priestly tribe of Levi. It was right, Yosef thought, that these would bear the mother and child to the home of Rachel and Zadok.

Yosef rose and brushed his clothes as Rachel parted the curtain. All heads nodded in unison at the sight of Mary, cradling the promised King of Israel in her arms.

Mary, covered by a double fleece, reclined on the straw. After glancing down at the infant, she lifted a beaming face to Yosef. "Good morning, Yosef. He's a good baby. Exceptionally good, Rachel tells me. He's had his breakfast. See? Look! He's asleep."

You are Lord of All the Angel Armies from all eternity, Yosef thought, *yet you rest in the arms of your earthly mother! Look: a tiny face turned toward a mother's breast. From before time, you chose her to carry you; to bear you in suffering; to love, protect, and care for you. What am I to learn, O Lord, from your willingness to be vulnerable? What is the lesson, Sovereign Lord, that you trust us with the life of your Son before we have learned to trust you with our lives? What must the eyes of my heart see in this true vision by which you reveal your eternal attributes? What must I learn on your first morning living among us as a human child?*

The color had returned to Mary's cheeks, Yosef noted, but she was clearly exhausted from the long night. What a failure he was in his first assignment as caretaker of the Messiah and His mother!

Yosef stammered, "I-I'm so glad, Mary. I was worried. I mean, I'm just . . . this is not what I intended. . . . I'm so sorry." He raised his arms and let them fall in a gesture of helplessness.

"It's as it should be." She smiled and tugged the swaddling cloth close around the baby's face. "Always meant to be." She motioned for Yosef to come close and grasped his hand, pulling him down beside her. "A fine stable. A night to remember! We'll laugh about it one day when we tell the story!"

Rachel hung back and let the curtain fall, allowing them a moment of privacy.

Meant to be? Was it true? Yosef wondered. *Messiah born in a sheep pen?*

He brushed his lips lightly over Mary's brow. Struck by the nearness of the little one, he was overcome with awe. He reached out to touch the newborn's head . . . then remembered who the baby was and drew back.

"Go ahead," Mary urged.

"He's sleeping."

"Babies sleep. Don't be afraid. Touch his cheek." She hummed as she stroked the newborn's face. He did not stir but seemed content. "So soft. Yosef, don't you know? It's why he was born. Why he chose to live with us. He's here, like this, because you and I—everyone, I think—couldn't imagine what he was really like." She kissed the baby's head. "You see it, don't you?"

Blessed are you, O Adonai! How could we approach you as you were in heaven—The Eternal Light, God's Son—so lofty and holy and beyond ourselves! Before this day our minds could not grasp you!

Mary's explanation tumbled out. "I've thought about it a lot. The why of it all. I knew the minute I saw his sweet face, looked in his eyes. He came to earth the same way we all have come. He came so you and I can see him and hear his voice and, yes, love him. He came to live in our family so we can learn how a family is meant to live. So we can care for his needs for a while and love him as our own child and let him love us—mother and father, aunts, uncles, and cousins—his family, you know? And I think he will show us how to forgive one another too. He came to us like this so we can rock him gently in our arms and sing to him. And you will carry him on your shoulders and never, never be afraid of him again."

Instead of angel songs like the night before, the morning was filled with a discordant chorus of hungry sheep milling in the pens. The hymn of the Temple flocks—ten thousand voices strong—swept over Beth-lehem like a tide. Bass and treble, hungry, impatient, angry, lost, found—the herds sang welcome to Israel's Shepherd-King. Havila's sweet voice added lyrics to the world's welcome.

The four men who carried the litter were used to the din. After a lifetime in Beth-lehem, they barely noticed the uproar. But the baby's unfocused eyes were attentive during these first few steps from the lambing cave toward the City of David. Blinking at the gray light, He drank in His first impression of the world of mankind. Lips pursed, as if murmuring a silent *oooh!* He glanced at the red stripe of Yosef's cloak; then the blue border of Mary's blanket caught His attention. The distant barking of a sheepdog caused Him to look up, up . . . searching . . . where? Where did that sound come from? He blinked rapidly at the stormy sky as the litter swayed like a boat, then closed His eyes and was asleep.

"Poor little lad," Mary cooed and kissed His warmly wrapped head. "The cave was dim and cozy. But this light. The noise of the world. So much suddenly. Almost too much to take in."

Her face was illuminated with love. Lips curved in a smile as her breath warmed the baby's cheek, keeping the chill from touching Him.

Yosef, overwhelmed by the tender intensity of her gesture, looked away and wiped his eyes.

Blessed are you, O Lord! Sweet one, innocent one, so vulnerable. It is you who will teach the heart of every mother since Eve to love her child more than she loves her own life. Just as you show your love for us.

The stretcher was made of a wool carpet suspended from long poles. The midwife walked ahead, scouring the path and issuing warnings: "It's rocky here! A rut there! Watch your step!"

The bearers must not stumble or jostle their precious cargo.

The Eternal bless and preserve you![7]

Yosef followed alongside. Wind—weighted with the aromas of earth, damp animals, and dung—stirred his cloak. Baby and mother were protected from the elements by layers of soft, clean fleece.

The Eternal cause His countenance to shine upon you, and be gracious unto you![8]

The first snowflake of winter spiraled downward, landing on the baby's brow as He nestled in the crook of Mary's arm. At the sensation of cold, tiny lashes fluttered. Mary brushed away the crystal with her thumb, pulled Him closer, and spread her fingers to shield His face beneath the palm of her hand.

He who dwells in the shelter of the Most High will rest in the shadow of the Almighty.[9]

O Lord! How effortlessly she protects him even from the snowflake. Is this the way you protect us?

He will cover you with His feathers, and under His wings you will find refuge. His faithfulness will be your shield and rampart. You will not fear.[10]

Yosef silently recited the morning prayers. His heart rejoiced as comprehension of God's message unfolded like successive waves against a desolate shore. *In every gesture of her love for this little one . . . this One . . . your beloved Son . . . O Lord! Through a mother's heart, you reveal how much you love your children!*

Only several short strides separated the birthing cottage and the back door of Rachel and Zadok's home. An arbor covered the graveled path between the two structures. The convenience of the arrangement enabled Rachel to remain at home and still keep her patients, near to full term, under her watchful care.

The structure had been a house generations before anyone could remember. Some said the north and east walls were all that remained of the ancient home where David had grown up. Rachel liked the legend. Pregnant women who lived here at the end of their confinement took comfort in the thought that the walls retained some memory of the shepherd boy who grew up to be king of Israel. They touched the rough stones and imagined him singing psalms to the Lord. Many generations of women from Beth-lehem had given birth here. It was a sort of sacred place, redolent with the pathos and joy that accompany the birth of children.

This year the room had been occupied year-round by new mothers. Beth-lehem had been blessed with more baby boys than anyone could remember. One woman would give birth, remain under Rachel's and Havila's care for seven days, present her child for circumcision on the eighth day, then return home. Within a few days, the next patient would move in. Fortunately the cottage had been vacated three weeks before Mary and Yosef arrived. Except for Havila's delivery date, still two months away, no babies were due until late spring.

David's house was, in everyone's opinion, the perfect dwelling place for Mary, Yosef, and the future Deliverer of Israel.

The space consisted of only one room with tall ceilings, built of thick limestone blocks. Lavender hung from the rafters in profusion as defense against the stink of the vast flocks of sheep and goats. Windows were high, allowing heat to escape in the summer while thick shutters kept out the winds of winter. Stone floors were covered with sheep-fleece rugs that were rolled up once a woman's labor began. Light was provided by two oil lamps set in niches in the walls. A curtained alcove served as the water closet. A fire crackled on the smoke-blackened hearth built into the oldest part of the north wall. Furnishings consisted of a table, a cabinet for Rachel's supplies, a single bed on each of three walls, a birthing stool, and a plain acacia-wood cradle.

"Shalom be upon you and your family." Mary sighed with relief and sank stiffly onto the bed nearest the water closet. Yosef, extraordinarily awkward and in the way, was banished by Rachel into the main house to breakfast with Zadok and the men.

The midwife moved the cradle within Mary's reach, took the slumbering baby from her arms, and placed Him in His bed.

"Life makes these little ones very sleepy at first." Rachel tugged the blanket up around His chin.

"Me too. I don't know that I have ever been so tired."

"A few days. Rest. Quiet. Good food. You'll be good as new by the time he's circumcised." Rachel stroked the young woman's thick chestnut hair that fanned out on the cushion. It was tangled. Bits of straw remained as evidence of the difficult night. "How old are you, Mary?"

"Sixteen years."

"Sixteen."

"My mother will want to know."

"Can you write?"

"Yes."

"I'll fetch you parchment. There are so many pilgrims heading north through the Galil. Someone will carry a letter home for you."

"I always imagined she would be here when the time came."

Rachel paused, then asked quietly, "Mary? Our men say . . . they told us women last night . . . they saw . . . angels."

Mary did not reply but turned her face toward the cradle and rested her fingers on the top rim. Then she touched the well-worn stones of David's house.

A resolute peace in the gesture conveyed to Rachel that the young mother was not surprised that angels had come to announce the birth of her son. Son of David. Son of the Most High.

Rachel studied the infant . . . red-faced, thick dark hair. She remembered His spindly limbs, big belly with an inch of umbilical cord tied off as she had bathed Him. He looked so ordinary, so like any baby born in Beth-lehem since the time of David. And yet . . .

Mary smiled and said hoarsely, "I'll be glad for a bath."

Rachel inclined her head toward the alcove. "A bath will do wonders. But you mustn't get up on your own. Another day at least. Then I'll help you bathe all over. For now I'll bring a basin of warm water before breakfast. We'll wash and plait your hair. You'll be amazed at the difference that will make. I'm going to fetch your breakfast now. You mustn't fall asleep until you've had bread and oxtail soup. Lots of fluids will bring your milk in strong. Havila worked much of the night to get everything ready for you."

Mary blinked at the snow falling softly outside the window. "So good here. Warm. Clean. Tell Havila how much it means to me . . . to us. How can we thank you all? Especially you, Rachel. You stayed with me . . . with us . . . all night in the barn. Every time I opened my eyes, there you were. Like an angel here on earth to help me."

Rachel laughed and waved away the compliment. "I may vanish for a bit later, never fear. Just stay awake a little while longer. The worst is over. You'll eat. The baby will eat. I'll eat. A good wash and we'll all get some rest, eh?" She patted the end of a rope attached above Mary's bed. "If you need anything, pull this. A bell will ring inside my house, and I'll come."

The Judean sky, so clear and vibrant with stars the night before, was now a solid mass of dark clouds. As Zadok and Eliyahu trudged along, more tiny snowflakes fell. The temperature dropped noticeably with each passing minute.

Zadok tugged his cloak more firmly around his shoulders and under his chin. His frosty breath exploded in a counterpoint to each emphatic stamp of his staff.

Eliyahu trotted two steps to Zadok's one in order to keep up.

"Do y' see this storm?" Zadok waved his staff overhead. "What if it had come before sunset, last evenin', eh? What would have happened t' the maid then? And the babe? I tell y', Eliyahu, this won't get over quickly. I know the feel. This is a big storm, this is. And a colder one I've never felt. It's a time for pregnant ewes and newborn lambs t' be in shelter, like in the lambin' cave. Came just in time, they did. And right t' my Rachel. And who else—savin' your wife, my sister, of course—where else in all the region of Ephratha could they have got the help needed? Eh? Tell me that!"

Eliyahu blew into cupped hands to warm his freezing fingers. "Do you think the Almighty, blessed be he, left any of this to chance? No, Zadok, no. In Beth-lehem the child was always to be born.[11] And that means Rachel—and you and me too—were seen and made part of his plan from ages long past."

That suggestion stopped Zadok's torrent of words. How could that be right? Zadok—honest, hearty, generous Zadok—knew he had a temper and other failings. Was it possible the Lord God Almighty had prepared Zadok, a rough-hewn man at best, to receive the child sent to be the Restoration of Israel and the Light of the World?

It was too much. The wonder of the angelic announcement and the fulfillment seen in the babe in the manger were already enough. Making himself part of that miracle felt wrong, almost blasphemous. Zadok was prepared to testify to what he had been privileged to witness . . . but to be prepared by Yahweh to play a role in the event?

"That's too deep for a poor shepherd," Zadok demurred. "I don't begin t' understand half of what's happened. But I can't just keep pourin' it out t' you and Rachel. You already know it!"

"And isn't that why we're rushing off to Yerushalayim this fine, warm morning?" Eliyahu panted, rubbing his cheeks and nose to get some feeling back in them. "Don't you sense that if you keep it in one moment more you'd burst?"

All the shepherds of Migdal Eder, the Tower of the Flock where the lambs for Temple sacrifice were raised, were brimming with the news. Well before sunup all the people of Beth-lehem had been roused and regaled with stories of astonishing sights, angelic announcements, and heavenly choirs.

And now Zadok and Eliyahu were the advance guard of those carrying the news to the Holy City.

"To Simeon the Elder," Zadok restated firmly. "First to him. That good, righteous old man. To him first, before any other. It's only right."

Simeon, an aged elder of Israel, was the keeper of many secrets having to do with the advent of Messiah. It was altogether fitting that he be the first outside Beth-lehem to hear the report.

By the time Zadok and Eliyahu reached Simeon's house, the snow was falling in earnest. It dusted Zadok's shoulders and whitened the braids of his jet-black beard. The walls of Jerusalem reached upward until they disappeared into the dense white veil. The Temple, normally gleaming majestically on the Mountain of the Lord, could not even be glimpsed.

Zadok wasted no time knocking politely on Simeon's door. Instead he rapped on it with his staff, calling out, "Ho, Simeon! Let us in! I have news!"

As the door creaked open, Zadok gratefully received a wave of warmth. Simeon peered out, squinting to recognize his callers against the curtain of white. "Zadok and Eliyahu? Such a storm, eh? Come in, come in."

Zadok had already barged past Simeon before the invitation was completed. Without preamble he announced, "He's here! The child of promise! He was born last night in Beth-lehem. I've seen him! Eliyahu too. Many others! You were right, Simeon. This was the year!"

Simeon's frail, gnarled hands grasped both Zadok's brawny forearms. "Is he here, indeed?" he asked urgently. Without relinquishing his grip on the shepherd, Simeon looked at Eliyahu for confirmation.

The rabbi nodded vigorously.

Then the story tumbled out, alternating from the mouths of Zadok and Eliyahu:

"Last night. In the fields."

"I was with them. One of the shepherds was sick."

"The two wandering stars were just settin', when between them . . ."

"Brighter than anything!"

When Eliyahu paused for breath, Zadok took it as a signal for him to forge ahead alone. "An angel appeared. No doubt that's what he was. And he told us about the child. Born in a manger, he said. In little Beth-lehem. Then, *whoosh!* Like a fire in dry brush, suddenly there were hundreds—"

"Thousands," Eliyahu corrected.

"Thousands of angels! 'Glory to God in the highest!' they chanted. 'And peace to God's people, on whom His favor rests!' Then their spokesman—huge, he was, and shinin' like gold . . . no, more like molten brass! Anyway, he told us t' go. T' find the babe. And we did just that. In the lambin' cave is where we found them. A newborn and his mother and their protector.[12] My Rachel helped her."

Simeon, eyes brimming with tears, sank onto a cushion on the floor. He rocked forward and back, apparently caught in the grip of emotion too powerful for words.

Zadok, concerned that the shock of the announcement had been too much for the old man, knelt beside him.

Tears flowed freely down creviced cheeks and into Simeon's snow-white beard as he patted Zadok's arm reassuringly. "Just . . . give me a moment. All my life I've been waiting for this day. The Almighty promised . . . and I've lived to see it come to pass."[13]

"But don't die now!" Zadok countered in a worried tone. "Not now! Not yet!"

Simeon's face cracked into a smile. "Don't worry, Zadok, Eliyahu. I'm all right. No, I won't die yet. You must tell me all."

"All?" Zadok repeated in a puzzled tone. "What else is there?"

"What exactly—*exactly*, mind you—did the angel say?"

Eliyahu's scholarly, trained memory stepped in. "His exact words were 'Do not be afraid. I bring you good news of great joy that will be for all the people. Today in the town of David a Savior has been born to you; He is Messiah the Lord.'"[14]

"Messiah the Lord," Simeon murmured as Eliyahu paused to capture anew the angel's exact phrase.

"Then he added something else," Eliyahu resumed.

"Aye, that's when he told us—"

Shushing Zadok with a sharp look, Eliyahu elaborated. "The angel said, 'This will be a sign to you. You will find a baby wrapped in cloths and lying in a manger.'"[15]

"And so we did! All of us. Lem, and the boy, Jesse, and—"

"Too much! Too much!" Simeon warned. "One bit at a time. Everything means something, Zadok. Don't rush ahead! There has never been a proclamation like this since the world began, nor will there ever come such a message again. Stop now and let me think!"

CHAPTER 4

almai, Herod's chief steward, and Hermes, the captain of his bodyguards, stood together atop the battlements of the palace. Alternate moaning and raging rose through the open window of Herod's bedchamber, as if coming from beneath their feet.

"Did you tell the physician to increase the dose as I instructed?" Talmai asked.

Hermes shrugged. "The doctor is a fool. Says he already gave the king enough poppy juice to make him sleep a week instead of two hours. He's afraid to suggest more. Says the king accused him of trying to poison him."

The officer paused. He and Talmai exchanged a significant look but voiced nothing further. The two men were accomplices in currying the king's favor, but neither trusted the other with such dangerous thoughts as assassination. Both had made many enemies as well.

"When I strangled Ari and Alex and stuffed them in their tomb, I thought we were burying the king's fears." Hermes sniffed. "Now that Antipater is the lone heir, and away in Rome besides, what has Herod to fear?"

"His own death . . . or rather, what comes after," Talmai said. "He sees the ghosts of old victims gathering around him."

"Rubbish," Hermes retorted. "No ghosts. Dead is dead. That's all."

"Yet *something* whispers in Lord Herod's ear," Talmai mused aloud. "He burns the genealogy records so no one can prove descent from King David. Sends riders far and wide because some aged priest's equally aged wife supposedly had a miracle baby. Demands an investigation every time someone uses the word *messiah* in a sentence. Even the loyalty oath and the census did not satisfy him."

"Perhaps Lord Antipater should come back from Rome soon?"

"Not now!" Talmai rebuked sharply. "Stick to your soldiering, Hermes, and leave politics to me. What if the king's suspicions *are* true? What if there *is* a rebellion brewing to restore a real Jewish king? Caesar would send in the legions to put it down, and that would be the end of any hope of a Herodian dynasty in Judea . . . and of you and me."

"I still say any talk of revolt is nonsense!" Hermes countered. "We crucified dozens, executed hundreds more, all in the last year. I smell the stink of their fear whenever I go out in the streets. When I ride through villages, the rabble keep to their hovels. There's no one living who can challenge Herod's throne. No one!"

Talmai brooded. "I hope you're right. But hoping isn't enough. Double your patrols. I'll do the same with my spies."

After Zadok and Eliyahu had hurried off to Jerusalem, Havila and Grandmother finished the baking. Rachel helped Mary and Yosef settle into the cottage. By midmorning, lack of sleep the night before began to take its toll on Rachel.

Grandmother seemed unruffled by the unusual events. She was more troubled by the loss of the gold coin. As Rachel nursed Obi, Grandmother played with the boys on the floor. "Did you hide the shiny gold thing, Enoch? Did you eat my money, Samu'el? Tell Grandmother where it is, eh?"

Havila appeared to possess an endless well of energy. "Look at you, Rachel. Dark circles under your eyes. Grandmother and I will take the boys home for the afternoon, eh? You take a nap. Tonight Mary will need you."

Rachel nodded. In her weariness, thoughts swirled as thick as the snow. Everything in Beth-lehem had changed overnight.

As Havila wrapped baby Obi in warm blankets and Grandmother bundled Enoch, Samu'el, and Dan for the short walk to Havila's house, there was a knock on the door.

Havila peeked through the shutters. "No one I know. Travelers?"

The knock sounded again.

"A man and a woman," Havila announced. "Four girls from about twelve years to maybe six years. Out in such weather?"

Grandmother laced Enoch's leggings. "It's this Herodian edict. Never mind the weather. Rome will have its census and Herod will have his taxes. The inn is full. They're probably looking for shelter before Shabbat." She scanned the corners and the cracks again for her lost treasure.

Havila opened the door only a crack. "Shalom?"

A man's bass voice reached Rachel's ears. "We've come about the baby born last night. We saw the star in Ramah. We heard a miracle has happened."

Havila explained, "The mother is resting. She can't have visitors at least until after the *Bris*. That's eight days from now."

The woman broke in. "We didn't mean that we wanted to see him. No, not that. We brought a bushel of cabbages and carrots for soup. A gift for the mother of the Messiah. Date cakes too. And an embroidered blanket for the baby. I am also expecting, you see. My mother, a weaver, made it for my baby before she died. I dreamed last night that I must bring this gift to the infant who is born King of Israel. 'What king?' I asked. I was told we must bring our four daughters to Beth-lehem, but we must not enter the house where the King resides. Only leave our gift and return home. I was very troubled this morning until we heard the rumor that the promised baby had been born and angels appeared over Beth-lehem. At synagogue they said the baby and his mother are with you."

Havila, flushed with surprise by the stranger's dream, threw back the door. "Come in! Come in, and welcome! Warm yourself!"

"Oh no!" The man passed a heaping basket to Havila.

The woman added, "I was told we must not enter."

In spite of the freezing weather, complete strangers had traveled to the house of Zadok. "We heard the good news. Angels. Is it true? We just wanted to say Mazel tov! Tell them we're very happy! All Israel rejoices today. Except for those who don't."

After the family presented their gifts, they trudged away in the snow.

Grandmother fumed, "Everyone but me! Something to give him. But I have nothing. Lost! Lost! Eaten by a child!"

Havila shut the door and slid the bar. She turned in amazement. "What do you think of that? All the way from Ramah? In the snow."

Grandmother cooed, "If only these boys could talk plain! Eh? Tell Grandmother what you've done with it! Did we eat the pretty gold thing? Tell Grandmother where it is."

Another rapping sounded.

Rachel's neighbors, arms heaped with bundles and baskets, came too. They did not expect to be invited in, so they remained outside. With whispered exclamations, they left their gifts at Rachel's threshold. All shared what they had, and no matter how little, it was more than enough.

The blessing of shalom that Mary recited over Rachel and her household had already taken effect, it seemed. The blessings of peace and prosperity overflowed the little house. The table was heaped with bread, winter vegetables, and clothing.

Last and least expected of the visitors was Hamid, the olive-oil broker. Hamid, a man of great wealth, had lived a bitter and miserly life for forty years after the death of his wife and only son in childbirth. It was said he blamed Rachel's family for his loss. He had never spoken to her.

Like all the visitors, Hamid remained outside. In spite of Rachel's invitation to enter, he would not be persuaded.

"I am not worthy," the proud man replied.

To Rachel's knowledge, before today Hamid had never smiled. Before today he had never looked Rachel in the eye.

But this morning Hamid beamed. He bowed extravagantly. "I know, I know. I should not trouble you, dear lady. My apologies. I will not stay long."

Rachel noticed for the first time that Hamid the Oil Merchant had bright blue eyes.

"I do not come to disturb but rather to bring a small gift. My dear woman—Rachel, wife of Zadok—my neighbor!"

Rachel marveled. His words were unlike any he'd ever spoken to her!

"The news is very good," Hamid continued. "This baby. Everyone is talking about him! How could I not come too? I have heard the mother had difficulty bearing the child. It is said that this bringing forth of a Prince in the House of David was very difficult for her. So. In days long gone I lost my own beloved in childbirth. She perished, and my life seemed to end in the very cottage where now the Anointed sleeps. Your mother's mother was the midwife in that day."

Hamid frowned and looked down. "For forty years I have not spoken to your household. But this morning I said to myself, 'It is no different for a woman bringing forth the King of Israel than it was for my dear wife. The curse of Eve upon all daughters of Eve. What can I, a frail son of Adam, do for this poor, dear woman who has given us Israel's King?' It came to me: 'She will need to regain her strength. Good food will help her regain her strength,' I said to myself. And so my servant, a dull and slow-witted fellow, is coming along after me. I bring to the house of Zadok and Rachel, who are blessed by The Eternal to care for the young Prince . . ."

He paused as though he had forgotten why he had come. "Ah yes! And so I offer to the parents of the young Prince a gift of seven chickens. One plump chicken for supper each night until the baby boy's circumcision, if you please. Eh? Eh? A chicken to cook every day? This should get them off to a good start. She will recover! And—" Hamid patted his broad belly—"seven jars of wine and seven jars of oil I offer to the synagogue and also a yearling calf to feed everyone at the synagogue on the day of the *Bris* of the Son of David, eh? Eh?"

After Hamid left, Rachel wondered at first if Hamid's generosity was motivated by shrewd business. Did the old man have in mind that one day the infant would grow up, become king, and need olive oil? In that day would Mary approach the throne of David's Son? Would Mary remind her royal offspring that, at His birth, old Hamid the Oil Merchant had provided seven pullets for the week? And also wine and oil and a calf for the entire synagogue to feast on? But Hamid was old and would certainly not be around long enough for the true King of Israel to purchase his oil.

Rachel had seen something in Hamid's expression she had never seen before. The same expression worn by every member of each poor family who had offered their best gifts to the infant today. The expression that asked *What is it, Lord? How is the birth of this one little boy different from all others?*

Babies often brought out the best in people. Rachel had observed it a hundred times before. Even the most cynical heart could be touched when confronted by the vulnerability of a newborn. But there was so much more in this day!

Havila and Grandmother gathered the boys and headed to Havila's house. Rachel lay down and gazed at the bunches of lavender in the rafters. She tried to sort out her questions.

Mary had not been surprised to hear that angels had sung about the birth of her child. What mystery did Mary comprehend that no one else grasped?

Rachel closed her eyes and let much-needed slumber overtake her as the muted bleating of sheep from the pastures of Migdal Eder drifted up to Beth-lehem.

News that angels had appeared to Beth-lehem's shepherds was greeted by Mordechai, proprietor of the inn, with ridicule. He wiped his greasy hands on his apron and sneered at his thirteen-year-old daughter as she told him the rumor. "Angels, eh?"

"So they say. A huge host of angels! I heard all about it at the souk when I bought the cabbages."

"Huh! Dim-witted child that you are, you believe every word of it. Angels? Appeared to Zadok and Lem and the others?"

"Yes, Papa. They say it was something about that man and his wife. You remember. The woman was in labor. The man came and asked for a room. Remember?"

Mordechai scratched beneath his scruffy double chin. "I have a slight memory. The inn was crowded. It was a long night."

"I remember them. The fellow came to the door, and you turned them away. Sent them to the stable. They say after the baby was born, angels sang to the shepherds."

Mordechai sucked his decaying teeth as he reflected. "A heavenly lullaby, I suppose? Huh! Drunk. All of them. Last night of Hanukkah. They was in their cups a bit, I'd say! Heavenly visions of angels indeed!"

"The rabbi was with 'em, Papa. Out there in the fields. Sober, all of 'em. And Rachel the Midwife was called to attend the birth. They say a great light shone in the heavens when the babe was born."

Mordechai quaffed his barley beer and belched. "You're a fool. They say so, do they?"

"Aye, Papa. They say you have missed a heavenly blessing that would have come upon our house. They say you turned away the one who will grow up to be the Messiah."

The innkeeper waved his hand dismissively. "You know I'm hated by the townsfolk because we accept the business of Romans and tax collectors. They've made this up to shame me. It's nothing, I tell you. A wild story meant to make me jealous and meant to make you out to be a fool."

"Everyone in the village is talking about it," she insisted. "Everyone. People are going to see the babe. At the house of Zadok, he and his mother are."

Mordechai poured himself another drink and plucked meat from the plate. "'Tis a joke. Aye. Daughter, sooner you know we don't mix with them folk the better off you'll be. They're having us on. They've made up this story hoping to draw us into their joke. A conspiracy so's they can draw us in. Excite our curiosity, like."

"I'd like to see it."

"See what?"

"The baby."

"One brat's the same as another."

"Even so, I'd like to see it."

Mordechai wagged his fist at her threateningly. "If you do, I'll . . ."

She flinched and drew back. "All right, Papa."

"Mind what I say now," he growled. "Not a word of this to anyone! It's a made-up story, I tell you. No use you repeating that I turned out a man and his pregnant wife. We'll be the butt of a joke forever. Not a word of the lie to anyone! Messiah born in Beth-lehem. Messiah turned away. It's a lie, and you'll not be shaming us by repeating such a falsehood."

While Zadok and Eliyahu warmed hands and insides with mugs of barley broth in Simeon's study, the Levite scholar pondered and pondered. Neither younger man dared speak and disturb the elder's reverie. Eliyahu even hushed Zadok when the shepherd made slurping noises.

Not that Simeon noticed or seemed aware of their presence at all. His eyes stared into the ceiling, as if all the answers he sought were displayed there. His lips moved soundlessly. Sometimes he shook his head violently from side to side as his internal argument progressed.

Then, when the older man grew so still Zadok wondered if he had drifted off, Simeon gave a savage nod and jumped up. He threw back the panels of a dark, wooden press in a corner of the chamber to display its contents. Heaps of scrolls, ends outward, filled the entire cupboard . . . but only momentarily.

An instant later Simeon began dragging book after book from the recesses of the closet. Scroll upon scroll welled up in the center of the oak-plank table. They spilled from it onto the flagstone floor, like a fountain overflowing a well of parchment.

Snatching up a final cylinder, Simeon let it unroll across the table, then scanned it furiously. "Ha!" he exclaimed. Keeping a silver-tipped pointer on the exact spot, Simeon raised his eyes and examined the expectant features of his guests. "'Good news,' the angel said, eh? *Shemuah tov. Shemuah*: an announcement, a report, tidings, yes. Sounds like the word for the heavens: *shamayim. Tov*: good news. So! A report so good as to be heavenly, true?"

Eliyahu nodded vigorously. "And where in Holy Scripture is such a phrase used except in—"

"Proverbs!" Simeon confirmed, gesturing at the scroll. "One place only! Listen: *Like cold water to a weary soul is good news*—shemuah tov—*from a distant land!*[16] What a sense of humor has the Almighty, blessed be he! Heaven is indeed a 'distant land'!"

"And that relates to a newborn Messiah?" Zadok questioned calmly. He struggled to keep up but was unwilling for his brother-in-law to note his mental exertion.

"Exactly!" Simeon praised, as if Zadok had uttered something profound. "See here what Isaias says of Messiah." Simeon swept aside the Proverbs scroll to reveal one of the prophet Isaias. *"I will make you a covenant for the people, to restore the land. . . . He who has compassion on them will guide them and lead them beside springs of water!"*[17]

"Shemuah tov! Good news from heaven, indeed," Eliyahu murmured. "Messiah refreshes our souls like a cool spring of water."

"And further it says, *I will also make you a light for the Gentiles, that you may bring My salvation to the ends of the earth."*[18] Abruptly Simeon broke off quoting to ask, "Have they said what the baby will be called? His name?"

"Not a hint." Eliyahu frowned.

Simeon tapped the Isaiah scroll with his forefinger. "His name is written here. It will become known to the ends of the earth. But for now, silence! Above all. No one must know of this outside the circle of your families. Herod hears the whispers of evil within his soul. Demons will tell him of the threat to his rule, even if we do not speak of it. His madness grows worse each day. He'll be searching for the baby. Aye, he will feel that the Light has entered the world. He'll stir himself to look for the Light and do all he can to put out the flame. You'll need to find a place for the family to stay. Someplace quite safe."

Zadok rested his chin on his broad, calloused palm. "The whole of Beth-lehem knows the news by now. Yerushalayim will be buzzin' with it soon. There's no puttin' the cork back in that bottle of news, I fear.

But none of Migdal Eder will betray him—that you may count on. We'll put our minds to it, eh, Eliyahu? And now we'd best be headin' home. We may have t' fight our way through snow in the low places as it is. Soon as we can, we'll come back t' hear more."

"Go with God," Simeon said, blessing with upraised hands both rabbi and shepherd. "May he who blessed you first among all men of earth guide and protect you and the babe."

Old Balthasar's caravan and six other westbound parties were stuck in Tadmor. The senior Roman military commander had been called away. The junior officers were unwilling to take the responsibility of admitting foreign travelers to Roman territory without his permission. The caravansary grew more and more crowded, and Old Balthasar more and more impatient.

"I wanted to be among the first to welcome Messiah," he fumed.

Esther was content to be practical. "The Almighty knew you needed rest, Grandfather. Now it's been forced on you."

Melchior, while caught up in Balthasar's fervor to see the newborn King, admitted to himself that the time with Esther was very pleasant. Together they strolled through the markets and souks that sold to pilgrims.

"The tradesmen don't mind this delay at all," Esther noted. "As soon as the border shut down they raised their prices."

To get away from the crowded conditions in the caravansary the couple wandered outside the gates. They were a half mile beyond the edge of the campground when the ground rumbled beneath Melchior's feet.

"Earthquake?" Esther guessed.

Tremors were not uncommon back in the mountains surrounding Ecbatana, but here they were on an open plain.

"I don't think so," Melchior began.

A swirl of dust appeared on the southern horizon. In seconds it resolved into a crescent-shaped array of horsemen sweeping toward them.

Bandits?

Melchior counted the numbers. Far too many to fight.

He judged the distance back to the settlement. The riders would be on them before they reached it.

There was only one option left: "Come on! We'll hide in those rocks." Melchior's pull on Esther's arm propelled her into the scant cover of a brushy mound. "Duck down. Maybe they won't see us."

As the horsemen drew closer, Melchior saw that the riders wore conical helmets and short swords. Each carried another weapon, either a lance or a double-curved bow slung over his back. Melchior had never seen soldiers outfitted like this before.

Melchior directed most of his attention toward the obvious leader at the center of the formation. The man positioned between the horns of the crescent was tall and dressed all in black. Both his form and his motion blended with the black horse he rode.

The riders galloped toward the caravansary at full speed, showing no signs of drawing their weapons.

Who were these fierce-looking horsemen?

Melchior thought he and Esther had escaped detection as the leading points of the squadron cantered by. He had just gained a sense of relief when one of the troopers gave a sharp whistle of alarm.

Instantly half a score of horsemen spun their mounts toward the small hill and completely encircled it. Lance heads flashed in the light. The bowmen nocked arrows without stopping and took the reins in their teeth. The warriors advanced their steeds at a walk.

"Wait!" Melchior pleaded, rising to his feet. "We're from a caravan. From Parthia."

With his men ringing the knoll, the leader rode directly up to Melchior and Esther. He was a good head taller than Melchior and as dark as Melchior was fair. The horseman's thin-lipped mouth was cruel, his face was lined from the sun, and his eyes held no pity.

When he spoke, his voice was as harsh as a desert sandstorm. "So! Finally something worth looking at in this pestilential hole!" The captain spurred his horse, making Melchior jump back. The prancing stallion jogged a tight circle around Esther. "What's your name, pretty one?"

The troopers laughed and passed appreciative comments back and forth.

This man felt dangerous! Melchior wanted to come to Esther's aid, wanted to step between her and this desert chieftain.

Esther kept her eyes on the ground. She gave no reply, no sign of acknowledgment at all.

"There are bandits hereabouts," the horseman said. He jutted his chin toward Melchior. "If this is all your protection, you'd best stay in camp." The captain offered Esther a curt bow. A simple jerk of his head and the riders trotted off toward the caravansary.

Later, safely back in the campground, Melchior inquired about the identity of this strange figure.

"You haven't heard of Zamaris?" was the surprised response.

"Who's he? Bandit chief? Warlord?"

"Zamaris? Why, he's the greatest Jewish warrior who ever lived. Rules Batanea for King Herod. His fighters are the toughest cavalry troopers in the world."

The face on the other side of the door was a surprise to Rachel. Mordechai, innkeeper of the Beth-lehem caravansary, bowed slightly. His rotten teeth were bared in a smile as he tried to peer around her into the house. "Shalom, woman." His eyes did not meet hers.

Rachel instinctively closed the door to a slit. "Shalom . . . Mordechai. My husband, Zadok, is sleeping." She was unwilling for such a creature to know she and the children were alone in the house.

"Ah. Well." Another bob of the head. "No matter. I have come to see the baby they say is the Messiah, eh?"

"Who says such a thing?" Rachel felt herself bristle. A fellow like Mordechai had not come out of goodwill. And, unlike all the other neighbors of Beth-lehem, Mordechai was the only visitor who had not brought even some small gift.

"My daughter—you know her, stupid girl that she is—came to me saying that she heard of some miraculous sign . . . something to do with the birth of a baby. Messiah, she says. A baby boy born in the lambing cave."

Rachel braced herself against the door, blocking the threshold as Mordechai leaned closer. He reeked of sour wine and vomit. "I am the midwife of all Ephratha. Babies are born here all the time. I don't know what your daughter might have heard. A miracle? Messiah?"

"Stupid girl that she is. Like her mother." The obsequious grin vanished. Pitiless blackness showed in his snakelike eyes. "It's nothing, then?"

"Nothing at all. As you know, there have been seventy baby boys born in the territory over the last two years. If the Messiah is among them, it would be a surprise, eh?"

His lip curled in a human snarl. "I'll teach her to repeat wild tales. Just so." He brandished the back of his hand. "Stupid girl. Make a fool of me."

At that, he turned on his heel and stalked off.

⊕

"Mordechai wasn't like the others who came to visit." Rachel rubbed her arms as though the memory of the innkeeper at the door gave her a chill. "His eyes. Dead. Like a serpent's eyes."

Zadok inhaled deeply and clapped Yosef on the back. "Aye. An evil creature, Mordechai is. You know what he looks like, this innkeeper?"

Yosef nodded. "He was drunk that night when I spoke with him. He may not remember my face."

"That's good. Good if he's forgotten. It gives you some advantage over him. He can't tell the authorities, 'Well, the child's father looks like . . . this or that,' eh?"

"It was dark that night. I was in shadow. I don't think he'll remember my looks."

"There's a blessin'. Mordechai'll work for anyone who pays him. Herod pays well for good information. And bad information. Herod sees traitors everywhere. Aye. And there are always those who'll sell their own souls and the soul of another for cash. But here's the rub: Informants often become suspected themselves. They end up nailed to a cross as well."

Yosef patted his sword. "No one will get to Mary or the baby. No one will get past me while I breathe."

"Aye. You've got shoulders as broad as an oak," Zadok concurred. "We'll make a shepherd of you while you're with us. One of us, eh? Yosef, good shepherd of Beth-lehem. Descended from David.[19] Aye. And as for Mary . . ."

"Her family also of David's line."

"Well then, if anyone asks, Mary's one of us. Family. A daughter of Beth-lehem all her life. None our folk will tell it any different t' Mordechai or his Roman guests or Herodian pigs."

Yosef frowned. "I don't want Mary to know there might be danger to the baby."

"Mordechai's mouth is dangerous. He's no physical threat. One flash of your blade and he'd run for cover."

"I'll sleep across the threshold."

Zadok grinned. "Aye. You do that. And in that case I'll knock loudly and ask your permission before ever you see me cross your threshold. The password'll be, 'Yosef, it's me, Zadok! Don't kill me, brother!'"

Rachel added, "The bell rope. Above Mary's bed. Pull it hard if there's any trouble."

Yosef ceremonially washed in the mikveh of the synagogue in preparation for Shabbat's arrival at twilight. His tallith was laid out and examined. Polished agate phylacteries from Sinai, handed down from generation to generation, were removed from their pouch.

Everything was in order.

With Rachel's help Mary had bathed and brushed her hair.

The baby was washed in warm water from David's Well. His pink skin was anointed with olive oil. The stump of his umbilical cord was coated with strong wine. Rachel helped Mary walk unsteadily to the main house, where she was made to recline on cushions. Yosef carried the baby, who was then placed in Mary's arms.

Havila and Eliyahu arrived with little Dan and Grandmother.

The quartet of women—Rachel, Havila, Grandmother, and Mary—sang the Shabbat psalms as preparations for the Shabbat meal were completed. The baby listened with rapt attention while treble voices recalled the songs of Shabbat eve sung by generations of women for over a thousand years.

Tonight the words took on new significance:

"Sing to the Lord a new song, for He has done marvelous things!
Shout for joy to the Lord, all the earth!
The Lord has made His salvation known and revealed His righteousness
to the nations!
Shout for joy to the Lord, all the earth!
He has remembered His love and His faithfulness to the House of Isra'el!
All the nations of the earth have seen the salvation of our God!
Shout for joy to the Lord, all the earth!"[20]

The sun balanced like a gold coin on the rim of the western horizon. Yosef, Zadok, and Eliyahu donned prayer shawls.

Zadok, as master of the house, began. "Blessed are you, O Eternal, our God, King of the Universe. The Lord of All the Angel Armies is his name! God, ever-living and enduring! He will reign over us forevermore."

Then everyone recited the Shema: *"Hear, O Israel: The Lord our God, the Lord is one!"*[21]

All eyes were riveted on the baby in Mary's arms as Eliyahu sang: "Permit our prayers to come before you and be regarded! Remember the promise you made to our ancestors and the promise of Messiah, the Son of David, your servant. Blessed are you, The Eternal, who restores his divine glory to Zion."

At the instant before sundown Rachel lit the two havdalah candles. She blessed all the sons gathered in the room. "May the Lord make you like Ephraim and Manasseh. The Eternal bless and preserve you, Enoch, Dan, Samu'el, and Obi. And you, little one. You, whose name has not yet been revealed to the congregation of Israel. You, who are the One we have been waiting for, now resting in the arms of your mother. May your name be blessed forever! May you be known and revealed to Israel soon!"

In that instant, the newborn worked His hand free and extended His right arm upward. Perfect fingers spread as if to touch Mary's face. Rachel smiled at the interaction between mother and child.

Mary, propped up on pillows, tilted her head as though she was hearing another song . . . a harmony meant first for her. She kissed the baby's fingers and her countenance brightened. Shadows from the candle flames danced on the whitewashed walls as Rachel's prayers came to an end.

The room fell silent with expectation. Mary uttered her first Shabbat blessing to her child. Her greeting was a barely audible whisper intended only for the ears of the baby. "Shabbat shalom, little lamb. Perfect lamb. The breath of whatever has life will bless your holy name. Every knee shall bow and every tongue shall confess you are Messiah and Lord.[22] All the earth will proclaim your sovereign power."

The ceremony of blessing the children was completed.

Mary said to Rachel and the other women, "His first Shabbat evening. Supper with friends. I'll keep this memory always. How you took us into your own home. Your kindness. A treasure in my heart. He mustn't miss attending his first Shabbat service on earth among his people! Tomorrow morning I'll be strong enough if you will help me. We'll walk together and bring the baby into Beth David, the House of David Synagogue. He'll attend his first Shabbat service in your synagogue, Rabbi Eliyahu. He'll worship the first time in Israel in the midst of your little sons. It was always meant to be. Right here in Beth-lehem!"

"What is it you are searching for, Melchior?" Esther passed him a platter of hummus and lamb rolled in grape leaves. The candlelight shone in her dark eyes.

His breath caught when she smiled at him. "Searching?" he asked dumbly, barely able to think through her question.

"Yes. Well, we're all traveling so far. Grandfather's hope? I think I know what he is looking for at the end of the journey. The others we've met on the road from the East. But you, Melchior? You are a man of so few words, yet . . ."

He exhaled loudly and craned his neck to gaze at the heavens. He pointed at the cluster of stars that formed the constellation called The Pleiades by some. "Look there. The Seven Sisters they are called. But on a clear night from the top of the mountain, you can see there are more than seven. And some say they aren't pinpoints of light but giant fires, as big as the sun. So distant."

"I believe it. A very big place, the heavens." Esther wrapped her arms around her knees and rocked back.

"Yes, very big. And beautiful too. Your grandfather has taught me over the years to believe that someone . . . wonderful and mighty beyond our imagination . . . has created the stars."

"We Jews call the Pleiades *Ki-Mah*."

"Yes. It means 'who made?'" Melchior spread his hands. "And that is what—or rather, whom—I am searching for. The One who made the stars and ordered the heavens so that even the night speaks to men's hearts. It is written in the book of Job. I looked it up. *Can you bind the beautiful Pleiades? Can you loose the cords of Orion? Can you bring forth the constellations in their seasons?*"[23]

"You speak almost as though you are one of us. A Jew."

"I wish I was. I wish . . . for many reasons . . . I had been born one of your people."

"What reasons?"

"I can't . . . tell you."

"Not even one reason?"

"Not . . . tonight. Maybe not . . . ever."

Esther shrugged and did not pursue the question further, though he wished she would.

"You have a good heart, Melchior. Grandfather says it. He says you are a good man."

"Even though I'm not a Jew?"

"Even though." She reached toward him, as if to touch his cheek but drew back. "Why do you shave? You would be very handsome if you had a beard. Like a Jew. It would be gold? Or red, I think. Like your hair."

He felt the color climb to his cheeks. "Oh." How he hated blushing like a schoolboy!

Esther laughed. "A red beard would hide your red cheeks."

"It's . . . from the time I was a boy. I could never lie. Blushing has always given away my thoughts."

"Then you might as well tell me what you are thinking . . . or . . ."

His mouth worked like a fish out of water. He felt his color deepen. Why could he not look at her? Why could he not make his arms draw her near to him? "Oh, Esther. If only I could say . . . you know."

"Well?" Her head was tilted quizzically to one side.

As though she was waiting for a kiss?

"I . . . I . . ." He cleared his throat and rose suddenly, spilling his cup of wine. "Sorry. Sorry. Such a waste. Oh . . . I . . . I'll clean it up."

She stared up at him for several heartbeats. Did she think him the clumsiest creature she had ever met? "Melchior, it's only a cup of wine that's spilt. The ground will drink it. But when a man wastes a chance to tell someone how he feels? . . . He may never have another."

With those last words she rose and disappeared into the tent of her grandfather.

ϕ

"How many Jewish children were conceived on Shabbat, I wonder?" Rachel lay with her head on Zadok's broad chest.

He sighed and wrapped his arms around her. "Aye. Blessed be the Lord who commanded us t' be fruitful and multiply. A mitzvah, it is, for me t' take you in my arms on Shabbat night. No wonder we men look forward t' Shabbat night all week. And no wonder we sleep so deep and rest so well."

She stroked his beard. "If loving you is so wonderful here in this life, what will it be like in *olam haba*?"

"Ah, Rachel. My Rachel! I can't think that far ahead. Lovin' you on earth is my one great joy. And the boys . . . our sons . . . the best gift from heaven."

"The best gift," Rachel reflected. "Our children."

"I've thought of it more than ever these last days. Babies and such."

She knew he was not speaking of their own children now but of the infant who was but a handful of paces from them. "The baby. He is beautiful, isn't he?"

"Aye. Perfect, as we would expect him to be. What will his name be, do you think?"

"It's a well-kept secret. I suppose we won't know until the *Bris*."

"Old Simeon has some idea." Zadok stroked her back. "But he wouldn't tell us right out."

"Hmm. Whatever it is, it will be wonderful."

The two lay in a contented embrace for a time as the embers of the fire winked and began to fade. Bear Dog whined to be let out. At last Zadok rose, wrapped himself in a blanket, stirred the coals, and tended to the dog.

Rachel, drowsy, clinging to consciousness, followed him with her eyes as he moved about the room. "Check the babies? Make sure they're covered up."

"Enoch. Hot-blooded like me. Kicks the blankets off even when it's freezin'."

Zadok tended the children, then climbed back into bed and snuggled against Rachel.

"Your feet are cold."

"That's nothin' compared to what the unmarried lads down in the pastures are feelin' tonight. After such a winter they'll all be eager t' marry so they won't have t' stand watch on Shabbat night."

"There are some advantages to marriage if you are a shepherd of the Temple flock." Rachel laughed and pulled him closer.

"Aye. Some." As Zadok kissed her, the fire blazed once again. "Rachel, my ewe lamb. Strange, isn't it? We call this Shabbat night our day of rest. . . ."

⚶

"Eliyahu? Love? When will you come to bed?" Havila turned back the blanket and patted the mattress.

Eliyahu did not look up or seem to notice her inviting gesture. Hunched over an open scroll, he studied the text by the flickering light of an oil lamp.

On Shabbat night Grandmother stayed down the lane with the widow of Zebulun the Shoemaker so the couple could be alone. This was the first Shabbat night since their marriage that Eliyahu had not eagerly said his prayers and come to bed to caress her. To make love on Shabbat night after the meal was a custom so ancient that it had almost become a law.

A very good custom, Havila thought. She had no doubt that Dan had been conceived on a Shabbat and also this new baby.

When Eliyahu did not reply, Havila sighed and rolled over on her back. Both hands on her expansive stomach, she drummed her fingers as the baby tapped an infant greeting.

"I am too fat." She sighed, convinced that Eliyahu was repulsed by her condition. She began to cry. Little sniffles dissolved into sobs.

Eliyahu, startled by her outburst, looked up. "Havila? Wife? Are you unwell? What's this? What's this? What? Shall I fetch Rachel? Are you in labor?"

"I'm too fat!" she moaned.

"Too fat? Blessed be The Eternal Lord for your fatness! You are seven months pregnant, dear wife. If you weren't fat, what would be the point? May you be fat with new babies forever!"

"If you don't find me pleasing, I'll never be fat again, God forbid!"

His expression displayed absolute confusion. "What? What? I? Not find you pleasing? My life? My lamb? My treasure?"

"It's Shabbat! *Shabbat*, and you haven't even looked at me since you and Zadok came home from Yerushalayim! No wink. No touch. Usually you are so eager. Always the day before I'm fending you off. 'Wait until tonight! Almost time for Shabbat, sweets!' You haven't even looked at me! I know you think I'm too fat! I'm ugly and . . . fat! You don't want me anymore!"

Eliyahu rubbed his hands over his face in frustration. "Oh, love. My precious Havila. It's this . . . it's not you! Surely you know! Nothing has ever happened like this before. Tomorrow is the service. The first Shabbat since his birth and . . . there's so much here! The Parashah tomorrow is . . . is . . . ."

"You don't love me anymore." She buried her face in her hands and wept. Had she ever felt so miserable? Even when she had been a full nine-months' term with Dan, her husband had seemed to relish the largeness of her body. But now? Now? What had happened?

"It's Shabbat," she cried again. "Grandmother is gone to Widow Zebulun's, and you didn't even notice!"

Eliyahu flung himself onto the bed beside her. "Grandmother is out of the house! My love! How selfish I've been! My treasure! There is no land I wish to explore but you!"

"You don't mean it." Havila rolled over with her back to him.

"Blessed are you, O Lord, who gives us this mystery called 'woman' and leaves her to us to decipher!" He tugged on her shoulder. Gently. Gently. "Havila? Havila?"

"Huh?"

"Shabbat shalom, my little doe. My delicate gazelle."

"You're just saying that because you've wounded me beyond healing."

He coaxed her with verses of Solomon's song: "*My dove in the clefts of the rock, in the hiding places on the mountainside. Show me your face, let me hear your voice, for your voice is sweet, and your face is lovely.*"[24]

"It's the rest of me you don't like."

"Come now, my delicate fawn. *Catch for us the foxes, the little foxes that ruin the vineyards."* He kissed the back of her neck and slid his hand around her middle. *"Our vineyards that are . . . in bloom."*[25]

She chuckled and yielded to his touch. "In bloom all right."

"How's the rest of it go?"

She wrapped her strong arms around him. *"My lover is mine and I am his; he browses among the lilies. Until the day breaks and the shadows flee."*[26]

"Ah, my Havila. I forgot for a moment my Shabbat gift to you. Would you forgive me? Now we'll say the rest of the passage with a kiss and a sigh, eh?"

"Turn, my lover, and be like a gazelle or like a young stag on the rugged hills!"[27]

The amber coals of the banked fire peeked out from beneath heavy lids of gray ash. Outside, the hills were blanketed with snow. Nazareth, with its backbiting, tale-bearing neighbors, seemed a long way off . . . worries about King Herod further still.

Beth-lehem felt snug and protected in many ways, Yosef thought. Nestled here in its own valley, the House of Bread—David's House— was a house of compassion and caring. The shepherds lived rough, *were* rough, but Yosef had never sensed more immediate acceptance anywhere. Here genuine concern was shown for Mary and the child and himself. Tribe of Judah and line of David as he was, Yosef had not expected such a reception.

Tomorrow morning's Shabbat readings: *Vayigash!* "Draw near!" How the villagers had taken that admonition to heart! It was as if every shred of consideration that gossipy Galilee had failed to provide them had been offered here ten times over.

And yet . . . and yet . . . Beth-lehem was also the place of the drunken innkeeper.

And though it might be cloaked by clouds and masked with snow, Herodium still lurked above the plain.

So Yosef slept across the doorway. His sword lay near his right hand. His left touched a timeworn shepherd's staff, loaned to him by Zadok. And Rachel had repeated, "The bell, remember. Ring it if you need anything."

"Yosef?" Mary murmured sleepily. "Are you awake?"

"Are you all right? Do you need anything?" Worry flooded in. Had the too-soon Shabbat evening with the shepherd's family injured Mary's recovery?

"No, nothing. I'm fine. Just worried about you on that cold floor on such a night."

Lying atop a heap of sheep fleeces with two more and a wool blanket over him, Yosef could truthfully reassure her. "Plenty warm. I've slept a lot rougher than this many times, believe me."

"Everyone here is so kind. Rachel. Zadok. Havila. If only Mama were here. She'd love it here. Love these folks. Everything would be perfect." Her words drifted away in the stillness.

A coal popped and hissed, spurting a dying jet of flame. It was good Mary felt no concern to mar her rest. It was as it should be, Yosef thought.

He tucked the sword hilt nearer his fingertips, making certain the blade was not tangled in the fleeces.

S habbat morning. The snow had frozen to a hard, dirty crust. Soggy
sheep, burdened with the weight of water in their coats, pawed the
ice in search of a blade of grass.

The rabbinic laws of work on the seventh day did not apply to shepherds. Prophets like Mosheh knew livestock had no respect for Shabbat
customs. When a ewe fell into a ditch, a shepherd was required to carry her
out even on the day of rest. When animals required feeding, the shepherd
was always obligated by the greater law of mercy to care for his flock.

Zadok, back from predawn chores, put his arms around Rachel and
kissed her.

"Even your lips are cold." She laughed.

"After service this mornin' me and the lads'll be movin' the flocks
down the pass. A couple miles t' greener pastures. Ewes scratchin' t'
find the green beneath the white. I've not seen a colder winter than
this in my life."

"Will Eliyahu call on Yosef to make aliyah in synagogue this
morning?"

"Aye. Yosef must read a seventh part of today's Torah portion.
Customary for a new father. It's proper, him bein' thought father of a

newborn son. So he will be called up for the readin' and six of us others who met the angels in the fields. Me among them. Seven of us. We'll read the Torah portion. It's a fine readin' today. Fits the occasion, I should say. Now, I've got to wash and change. Is Mary still intent on bringin' the wee lad to synagogue?"

"She's a strong girl, Zadok, or she wouldn't have survived. She did well last night at supper. This morning she had a purpose in her eye when she spoke of the baby not missing services on his first Shabbat. 'But a baby so new out in the cold?' I asked her. She says to me, 'I must bring him.' She'll carry him in her arms, she says. She won't be carried to the synagogue. She says she'll walk the distance on her own. Herself. She won't be denied. I think the snow affects reason."

"Eliyahu has asked Lem t' blow the shofar from the roof of Beth David as they approach. To welcome the babe t' our village. No match for the trumpets we heard that night. But a fittin' gesture, I reckon."

"Fitting. But I wish Mary would stay in bed one more day."

"Well then. After what we've witnessed, who are we to question her resolve? The girl hears voices from a distant land. I believe her. A different song, she hears, from the songs we sing. She gives birth, and the stars break open above our heads. Snow falls like it hasn't fallen in a hundred years. Whatever the girl says, I'll believe it. If Mary says the babe must attend synagogue even on the first Shabbat of his life among us, then he must."

Lem stood on the parapet above the entrance to Beth David Synagogue and blew the shofar as the procession from Zadok's house approached.

Mary raised her face and cheerfully waved at the red-haired trumpeter. The baby, bundled up against the chilly breeze, awakened at the blast from the ram's horn.

Men and women who had heard the shepherd's tale lined the approach and applauded as Mary and Yosef entered the house of worship.

Behind the lattice screen that separated the women's from the men's section of the Beth-lehem synagogue, Rachel and Grandmother, arms full of wriggling toddlers, flanked Mary and her baby. Havila and

Sharona sat behind them. The women's alcove teemed with small children who chattered and giggled and nursed and whined. The usual commotion in the Women's Gallery did not disturb the noisy rhythm of worship in the main hall.

Beyond the women's lattice, over two hundred men of Ephratha swayed as they murmured their Shabbat prayers. Shoulder to shoulder beneath their white prayer shawls the worshippers were like a flock of sheep jostling to be fed.

The sanctuary was overflowing its capacity today. Rachel believed many had come for a glimpse of the miraculous child. The baby, unperturbed by the curiosity of the villagers, nursed for a few moments. His lids were heavy, as though the noise were a lullaby. A drop of milk hung on his lower lip.

Rachel spotted Mary's husband, Yosef, standing beside the chair of honor behind the bema. Eliyahu, a *cohen* of the tribe of Levi, presided over the service. Zadok served as an elder of the tight-knit congregation of shepherd families.

This morning Mary wore the pale blue wool dress she had brought from Nazareth. Her thick chestnut locks were plaited in a single braid draped over her left shoulder. A woven garland of Rachel's lavender crowned Mary's brow. She held the infant in her arms and sat erect and attentive as the clamor of Shabbat morning prayers competed with the chatter of Beth-lehem's mothers and children.

A hush fell over the congregation as each of the shepherds who had witnessed the angel's proclamation made aliyah to read from the Torah portion *Vayigash*, which means "Draw near to me."

Rachel, with Enoch and Samu'el on her lap, sat close on Mary's right side in the Women's Gallery. Grandmother held Obi. Rachel observed the tiny infant sleeping in His mother, Mary's, arms. Messiah! Light who shone in the heavens before the stars were created!

What message was contained in today's reading? Would heaven speak on this first Shabbat after the birth of Messiah?

"Vayigash!"

Zadok, his powerful voice thick with emotion, read part of the story that told of the reunion of Joseph the Dreamer with the brothers who had betrayed him and sold him into slavery in Egypt. The Lord had delivered Joseph from bondage and raised him to be ruler. Now Joseph's brothers had come to Egypt to purchase food because of a famine in their own country. Joseph did not reveal his true identity to them until he had tested them to see if they had changed.

And the test was all about family and loyalty and doing what was right even at personal risk. Would the brothers now also betray Joseph's full brother, Ben-Yamin, youngest son of old Jacob and Rachel? After Rachel's death near Beth-lehem while giving birth to him,[28] Ben-Yamin— "son of my right hand"—was the main prop of Jacob's old age.

Would the brothers allow Ben-Yamin to be arrested and enslaved in Egypt as Joseph was? Would they let their youngest brother be punished for a crime he did not commit so they could go free? The congregation of Beth David had heard this Torah passage many times, but it seemed to Rachel this was the first time she had really listened to it.

As Zadok read, his rumbling bass voice broke.

"Then Judah, in terror, drew near the throne of Joseph and said, 'If you please, my lord, may your servant speak a word in my lord's ears and let not your anger flare up—for you are like Pharaoh. If I come to my father and the youth is not with us, when my father sees the youth is missing, my old father will die. I took responsibility for the youth. Let me remain here instead of the youth. I will be a slave to my lord. Let the youth go home. For how can I go up to my father if the youth is not with me, lest I see the evil that will befall my father.'"[29]

Zadok inhaled and studied the scroll for a time. His glossy black beard rose and fell with some inner turmoil. What had moved him so deeply? Rachel wondered. Was this only a story of a long-past event, or did it also contain the events of a present reunion between God's Son and the children of Israel? Was it a future glimpse of the great reconciliation between God and His covenant people in the world to come?

"Vayigash! Draw near to me!"

The baby stirred in Mary's arms. She gently smoothed the soft dark curls on His head. He turned His face toward the bema as Zadok bowed and said, "This is the word of Adonai. Blessed be the name of Adonai."

Zadok moved back and passed the silver-tipped pointer to Yosef of Nazareth. Yosef, the seventh reader, drew near to the bema. Mary's face radiated peace as she observed her husband. The baby's fingers closed around His mother's right thumb.

Yosef raised his eyes to gaze above the heads of the men as though he could see Mary and the Holy Child behind the latticework. His voice boomed across the auditorium, filling the space.

As he spoke, Rachel felt certain that from the beginning of time this moment had been ordained. On this day, in this place, *Vayigash* was the Torah reading that would announce God's plan to redeem, deliver, and heal His broken relationship with man.

"Draw near to me!"

Yosef scrutinized the page. "Blessed be the one who comes in the Name of Adonai! This is the word of Adonai to his people. I begin the seventh part of Parashah *Vayigash*. From the Book of Beginnings."

The carpenter bowed and touched his hand to his heart in what appeared to be a silent salute to Mary and her baby. He began to read:

> *"At the words of his brother Judah, Joseph could not restrain himself in the presence of all the court who stood before him, so he called out, 'Remove everyone from before me!' Thus no one remained with him when Joseph made himself known to his brothers. He cried in a loud voice, 'I AM JOSEPH!'"*[30]

At that instant Mary's baby opened His mouth and began to cry. It was not a whimper but a lusty wail—an exclamation so loud that heads turned to see who and what was making such a racket behind the screen. A collective sigh of relief and pleasure passed through the congregation. Like Joseph of old, the Messiah was revealing His identity to His brother shepherds. *"Vayigash,"* the ancient prophetic words of Scripture declared. *"Don't be afraid! Draw near to me! I am your brother!"*[31]

Enoch, concerned at the newborn's cry, wriggled free from Rachel's lap. "Oh!" he crooned. "Poor baby!"

Rachel stretched her hand to hold him back.

Mary shook her head. "Let him come. Come closer, Enoch. Draw near. He's just so glad to be here with you all, and he can't say it any other way." She drew Enoch to her and let him touch the baby's hand.

Enoch laughed. "Is he my brother?"

From the bema Yosef spoke. *"Vayigash!* Blessed be the Name of the Lord!"

A cheer arose from the people of Beth-lehem. Mary's eyes brimmed. Rachel patted her and smiled down at the Messiah.

The carpenter closed his eyes. His lips moved in a silent prayer of adoration. His head nodded as the importance of *Vayigash* penetrated every mind and flooded every heart with joy. The roar of approval increased.

Joseph, ruler of Egypt, despite the ill treatment he had received at the hands of his brothers, still loved them. For the sake of loving his father, he wanted good for them. He stepped down from his throne and made his identity known to them at last!

Yosef raised his hands for silence.

Now only the baby's undiminished wail accompanied the *Vayigash* reading. It was, Rachel thought, a holy cry, as though when the humble carpenter read from Torah he was speaking on behalf of the baby who could not yet speak.

Yosef's words boomed in concert with the newborn's bellow.

"But Joseph's brothers could not answer him. Then Joseph said to his brothers, 'Vayigash! Draw near to me, if you please. Vayigash! Draw nearer still!' And they drew near. And he said, 'I AM . . . your brother—it is ME.'"[32]

At this the infant Messiah bellowed louder than before!

"'I AM your brother . . . whom you sold into Egypt. And now, be not distressed, nor reproach yourself for having sold me here. For it was to be a provider that Yahweh SENT ME ahead of you. For this has been two of the hunger years in the midst of the land, and there are yet five years in which there shall be neither plowing nor harvest. Thus the Lord has sent me ahead of you to ensure your survival in the land and to sustain you for a momentous deliverance.'"[33]

Again a mighty cheer arose in Beth David Synagogue!
Yosef shouted the rest of the passage above the tumult:

"'And now! It is not You who SENT ME here, BUT YAHWEH!' And Joseph fell upon his brother Ben-Yamin's neck and wept. He then kissed all his brothers and wept upon them; afterwards his brothers conversed with him."[34]

Yosef of Nazareth could not complete the reading! A tremendous roar of joy increased from the people of Beth-lehem. They leapt to their feet with clapping and cheering the good news. "*Vayigash!* Draw near to me! *Vayigash!*"

Had the angels not called out this very same thing? "Go, now! You will find Him lying in a manger! Draw near to your Lord and Savior!"[35]

The identity of the Deliverer of Israel was revealed. The Savior was in their midst! The Lord, who had existed before time, had stepped down from His heavenly throne to enter time and live in the world of men. The long-awaited baby promised in all the Scriptures was here now. Born in little Beth-lehem! Born in the place where Rachel of old had died giving birth to Ben-Yamin. Here, where Joseph's beloved mother was buried. Beth-lehem, House of Bread. The One sent from heaven by Yahweh would provide for the flock of Israel. He had been laid in a feed trough—the sign that He would one day become the Living Bread that would nourish the aching spiritual hunger of all who came to Him. He was born in the very place where David, descendant of Judah, had been born. Here, in the land belonging to that same Judah of old, who passed the test!

"*Vayigash!*"

Joseph of old had proclaimed his identity to his brother shepherds, telling them he was sent by Yahweh to deliver them. Now, here in Beth-lehem, Yahweh had sent a fulfillment of that prophecy. *Vayigash* was the message of love, forgiveness, and deliverance to the shepherds of the Temple flocks and to a people yet unborn!

Vayigash! Draw near to me, declares the Lord. I love you so much I lay aside my awesome power and open my arms to embrace you as the brother you rejected.

The family rift between God and His beloved children, as foretold in Scripture, was about to be healed forever by the only Son of the Living God of Israel!

In the Women's Gallery women and children drew near and surrounded Mary. Young and old, they worshipped the infant King of Israel. They clapped as they sang the Great Hallel!

In the hall men raised their hands and began to spin and dance and chant, "*Vayigash!* Bring forth the One who is sent! Lift high the Lord! *Vayigash!* Draw near to the One who is sent to deliver his brothers!

Reveal our Savior to his people! We have not come to him! Our Savior is sent to us from heaven!"

The baby no longer cried. Could the face of one so small reflect joy in the understanding of others? He acted serene and content in the celebration . . . happy to be surrounded by the laughing, singing children of Beth-lehem. His tiny hands stretched up toward their beaming faces, as if to thank heaven for this occasion.

The lattice barrier dividing the congregation between male and female, young and old, came down.

"Vayigash! Vayigash!"

Seven shepherds from the fields drew near to worship. Mary and the Holy Child were lifted high in their chair and held above the heads of the dancing congregation of Beth David Synagogue.

"Vayigash! Vayigash!"

In this reunion between God and man that first Shabbat morning, the Savior of Israel was embraced and adored by His family, the shepherds, and their families in Beth-lehem. Those who had given up hope that they would ever see Him face-to-face danced and sang as they drew near to Him.

It was, Rachel thought, as she whirled to the music with her boys and Zadok, something like a wedding celebration. Only this time the Bridegroom was only a few days old, and His bride was the nation of Israel.

And the reading was a promise to all who worshipped the newborn King that morning: *Vayigash!* Draw near to me and do not delay! And you will be near to me—you, your sons, your grandchildren, your flock and your cattle, and all that is yours. And I will provide for you there. So you will not be destitute, you, your household, and all that is there.

CHAPTER 8

A squad of Herodian soldiers tramped ahead of the royal party, and another followed after. A stiff breeze from the sea plastered red tunics against bodies. Green cloaks flapped toward Parthia. Helmet plumes drooped in the drizzling rain and leather fittings creaked.

Herod's litter bearers were shod with Roman boots like his soldiers. Hundreds of hobnails screeched on the slick paving of the ascent. Despite the inclement weather and his many ailments, Herod still insisted on this trip to the Hippodrome.

Caesarea Maritima was Herod's salute to all things Roman. Named for Herod's patron, Caesar Augustus, the city displayed all that was fashionable in Roman architecture. Now, nearing the end of his life, Herod was not satisfied with any of it. The cargo docks needed renovating. The aqueduct bringing fresh water from Mount Carmel was inadequate. The sewers did not work properly. The Hippodrome, 1,000 cubits long and 175 wide, with elaborate facilities for horse and chariot racing, was too small. Herod wanted additional balconies built.

The king's palanquin was completely enclosed. The ebony frame was hung with woolen drapes. Like the bearers, Chief Steward Talmai and the Jewish high priest Boethus splashed through the puddles. They trudged, one on either side of the litter, straining to hear the king's commentary.

"I had another dream about a usurper—a traitor!" Herod's wheezing voice asserted from within the tapestry. "A child with a star on his brow. What else can it mean but a conspiracy to replace me?"

Talmai dropped back a pace so he could exchange a glance with Boethus. All known and even suspected rebels had been either murdered or imprisoned. The *am ha aretz*, the simple country folk, were gripped with fear. Voicing anything remotely suspicious that might be overheard by Herod's spies led to torture or crucifixion. With Roman troops to keep order and this miserable weather, the present likelihood of revolt was miniscule.

Still, it was not safe to argue with the monarch. Better to listen and speak soothingly.

Reapproaching the fold in the hangings, Talmai observed, "But a child is not threatening, sire. Perhaps the dream foretells the dynasty that will come after you."

But Talmai himself did not find that explanation likely. Since Herod had executed or disowned most of his sons, the possibilities of the royal lineage were getting very limited.

Herod's voice cracked as he strained to overcome the thumping tread of the marching men. "I heard a voice. Like it was warning me. 'A virgin and a child,' it said. 'One born to be king!' What do you say to that, Boethus?"

The high priest's face clouded with alarm. He stammered, perhaps hoping Talmai would come to his aid.

The steward had no intention of pulling the king's attention back his way. Let the priest fend for himself!

At the last possible instant before Herod could repeat the inquiry, relief replaced the terror on Boethus' face. "Not a warning, Majesty! An omen of good news."

"What is that?" Herod demanded.

"Your highness is cleverly remembering the words of the Cumaean Sibyl as quoted by the Roman poet Virgil. How did that go? 'Now the virgin is returning.' Something about a new human race. And then, 'The birth of a child when the iron age of humanity will end and the golden age begin.' It's the prophecy about Caesar Augustus, delivered a century or more ago," the *cohen hagadol* asserted. "It's a sign, a good omen. Caesar will be pleased with how you honor him with this city."

Herod's black-wigged head was thrust out of the curtains. His scraggly beard waggled in the breeze, and he kept the drapes tucked beneath his chin. "A good omen, you say?"

Boethus reassured the king. "The emperor will be delighted with your tribute to him. The dream confirms this."

"Yes, yes, you are right," Herod concurred. "I see it now. A good omen. All about Caesar."

Just then one of the litter bearers tripped slightly on the uneven pavement, jostling the king into a sharp cry and an extended groan.

"Have that man flogged," Herod ordered. "And if it happens again, flog him to death." Speaking again to Boethus, Herod concluded, "Of course, you are correct. Thank you for the reminder. A good omen. I feel much better now."

It was two hours past sunset. Shabbat was over, but the lamp in the study room of the synagogue continued to burn. The glow spilled out onto a patch of snow.

Havila glanced out the window of their house and toward the synagogue. "Maybe he's fallen asleep."

Grandmother took a bite of a date and spit the seed into a bowl. "Love of Torah is better to some men than love of a woman. Your lot in life is to be second to the Law and the Prophets."

After this morning in synagogue, Havila understood why Eliyahu had wanted to study Torah before they made love.

Eliyahu had not come home for supper. Havila had taken him his meal on a tray, but he did not look up from the text of the open scroll on the table. He promised to eat but barely noticed when she left him.

Havila tucked Dan into bed, prayed, and sang with him.

Grandmother, eyes milky with age, gazed at the light of the fire. "If you don't go now you won't see him till morning."

Havila kissed Dan good night and joined the old woman. "Such a day. Like no day ever before." She stretched her hands to the warmth. "Everyone so happy."

"I prayed as I danced. Prayed I would find my coin." The old woman spit a date seed with precision from a lifetime of practice.

"We all prayed for something."

"Go, Havila. Go to Eliyahu. Ask him what he is searching for. Remind him you are warmer than Torah, eh?"

Havila nodded and wrapped a blanket around her shoulders. She stepped out into the night without a lantern and walked the short distance to the synagogue.

It was unlocked, dark and silent. She threaded through the benches of the unlit sanctuary to the Torah room. Knocking twice at the door, she called, "Eliyahu?"

When he did not answer, she opened the door and peered in. His supper remained untouched on the table beneath the window. The lamp cast long shadows on the white walls. Eliyahu sat, with his head in his hands, on a bench in front of the table. The Ezekiel scroll was open before him. He did not look up when she spoke.

"It's freezing in here."

"Warm enough."

"You've almost let the fire die." She threw a dried grapevine branch onto the coals of the brazier.

"I haven't thought of anything but this morning. Enough to warm a man inside and keep him warm."

"You haven't eaten." Havila regarded the slightly built form of her husband with affectionate exasperation.

"There's food enough for me. Enough for a lifetime and then some."

Havila frowned at the uneaten chicken and unbroken bread. The bowl of dates, Eliyahu's favorite snack, was still full. "What are you looking for?"

A crimson ember, nestled against the grapevine, touched it with a tentative flame.

"His name."

"They haven't told anyone. Rachel says they won't speak his name until his *Bris Milah*. The angel spoke the name to Mary. And Yosef knows what it will be. They've kept it secret from everyone. Everyone. We'll just have to be surprised."

He raised his head at her remark. "I think I know."

"Know what?"

"What the Haftarah means."

"Are you all right?" Havila's hands were on her hips—a sign she knew her husband would normally perceive as an imminent warning. But tonight he paid no attention.

The entire length of the vine cutting burst into yellow fire.

"We didn't read the Haftarah this morning. Only the Torah portion," he said slowly.

"It seemed to be enough to read about Joseph the Great and his reunion with his brothers. Anything else and the foundations of this building would have cracked from the dancing. Or the want of it, perhaps. And no one would sit still for any more words." Havila added a handful of sticks to the flames, now crackling and popping.

Eliyahu tapped the table with the silver-tipped pointer. "The prophet Ezekiel. The Haftarah for this morning. The first Shabbat of the child's life." He patted the bench beside him. "Sit, Havila. I have to tell someone now or I'll burst. I'll never be able to sleep."

Eliyahu had never before opened his thoughts to her about the deep matters of Torah. "Tell me, then. Please, love!"

"Listen." Eliyahu sounded eager.

She sat beside him and studied the unbroken lines of writing that appeared to her eyes like pictures of dancing flames in the soft light. She could not read well enough to study the Scriptures or parse out the individual words from the text. Excitement filled her as she waited for Eliyahu to share what he had discovered.

"Here is the word of the Lord," he said. "The word given to us in the Haftarah message at the infant Messiah's first Shabbat on earth among his people. This is the message concerning the Sixth Covenant that The Eternal promises for the salvation of Israel." He pronounced each word distinctly as the pointer slid across the page:

"This is what the Sovereign Lord says: I will take the Israelites out of the nations where they have gone. I will gather them from all around and bring them back into their own land. . . . There will be one King over them. . . . I will save them from all their sinful backsliding, and I will cleanse them. They will be My people and I will be their God! My servant David will be king over them and they will all have one Shepherd!"[36]

Havila nodded. "One Shepherd. For this reason he is born among us shepherds. Will he live here with us too? grow up among our sons?"

Eliyahu raised one finger, urging her to be patient. He continued to read: *"They will follow My laws and be careful to keep My decrees. They will*

*live in the land I gave Jacob. . . . They and their children's children will live
there forever. And David My servant will be their prince forever. I will make a
covenant of peace with them. It will be an everlasting covenant. I will establish
them and increase their numbers. I will put My sanctuary among them forever.
My dwelling place shall be with them. I will be their God and they will be My
people. Then the nations will know that I the Lord make Israel holy, when
My sanctuary is among them forever.*"[37]

Eliyahu lowered his head until his brow touched the scroll. His
hooded eyes and hunched shoulders expressed such reverence that
Havila shivered.

"This is the Word of the Lord. This morning we have seen this
prophecy come true before our eyes! Havila! This child is the sign of
the Sixth Covenant. Of salvation! God has come down to dwell with us
as he promised when he spoke to Ezekiel the prophet. Immanu'el, the
angels called the Prince, 'God-with-us.' It is his royal title. He is the
one Shepherd of Israel."[38]

"But what is his name?"

"The name of the Sixth Covenant is Yeshua! Salvation! The One
True Shepherd who will save Israel! Our Salvation. He will wipe away
our sins and make his dwelling place with us forever!"[39]

Melchior quit shaving. His beard sprouted a beautiful red-gold as
Esther had predicted, but she did not seem to notice.

Like wine spilled from the cup into the sand, Melchior was convinced his chance to tell Esther he loved her was lost forever.

She hardly looked at him now. As they traveled, she protected her
skin against the weather with a veil. Was she hiding smiles, hiding longing, hiding her feelings for him?

He trudged along behind her in the camp in misery. When she
came near, his heart felt as though it would break. When he slept he
dreamed of her. When he was awake he tried not to catch her eye lest
she somehow see last night's dreams in his hungry gaze.

If Melchior had ever been so miserable, he could not remember
the occasion.

Perhaps it was just as well he had been so clumsy and spilled the wine.
What hope did he have of being loved by such a woman as Esther?

The snowy backs of firstborn male lambs stretched as far from Migdal Eder as Yosef could see. The late-afternoon sun completed its circuit low in the southwestern sky. The sky was pale blue, streaked with high clouds.

Yosef said to Zadok, "The Tenth of Tevet. A fast day tomorrow. A day of mourning. The anniversary of the beginning of Nebuchad-nezzar's siege of Yerushalayim. A strange day for him to be circum-cised."

"A week gone since the world changed." Zadok turned his face to the heavens and closed his eyes. "Yet I see them still. Angels. Hear their voices singin' hope t' us poor fellows out in that field. Never expected it . . . not for me t' witness. We were there. Just there." He swept the tip of his staff toward a watch fire on the verge of the pasture. Sheep cropping the stubble resembled dirty heaps of snow.

"You. First witness," Yosef murmured. "So it is you and Rachel must stand with me and Mary at the circumcision."

Zadok's eyes opened wide, and he lifted his staff to point in the direction of Jerusalem. "And this is what I say t' the Fast of Nebuchad-nezzar's Siege. Aye, if I were a learned man, which I am not, I'd say the day of his circumcision is the very day the siege of darkness against all of us is finally broken. All the world will remember his *Bris Milah* and celebrate our freedom! And we'll have a banquet t' mark the day he was circumcised."

"Well spoken. You should have been a rabbi."

"Aye. I'm shepherd to dumb sheep, which makes me the next thing t' a rabbi."

Yosef pondered what Zadok had said. "But you didn't answer my question. You and Rachel? Will you stand as his guardians? *Kvatter* and *Kvatterin*? Beside me and Mary at the *Bris Milah*? Our family's so far away. You've treated us like your own."

"It's all too much, Yosef. I tell y', lad! My heart can't hold such a great thing. It'll burst if I taste even one more sip of happiness."

"But there'll be no supper after the shedding of his blood at the *Bris Milah*," Yosef noted grimly. "That will have to wait until the present siege of Yerushalayim by Herod and Rome is finally at an end."

Zadok spit and made the sign against the evil eye. "May the Lord grant that day be in our lifetime, eh?"

Yosef clapped Zadok on the back and said relentlessly, "But . . . if you and Rachel would do us the honor? You will sit in Elijah's throne and be the baby's *Sandek*?"

Zadok, silenced for once by the enormous responsibility of Yosef's request, sat on the boulder overlooking the Pasture of the Firstborn Lambs. The scent of woodsmoke was in the air.

He tugged the braid of his thick black beard. "Who am I that y' would ask me? Me? Stand at your right side? Hold the baby during the *Bris*? The circumcision and namin' of Messiah, our King? Could a shepherd be chosen protector and guardian t' such a one as that? I'm only Zadok. I have no wealth. The only thing in life I care for is my wife and our boys. Who am I . . . yet y' ask me t' take the oath before The Eternal that I can raise the boy properly if you and Mary should die?"

"No man in Israel but you could I trust at such a time." Yosef looked away, lest Zadok see the emotion in his eyes.

"Ah, Yosef. I'll make no lastin' mark upon this world. Poor shepherds are no more remembered than sheep." The staff rested on his shoulder, and he spread his broad palms as he spoke.

"Like me. Who'll remember the name of a carpenter from Nazareth? But, Zadok, like you, I've heard the voices of angels! They call me to carry him on my shoulders. I'll teach him how to make a beam level and smooth and how to drive a nail straight in with one blow. That's all I have to offer."

"Me! Stand as guardian at the *Bris Milah* of the Messiah. And my own Rachel support the mother of the King! He's King, though none know it yet. None but the righteous must know he's here. Herod would seek t' kill him. Think of it! Herod kill the One who commands the angel armies," Zadok reflected. "Till the end of my days I'll not forget his heavenly troops shinin' there above the field!"

"That's why you must stand with us at the circumcision. You and your Rachel. Rachel, whose gentle hands helped guide the Lord into this world from *olam haba*."

"Rachel. My own ewe lamb. Rachel. Aye. Now she's worthy t' stand as witness. She knows a mother's heart. She knows what it means t' bring forth life. Many's the child she's helped into this world. Seventy sons born in Beth-lehem over the last two years and my Rachel the midwife of them all. Seventy boys . . . may all grow up t' serve their King!"

"It came to me and Mary . . . yes! She said the vision of your faces was clear in her mind as we prayed. The two of you as honored witnesses. You two on the right and the left at the circumcision. The shepherd and the midwife as we speak aloud the name for the first time. His name. The name the angel commanded we must call him. And you, Zadok, by standing there with us, pledge you'll care for him if we should die? You'll take him in so he'll never be hungry or in want?"

They were questions, not commands. Yosef had pondered his own death many times. Suppose he died before the child was a man. Who would care for Him? This greathearted shepherd of God's Temple flocks seemed to be the only trustworthy man.

Zadok nodded. "Aye! I think often on the same thing. If I should perish, who would care for my widow and three children? 'Tis a worry when a man loves his family so much. Count on me, Yosef! That I can pledge to you. Me and Rachel . . . we'll embrace the honor of guardin' the wee lad with our very lives. Aye!"

Zadok patted his battered staff like a weapon. His eyes narrowed as he considered the glowering fortress of Herodium in the distance. "None of them dark hearts will harm one hair of his head or threaten his life while I breathe. Count on me, Yosef. Herod is a wolf. This babe is the Firstborn Lamb of The Eternal. Rest easy. I'll prepare and pray and wash and dress for his *Bris Milah*. And me and my Rachel will come with our family t' fetch you."

Talmai and Boethus stood together under the arched colonnade at one end of the harbor. While Herod conferred with his architect and the master mason, steward and priest likewise put their heads together, out of the king's hearing.

"Cumaean Sibyl, eh?" Talmai said with a sideways glance and a smirk. "Quoting a Greek prophetess of Apollo? And our Roman emperor is a deity? What would your Jewish council, your Sanhedrin, say about those words if they heard you?"

Boethus stiffened, then replied haughtily, "Just because I serve

Lord Herod in Jerusalem doesn't make me one of the superstitious, illiterate *am ha aretz* of Judea. I was educated in Alexandria, remember."

"Truly," Talmai acknowledged with a mocking bow. "And you're the king's father-in-law as well. Perhaps he calls you Abba in your private moments? But I meant no disrespect. Your response was well made. My informers are running out of beggars and Pharisees to denounce in Jerusalem. I'd hate to start in on Caesarea. Bad for the economy. Might cause the very revolt the king already expects. Besides, His Majesty still frets about Caesar's disapproval of the execution of the two princes. Smart of you to connect his dream with Caesar and turn a nightmare into a good thing."

"I spoke the truth," Boethus protested. "The Sibyl delivered the prophecy about a virgin-born child a hundred years ago."

Talmai's head already bobbed in agreement before the high priest's sentence was complete. "And our emperor reaped the benefit by spreading the story far and wide that he is that child. Remember hearing of the comet that appeared on the day of Julius Caesar's funeral? His spirit was a new star, set in the heavens, Augustus announced. Then, after his father was promoted to godhood, instantly Augustus was . . . the son of god. Very timely, very convenient. All Rome buzzed with how the Sibyl's words applied to the emperor. Prophetic! Divinely inspired! Not virgin born, but you can't have everything, can you? Still, he was called 'Augustus: The promised child who ushers in the Golden Age!' And the lion and lamb will lie down together . . . heaven on earth, courtesy of Augustus Caesar, the son of god."

Boethus archly observed, "Such scornful talk would get your tongue cut out in Rome. Might even in Judea."

A lazy smile crept across the steward's face. "Don't try to threaten me, priest. For one thing, you're no good at it. For another, you need my goodwill even more than I need yours. We have both staked our futures on Herod and on his son Antipater as his successor. Keeping Herod happy and reassured is our mutual duty."

Talmai noted that Boethus was no longer listening. Instead the high priest stared off into the slate gray sky above the southern horizon. His eyes narrowed in contemplation.

"What is it?"

Boethus gave a start but attempted to mask it with gruffness. "Nothing! Nothing of consequence. It's just . . . something I remembered . . . a star . . . and the child of a virgin."

"Barracks-room joke, no doubt!" Talmai suggested coarsely.

When the high priest offered no further explanation, Talmai studied him curiously. The hair on the back of Boethus' neck, right below his white turban, stood erect as if from a sudden chill.

9

CHAPTER

I t was shortly after sunset when the caravan reached the outskirts of Damascus. Twilight had little effect on the already colorless obscurity of land and heavens.

The travelers had lived with leaden skies and intermittent rain for many miles. Ever since entering Roman-occupied Syria, the pilgrims faced winter travel at its most exhausting. The trek from the Parthian border slogged through low-lying, swampy marsh. Even the brief periods of relief from mud were little improvement. Ridgelines of jagged volcanic rocks wore out donkeys' hooves and made both human and camel feet sore.

Melchior, trudging near the head of the procession, was the first to see the torches blazing on the Roman battlements. Blinking through the mist, Melchior stopped to brush aside a lock of soggy, light red hair from his eyes. His first reaction on sighting Damascus was relief, followed immediately by recognition of the bone-deep weariness he had been ignoring for the last five miles. If he, strong and fit at age twenty-six, was so tired as to be staggering, what must his companions be experiencing? Melchior was especially concerned for Old Balthasar, even though the elder man rode a donkey.

The camel drover at the head of the line glanced once at the city's outline, grunted, and pushed Melchior out of the way. The string of camels he led plodded stoically on, as if the difference between five hundred additional yards or five hundred miles was of no consequence.

Melchior trotted back over the ridge past the spice merchants and silk dealers. He stopped when he reached Balthasar's brown donkey. Esther rode a rust-colored animal close by his side.

"It's just ahead. Damascus," Melchior reported, waving vaguely over the slope.

Old Balthasar nodded. His shoulders drooped and his complexion was pale. "Thanks be to The Eternal," he murmured.

"Thanks be to The Eternal," Esther echoed. Gesturing for Melchior to come nearer, she added in a lower tone, "Grandfather's not at all well. He won't admit it, but his breathing trouble continues."

"Don't worry," Melchior offered stoutly. "A quarter hour and we'll have him snug at a caravansary by a hot fire. Let him get a quart of lentil stew inside him and he'll be right as—" Melchior stopped himself from mentioning the hated word *rain*.

Despite her own weariness Esther favored Melchior with a smile that warmed him better than fire or stew ever could.

Despite the cheerful thought of a hot, rain-free meal, their travels were still far from over. Miles of bandit-infested Trachonitis lay ahead of them. One hundred and fifty miles still separated them from Jerusalem.

Before he reached the other side of the hill again, Melchior was surprised to hear camels bawling and donkeys braying. There was much milling around but no forward progress.

"What is it?" Melchior demanded of Gaspar. "Why are we stopping?"

"Roman guards shut the gate at sunset. No exceptions, they say. We have to camp outside tonight and enter tomorrow."

Another night in dripping tents, trying to dry clothes and warm spirits by the feeble efforts of charcoal braziers, Melchior thought. Nor would arguing help. Here, Roman law was master.

"Help me get Balthasar into shelter, please," Melchior asked Gaspar.

"Willingly," the other returned. "And cheer up, young Court Astronomer Melchior. Even reaching the walls of Damascus is something, eh? Remember why we are here. Soon we will see *him*, and all this will be forgotten."

Such a party in the house of Rachel and Zadok! There were no men in the room, only mothers and children. Havila, Dan on her hip, handed out honey-dipped dates to scores of jostling toddlers. Sharona, youngest sons in tow, wiped faces and hands. Grandmother held Samu'el in one arm and little Obi in the other as she talked animatedly to the wife of the butcher about the price of a chicken in a world dominated by lamb chops.

Tonight, the night before the baby's circumcision ceremony, was *Leil Shimurim*, which means "the night of protection." Mary and Yosef followed the custom that had existed for 1,365 years since the Exodus. The sages taught that the mitzvah of *Bris Milah* was so spiritually important that the powers of darkness wailed and gathered together to prevent the circumcision of a newborn child of the covenant.

Young children, souls pure and unblemished, were invited into the household. Prayers from innocent hearts, it was said, pierced the heavens and formed a spiritual protection that called down blessings on the baby, the household, and the family.

Tonight Yosef, Eliyahu, and Zadok, all of whom would participate in the ceremony tomorrow, were absent from the house. They were together at the mikveh, the ritual bath.

Since the birthing cottage was too small, Rachel's home hosted Mary's baby. It overflowed with seventy toddlers, all boys under three years of age, and their mothers. The sweet scent of lavender drying in the rafters mingled with that of grape juice spilled on the paving stones. Those children who could speak recited simple prayers and sang songs and uttered halting blessings over food. The littlest of the congregation, like Obi, whose souls had only recently come down from heaven, were counted as honored guests. Even though the smallest revelers could not yet pray or sing, the noise of squawks and squeals was deafening.

Rachel coached Enoch in his name verse: "*And Enoch . . .*"

The boy frowned down at the baby and recited. "I am Enoch. *And Enoch . . . walked . . . with Adonai . . . and was no more. . . .* That's ME. Baby! I'm Enoch!"

The baby Messiah wriggled in His mother's lap and opened His mouth with an *oh* of approval.

Rachel hugged her son. "He likes that last part especially, Enoch."

Mary laughed and patted Enoch's head. "Well spoken, Enoch! The baby likes your verse very much."

"What's his name?" Enoch asked.

Mary leaned forward and put a finger to her lips. "It's a very secret name, wonderful and mighty! Until tomorrow, Enoch, we can't tell anyone. Then we announce it at his *Bris Milah*, and everyone will know!"

"Everyone in the world?" Enoch asked.

"Yes, Enoch. Someday. Everyone." Rachel pushed Enoch's dark curls from his brow.

"Does he have a name verse like mine?"

Rachel confided, "Oh, Enoch, he has so many name verses we can't count them."

The wind howled up the pass and whistled fiercely round the corner of the house, giving credence to the tradition that demons flew to the site to attempt to take the soul of the baby. But their moaning was drowned out by the cheerful piping of seventy small voices, all speaking at once.

Havila clapped her hands for attention. Mothers, arms laden with precious bundles, turned to her. Here was the real reason they had come. The babble of conversation and assorted squawks died away until only the wind wailed.

Rachel, as honored *Kvatterin*, godmother, passed an unlit candle to Mary.

Mary dipped the wick into the flame of an oil lamp and recited, "Blessed are you, Lord God of the Universe, who has given us One True Light in this world and in the world to come."

The children cheered and applauded.

Havila stepped forward. It was right for Havila to lead the young congregation because she was the rabbi's wife. "Attention, everyone! A big day tomorrow and all of you must go home and go to bed, eh? But first we say the evening prayers for the newborn baby boy on his *Leil Shimurim*! We'll sing it like we do at school. Yes. You on the right sing first. On the left you answer. Mothers, sing for your babies if they have no words."

Havila raised her hands. Shining faces turned upward. The mothers of Beth-lehem knew the words and sang for their sons.

Mary picked up her baby from His cradle and supported His head so He faced His young congregation.

The Song of Shimurim began in Mary's clear, sweet soprano:

"Hear, O Israel, the Lord our God,
the Lord is one.
    You shall love the Lord your God
With all your heart
        With all your soul,
With all your might.
    And these words
Which I command you today
        Shall be upon your heart."⁴⁰

The song died away, and Havila pronounced the blessing on the Innocents of Beth-lehem. "May the angel who has delivered us from all evil bless the lads, and may our names and the names of our fathers Avraham and Yitz'chak be called upon them, and may they increase abundantly like fish in the midst of the earth!"

The wind sighed, scraping dead tree branches against the stones of the house.

Mary's smile faded for an instant as she gazed down at her baby and kissed His cheek. What message was on the wind? An ominous silence hung in the room.

Havila kissed little Dan. "And now we all say the final benediction: 'Blessed are you, Lord our God, King of the Universe, by whose word all things came into being.'"

Enoch asked, "Mama, will they hurt him? Will him bleed, Mama?"

Obi began to cry. Near the back of the room another baby joined his wail. Then another and another.

"He made . . . even the wind." Rachel brushed her lips over the brows of her three boys. "Don't be afraid, Obi. Don't cry. Even the wind will obey his word."

Charcoal braziers blazed along every wall of King Herod's audience chamber. Every window was carefully shuttered. Every opening, both windows and doors, hung with brocaded fabrics. To Chief Steward

Talmai the heat in the room was oppressive, but no amount of warmth was enough to suit the monarch. He complained incessantly about the ache in his bones, the stiffness in neck and shoulders, the fingers and toes that had no feeling, and the sense that a block of ice rested in his chest.

It was the coldest winter anyone could remember, but no one in Herod's court suffered from it as he did. As a consequence, to be in Herod's presence was to sweat. Woe to anyone who suggested a need for fresh air. A slave overheard making such an incautious statement had been flogged to death. Even a courtier of high station might find himself banished to Galilee for such a complaint.

After the trial, sentence, and execution of Herod's sons for their parts in an imagined conspiracy, Talmai had hoped the king's mental state would improve. Every day the steward offered soothing words about how loyal his remaining son and heir Antipater was and what a fine job Antipater was performing as a diplomat in Rome before Caesar.

But Herod grew more petulant than ever. Nothing satisfied him. His bathwater was either too cold or dangerously hot. His food was tasteless or overseasoned. Dinner conversation was either boring or suspiciously flattering.

At least the king's nightmares had decreased. No longer was a massive dose of poppy juice required to stave them off.

It was an enormous relief to the household. Even when drugged into slumber, Herod had awoken screaming, rousing the entire bodyguard and insisting all lamps and torches be lit and the palace searched for intruders.

The last such episode had been some days earlier.

Today the king entertained emissaries from Nabatea and Cyprus. He was not jovial, but he was cordial, and no sudden executions had been ordered either. The report from his copper mines on the island of Cyprus was encouraging: New veins of the ore had opened at the same time sources elsewhere diminished. The Empire craved ever more of the red metal for use in bronze armor and brass lamps. The demand drove up the price. Herod was richer than ever.

Talmai saw the change of mood come over King Herod in his audience chamber, despite the flow of good financial news. The chief steward had seen this happen many times before.

The king, who had been questioning the Cypriot mine foreman, stopped doing so. Leaning back on his throne, he inclined his head toward his right shoulder. His gaze fixed on a spot high on the south wall, and he began nodding, as if listening to an unseen whisperer standing just behind his shoulder.

Without warning he demanded, "Where is the messenger from Yerushalayim? Why have I not received a report? It is overdue!"

Talmai knew the courier had arrived from the capital two days earlier, but the king had refused to see him. Herod could not be bothered with insignificant details of governing, such as how many citizens had died of diseases rampant in the poorer quarters of the city.

Talmai did not remind the monarch of this fact.

Bowing and stepping backwards, the mine manager was wise enough not to question the interruption.

Summoning the messenger from an antechamber, Talmai presented the soldier to Herod, who glared and demanded, "What news of the new rebellion?"

"Sire?" the man said doubtfully. The officer, one of Herod's Thracian mercenaries, was bewildered. "There's no rebellion. With the cold so intense I've never seen the city so quiet. There's no crime. Hardly anyone goes out at all."

"You are lying! The Pharisees are whining again! They whisper that when Messiah comes, I will be deposed!"

"Sire?" the courier repeated.

"It is going on there now! In Yerushalayim! They are talking about him!"

"There is always talk, Majesty," Talmai suggested. "But you know my informants are everywhere. At the slightest hint of some usurper being pushed forward, I'll know at once and deal with it. Never fear."

"They will not stop unless they are all crucified," Herod shrieked. "All of them!"

Three of the *doryphoroi*, Herod's bodyguards—huge, blond-haired northerners—drew their swords and advanced from the corners where they had been posted. Idle conversation in the corners of the room came to an abrupt halt.

Despite the swelter, Talmai knew every person in the chamber felt the draft of death on the back of his neck. Summoning his nerve, he suggested, "We have already executed all the ringleaders, Majesty. There is nothing to fear."

Herod focused baleful eyes on his servant. "I hear otherwise. No more reports just once a week. I want the news from Yerushalayim every day! Every day, you hear? The slightest hint of revolt and we must know at once."

What else could Talmai reply? "It shall be done, Majesty."

In the mikveh, the stone bath beneath the synagogue, Yosef, Eliyahu, and Zadok completed their ritual immersion in preparation for the morning's ceremony. The walls had been recently whitewashed, but the ceiling remained soot-streaked from long ages of lamp smoke. It was said that this was the mikveh where David had washed on the day he killed Goliath.

Eliyahu, though he was the rabbi, would double as the *Mohel*, performing the circumcision. Zadok was *Kvatter*, godfather, and honored *Sandek*, the one who would hold the baby during the circumcision.

Zadok grinned. "Look at these." He held out his enormous hands. "Clumsy, these paws. Now y' give me a lamb I can sling round my shoulders and I never fear hurtin' the wee thing. Ah, but a baby! One so small. Hold him for the *Bris*. I'm not much good with child blood. And when a baby cries, I'm lost. Ask my Rachel. No good at it, she says. So. At the *Bris*. Now, there's a knife involved in this. If I hold him too tight, that's not good. If I hold him too loose at such a moment . . . that's no good. Never cease worryin'."

"Just hold him steady for the knife," Eliyahu instructed.

"Aye. That I will. Do my best." Zadok wagged his shaggy head.

"Imagine. Zadok. *Sandek* at Messiah's *Bris*. An honor, Yosef, which this simple shepherd is not deservin'. Hope I'm steady on the job."

The trio of men said farewell at the gate of the synagogue. Eliyahu placed a box of study scrolls in Yosef's arms. "Tonight, Yosef, is the Night of Protection for the little one. Tomorrow we will all hear his name revealed at last, eh? I've felt a stirring in the air. Something I've never felt before. As though the darkness has turned its eyes this way."

Zadok gestured toward the broken teeth of Herodium's towers. "Glad t' know it isn't just me. An evil time he's been born to."

Eliyahu concurred. "You must keep the light burning for him in the room. Your sword in one hand and the Word of the Lord in the other, eh? Read the passages marked down on the parchment. Of all nights, this night the Word of Yahweh will be a shield. The name—*his* name—will be a declaration of war against Satan. I'm sure of it."

Yosef and Zadok trudged together back to the house and the cottage. "The women and children have gone," Zadok said. "I'll stay dressed. Keep my shoes on. Remember the bell rope if you need help with his defense."

Yosef raised his face to the wind. "It isn't the sword I fear tonight. But something . . . else. You and Eliyahu confirmed it for me. Nothing I can see. Nothing I can explain. But some danger."

"Aye. Like the scent of a jackal when the flock is sleepin'. It's there. Though a man can't see it in the dark. Tomorrow we welcome him into the covenant. His name will be spoken t' the congregation. Will the danger t' his life pass then?"

Yosef could not answer. "Tomorrow seems a long way off."

Mary lay with the baby in the crook of her arm. The candle burned low. Three unlit tapers were on the table . . . each to follow the other through the night watches.

"It was a fine party." Mary's mood seemed lighter than Yosef had seen her in a long time. "So many little boys! Their mothers all with funny stories about their circumcision. It's good to laugh. So good to laugh again, Yosef."

What a contrast her happiness was compared to the concerns of Zadok and Eliyahu. Yosef set the box of scrolls onto the table and peeked at the baby. He was awake. Bright eyes reflected the joy of His mother. "I'm glad to hear it went so well."

"The women are so kind here. Not like . . . well, you know. So different here."

"They believe what the angels told them. They love him and you too, Mary. You're easy to love."

"If only Mama could be here tomorrow. And Papa. My sisters."

"Yes. Well. Now you should get some sleep. A big day tomorrow for you and the baby. I'll stand watch. Read a bit. Eliyahu gave me a list of Scriptures to study. Enough to last till morning." He kissed the top of her head, then the baby's brow.

"Yes. I am tired. I'll just lay awake awhile and listen."

Yosef read aloud for several hours, following the order Eliyahu had given him. Mary nodded off long before the first candle guttered.

Halfway through the second candle exhaustion settled on Yosef. His voice had become a hoarse whisper. His eyes blurred as he read the final passage: Messiah's naming prophecy from the book of Isaiah. *"For unto us a child is born. To us a Son is given. And the government will be on His shoulder. And He will be called Wonderful, Counselor, Mighty God, Everlasting Father, Prince of Peace. Of the increase of His government and peace there will be no end. He will reign on David's throne . . . from that time on and forever."*[41]

Yosef did not roll up the scroll but left it open on the table as he prepared for a few hours of sleep. Keeping his sword by his side, he lay down across the threshold and closed his eyes. The image of the candle flame danced on his lids. The question burned in his mind.

Blessed are you, O Adonai, for giving us wisdom and insight into eternal mysteries through your Holy Word. You do not mind if I ask a question, eh? You have written that the Messiah will be called Wonderful, Piliy. Secret. Remarkable. Miraculous. Also Mighty God and Everlasting Father. But here he is. Messiah. Son of David. Just a baby sleeping beside his mother in a little cottage. How can it be that The Eternal One is contained in a form that we can see with our eyes and hold in our arms?

Yosef listened to the wind stirring the dry branches of the trees outside the cottage. But the answer was not in the wind. He gazed for a time at the fire crackling on the hearth, but there was no reply in the fire. He gazed to where the baby lay beside Mary . . . dark curls and perfect head against her breast.

There he is. Real and wonderful. But how does it work? That the Immortal One, who has existed since before time, can inhabit a mortal body? How can this baby, who will be called son of Yosef of Nazareth, also be named Wonderful, Counselor, Mighty God, Everlasting Father, and Prince of Peace?

With that question still unanswered, Yosef fell asleep.

Had hours passed, or only minutes?

The faint tinkle of bells disturbed Yosef's slumber. He lay on his side, facing the door. His hand closed around the grip of his sword. The sound of bells increased. Someone was standing at the threshold.

Yosef . . . son of Jacob . . . son of David.

"Who's there?"

The voice, richly resonant, repeated, *Yosef . . . son of Jacob . . . son of David . . . where are you?*

Yosef had heard this voice in his dreams before. "Here I am. Asleep on the floor of a cottage in Beth-lehem. Guarding the baby Messiah on this night before the covenant is sealed by his circumcision."

Open your eyes, Yosef, and see.

Yosef opened his eyes. He was dreaming.

Beside Yosef stood the angel who had appeared to him in his dreams before. Gabriel! Messenger of the Most High. His skin shone like molten silver. Clothes shimmered in the light.

The next thing Yosef knew he lay on a grassy slope beneath an olive tree. The day was warm and bright. A woman sat weeping beside a pasture where a handful of sheep grazed.

She cannot see us, Gabriel assured Yosef.

"Who is guarding Mary's baby if I am here?"

Do not fear. Your question has been heard.

"So many questions. Which question?"

Tomorrow in Beth-lehem, the town of David, Messiah's name—the name I spoke before He was conceived—His name will at last be revealed. And by His name His purpose on earth will be revealed. All the world will know the

Salvation of the Almighty has come to mankind. His name is wonderful as the prophet Isaias has written. Heaven and earth cannot contain all the names by which the Lord is known. The one Name I revealed to Mary, His mother, and to you, Yosef . . . by this Name He will be known on earth.[42]

"But shouldn't I stay at the house? Shouldn't I be lying in front of the door, preventing enemies from entering? protecting the baby and his mother? Why have you brought me here?"

The angel extended his shimmering hand and lifted Yosef to his feet. *Stand, Yosef. Observe the past and see the future. See the face of Mary's Child before He was born on earth. He is the One whose origins are from of old. He who was . . . and is now . . . and will be. See for yourself the origins of the Salvation of Israel out of the hand of the Philistine people who are called The Uncircumcised.*

Yosef wished he had his sword. Why had the angel brought him near the powerful and ancient enemies of Israel without a sword? "What time is it?"

It is a time like your own time. A time when the judges of Israel have forsaken the Lord and done evil in His sight. Because of their evil deeds the Lord delivered Israel into the hand of the Philistines for forty years.

"Who is the woman I see weeping?"

She is the wife of Manoah of Zorah. She became the mother of Samson. She weeps and prays because she is barren and has lost all hope for the future. Like all of Israel. Is it not always so? In such a time when hope is dead, a miraculous Baby is born . . . a Deliverer. Look up!

Yosef raised his eyes and there, beside the woman, was a man, tall and strong. He seemed to be human, yet Yosef sensed He was far greater than Gabriel. He was wrapped in light. The air around Him sparkled with color.

On the breeze Yosef heard a sigh of adoration. *Holy! Holy is the Lord of Hosts!* The song of praise split and multiplied.

At the sight of the Great One, Gabriel bowed low. Yosef dropped to his knees, no longer able to stand. But the woman did not seem afraid. She looked full into the Great One's face and smiled.

Yosef squeezed his eyes shut, afraid to look. The Great One spoke to her quietly, while Yosef felt the ground tremble beneath him at the words. **You are barren and childless but you are going to conceive and bear a son. Now see to it that you drink no wine and do not eat anything unclean, because you will conceive and give birth to** a son. **No razor may be used on his head because the boy will be a Nazarite and he will begin the deliverance of Israel from the hands of the Philistines.**[43]

Then there was silence. Yosef knew some time had passed. He raised his head at the sound of the woman's voice.

She was with her husband. Words tumbled out. *"Manoah! A man of God came to me. He was like an angel when He spoke, very awesome. I didn't ask Him where He came from, and He didn't tell me His name. But He promised me. I will bear a son who will begin the deliverance of Israel!"*[44]

Then, as Yosef watched, Manoah began to pray. It was like the prayer of desperation Yosef had prayed every day from the first hour Gabriel had spoken in his dreams and told him about Mary's child.

Manoah cried out, *"O Yahweh! I beg You, let the man of God You sent to us come again to teach us how to bring up the boy who is to be born."*[45]

Yosef whispered to Gabriel, "I have said the same prayer as Manoah many times in the last months."

Gabriel responded, *And so a father's prayer, asking for wisdom about his children, is answered. Look again, Yosef! There, with Manoah and his wife. They speak with the great and mighty Counselor about their child.*

Manoah stood beaming as he spoke to the Great One. *"We would like You to stay until we prepare a young goat for You."*

The Great One replied, **Even though you detain me I will not eat any of your food. But if you prepare a burnt offering, offer it to the Lord.**

Then Manoah asked, *"What is Your name, so that we may honor You when Your word comes true and the baby is born?"*

The hills resounded with the reply, **Why do you ask my name? My name is . . .** *Piliy* **. . . Wonderful.**[46]

As the flame of the altar blazed toward heaven the Great One—Wonderful!—ascended up and up on the flame.

A thousand, thousand voices echoed His Name.

Wonderful!

>*Wonderful!*

>>*Wonderful!*

Manoah and his wife fell to the ground, realizing they had seen the Lord Himself. *"We are doomed to die! We have seen God!"*[47]

Yosef covered his face as if Manoah's terror were his own. Suddenly there was darkness, as though a candle had blown out.

The warmth of the fire touched Yosef. He was back in the cottage in Beth-lehem. He could not hold his eyes open. The light of Gabriel's presence began to fade. Once again he felt his sword at his side.

"What does it mean?" Yosef mumbled. "The Lord's name is Wonderful. He appeared to men like Manoah in days long ago, and they were terrified. What does it mean to me?"

The angel's head was respectfully bowed. *It is written in the book of Isaiah*, he whispered. *He is Wonderful and for unto us a Son is given. Mary's son—Son of David, Son of the Most High—He who was . . . is now . . . and evermore will be. The government will rest upon His shoulder.*

"Don't leave until you tell me," Yosef cried as he struggled to hear the receding voice. "What does the vision you have showed me mean?"

Tonight in a dream you saw the Lord as He appeared to men of old. They feared His awesome presence even though He was merciful and kind. But in this hour—the Babe born in Beth-lehem, the Child in Mary's arms. As it was prophesied by Isaias, The Lord of Eternity now reveals Himself to mankind in a new way. His name is Counselor! Mighty God! Everlasting Father! Prince of Peace! His name is Wonderful! Secret! Miraculous! Powerful! But those who draw near to Him need not be afraid. Is it not wonderful, Yosef, son of Jacob?

11

Damascus was the largest and most important city in Roman-occupied Syria, after Antioch on the seacoast. Located in an otherwise waterless stretch of desert, it owed its existence thirty miles northeast of Mount Hermon to an oasis fed by a river.

Most weary travelers reaching the city after a long journey immediately took advantage of the wine and food of the Damascus bazaar. Despite having just reached their inn, Old Balthasar insisted his party observe a fast. There were two reasons for this, he explained. Firstly, they had arrived on the Tenth of Tevet. It was the date pious Jews mourned the anniversary of the tragedy when Nebuchadnezzar of Babylon laid siege to Jerusalem.

"We will keep the day as a fast until after sunset," Balthasar instructed.

The second reason was more practical than pious.

Damascus was full of debauchery.

The elder Jew pointed into the street outside the caravansary wall. Brawlers spilled out of a tavern like a frothing ferment of men. A pair of beggars stole a cart of bread. When they attempted to round the first corner on their escape, the wagon dumped its load into the mud.

Onlookers laughed. No one moved to help the baker recover his property or to stop the would-be thieves.

Nor were travelers immune to the infection of drunkenness. A Bactrian camel trader with Old Balthasar's caravan had quickly imbibed. Now the normally tactiturn man staggered as he bellowed ribald songs at the top of his lungs and wandered arm in arm with a seemingly stunned Kashgari wool merchant. The two had been bitterest enemies until drowning their hostility in wine.

And it was still morning.

"We need to be watchful and keep our wits about us. This is the Roman New Year," Balthasar explained. "Their usual behavior, as wretched as that may be, is turned on its head. This has been going on for ten days already, but tonight is the climax. It will be the most dangerous for—" Balthasar paused and glanced at his granddaughter before continuing— "us. By tomorrow there will be more hangovers than rioting."

Romans had celebrated the midwinter solstice called Saturnalia for hundreds of years. It had been separate from the New Year revels until Julius Caesar tinkered with the Roman calendar about forty years earlier. As a result of his machinations and several others since, Saturnalia now ran right into the carousing honoring Janus, the two-faced god who looked both forward and back. The combination produced an extended time of unparalleled drunkenness.

Old Balthasar concluded, "So we will remain in the courtyard of the caravansary with our belongings. We must defend ourselves against theft. And . . . other abuses."

Yosef, his head covered with his prayer shawl, prayed silently through the eighteen morning prayers. Near him in the cottage Mary and Rachel prepared for the *Bris Milah* of the baby. From the days of Abraham, a baby boy was consecrated and brought into the covenant of Abraham to inherit the promises as one of God's people. Just as Abraham received his name at this time of his circumcision, so the name of the infant would be revealed today.

O Lord! We will sanctify your name in this place!

Mary, dressed in her one good dress—white wool with blue borders—sat in front of Rachel as the midwife plaited her thick hair.

Yosef glanced at her. *How beautiful she is, O Lord.*

Mary sighed, "It's good that Yosef will say his name. I don't know that I will have the strength to speak."

Rachel coaxed as she worked. "But, Mary, sweet Mary, you must eat breakfast. Today's a fast day, yes. But a fast for the siege of Yerushalayim has nothing to do with you. It does not apply to new mothers. Nursing mothers. You need to eat so you'll have milk and he'll be able to nurse. Believe me! After such an experience every baby boy wants only to nurse. So, you? Fast today? And especially not on the day of your baby's *Bris Milah.*"

Rachel clucked her tongue. "I've seen new mothers faint when the rabbi takes out the knife. No wonder Avraham didn't tell Sarai he intended to sacrifice her boy on Moriah. There would have been an argument. Every woman feels the circumcision of her baby boy, I can tell you! And few first mothers can stand up without help when the flint touches their newborn's skin. That's why I'll be at your left hand. To help you stay on your feet. Don't be ashamed if a tear or two falls from your eyes. It's normal. He cries. You cry. You may think you'll be strong, eh? Yes, you're a strong girl. But when he cries, your heart will break. And the sight of your baby's blood . . . there is nothing you can do to stop the pain he must feel. Please, eat something!"

Yosef prayed, *Blessed be the Presence of the Lord in this place.*

Mary turned her eyes to where the baby lay loosely wrapped in swaddling clothes that would be easily removed for the ceremony of the covenant. She replied softly, "The rabbis say—don't they?—that a baby is circumcised on the eighth day because if he survives his first Shabbat he's gained a measure of strength to live? Rachel! I won't eat. I'm fasting . . . for his sake. For the first drop of his precious blood that is spilled for the sake of Avraham's covenant. He's such a sweet little lamb. We shared the same heart for nine months. I can't eat this morning. I promise I'll eat again when it's finished."

Yosef listened to the women talk as he prayed. Was even this day a prophecy of what was to come?

Forgive us, O our Father, for we have sinned: pardon us, O our King, for we have transgressed. For you pardon and forgive. Blessed are you, O Lord, who is merciful and always ready to forgive.[48]

Rachel patted Mary's shoulders. "You'll live through it. Three little sons I have. Three circumcisions. Every son cried a little. Havila stood at my side to support me. I needed her there too. It's not the same for our men. I suppose they think, *Well, I lived through it*, eh? But we who are mothers . . . we see the knife, and it pierces our own hearts to hear them cry."

"I promise," Mary said. "I'll hold on very tightly to you." She placed her hand on Rachel's hand.

Yosef's lips continued to move silently, but he was certain the Presence of the Lord was near enough to hear. *Redeem us speedily for your name's sake, for you are a mighty redeemer. Blessed are you, O Adonai, the Redeemer of Israel.*[49]

No one among the residents of David's village would willingly miss the *Bris Milah* of the baby boy at whose birth the angels had sung hymns of praise. So the flocks of Migdal Eder were tended by men chosen by lot.

And now, on the Eighth Day, the day of the circumcision, the hall of Beth David Synagogue was filled with familiar faces.

In the center of the room the empty chair called the Throne of Elijah was covered in fine purple cloth. Thirteen candles were lit to commemorate the thirteen attributes of Yahweh's mercy.

Zadok, dressed in his finest tallith, stood at Yosef's right hand. All the men wore prayer shawls, with phylacteries upon their brows and forearms.

It was a fast day, so no adult could drink the wine that symbolized the covenant. The cupbearer was Sharona's ten-year-old son, Jesse, who had been at the lambing cave the night of the birth and helped Mary and Yosef. Being under the age of thirteen, he had been chosen to drink the wine in place of an adult.

Rabbi Eliyahu wore the priestly robes of a *cohen*. The implements used for circumcision were concealed beneath a cloth on the table. The ceremony would begin when the women carried the baby into the hall from the preparation room.

Yosef saw Mary, very pale, framed in the doorway. Rachel, as honored *Kvatterin*, held the infant Messiah and waited for Eliyahu to give the signal.

With a nod, Eliyahu stepped forward and shouted the proclamation: "Blessed is the one arriving!"

Rachel followed Mary into the room.

All the congregation joined in: "Blessed is the one arriving! Happy is the man you choose and bring near to dwell in your courtyards! We will be satisfied with the goodness of your house! Your holy Temple!"

Eliyahu responded, "The Lord spoke to Mosheh, saying, 'I grant him My covenant of peace!'"[50]

Rachel walked to where Yosef waited and placed the baby in his arms. Yosef's tears overflowed as he looked down at the fulfillment of two thousand years of Israel's hopes and yearnings. The baby's eyes were wide. He peered at Yosef then focused on the light of the tallest candle beside the Throne of Elijah.

Eliyahu continued, "Oh! Blessed are you! Holy Child of the Most High God! We welcome you! Blessed are you, Son of David! Blessed are you, Messiah, who has arrived to dwell in our midst!"

Yosef glanced up. Mary's expression radiated love and joy. She nodded at him and mouthed the words *thank you!*

How far they had come in the past year, Yosef thought. It had not even been twelve months since a whole series of miracles had begun with an angel's visit to Mary. Yosef's dreams, their wedding, the angel-attended travel to King David's town—all those mind-swirling memories seemed nothing compared to the reality Yosef held in his arms.

Proudly, Yosef placed the baby Messiah in the Throne of Elijah.

Eliyahu and Zadok stretched hands over the child.

Yosef recited the words that had been spoken during generations of circumcisions as the people of Israel waited for this moment, when the One worthy to fill Elijah's throne came at last to His people.

Yosef was not speaking to some far-off heavenly being but talking directly to the baby: "This is the *Kissay Shel Eliyahu*, the Seat of Elijah. May he be remembered for good. For your salvation I hope, O Lord. I have hoped for your salvation, Lord, and I have performed your commandments. Elijah, angel of the covenant, here is yours, before you. Stand at my right hand and support me. I rejoice in your word, like one who finds an unexpected treasure. Those who love your Torah have abounding peace, and there is no stumbling for them. Happy is the man you choose and bring near to dwell in your courtyards! We will be satisfied with the goodness of your house, O Lord! Your holy Temple."

How many families, how many generations of families, had gathered in this place to repeat these same vows? Since David—no, since

David's great-grandmother Ruth—the stones of this place had borne witness to the continual renewing of the covenant.

How many fathers had stood here hoping and praying, *Lord, let Messiah come in the lifetime of this, my son.*

Rabbi Eliyahu gathered the baby in his arms, then handed Him to Yosef to hold. The infant twined His fingers in Yosef's beard and kicked His feet as if to show His pleasure.

Well spoken! Well done!

Zadok, as *Sandek*, his weathered face trembling with emotion, sat in the Elijah seat. Yosef placed the baby in his lap and drew back the last layer of white-linen blanket that covered him.

A sigh of pleasure passed through the congregation.

Yosef uncovered the flint knife and bowed slightly as he passed it, and the responsibility of the cutting, to Eliyahu, the *cohen*.

Mary clung to Rachel's arm. Her face was ashen at the sight of the knife poised over her naked child.

Young Jesse frowned and stared into the cup he held, as though he could not bear to watch.

Holding the knife high for all to see, Eliyahu pronounced the blessing: "Blessed are you, Lord our God, King of the Universe, who has sanctified us with his commandments and commanded us concerning circumcision."

Zadok, his big hands awkwardly restraining the baby, questioned Eliyahu. "Like this? Hold his hands?"

"His legs. Careful now. That's right. Hold him still, Zadok."

Mary buried her face against Rachel's shoulder. Jesse's eyes reflected apprehension. A nervous twitter passed through Beth David Synagogue. This was not just any baby, after all.

Eliyahu adjusted Zadok's grip. "All right now. Don't let him kick." The rabbi went to work, wielding the flint with a practiced hand. The cutting of the foreskin of the Son of the Almighty was accomplished in seconds, accompanied by a lusty cry from the child. Blood flowed. A strong arc of urine shot over Zadok's arm and hit the floor near Eliyahu's feet.

The big shepherd cried, "Now there's a true Israelite!"

The people of Beth-lehem cheered.

Mary smiled weakly and leaned against Rachel.

Yosef laughed with joy that the sign of the covenant had been accomplished. The murmur of approval reverberating from the ceiling was almost musical in the way it rose and fell, swelled and rebounded. The melody felt both sweeter and fuller than the chatter of a room packed with shepherds and their families. Or was Yosef hearing the echo of a hymn of praise and wonder whose origin was not inside this room at all, but from somewhere bigger . . . much bigger?

Eliyahu blotted the blood and applied oil. "Blessed are you, Lord our God! King of the Universe, who has sanctified us with your commandments, and commanded us to enter him into the covenant of Avraham our father!"

All the congregation responded in unison: "Just as he has entered into the covenant, so may he enter into Torah, into marriage, and into good deeds!" A second cheer rocked the hall.

Eliyahu completed the *Bris* and wrapped the baby in His white blanket. He lifted the bundle to show the people as they applauded before he returned Him to Yosef's arms.

At last it was time for the revealing of the name.

Crimson blood stained the baby's white linen blanket. Tiny fists, raised in the air, shook.

"Oh, little one," Yosef comforted. "Oh! What you go through to be one of us." One foot kicked free from the blanket. The wail finally softened to a bleat and then, at Yosef's touch, quieted.

The long-awaited Messiah, Son of David, Son of the Most High, sucked His fist. Yosef gazed down at Him and crooned, "Like us. You are . . . yes! One of us."

Zadok rose from the chair of Elijah and took the cup of wine from young Jesse. He raised it before the whole congregation and blessed it in a loud voice choked with emotion. "Blessed are you, O Lord our God, King of the Universe, who creates the fruit of the vine."

The shepherd held out the cup to Rabbi Eliyahu, who placed a single drop of wine on the trembling lips of the infant and recited: "Blessed are you, O Lord our God, King of the Universe, who sanctified his Beloved One from the womb, set his statute in his flesh, and sealed his descendants with the sign of the holy covenant in blood! Therefore, as a reward of this circumcision, the Living God, our Portion, our Rock, has ordained that the Beloved of our flesh be saved from the abyss. He will live for the sake of the covenant that he has set in our flesh. Blessed are you, Lord, who makes the covenant!"

The cup was returned to Jesse's sure grip.

It was Yosef, the baby's chosen father on earth, who had the honor of speaking His Name for the first time.

Yosef swayed with the baby in the loving dance of father and infant son as Eliyahu prayed, "Our God and God of our fathers, preserve the child for this father and mother. And His Name in Israel shall be . . ."

Yosef inhaled and raised his chin, "His Name shall be . . . YESHUA!"

*Ahhhh*s of pleasure passed through the crowd. It was a good name.

Eliyahu grinned. "So! His Name shall be YESHUA, Salvation! Son of Yosef of Nazareth!"

A roar of approval resounded.

"Yeshua!"

"Of course, Yeshua!"

"Salvation is His Name!"

"Salvation has come at last to Israel!"

"The descendant of David will bring us Salvation!"

"His Name is in every prayer we pray!"

"Grant us Salvation . . ."

"And now! Here he is!"

Eliyahu signaled for Rachel to guide Mary close to Yosef. The ancient blessing prayer that Eliyahu now prayed took on new meaning as he stretched his hands over the couple and the child. "May the father rejoice in this offspring, and may the mother be glad with the fruit of her womb. As it is written, *'May your father and mother be glad; may she who gave you birth rejoice!'*[51]

Eliyahu placed his right hand on the head of the infant. "And it is said by the Almighty, *'As you lay there in your blood, I said to you, "Live!"'*"[52]

The rabbi turned to his flock. "The Lord has remembered His covenant forever, the word which He commanded to a thousand generations; the covenant he made with Avraham, . . . to Israel as an everlasting covenant.[53]

"Avraham circumcised his son Yitz'chak when he was eight days old, as God had commanded him."[54]

Eliyahu concluded and all the congregation joined him. *"Give thanks to the Lord, for He is good;*[55] *for His kingdom is everlasting."*

Then Eliyahu blessed baby Yeshua. "May this infant—Yeshua—become great! Just as he has entered the covenant, so may he enter into Torah, into marriage with his holy bride Israel, and into good deeds."

At Eliyahu's signal, young Jesse drank the cup of the covenant wine on behalf of those men who were fasting.

Together Yosef and Eliyahu recited the prayer for baby Yeshua: "Sovereign of the Universe, may it be your will that this circumcision be regarded and accepted by you as if I had offered him before the throne of your glory. And you, in your abounding mercy, send from your holy throne a holy and pure Spirit to Yeshua bar Yosef, who has now been circumcised for the sake of your Great Name. May his heart be an open portal of the Great Hall in the Temple in your holy Torah, to learn, to teach, to observe, and to practice. Grant him long life. A life imbued with fear of sin. A life of wealth and honor. And fulfill the desires of his heart for good! Omaine, and so may it be your will."

And all the people of Beth David echoed the last Omaine. A long rolling applause erupted and continued.

The shedding of the blood of the covenant was completed. Rachel embraced Mary, then retrieved the baby from Yosef and returned him to his mother's eager embrace.

Zadok wrapped his arms around Yosef and thumped him on the back. Eliyahu mussed Jesse's red hair and congratulated him for doing such a fine job.

The celebration of Beth David was heard in the fields and pastures of Migdal Eder.

At last the rumble of joy quieted. Eliyahu recited the final priestly blessing over all the people. *"And the Lord spoke to Mosheh, saying, 'Speak to Aaron and to his sons, saying, "Thus shall you bless the children of Israel and say to them, The Lord bless you and guard you. The Lord make His countenance shine upon you and be gracious to you. The Lord turn His countenance toward you and grant you peace." And they shall set My NAME upon the people of Israel, and I SHALL BLESS them!'"*[56]

Thus the law of the covenant with Abraham was fulfilled.

"Wait!" Eliyahu proclaimed. "One more thing, if you please. My wife, Havila, has an announcement."

Havila, balancing Dan, said, "Because this is a fast day, the celebration feast will be here in the hall this evening when the fast is ended.

Return at sunset! Bring your own food to share. The main dish of a roasted calf, donated by Hamid the Oil Merchant, will be roasted by the shepherds of Beth-lehem!"

Puffing from exertion, Mordechai climbed the steps to the second-story parapet of the caravansary. He joined his daughter and peered across the rooftops of Beth-lehem. The aroma of roasting beef on the spit made his mouth water. Music warmed the night.

"Well?" he asked the girl.

"A great celebration at the synagogue."

Mordechai scowled. "Put two Jews together and there is something to celebrate. What is it this time?"

"The baby. His *Bris*, I heard."

"What baby?"

"The one you said I shouldn't speak about."

"Their newborn Messiah, you mean? The stuff of treason. The brew of Herod's nightmares." Mordechai's eyes narrowed with resentment.

"They say angels—," the girl began, only to be slapped to silence by Mordechai.

"Shut up! Angels? It's that brat, isn't it? The one Rachel, wife of Zadok, would not let me see. And now no word of inviting us to their little celebration? We aren't good enough to join them, I suppose."

The girl rubbed her cheek and wiped her tears. "We could have gone, Papa. If we ever went to synagogue. But since we never go, I suppose they didn't think about inviting anyone from outside."

"Aren't I a Jew? As good as any of them? So. They exclude us. They shun us because on a certain night this inn was too full for her to deliver her brat indoors!" He spat over the railing. "Well, let them revel! What is it to us, eh? They'll all be hanged for celebrating a new Messiah while old Herod still reigns over the land. This is not the celebration of a circumcision. It is the wake after a funeral. Mark my words! The king will hear of it soon enough!"

12

y two hours after sunset the streets of Damascus were deserted. The freezing wind swirling down from the craggy summit of Mount Hermon drove travelers and citizens alike to nurse their barley beer and headaches indoors next to warm fires. Old Balthasar rested quietly, dozing in the tent, attended by Esther and Prince Aretas.

Melchior, wrapped up to his eyes in a dark red cloak, poked his head out of the pavilion to inspect the sky. In the west a patch of blue appeared, framing the setting Mars—The Adam—in the constellation known as The Water Bearer.

As the young astronomer watched, the clouds peeled back, revealing Jupiter—The Righteous—still high in the southwest in company with Saturn—The Lord of the Sabbath. Melchior was pleased to see the two bright lights again. He had not been able to observe them since the last night of Hanukkah, the night of the miraculous star.

Gesturing for Prince Aretas to join him at the tent flap, Melchior whispered, "I'm going up on the city wall to observe. Who knows how long this break in the weather will last?"

The teenager protested, "Old Balthasar said we shouldn't venture out. Too dangerous."

Melchior acknowledged the warning. "I know, but that was earlier. There's no one around. See for yourself. I'll be alone, and in this cold I won't stay long either."

"Shall I send my guards with you?"

"No need. Besides, any trouble will come from the inn or the taverns. You and your men stay here and look after things. I'll be back soon."

The city gate was shut. There were no guards posted either there or on the wall. Melchior heard slurred singing coming from the sentry post beside the portal.

Once atop the south-facing battlements, Melchior almost regretted his commitment to his craft. Dominating the near horizon like a gigantic pyramid, Mount Hermon might have been a block of ice. The mountain's wintry blast cut through his wool cloak like a knife. Each intake of breath made Melchior gasp.

The rift in the western clouds tore apart into a larger triangular patch, revealing all of the sign of The Two Fish and then that of Aries, called by Jews The Lamb. The hole in the fabric of the weather ripped still farther. Near the peak of the heavens the moon flooded the sky with silver light.

The gibbous moon—the light of the Holy Spirit according to Balthasar—rode high above Orion's shoulder. The constellation of Orion was named in Hebrew *Chesil*, Coming Forth as Light. Because of the brilliance of the moon, all but Orion's brightest stars—like Rigel, the one known as The Treading Underfoot—were washed away in the glare.

The wind whistled through the battlements. Melchior's ears ached and he had lost the feeling in his fingers and toes.

It was enough. Melchior was satisfied. He had renewed his covenant with the sky. He could enter these observations in his journal . . . after returning to the fireside.

It was not until he turned to leave that he noticed a man in the shadows at the head of the stairs. Melchior's heart thudded in his chest. The figure was a head taller than him and broader as well.

A bronze lance head glistened as the man swung in a swift arc to point at Melchior's midsection. "What're you doing there?" a guttural voice demanded. The figure advancing into view in the moonlight was uniformed as a Roman soldier.

Melchior puffed a sigh of relief. In Aramaic, the common language of trade, he replied, "Guard? For a moment there I thought you were—"

"I said, what's your business here?" The bluntly repeated inquiry was accompanied by the sharp prod of the lance tip into Melchior's stomach.

"Stars. I came to watch—"

A blast of breath freighted with sour wine asserted, "Parthian, eh? Accent gives you away. Spying out defenses!"

"No," Melchior protested. "Astronomer. Traveling to Jerusalem."

The press of the spearpoint angled toward Melchior's heart stopped his mouth and backed him up a pace. "Wait!" Melchior croaked.

"Stinking Parthians! Killed my brother. Can't trust 'em. Crucify spies here, we do." Another jab of the lance ripped fabric.

The next time it would be skin.

There was no point in arguing.

Melchior turned to flee. After only two strides he plunged straight into the chest of another guard who had approached, unheard in the howling wind, from the opposite end of the parapet.

Melchior's shoulder knocked a gasp out of the second sentry, followed by an oath.

Then a fist against Melchior's temple clubbed him to the stones.

"Caught us a spy, Junius," the first guard exulted. "Let's kill 'im and heave 'im over the wall."

Melchior, urging his head to stop throbbing and his eyes to refocus, shrank back against the blocks that separated him from oblivion.

Would Esther ever know what had happened to him?

The two closed in.

"Wait! Don't forget the reward," Melchior babbled. "No good to you dead."

"He's right, Cato," Junius announced. "Spies is worth at least a drachma . . . before they nail 'im up."

Poking Melchior with the spear tip, Junius urged him to his feet. Dragged by his elbows, Melchior and his captors stumbled awkwardly down from the wall in search of an officer.

Yosef penned the letter to Mary's mother and father first of all. Perhaps some thoughtful angel had stopped by to tell Anna and Heli that they were grandparents to the Messiah, but Yosef did not count on it.

Sharpened duck quill dipped in ink made from the blood of a sea snail formed words on a fragile scrap of parchment at the rabbi's house.

Honored parents, family of my wife, Mary,

Blessed be the name of Adonai! Great news! We stay at the house of Zadok the Shepherd in Beth-lehem, and you may send word to us here. The house is near the well of David. We will remain until time for the Redemption of the Firstborn and purification offering at the Temple. We will come home to Nazareth soon after when the baby can travel safely. Mary sends her love. The Bris was celebrated and the covenant sealed. His name will be as we were told. His name is Yeshua.

Greetings to all.

May Adonai cause his face to shine upon you!

Your son-in-law,

Yosef

Eliyahu took the parchment from Yosef, blew upon the ink, then rolled it tightly and sealed it with candle wax. "I'll take it to Yerushalayim to the pilgrim stand in the Temple. Someone from the Galil will carry it home to Nazareth for a penny."

Yosef scrawled out the address of Heli, Carpenter of Nazareth, and produced a penny for the rabbi to carry.

"She misses her mother very much." Yosef sighed. "It was not the way I had planned it. I thought we would be home again. And she would be cared for by her mother when the time came."

Eliyahu pocketed the message. "It was meant to be as it is. The watchers of light. Why here in Beth-lehem? Yet it was meant to be. I'm certain of it, though I don't know what it means."

"You're a learned man. A rabbi."

"It is all too high for me to understand. Zadok and I are going to meet with Simeon the Tzadik again at his home in Yerushalayim. He is the last of the righteous generation. Herod has murdered most of them. But Simeon has survived somehow. He expects Messiah's coming. He'll know much more than we."

Yosef ran his hand through his hair. "This morning I glanced up at Herod's fortress on the hill. I felt a chill more intense than merely the weather."

Eliyahu nodded. "Herod is at the seacoast. Most of the religious leaders . . . Herod's men . . . the rich men . . . have villas in Caesarea Maritima. They pack up their households in the autumn after Yom Kippur and leave Yerushalayim in peace during the cold months. It's several days' travel. With the snow, the baby is as safe here as anywhere in Eretz-Israel."

Yosef considered Eliyahu's assurances. "Is there any place in Eretz-Israel where Herodian spies aren't paid to bring the Butcher King news?"

Eliyahu patted his pocket. "I'll find some fellow from the Galil who looks the part of a rebel to carry the letter to Nazareth. Not like a Galilean would spy for the Herodians."

"When I saw the fortress I had the thought of Herod standing over Mary and the baby with a sword."

"I can't imagine Herod will think of the birth of a baby as a threat to his power. I suppose it could be that the demons will whisper to him that Messiah is born in the City of David, just as angels have shouted the news to us."

"Mary won't be strong enough to travel for some time yet."

Eliyahu threw his cloak over his shoulders. "It's good you stay here awhile. No better folk than Zadok and Rachel. No place more filled with hope for the Son of David than David's hometown. Our folk will be careful with the news."

Melchior was dragged across several miles of Damascus, but he experienced only part of it. While being hustled past the street of the caravansary, he made the mistake of calling out for Gaspar and Aretas. Neither friend heard his shout, but trying to get help earned Melchior another clout on the head, this time with the butt of a lance.

Thereafter Damascus was no more to him than a blur of torchlights and shadows. The blare of drunken revelry merged with a continuous roaring in his ears. Sometimes inquisitive faces floated in and out of his vision like sneering apparitions drifting on the breeze.

His captors twice stopped to extort freshly filled wineskins from taverns. Far from diminishing with the exertion and the cold, their exuberant plans for spending the reward money increased with the journey.

Some walled-off portion of Melchior's mind recognized a columned building as he was towed past it. The temple to Jupiter was devoted to the highest Roman god—highest, anyway, before the ascension of the caesars to godhood. Towering overhead, carved limestone capitals supported massive lintels and arches.

Why had Balthasar mentioned this pagan structure?

The correct answer came to Melchior's befuddled brain at last. It was because King Herod, the king of the Jews, helped finance the restoration of this building, as he had the temple of Baalbek in Lebanon and other pagan shrines.

It was at a porticoed villa not far from the temple that Junius and Cato finally located their centurion. The elegant, mosaic-inlaid entry on which they dropped Melchior belonged to the junior tribune of Syria, Flavius Severus. The second-highest military commander in Syria was related by marriage to the emperor.

Melchior's cheek lay pressed against the figure of a mermaid riding on a dolphin's back. He prayed for the world to stop spinning. One side of his head felt twice the size of the other.

The centurion, serving as part of the tribune's honor guard for the night's celebration, was mortified when summoned from inside the villa. "What is this?" he demanded.

"Caught us a spy," Junius asserted. "Guard sergeant said bring 'im to you."

Cato agreed. "Top of the wall. Signaling to some accomplice maybe." Then, spoiling the gravity of his report with a loud belch, he added, "Come about the reward too."

"Idiots! Throw him in the brig. I'll deal with him tomorrow. Get back to your posts!"

Drunk as they were, the two legionnaires knew better than to argue with their officer. Crestfallen, they yanked Melchior to his feet.

Their departure was interrupted by the arrival of a dignitary. A slim man in a purple-trimmed white robe swam into Melchior's trembling vision. As both soldiers and centurion snapped to attention, Melchior was unceremoniously dumped again, as were the sloshing wineskins.

"What's this disturbance about, centurion?" the newcomer demanded. "I heard someone bellowing about spies and rewards. Are these men drunk on duty?"

"Tribune Severus, sir," the centurion acknowledged. "These men have been drinking, for which they will be flogged. But they came to report the capture of a spy."

"By his dress he's Parthian, eh?" the tribune surmised, gesturing toward Melchior's trousers and his peaked cap. "But he doesn't belong here. Take him away and we'll interrogate him tomorrow."

"My orders exactly, sir," the centurion replied.

One of Melchior's eyes refused to focus and his tongue felt leaden and uncooperative, but he had to try. "No spy, sir! Court astronomer to King Phraates. On the wall to observe stars."

The centurion, hearing Melchior's credentials, backed up a pace. Cato did the same. Junius stood rooted, staring stupidly, until his comrade plucked him by the elbow.

"I've had no word of an official deputation," Tribune Severus countered.

Melchior admitted, "Not here officially. Traveling by caravan to Jerusalem, sir. Old Balthasar of Ecbatana can verify my story."

By now a handful of onlookers had emerged from the warmth of the villa to investigate the tribune's absence. Melchior noted that one of these was an immensely large black man. The shine of the skin of his broad face in the lamplight was not the dark brown some term *black*, but a true, lustrous blue-black, like the reflection of a moonlit sky in a lake. His embroidered trousers were trimmed with gold thread, and he wore an ostrich plume in his tightly wrapped turban.

When the black man spoke, it was in a deep rumble, like the bass note of an earthquake. "Your pardon, Tribune. Did I hear the name Balthasar of Ecbatana mentioned? I myself have corresponded with him. If this young man is vouched for by Balthasar, then he is truly a man of peace with knowledge of the stars . . . and perhaps of the very matter we discussed earlier tonight."

Even to Melchior's cloudy view the tribune's eyes flashed dangerously.

The centurion's back was already against the wall, so he could not retreat farther, except by what he said. "Grave mistake, sir. Very fortunate this man was brought here to my attention. Shall I take him back to the caravansary?"

Melchior was relieved to hear the tribune disagree. "And have him disappear along the way? Bring him to my library. Then you will escort these two . . . soldiers . . . to the guardhouse. I will attend to them tomorrow myself!"

Enoch, some months past his second birthday, was weaned and proud of it. He was scornful when his two younger siblings nursed in Rachel's arms.

Enoch lived up to his namesake. Like Enoch of old, the ancient city builder in the book of Genesis, the child was happiest when stacking wooden blocks to build his version of Jerusalem's Temple or digging imaginary roads in the dirt.

Enoch's dark eyes flashed a warning and his voice raised in a yell of frustration as Samu'el crawled toward Enoch's latest construction project.

"Share with your brother, Enoch!" Zadok growled.

Enoch began to cry as Samu'el thrust himself upon the stack, turning Enoch's holy of holies into a heap.

Rachel burped Obi. "Enoch looks just like you, Zadok. Just as I remember you before you had a beard."

Zadok rubbed his nose and tucked his chin. "Poor boy. Ah well, Enoch! As long as y' have your father's brains, eh?"

Obi belched.

"Brains, is it?" Rachel added. "Your heart is what I'm after in my sons."

"Well then, a wife for each son t' one day love as I love you. That's my prayer. My heart can't contain what I feel for you when I see you here. When we sit together. You. Me. These three little ones."

Enoch wailed on. Samu'el lifted a block to his mouth and tasted it. Obi plucked at Rachel's ear.

Zadok's eyes warmed her as he held her in his gaze.

She flashed a smile. "Dangerous talk when you'll be leaving for the night watch in less than two hours. You should be sleeping."

"To sleep is t' dream. And when I dream, I dream only of you. So what's the point of sleepin'? I can dream better if I am wide-awake."

"The boys . . ."

"Put them to bed."

Enoch jerked up in alarm. Bed? It was plain he wanted to rebuild his city. The words *bed* and *sleep* were an interruption he could not bear.

"Enoch, Samu'el, Papa says wash and lessons and prayers and bed."

Enoch's lower lip quivered. "Mama!"

Zadok scowled. "You call on your mother when I have spoken? I'll handle this." With a growl he scooped Enoch up, lifting him high upon his shoulder. He danced around the room, brushing the boy's head in lavender until Enoch howled with laughter.

Zadok balanced the child in one hand and swooped toward the fleece mattress. "What a fine big rooster you are! Into the nest! Into the nest!"

Enoch flapped his arms and crowed, forgetting entirely whatever he had intended to accomplish with the blocks.

Wash. Song. Prayers. No lesson. All were accomplished in record time. Within a few minutes all three boys were fast asleep.

It was, Rachel thought, an answer to Zadok's prayers.

"You see? It takes a man, eh?" Zadok remarked later as the fire crackled and Rachel lay in his arms. "I knew it was time for bed." He kissed her lips. "Here we are. And there is no dream I'd rather dream than you."

Seated in Tribune Severus' opulently furnished study, Melchior was for a time bewildered at his changed fortunes. Wrapped in soft blankets, with a charcoal brazier at his feet and a pack of ice pressed to his temple, his thoughts struggled to find reality as his body vacillated between sweating and shivering.

"My name is unpronounceable in your tongue," the black man announced. "But here in Syria I am called Perroz." Perroz, since hearing of Melchior's connection to Old Balthasar, had taken complete charge of the young Parthian's well-being. A cup of hot, spiced wine was pressed into Melchior's hand and his scraped knees and elbows rubbed with sweet oil.

Even the tribune hovered around for a time. "Shall we send a litter to bring Balthasar?" he asked.

Melchior shook his head . . . gently. "He's an old man, and the journey has been hard on him. But they'll be worried about me. Perhaps a message?"

"Caravansary nearest the south gate? Done!" At a snap of the tribune's fingers a slave leapt toward the door. Severus apologized, "Please excuse me. I must see to my other guests. If there's anything else you need, my stewards are at your call."

"So Old Balthasar has come all the way from Ecbatana, eh?" Perroz ventured. "I always knew he would try. He's waited so long."

"You know him, sir?" Melchior inquired.

"We've never met, but we have exchanged letters for years. There is always at least one caravan a year going to Parthia from my home in the kingdom of Axum—what the Greeks named Ethiopia—'the country of burnt faces'!" Perroz threw back his head and laughed so that the flame of the oil lamps trembled. "Yes, Old Balthasar has taught me much. And I have shared a few things with him as well."

"But Ethiopia is not a Roman province, and you must have passed near Jerusalem before coming to Damascus from your home." Melchior felt even more confused.

Standing in a corner of the room was another man. Because he was dressed modestly in tunic and robe compared to Perroz and the Roman tribune, Melchior assumed he was another servant waiting for orders.

Then he spoke. "Our friend Perroz is only cryptic because he is so modest about himself. He's not just *from* Axum; he is brother to Queen Candace herself. For him to be in Roman Syria requires that diplomatic niceties must be observed. So he finds himself in Damascus, conveying official greetings from his sister. Now as to me, I really am as lowly in my origins as I appear: Kagba of Tarsus. Born in Armenia."

Kagba's speech was so polished Melchior doubted that "lowly origin" was a full explanation. Shifting his attention from the jovial giant Perroz to Kagba, Melchior found a man a few years older than himself but of much the same medium height and build. Tarsus was in Cilicia, a Roman province on the southeastern coast of Asia Minor.

Kagba brushed a lock of straight brown hair out of his eyes and stroked his short, pointed beard. Drawing a chair close to Melchior's, he leaned forward and said with intensity, "Did you see it?"

There was no doubt in Melchior's mind what sight Kagba meant. "Of course. At the desert caravansary at Tadmor. Only a brief time before it faded."

"You see, my brother!" Perroz exulted to Kagba. "It calls to all who have been watching! Tell me, young Melchior . . . are there more in your party besides Old Balthasar?"

Melchior explained how Prince Aretas of Nabatea and Gaspar the

Zoroastrian had joined their company at Ctesiphon. "The young prince was my pupil in Ecbatana. Queen Musa suggested he be allowed to come, and his father allowed it. Gaspar watched the signs from India before first sailing through the Arabian Sea and then going overland to Ctesiphon."

"Can you any longer doubt that the power of the One God draws us?" Perroz asked Kagba. "India. Parthia. You who say you sorted ancient Greek manuscripts to separate myth from prophecy. My people who learned of his worship from the wisdom of Solomon. Yet here we meet, all part of the same journey, it seems."

Melchior ventured, "To see the newborn."

Abruptly Kagba shouted to the servants, "More wine for this man. He is cold. Hurry! Be quick! And a fresh pack of ice. This is all melted."

"I really don't need any more," Melchior protested as servants scurried off to carry out Kagba's demands.

Bending his frame next to Melchior's ear, Perroz whispered, "Thank the One God for Kagba's quick wits. We must warn Balthasar as well. The Idumean Herod . . . he is only king of the Jews because the Romans wish it so. Our host knows only that we seek to understand certain signs in the sky. Let's not upset him by offering any conclusions . . . just yet."

PART II

The Lord is my shepherd. . . . Even though I walk through the valley of the shadow of death, I will fear no evil, for You are with me; Your rod and Your staff, they comfort me.

PSALM 23:1, 4

The snow falling on the Holy City had given way to icy rain. Thereafter, though it remained dry, the daytime temperatures barely rose above freezing while at night the chill tormented old men's bones. The bones of Jerusalem were likewise tormented. Paving stones were coated with a glassy layer of ice, endangering pedestrians and donkeys alike. The entire population of Jerusalem walked gingerly, as if all were elderly.

On the Mountain of the House the daily rituals continued as prescribed. The trumpeter still sounded the call from the pinnacle of the Temple, but the tempo of the notes was rushed as he hurried to escape the icy blast. Serving at the altar of sacrifice was now a coveted assignment, since it was one of the few warm places in all Judea, while the labor was less than usual. There had been a significant decrease in applications for sin offerings and fellowship offerings. Families needing to present their firstborn male offspring for redemption likewise took advantage of the flexibility in the law. They postponed the event until temperatures moderated.

In the open-air Court of Women, the priests assigned to inspect lepers and those who oversaw the Nazarite vows bustled about their duties with unseemly haste. No one was on hand to criticize. High Priest Boethus was in Caesarea with King Herod. His deputies gave instructions but never remained out-of-doors to see they were carried out.

In only one corner of the Temple Mount was it business as usual. Beneath the hazy shadows of the giant menorah in the southwest corner stood Old Hannah, preaching as always. Widely regarded as a prophetess, Hannah always seemed on the verge of being arrested for treason for denouncing evil and corruption. So far her age and her reputation had protected her. Since she always quoted from Scripture and because so many wealthy, highborn women consulted her, the over-eighty-year-old had been, thus far, immune from Herod's revenge.

Hannah's voice rang out above the muted clamor of the courtyard and even above the lowing cattle and bleating sheep. *"Come, let us return to the Lord,"* she exhorted. *"He has torn us to pieces but He will heal us; He has injured us but He will bind up our wounds. After two days He will revive us; on the third day He will restore us, that we may live in His presence. Let us acknowledge the Lord; let us press on to acknowledge Him. As surely as the sun rises, He will appear; He will come to us like the winter rains."*[57]

A woman who was doubtful of her husband's fidelity waited to consult Hannah. Was this citation from the prophet Hosea meant for her? And even if it were, what did it mean?

"Speak plainly, please," the housewife requested.

Hannah's eyes appeared fixed on a far-distant horizon. *"What can I do with you, Ephraim? What can I do with you, Judah? Your love is like the morning mist, like the early dew that disappears. Like Adam, they have broken the covenant."*[58]

"Exactly what I've been feeling!" the tormented woman cried. "I knew it! I was sure of it!" Dropping a coin into a basket at Hannah's feet, she covered her head with a shawl to hide her face and hurried away.

Another hooded figure who stood nearby watching did not advance, even when Hannah was alone. The prophetess pivoted to face the reluctant bystander. "Why have you come, Simeon the Righteous? Are not all the answers you seek to be found within the scrolls of the Book?"

Simeon, muffled so as to reveal barely his nose and bushy eyebrows, drew near to Hannah. "All the answers, yes," he agreed. "But I must know that I apply them correctly. May I visit you in your chambers?"

"Come tonight," she agreed softly. Then again raising her voice as Simeon drifted away Hannah quoted: *"Put the trumpet to your lips! An eagle is over the house of the Lord because the people have broken My covenant and rebelled against My law. Israel has rejected what is good. . . . They set up kings without My consent; they choose princes without My approval."*[59]

A spy in the pay of Steward Talmai started up from his bored reverie at these words. Locating a priest, he whispered urgently into the man's ear.

The *cohen* rubbed his hands and shook his head. "Hosea. It's in the book of Hosea."

The dejected informer went back to spying. His huddled posture indicated he hoped above all else that, treason or not, Hannah would soon be finished preaching and he could go home.

An emissary from Rome was on his way.

From Caesar Augustus' confidant, Rufus Valens, King Herod expected to hear if his attempts to regain Caesar's favor had been successful. Augustus had opposed Herod's execution of his sons. He had, in fact, advised clemency, but Herod had ordered their deaths anyway.

Very few of Rome's client-kings failed to take Caesar's advice and then continued as heads of state. Herod—and Talmai, who had advanced the scheme—hoped Prince Antipater had managed to renew the old bonds between emperor and Jewish monarch.

Unless amity was restored, Herod could not go forward with his plans to annex Nabatea to Judea and rule them both. He desperately wanted control of the enemy country on his eastern border. Much depended on Antipater's success in Rome, but not all. The outcome would also hang on the impression Herod made on Valens during his visit.

Because of the dangers attending sea voyages at this season of the year, Caesar's envoy was coming overland. A fast-riding *hipparchos*, a cavalry commander, had just arrived from Antioch of Syria to announce the ambassador's appearance there. He would reach Caesarea Maritima within two weeks and expected to meet Herod there.

"Double the guards on the roads between here and Antioch," Herod dictated to Talmai. "No bandits . . . no rebellion . . . may mar the peace of Judea. You understand? And order Zamaris to patrol everything from Damascus to the Decapolis. My kingdom must be in better order than ever before. Have Boethus make the Temple police more watchful than ever."

"I understand, Majesty," Talmai responded.

"See that you do. It is on your head, Talmai."

Old Hannah's sleeping quarters were thought to be in a rag-filled hovel inside one of the storerooms in the Court of Women. In reality she occupied a more extensive but secret space beneath the Temple Mount. One of her rooms was a long-forgotten hollow that had once been a storage cistern for cinnamon. The expensive, imported powdered bark, a component of the sacred incense, had long since vanished, but its ever-present aroma bore witness to its earlier presence.

Even before Simeon reached Hannah's chambers, the tang of the spice announced that his journey neared its conclusion. When a turn of a dark corridor brought him within sight of a glimmer of light, the elderly Levite heard Hannah call out, "Welcome, Simeon, the righteous and devout, he who waits for the Consolation of Israel, for the *nacham*, for the Comforter of Jacob. Welcome. I say to you, you shall not be disappointed, and you have not long to wait."

"You've heard of the child, then?"

"Who has not, except those who have no ears to hear with, or those whose ears the Lord has stopped until the time?"

"The *Ruach HaKodesh*, the Holy Spirit, promised me I would not die until I saw the Lord's Anointed, the Messiah.[60] And I hear he's come! All the scrolls of the prophets confirm this: Isaias, Micah, Mosheh the Lawgiver, the weeks of years in Dani'el's writing, and yet . . ."

"Yet you must be certain you are not deceived."

"Just so."

"Then here is how you may know for certain. Do you recall the words of the book of Numbers that speak of the Redemption of the Firstborn?"

"Where Levites redeemed the firstborn sons of Israel from being dedicated to the Lord? The priests each offered their service to the Almighty as a substitute for each of the children? Yes?" Simeon was unclear where this was leading. "Ever since that day all firstborn males must be redeemed at a price because at birth they belong to God."

"Correct, but you omitted part of the story. There were 273 more firstborn male children to be redeemed than there were Levites living. So Mosheh the Lawgiver was instructed to collect five shekels for each baby, and this money went into the treasury of the Tabernacle."[61]

Simeon was eager, impatient, to understand but so far did not. How could he be an elder of Israel and be so dense and slow of comprehension?

Hannah did not rebuke him. Gently she added, "Let the Comforter come to you, Simeon the Tzadik. We know when our ancestors left Egypt, and because of that we know when the first redemption of the firstborn males occurred, true?"

A dim light began to form in Simeon's mind, like glimpsing a flame far off on a mountainside. And like that feeble light, when approached nearer, it grew into a raging fire!

"Five shekels each!" Simeon exulted. "Five for each of 273 children! That's 1,365 shekels. The shekels are years, aren't they? One thousand three hundred and sixty-five years must pass until he comes who is the fulfillment of the redemption. It is the exact number to this year. It's true! He's come! He who is not a Levite will actually give his life in service to the Almighty. He is the Messiah, the Lord's Anointed."

Hannah held up a gnarled forefinger in admonition. "But first he will fulfill all righteousness, so he who needs not to be redeemed will still keep the covenant of redemption. If you are present when he draws near to be redeemed, then you will know, Simeon the Faithful Watcher. That's how you will meet the Comforter—the Consolation—of Israel, and you will know your watching has not been in vain."

Three days after leaving Damascus, Balthasar's traveling party, which now included Kagba and Perroz, reached the region called Batanea. They had left Raghana the night before and hoped to reach Bosra soon. Tonight they camped out on the broad plain southeast of Mount Hermon. There were no other caravans nearby.

Balthasar, scanning the horizon, clasped both fists to his chest. He announced, "It begins here. Here. We are in Eretz-Israel. Batanea was Bashan, conquered by the Israelites and given to the tribe of Manasseh as an inheritance."

"Not part of Roman Syria?" Melchior questioned.

"No-man's-land," Perroz interjected. "A land of brigands and out-laws. No place for lone travelers or groups too small to defend them-selves. A bad place."

Balthasar shook his head. "Only temporarily. Don't you know the story of King Og of Bashan, last of his breed of giants? Slept on an iron bed nine cubits long. The bed still exists, preserved by the Ammonites.[62] That was a dangerous time here too! But don't marvel that I claim this land again for Eretz-Israel. After King Messiah establishes his rule, Israel's law will extend back to where we crossed the Euphrates. When that day comes, the spot on which we stand will be over three hundred miles inside Israel and perfectly safe!"

"Grandfather is very talkative tonight," Esther remarked as she bustled past, pulling together their evening meal. Affectionately she brushed a lock of white hair off his forehead. "I haven't seen you this lighthearted since the night we saw the star."

Seeing the gesture, Melchior wished such a touch for himself.

"It's because we're getting close, Granddaughter. I feel it."

Intermittent rain still dogged their travel, and clouds continued to obscure the sky. Melchior stirred the campfire, adding another acacia branch to the flames. "How much farther to Jerusalem?"

Balthasar responded instantly. "A week, perhaps ten days. No more than that."

"And will the newborn King be hard to find?"

"Certainly not! All the land will be buzzing with the news. We need only go to the Holy City and ask the first person we see. By now, everyone must know!"

CHAPTER

14

With Enoch balanced on her hip, Rachel reached out to touch the mezuzah on the doorpost as they returned home from the day's lessons. Enoch placed his finger to his lips just as he had seen his mother and father do when they entered or departed the dwelling every day of his life.

Rachel laughed with pleasure at her firstborn son's imitation of Jewish tradition. "Two and a half years old. Very bright!" She instructed him in the blessing of the mezuzah. "The Lord shall preserve . . ."

He stumbled on the words but made every attempt to mimic her. "The Lord . . . shall . . ."

"Preserve . . ."

"Pre . . ." Enoch's somber dark eyes stared at her mouth. He could not get his tongue around such a word.

Never mind, Rachel thought. Enoch did not yet understand the need for a Jew to be preserved by the Lord in his goings and comings. She was glad the child had no sense of danger in the world.

Rachel continued the blessing of the mezuzah more slowly. "Preserve . . . your going out . . ."

"Out!"

"And your coming in . . ."

"In!"

"From this time forth for evermore!"[63]

"Ever . . . more!"

The education of children in Beth-lehem followed the traditions established before the written Torah existed. The first small lessons were taught by the mother. The sages said that knowledge of Torah may be looked for in those who sucked it in at their mother's breast.

Zadok remarked that if Rachel had been born a man, she would have made a wonderful rabbi, birthing the Word of God in the hearts of the young. She was learned in the intricacies of the Law and often joined with Zadok and Eliyahu in discussions over supper. Already she had begun to teach little Enoch the tribe, clan, and names of his ancestors by counting them, one by one, on the knuckles of his hands. Before Enoch could verbally ask for bread, his heart had memorized the names of grandfather, great-grandfather, great-great-grandfather, and so on back to the exile to Babylon.

Fourteen knuckles on the right hand led from the time of David to the Exile. Fourteen knuckles on the left led from the Exile to the present day. Fingers kept track of priestly lineage that reached to Aaron and the parting of the Red Sea.

"What about Obi?" Enoch had asked Rachel as he pointed to the stump where Obi's hand should have been.

She answered gently, "The time will come when Obi and all of Israel will count our ancestors in the stars of the heavens."

There was a school in every Jewish community. Formal education began in the fifth or sixth year, but teaching at home began before a child was weaned.

Morning and night Rachel sang the stories of the Book of Beginnings. Though her sons might not be capable yet of memorizing the story of Noah and the ark, Rachel held them entranced with her tales of great beasts and tiny mice scampering up the ramp onto the landlocked ship.

Eliyahu, the only rabbi in the community, was head teacher to all the children. From age six to ten the Torah was their only text. From ten to fifteen the Mishnah, or rabbinic commentary on traditional law, was added. Above that age those who showed aptitude were sent to the higher academies in Jerusalem. In Beth-lehem, however, formal education usually ended after the age of fifteen and the school of higher learning became long discussions beside the campfire with the glory of the stars shining above as evidence that Yahweh was too great to fully comprehend. The lessons of the flock provided the truest parable of God's love for His people Israel. This legacy of learning was passed from father to son on lonely nights in the fields.

Volunteers from among the older boys, like Sharona's son Jesse, were called upon in rotation to help instruct the younger children in their basic letters.

Three days a week Havila and Rachel taught basic religious education and practical household skills to a flock of twenty-two of Beth-lehem's little girls. Enoch, Samu'el, Obi, and Dan were passed from hand to hand as nine- and ten-year-old females played at being little mothers. Today, however, Havila had traveled to Ramah to visit her aunt. For that reason, today Rachel had decided to leave Obi and Samu'el at home in the care of Mary.

Unlike the opulent Torah academies that flourished in Jerusalem, the sons of Beth-lehem received their instruction sitting on the floor in a semicircle facing Eliyahu. This was in fulfillment of the prophecy of Isaias that proclaimed *"Your eyes shall see your teachers."*[64] It was said by the sages that the students encircled the teacher like a crown of glory. Thus Rabbi Eliyahu polished the jewels of the village.

The Torah was imparted to the youngest shepherds of Beth-lehem with patience and strictness, earnestness and kindness. It was first ingrained in little minds and hearts by the blessings of coming in and going out of every Jewish home. The story of Passover and the blood of the lamb on the doorposts of all the people of Israel was remembered by the mezuzah nailed on the doorposts of present-day Jewish homes.

Today, as Rachel entered the house with Enoch, she wondered if Mary's baby would have a rabbi teach Him. Would the boy grow up and attend a synagogue school like every other child in Eretz-Israel? Who would be worthy to teach Messiah? Would a learned sage appear somehow to recite with the Holy Child the laws of sacrifice and the redemption of mankind from the slavery of sin?

Rachel kissed Enoch on his forehead as the warmth of the house enveloped them. It took a minute for her eyes to adjust to the dim light.

Mary, with her firstborn son on her lap, sat beside the fire. Obi slept and Samu'el played quietly at her feet.

Enoch's face lit up. His somber eyes locked on the newborn in Mary's arms. He called out without hesitation, "Yeshua! The Lord shall . . ."

Rachel tried to coach him. ". . . preserve . . ."

Enoch seemed not to hear her. He touched his finger to his lips and stretched out his hand to the baby as though touching the mezuzah. Enoch's childish treble pronounced the words with surprising clarity. "Bless Yeshua . . . bless! You! Going out . . . and bless you! Coming in, from for evermore."

Rachel knew that, in part, Enoch had recited the blessing spoken over the mezuzah, but there was something else in Enoch's joyful cry when he saw the face of his Messiah.

Mary's face beamed. "What beautiful sons you have, Rachel! They have all been so good today."

Then Mary extended a gold coin that glinted in the firelight.

Rachel knew in an instant it was Grandmother's lost twenty-drachma piece.

Mary explained, "Look, Rachel! Enoch dropped this . . . this! . . . into my lap as Yeshua nursed. A very old coin. Pierced all the way through the heart of it, like a dowry coin. The temple of Judah Maccabee and the words *A great miracle happened here* on one side. On the other side, a menorah. A treasure, eh? I don't know where Enoch found it, but I'm sure someone in the house will be glad it's found!"

King Herod and Talmai waited beside the altar for the augur to finish his preparations for the ceremony. The wind, though not as biting, was still blustery, whipping cloaks and clouds.

Spread out below Talmai was the great seaport of Caesarea. The arms of King Herod's harbor embraced the commerce of the Roman Empire. Though little voyaging was done during the winter season, coasting galleys plied up and down the shore between Judea and Alexandria. The docks were packed with larger vessels waiting out the storms until it was safe to proceed.

If the breakwaters were the limbs, the central hill above the marina formed the head to the body of the city. Crowning that head was the Temple of Augustus. Herod had ordered its construction nearly two decades earlier to summarize his devotion to the emperor. In it was a many-times-greater-than-life-size statue of Augustus portrayed as Olympian Zeus—Jupiter to the Romans—a copy of the original idol in Greece. The figure showed the king of the gods in his most regal and imposing guise. Seated on a throne, the effigy with Caesar's features wore a diadem of olive branches. In Jupiter's right hand stood the winged goddess of victory; his left lifted an eagle-topped scepter.

Talmai never entered the temple without being struck by how odd the proportions were. If Jupiter/Augustus suddenly stood upright, he would hit his olive wreath on the ceiling.

Beside Jupiter, so much smaller as to appear an afterthought, stood a statue of Roma, patron goddess of the city of Rome. This was, or so Talmai believed, Herod's attempt to hedge his bets. If Augustus died suddenly or was deposed, the king of the Jews could denounce the fallen emperor while maintaining his loyalty to the Empire. It was not an idle conjecture since Herod had already successfully switched sides from supporting Marc Antony to the victorious Caesar in the Roman civil war.

At last the haruspex was ready. The smoke of the incense swirled in dense white vapor around Jupiter's marble feet until whipped away toward Egypt by the wind. The libation had been poured. The lamb and the knife were ready.

Hearing that Ambassador Valens was coming, Herod had come to the temple to offer sacrifice to Augustus and to take the auspices for success in the upcoming conference. Though the Jews had no toleration for the worship of other gods, this prohibition did not extend to their king. As in politics, so in religion Herod practiced expediency. He thought it best to placate the Roman gods, who doubtless favored Caesar. Besides, Caesarea was a Gentile city. No pious Jew was present to report on their king's apostasy.

If anyone did circulate such a report, it would be a clear sign of treason, Talmai thought. They might carry such a tale, but they would carry it only once.

For the omens to be properly read, Herod had to perform the sacrifice himself. This he did with the aid of two assistant priests, who held the bleating lamb, and the haruspex, the officiating priest who guided the knife.

One slice across the lamb's throat was followed immediately by one down the length of its belly. Herod thrust his hands into the entrails, clutching the liver with bloody hands and thrusting it into the grasp of the priest.

The organ was laid on a marble slab for the divination to proceed.

Though the haruspex tried to hide his gasp of astonishment, it did not go unnoticed by either Talmai or Herod, judging from the king's impatient demand. "What? What do you read there?"

"Majesty," the man said, clearly rattled by what he saw and unable to cover his nervousness. "Majesty, this liver is wholly without marks of any kind. See for yourself. It's perfectly smooth. It is unblemished, which means I cannot read it at all."

Herod's eyes widened, and his head tilted toward his right shoulder.

Spotting the onset of another fit of madness, Talmai hoped there was time to intervene. "Amazing," he said cheerfully. "A miracle for you, sire. Your relationship with the emperor will be wholly restored! Your friendship with the divine Augustus will be better than ever before—completely without shadow."

"Yes, yes, of course that's what I meant," the priest asserted, handing Herod the bowl of rose-scented water and a towel. "Perfectly restored. There can be no doubt."

Blood from Herod's fingers gave a rose-colored hue to the water and left scarlet streaks on the cloth.

Grandmother placed the coin necklace over Mary's head. "This is the one coin from my dowry that I have left. It was lost and now it's found. It's meant for you, my dear Mary, and for the little one."

Mary placed her hand over her heart. "Such a gift!"

Grandmother agreed. "My inheritance, yes? Though I did not tell Rachel, I lost it *two* Hanukkahs ago. But now it's found. So as I am washing the clothes, I think, *Which is better for my little boys to have? A gold coin from Grandmother or a place in the kingdom of the King of Israel?*"

"You don't need gold to buy a place in the kingdom for your children and grandchildren. Your love for him is the only gift he will ever want."

"Even so, when your son is ruler over Israel, may he remember my grandsons, eh?"

"He will remember. We will all remember you and your little ones. Your kindness. Your protection."

This assurance seemed to satisfy the old woman. "Good."

Mary started to return the gift. "Grandmother, give it to your little ones."

"No. No. Enoch found it. He gave it to Yeshua. A fine gift. Enoch will walk with God. So he says. An honorable gift for Enoch to offer to one so wonderful. And maybe it won't hurt when Yeshua is grown for you to keep a little reminder of my sweet boys, eh?"

Though the sky remained solid clouds, the rain stopped after supper. Because of the long day's travel behind, those still ahead, and the rapidly falling temperatures, none of the pilgrims desired long fireside conversations before bed. Melchior took Esther for a brief walk around the encampment as daylight slipped away. The glowing interiors of several tents announced that ongoing studies were in progress.

The attack came just after full dark, even as Melchior returned Esther to her father's tent. Brigands from the hill country of Trachonitis assailed the encampment from two directions in quick succession. Shouts of alarm and warning came from Aretas' guards as raiders thundered into the camp on horseback, stampeding the livestock and drawing the guards away after them as they withdrew to the south.

That was the moment the second party of attackers, having approached on foot up the creek bed near the camp, launched their assault. Slashing with short swords, they quickly incapacitated two of the servants. The others fled, running past Melchior, who had sprinted toward the cries for help.

Weaponless, he faced a dark-robed bandit who swung a curved

blade toward his face. Melchior ducked aside, feeling the rush of air from the sword as it narrowly missed his ear. He backed toward the fire in order to keep the light in his opponent's eyes and so no other enemy could approach him from behind. He scanned the area for anything with which to defend himself.

As he did so, Melchior saw Kagba on the offensive. The Armenian charged under the upraised arm of his foe, knocking the man off his feet by the force of his rush. Kagba helped himself to the robber's sword. Clubbing the downed man on the head with the pommel, he dashed off to help Prince Aretas.

The Parthian youth needed assistance because he faced a trio of bandits outside his tent. With only a small dagger, Aretas parried the blows of three larger men, all with bigger blades. The prince possessed skillful footwork, but he was too outnumbered for the contest to last.

Melchior barely had time to wonder where the prince's guards had gone. Had they been drawn away after the stolen animals? Then Melchior's own adversary closed in on him, and there was no further opportunity for speculation . . . only survival.

The next swipe of the brigand's sword ripped through a fold of Melchior's sleeve. Bending down, Melchior grasped a jagged chunk of black rock and threw it in his opponent's face.

The stone connected with the man's nose and forehead, making him drop his guard. Taking a cue from Kagba, Melchior lowered his shoulder and drove it into the bandit's midsection. The robber did not lose his weapon but did stagger sideways. Melchior seized the sword arm in both hands and snapped it over his knee, then wrenched the weapon free from the howling man, who ran off into the night.

As Melchior sped to help Aretas, he witnessed Perroz dealing with two assailants in his own way. Snatching a brand from the fire, the giant Ethiopian thrust its flames into one adversary's face, driving him backward so rapidly the robber collided with one of his own fellows. Tossing aside the torch, Perroz grabbed both men around their necks and bashed their heads together with an audible crack that felled both of them.

Kagba was already engaging one of Aretas' rivals as Melchior rushed up. Hearing the noise of Melchior's approach, the third of the prince's foes turned toward him. Their blades rang together with a shock Melchior felt clear to his shoulder.

Then Gaspar crowded into the scene, tangling his own enemy with Melchior's. The Indian scholar fought with a kukri, a short, heavy-bladed weapon much like a curved hand axe. His kukri flashed so furiously that both men gave ground before his attack.

Prince Aretas, tangled in a guy rope of the tent, gave a cry for help at the same instant Melchior heard Esther scream. Whipping around, Melchior saw Old Balthasar using a walking stick to try to fend off two aggressors who had seized Esther by the arms and were dragging her away.

Caught between two cries for help, Melchior could assist neither. Another raider rushed at him out of the darkness. With his blade lowered and on the wrong side of his body, all he could do to save himself was raise his right arm to deflect the blow.

The assailant's blade was dull and didn't pierce Melchior's woolen cloak, but the strike instantly numbed his arm and made him drop his weapon. Now he was at the mercy of his foe and unable to save even himself, let alone those he most cared about in the world.

Dull blade or not, the next strike Melchior suffered would probably kill him . . . unless he moved—and quickly. Throwing himself to the ground, he rolled clear of the descending blow. Sparks flashed from the clanging impact as his enemy's sword struck rock.

Melchior heard Esther cry out again. He saw Old Balthasar batted aside, causing the elderly man to land heavily across a camel's pack-saddle. The pair of abductors dragging Esther had her near the edge of the firelight. A score more paces and they would be swallowed up in darkness.

He had to save her!

Pounding hooves vibrated the ground. Another troop of horsemen thundered into camp out of the darkness. Melchior despaired. It must be the first set of brigands who had circled back to aid their comrades.

Another swipe barely missed him, the sword's tip striking mere inches from his head as he lunged aside. Melchior's lurch thrust him onto a pile of rocks in which he was wedged. He was stuck—trapped. He scrabbled frantically for a handful of gravel to fling in his attacker's face.

The man warded it off easily and sneered as he raised his weapon for a final blow.

A breath that was both prayer and apology for failing Esther escaped Melchior's lips. Then, just before his death, he watched with astonishment as a red flower bloomed from his foe's chest . . . where an arrowhead protruded.

Melchior was stunned. He could not comprehend what had happened.

The man collapsed, landing across Melchior's legs.

As Melchior shoved the deadweight aside, he saw the leader of the horsemen sweep into the firelight. Black robed and scowling, the captain wielded a lance. With it he rode down one of Esther's captors, spitting the bandit completely through the body.

Without drawing rein, the newcomer leapt from the saddle, tackling the other would-be kidnapper around the neck. Melchior noted the flash of a dagger in the captain's hand. He saw it rise and fall twice before the cavalry commander rose from the ground, leaving another inert body behind. Hands on hips, knifepoint held low but at the ready, the rescuer surveyed the scene.

The band of robbers attempted to scatter, but everywhere they dashed brought them face-to-face with a mounted man. With double-curved bows the riders routinely shot down the cutthroats.

At last Melchior recognized Zamaris in the fixed harshness of the captain's demeanor. As Melchior tried to make sense of this development, he watched as Zamaris drew a bow from across his own broad shoulders. Faster than Melchior had ever seen it done, Zamaris launched three arrows toward a fleeing brigand. The first missed, but the other two struck the man in the back and leg, bringing him screaming to earth.

And just like that, the fight was over. The remaining bandits were either shot down, hacked to pieces, or had fled, panic-stricken, into the night.

There was no question about Zamaris taking charge of the caravan after the battle. Within two hours all the survivors, their remaining pack animals, and the bodies of two dead servants had been transported to Bathyra, Zamaris' hilltop fortress.

The bandits, stripped of their weapons and clothing, were left for the jackals.

In a room of Spartan furnishing, Melchior sat with his back against a stone wall. The young astronomer listened but said nothing as Zamaris answered and asked questions. Relieved to be alive but feeling sadly useless, Melchior's thoughts were as much a mass of confusion as his body was a welter of bruises.

"I am master of Bathyra and of the hill country hereabouts." Zamaris' raspy voice scraped the air as he explained to Old Balthasar. "I came from Babylon with my five hundred mounted archers because King Herod pays me to patrol the caravan routes. The people of Trachonitis are *swine*." Zamaris spat out the name of the adjacent region as an epithet. "Someday soon we will have to reduce them and their city to ashes."

"Then you are a Jew?" Balthasar queried.

"To be sure, but of the practical sort. My profession leaves no time for handwashing and the like."

"Still, praise be to The Eternal you arrived when you did."

"Praise him, certainly, but he did not send me," Zamaris argued. "The king ordered me to redouble my patrols because some important Roman is visiting Judea, and he wants to make a good impression. Besides, we had already been following that band of Trachonite horse thieves since they struck a village earlier. So no miracle. I was already on their trail."

"You kept a divine appointment whether you know it or not," Balthasar argued.

Zamaris shrugged. "Consider this: If the Trachonites had known I was pursuing, they would never have stopped to attack your camp. Bad management, that. Also, I fear you have lost all your horses and many of your camels."

"But you saved my granddaughter!"

Zamaris turned his penetrating gaze on Esther, standing behind her grandfather's chair. "And well worth saving too, I say."

Even in the flickering firelight Melchior saw Esther blush and turn away from the compliment.

Zamaris studied the young woman for an uncomfortably long time before resuming. "But you gave a good account of yourselves even before I arrived. The Armenian, the one from the East who fights with an axe, and the big black man—brave men, good fighters all. Except for them, you'd have all been slaughtered before I arrived."

When Melchior thought about his contribution to the battle, it amounted to barely saving his own life . . . and he had needed Zamaris' rescue to do that. That thought, and others like it, kept him silent and his face turned toward the floor.

16 | CHAPTER

It was not yet daylight, but Yosef and Mary were up. The baby had slept the whole night through. Each day the rustle of Mary's movements as she cleaned and fed the baby awakened Yosef.

He arose and washed. The eighteen blessings were prayed. There were things to do before Yosef set out with Zadok and the shepherds for the distant pastures.

Yosef sat on the edge of his bed and sanded the shaft of wood.

The rough stone that marked the remainder of David's childhood home in the cottage was unpainted—a demarcation between past and present. Ancient and new blended into one dwelling place.

"The Lord is my shepherd," Mary sang as she swept the floor. *"I shall not want. . . ."*[65]

Yosef cut the last letter of the shepherd-king's psalm into the staff he had carved for Zadok.

"He makes me lie down in green pastures."[66]

A vine of flowers wound up the grain of the acacia wood. Hard as iron, the shepherd's crook would last Zadok's lifetime and beyond.

"He leads me beside still waters."[67]

Yosef blew away the sawdust and brushed it with his large calloused hands.

Mary's words trailed away as she stopped to admire the finished work.

"Oh, Yosef! You *are* an artist," she breathed, tracing the intricate detail with her fingertip. "I can almost smell the blossoms."

Yosef thumped the stick on the floor like the chamberlain of a king. "He won't accept payment. So this to thank him then."

"Worthy," Mary agreed.

"And I'll carve a medicine box for Rachel. There. For the corner."

"Good. Yes. Very good."

"This morning we move the flock to the lower pasture."

Mary's smile was gentle as she placed her hand on his cheek. "You love it, don't you?"

"Good people, these *am ha aretz*." Yosef gazed down at Yeshua, who observed him with serious eyes. "His people. The last true shepherds of Israel. The politics of Yerushalayim don't touch them."

"I've been wondering. Are we meant to stay here, Yosef? Raise him to walk the ancient shepherd paths? So he grows up following the footsteps of David?"

"A man could build a life in such a place. My father's family . . . all killed in the rebellion. None left alive in Beth-lehem. Strange, though, how there's some old memory of a thousand years of family that runs in a man's veins. You come home to a place your great-grandfather knew well, and it's as if his memories somehow become your own."

"David on the run from Saul, longing for a drink from the well we draw water from every day. Our souls thirst for the water of home like his did."

"Home. Going out with Zadok and the others, I walk paths I never walked and somehow it's as if they're all familiar. The wind blows over the flocks from Yerushalayim. I breathe Zion in the air and my heart is home."

Mary leaned on the broom handle. "They've opened their hearts to us, these people. Rachel. Zadok. Their boys. Havila and Eliyahu. All the rest. Is this why the baby was born here? why the angels spoke to the shepherds in the fields of Migdal Eder? So we would stay and live without the gossip we faced in Nazareth? raise him around people who don't doubt the truth of our story?"

"A man could settle here. Six miles from Yerushalayim. Plenty of work in the carpenter's trade."

The two stood silent for a time. Thoughts, following the course of two ancient streams, merged into one truth: *But you, Beth-lehem Ephrathah, though you are small among the clans of Judah, out of you will come for me one who will be ruler over Israel, whose origins are from of old, from ancient times!*[168]

Melchior awoke with a start as someone shook him by the elbow and softly called his name. With only the dying embers of the fire shedding any light, Melchior could not immediately remember where he was. Even worse, there was a moment when he thought they had all been captured by bandits.

When Prince Aretas whispered his name again, location and circumstances clicked into place.

"What? What is it? Have the robbers returned?"

"No, they wouldn't dare come here. But I have to talk to you."

"Why? What's the matter?"

Aretas summoned Melchior to join him on the battlements of Zamaris' stronghold, where they could speak without disturbing the others. A rosy hue suffused the Batanean plain beneath a layer of gray clouds.

"You know my guards didn't return after the attack?"

Melchior shook his head. He had been too concerned for Old Balthasar and Esther to notice the missing Parthian soldiers. "Captured? Or dead? Do we need to go search for them?"

Aretas shook his head grimly. "Zamaris says not. Seems one of the Trachonites was captured alive. From him they got a confession. I was the target of the attack."

"You?" Melchior responded stupidly, not comprehending. "For ransom? But who knew you are royalty, except . . ." On the eastern horizon a band of yellow light dawned. "Your guards sold you out!"

"Yes, and perhaps not merely to be kidnapped. The Trachonite said Queen Musa wants me dead. Wants no rival to her son for my father's throne. My bodyguards have been looking for a chance to do away with me. In Damascus they made a deal for the Trachonites to kill me in the raid and make it look like bandits only."

Aretas was the son of King Phraates and older than his half brother

Crown Prince Phraataces. Aretas had once been the heir. Since the king had remarried, his new queen had wasted no opportunity pushing her son forward at the expense of Aretas. No longer content with simply maneuvering, Musa had apparently wanted the issue settled forever.

Herod had executed his sons. The Parthian queen had planned to murder her stepson.

What a world the new King of Israel had been born into!

Aretas fretted, "If I remain with the caravan, I'll endanger all of you. Once my guards learn I'm still alive, they will have to try to kill everyone so the story doesn't get back to my father."

"But where can you go?"

"Perhaps I can hire some of Zamaris' men to accompany me. . . . I don't know. I don't think I'll live to see my father again if I try to return home. Perhaps I'll seek asylum in Rome. Caesar would not refuse giving refuge to someone of both Nabatean and Parthian royal blood."

Aretas' reasoning was sound. The Roman emperor had given asylum to many surplus princelings in the past. It gave him political clout and a potential future puppet ruler under his control.

Both young men stood silently, pondering.

Finally Melchior suggested, "I think you'd better stay with us. You'll be safer. From Jerusalem you can go on to Rome, if that's what you decide."

"We're all stuck here in Bathyra until we replace the animals we lost in the raid."

Footsteps approached the doorway from within the tower. Zamaris emerged into the morning air, giving a curt salutation to Aretas and ignoring Melchior. "Aren't you up early?" he growled.

Melchior was struck with the notion that Zamaris should not know everything. Not yet. "We're wondering how to replace the livestock we lost. We're eager to get on with our journey."

"Already taken care of." Zamaris addressed Aretas as if Melchior had not spoken. "Your death or disappearance would be a diplomatic problem for Lord Herod. It's my duty to see you safely to Jerusalem. I have plenty of horses for all."

With a bow for Aretas and a slight nod toward Melchior, Zamaris descended a stair toward the guardroom.

Melchior laid a hand on Aretas' arm. "Don't say anything to Zamaris about going to Rome," he advised. "For now we're all going to Jerusalem. That's all Zamaris needs to know."

Zadok stood on the knoll overlooking the vast sea of woolly sheep that moved slowly down the ravine. He clutched his new staff in his left hand. His rod, a blunt stick about the length of a man's forearm, hung from a leather strap on his right wrist.

Your rod and Your staff, they comfort me.[69]

A young ewe spotted green grass beside a steep drop-off. She left the trail. Zadok whistled for her to turn. When she did not heed his voice, he flung the rod with perfect aim to skim her nose. Startled by the rod, she scampered back among her fellows.

"She's a stubborn one, that one is." Zadok motioned for his dog to fetch back the throwing stick. "She'll go her own way nine times out of ten." He glanced at the crook of the staff. "That's the purpose of the hook on a staff. It'll see some hard use pullin' her up when she falls. Gettin' her out of tight places. A fine gift, Yosef."

Yosef kept his eye riveted on the errant ewe who, even though she came back into line, was still searching for a blade of grass to claim as her own. "I never thought of them as having their own minds."

Zadok laughed. "Just like humankind, they are! No different at all. It's no mistake the Lord has called us his sheep. Stubborn, stupid, timid, foolish, careless, greedy. Prone t' follow wherever the flock goes . . . even over a cliff if others was runnin' that way. And yet some'll find a way t' escape the lush green pastures we lead them to. Aye. Out of pure cussedness they'll run after a blade of grass on a desolate mountainside."

He thumped the staff and pointed toward a ledge on a precipice. "Last spring a ewe went off the edge, and Lem was climbin' up t' fetch her. Nearly killed himself, he did, tryin' t' save her."

"Why didn't you let her go?"

"There's a rule among us. It's written in here." Zadok tapped his chest. "There's lions and jackals in the desert pastures. A good shepherd'll lay down his life for the safety of the flock. That's the way it's always been with us. Since our father Avraham, the first shepherd of our people. Are there those who are in charge of sheep who don't care? Aye. When we reach the grazin' land, you'll see. There are hired men among the Arabs who'll turn tail at the first sign of danger. They let their master's sheep die and never think twice about it. But we men of Beth-lehem . . . we're hereditary shepherds of the Lord's own flocks. We walk the path David walked. Our shepherd-king. My boys will one day walk this path."

"You teach them young." Yosef observed Lem with three of his red-haired sons on the opposite side of the herd.

"Best for our lads t' learn the lesson early in life. The Eternal has used these dumb, stubborn sheep—of all animals on earth—t' teach us how much he loves his people Israel. That's why we carry the rod and staff. I can throw so as t' turn back a wolf from devourin' a lamb. Or I can use the rod t' correct and turn back a sheep who is goin' away from my protection. When I strike, it hurts the sheep. Aye. But at least she's alive."

Zadok waved the rod aloft. "Maybe that ewe will figure out one day that I do what I do for her good and the good of all. If not, one day she'll slip away out of range of my rod and staff. And she'll be pulled down and killed by a jackal who lies in wait. I will have done all I could. Some sheep refuse my protection. Some will not be saved. Aye. There's Torah lessons a'plenty in the sheep."

The gray clouds parted as they moved to the south and west. Yosef removed his outer coat and tied it around his shoulders. Perhaps he would carve himself a shepherd's crook—a simple one, nothing proud or fine. A strong humble staff so he could help Zadok and the others on the next journey. And he would make a rod of ironwood and ask Zadok to teach him the trick of throwing it so he didn't kill the creature he was trying to save.

Blessed are you, O Adonai! How many times you have thrown your rod at Israel's nose, not to destroy but to turn us back from wandering!

Yosef thought of Yeshua, a little lamb in Mary's arms. One day Yeshua would be the Great Shepherd. On that day, Yosef would carve Him a staff of such beauty! A staff like none had carried since the days of David's rule over Israel.

Blessed are you, beloved Lamb of God! Blessed are you, Good Shepherd who has come down from heaven to save your flock! "Though I walk in the valley of the shadow of death, I will fear no evil, for You are with me. Your rod and Your staff, they comfort me."[70]

❦

There was a single room in Mordechai's inn that served as the private office of the government officials in charge of Beth-lehem's census and tax collection.

"My lords, I have information of treason that might be of interest to the king," Mordechai whispered as he set the platter of mutton before the Herodian tax collector and the Roman census officer.

The red-haired, clean-shaven Roman and the bald, spade-bearded Herodian exchanged skeptical looks.

"How much money do you want to reveal the plot to us, Mordechai?" the Roman asked.

Mordechai brightened. "I knew you would welcome the news."

"How much?"

Mordechai's fingers twitched. He peered over the heads of his guests as though the payment for revealing treason was written on the wall behind them. "Twenty denarii."

"Twenty? So much?" The Roman scowled. "Treason is common these days. Twenty denarii is far too much for such a common crime."

"Or ten," Mordechai offered. "Ten would be good."

"So, Pliny"—the Herodian tore off a chunk of meat—"ten denarii. Mordechai the brothel keeper has news for Lord Herod."

Pliny, the Roman, chuckled. "A revolt among the harlots of a caravan master, perhaps? Ten denarii. Shall we pay him for this news, Tubal? A hundred concubines to take over the palace and poison the officers' wine?"

Mordechai drew his portly form erect. "You mock me."

Both patrons burst into laughter as the innkeeper attempted a dignified exit but was stopped by the Roman's upraised hand. The officer suggested, "Should we lock him up? Perhaps he's part of the plot! This stinking pig . . . master of this flea-infested hog wallow has information for Lord Herod!"

The Herodian tax collector stuck out his foot to trip Mordechai. The innkeeper plunged to the floor. His filthy robe flew up around his waist, sparking another round of uproarious laughter.

Tubal cried, "Our dear host reveals the bare truth, eh? The rumble of treason is heard in Beth-lehem!"

Mordechai reddened. He straightened his garment and slowly pulled himself up. "My lords, I have news. A baby has been born. Angels appeared. The people celebrated at the synagogue. Men and women dancing . . ."

The howl of amusement drowned out Mordechai's report. "Angels. *Oooooh!* Dancing in the synagogue. Little angels. Treasonous angels.

Babies born in Beth-lehem! An army of babies to take over the kingdom. The innkeeper's drunk!"

"Drunk again. Treason!" Tubal howled.

"Treason! Mordechai's meat is undercooked. Poison."

"Treason! Mordechai's wine is sour. Hemlock and death to all who
drink the wine of Mordechai!"

Pliny leapt to his feet and kicked Mordechai hard in the rump. "Get
out, pig! Fetch us more wine and shut up. We're not so drunk that we'll
pay you ten denarii or so much as a single mite."

Mordechai scrambled on hands and knees to escape.

The Roman, suddenly sober, roared after him, "One more week
and we are out of this cesspit you call an inn. I count the hours! Count
yourself lucky you aren't under arrest for attempting to kill us with
your foul food."

17

David's Pasture, it's called." Zadok gestured toward a mound of jagged boulders. "Just there marks the trail. A peaceful place, it is. A secret place. Hid in a swale between the mountains. Protected from the wind. The tableland. Aye. We shepherds cultivate it for the wee lambs and their mothers."

Yosef remembered David's psalm: *You prepare a table before me in the presence of my enemies.*[71] Was not the howling wind an enemy?

Zadok poured oil into the palm of his hand and rubbed it on his face. He poured a few drops into Yosef's palm. "Here. Put this on your face. Aye, rub it in for protection."

Then Zadok drew in a lamb with the crook of his staff and rubbed oil over the baby's eyelids. "This one has had a hard time of the cold. A fine big lamb . . . near perfect in every way. But wind burned his eyes. He'll go blind unless we anoint him. Aye, olive oil. That's the trick. We cover the faces of all the sheep against botflies in the summer. But I've see the cold do damage t' eyes just as much as worms from a botfly."

The lamb relaxed under Zadok's touch. Then, well protected, he scampered back to his mother.

"How many keep watch in David's Pasture?"

"We rotate. Four men on watch each week. The young shepherds. Boys of bar mitzvah age. Always with an older teacher. A good place t' learn. It's the best duty. There's a back way out. A way down t' the sea leads south. Those of us hereditary shepherds who know David's trail can make our way clear t' Egypt and never be seen by the bandits that haunt the main highway. They say David made use of this trail when he was on the run from Saul. I brought my brother Onias down t' the sea after he was crucified by Herod's soldiers and left for dead. Aye. And his wee lamb of a daughter too. Didn't meet one of Herod's soldiers. Not even one all the way t' Joppa."

Yosef scanned the heap of boulders that jutted into the sky. "I couldn't see the entrance to the trail if you didn't show me."

Zadok motioned toward Herod's palace in the distance. "Not even visible from there. Reserved only for the finest lambs of Migdal Eder, the pasture is. Korban. Them as is holy unto the Lord. The ones set apart. David's Pasture is meant for them.

"He wrote of it, the shepherd-king did. *'You make me lie down in green pastures. You restore my soul.'* [72] All that. He was speakin' of the place. A terrible hard journey t' reach it, but when we arrive . . . a clear spring of good water flows all year and fine green pasturage even in the worst of weather. Aye. We can be freezin' up here in Migdal Eder, and the weather at David's Pasture is lovely. Spring even in winter. We raise the best of the Temple flock there."

It was, Yosef knew, an honor to be asked to accompany Zadok as he moved a flock of two hundred ewes and their lambs along with one old ram to a lower pasture a mile distant through the hills.

A single sheepdog moved at Zadok's whistled commands. The shaggy, wild-looking creature seemed to be the extension of the shepherd's will. The beast protected right and left, front and rear as the flock of mothers and newborns followed papa ram toward a treacherous pass. Zadok raised fingers to his mouth and sounded three shrill signals. The black dog, half the size of the ram, tore to the front. He barked and snarled, halting the flock at the head of the trail.

"Aye," Zadok commented to Yosef with satisfaction at the canine's performance. "He's a good 'un, my Bear Dog. One man and two good dogs could move a thousand head. Bear by himself makes two. I, by myself, don't need more'n Bear."

Yosef noted how the dog seemed to enjoy the game, sometimes

nipping at the heels of his charges and other times baring fangs in the faces of sheep who resisted.

"Hold him there, Bear Dog!" Zadok commanded. Then to Yosef, "From here the path narrows. Steep. Five hundred feet straight to the bottom. I'll lead. You take the rear."

Zadok bent to retrieve a long stick of deadwood from the ground. He thrust it into Yosef's hand. "Not a proper shepherd without a staff. You'll need this t' extend your reach. If the young'uns get out of line, nudge them back. No need t' be too gentle."

Zadok brandished his new carved staff. "No room for a babe t' wander on this trail. We'd not be movin' them down t' lower pasture so early in their wee lives if the weather hadn't turned so bitter. Ewes are havin' a time of it. Water frozen. Home ground covered with ice. Wet fleece freezes at night. Too heavy a load for them t' bear on their own backs. They lie down and can't get up. But we can't shear them until the cold spell is ended. They'd freeze t' death for certain. The babies need warmth. A sheltered place out of this gale. David's Pasture. The grass is already green."

Yosef frowned at his staff of brittle deadwood. "It'll break at the first blow."

"Aye. Won't do for the long run. We'll get y' a proper stick. A good solid whack is called for sometimes. Not one step t' the right or left on this path. If they fall into the ravine, they won't survive. Up t' us t' keep them on the straight and narrow path."

The howling wind dropped away as they passed between the two gigantic pinnacles that marked the mountain pass. A profound silence, a warmth created by the absence of cold, embraced all of Yosef's senses. He sighed, like a man entering his house after a long day in the elements.

Blessed are you, O Adonai, who hides us in the shelter of your rock![73]

Yosef, at the rear of the shambling herd, noted how Zadok remained at the head, softly calling encouragement to his flock. "Come on then. Aye, girls, 'tis a lovely place to raise your babes! Come along. Careful! That's it. That's the way."

The precipitous trail clung to the side of the mountain. It narrowed down so only one at a time could move, nose to tail, after the other.

The high cliff walls rose on either side. Beneath them a rock-strewn canyon bore evidence of violent flash floods.

Zadok began to sing. His rich bass voice echoed on the walls of stone like a hundred voices. *"The Lord is my shepherd. I shall not want. I'll walk with him always. He makes me lie down in green pastures."*

Yosef joined him in antiphonal harmony as the two marched down and down, accompanied by a choir of two hundred echoes, into the valley.

> *"He leads me beside quiet waters.*
> *He restores my soul.*
> *He guides me in the path of righteousness for His name's sake.*
> *Even though I walk through the valley of the shadow of death,*
> *I will fear no evil, for You are with me!*
> *Your rod and Your staff . . . they comfort me!*
> *You prepare a table before me . . .*
> *in the presence of my enemies.*
> *You anoint my head with oil.*
> *My cup overflows!*
> *Surely goodness and mercy and love . . .*
> *will follow after me all the days of my life.*
> *And I will dwell in the house of the Lord forever!"*[74]

The little flock passed through a layer of clouds as it wound down the narrow path toward David's Pasture. Several paces ahead of Yosef, Zadok paused and waved his staff. As if by some miracle, they emerged into clear, bright sunshine. The air was warmer by twenty degrees.

"Look there." Zadok pointed into the narrow finger of green that stretched between two steep mountains for about a quarter of a mile. "The tableland. Where the flock can graze in peace. All the best food and clean water sheep could need. Safe from the jackals. Those devils travel in packs. They won't come down this path. Mountains too steep. Sometimes at sunrise a man'll glimpse them evil eyes watchin' the flocks from the crags above. Oh, they may wish for a taste of mutton, but they can't touch the lambs. Can't enter this valley."

You prepare a table before me in the presence of my enemies.

A ribbon of blue from a stream wound through tall green pastures where clusters of sheep tugged at the grass in languid contentment. "Sheep won't lay down if they sense danger, but look here," Zadok observed.

He makes me lie down in green pastures.

Zadok walked on. The switchback path widened so two men could walk side by side. Bear Dog at the fore controlled and slowed the descent of the sheep.

Yosef could clearly see the tents of the shepherds, unchanged from the days when Abraham first entered the land. The delicious aroma of meat on a spit floated up, rousing his hunger.

"'Tis a privileged place." Zadok waved his hand in the air. "By that I mean a man can't be unhappy in such a place. The stars . . . oh, the sky at night! We send the young shepherds here with their brides, after they wed. In days of old, Boaz and Ruth, great-grandparents of David—and your many times great-grandparents too, Yosef—spent their first days here after they wed. Me and my Rachel . . . we stayed here for a month. And when we came home again, we knew each other well. No weddin's of late. There's none but the old widowers here now and the young'uns, learnin' Torah by examples of the sheep. As your grandfather David did in his youth. And later, after King David sinned against the Lord, he came here alone to pray and find forgiveness."

He restores my soul.

Yosef gazed up at the high white clouds rushing on the wind above them—like white wings lifting and carrying the hidden valley through the sky. "So this is where David wrote his songs."

"Aye, many. Many more than he wrote down, I'm sure. And his one voice sounded like a hundred when he sang. He was never alone. Listen!" Zadok raised his face and began the chorus of the evening psalm that every righteous family in Israel sang each night before bed.

"He who dwells in the shelter . . ."

And as Zadok's deep rich baritone carried the words of David home, the rocks and clefts replied from a dozen directions:

"He who dwells . . ."
    dwells . . . dwells
"In the shelter"
    shelter . . . shelter . . .
"Of the Most High . . ."
    Most High . . . Most High . . . Most High!
"He will rest . . ."
    Rest . . . rest

"In the shadow . . ."
      shadow . . . shadow
"Of the Almighty! . . ."
      Almighty! . . . Almighty![75]

Men and boys in the camp of David's Valley emerged from their tents. They waved broadly to Zadok and began to sing with the rocks and trees. Yosef joined in, hearing more than the voices of mere mortals.

"I will say of the Lord,
'He is my refuge and my fortress,
my God, in whom I trust.'
Surely He will save you from the fowler's snare
and from the deadly pestilence.
He will cover you with His feathers,
and under His wings you will find refuge;
His faithfulness will be your shield and rampart.
You will not fear the terror of night,
nor the arrow that flies by day.
A thousand may fall at your side,
ten thousand at your right hand,
but it will not come near you."[76]

The song was complete the moment Zadok set foot on the valley floor.

"With long life will I satisfy him
and show him my Salvation . . . my Yeshua!"[77]
      Yeshua! . . . Yeshua! . . . Yeshua!

So. The psalm ended with the word *Yeshua* . . . Salvation . . . the name of the Messiah!

Yosef considered how much the stories—the history of the people and the Lord and the land—all fit together seamlessly. All things in Eretz-Israel seemed to sing the name Yeshua!

Suddenly somber, Zadok confided, "Yosef, you're here for a purpose. It came t' me strong, when I heard the babe's name, that I must show you David's Valley. And that marker . . ."

The big man pointed to a heap of stones on the opposite side of the enclave. "That marks a trail south. An unknown path. Only a few have traveled it. I, for one, have walked the distance in search of a lost ram some years ago. As I sat in the Throne of Elijah at the boy's *Bris*, it came so clearly t' me! The Spirit said t' my heart, *Yosef must know of it.* Aye. And if there should ever be a need t' escape . . . as it is written, the Red Sea parted and they walked across on dry ground."[78]

Yosef's eyes narrowed as he took in the implication of Zadok's revelation. A way of escape! But escape from what? from whom? He remembered Zadok's words: *"If there should ever be a need . . ."*

The coatless shepherd boys and old men hobbled up to greet the newcomers. Bear guided the lambs into the field and sat down to watch them as they settled in and began to graze.

"Zadok! Old friend. Just in time for supper. How's the weather up above?"

"Frightful cold at home in Beth-lehem, lads! Aye! As cruel a winter as ever I've seen. How's the fishin'?"

A grizzled old fellow with a marbled right eye winked. "Never better. For them that's eat enough mutton for ten lifetimes, fish is a banquet from above! We'll never go hungry, eh, lads?"

Old Balthasar was anxious to resume forward progress toward Jerusalem, but Zamaris convinced them to stay at least one more night in Bathyra.

"Using my horses you'll travel twice as fast as before," Zamaris claimed. "But what's the hurry anyway? Jerusalem won't disappear if you're later than you planned. It's been getting along nicely without you for at least a millennium, eh?"

Zamaris laughed at his own joke, and the sound was like the rasp of a stonemason's tool dressing a building block. "What brings you so far from home, eh? And the others? From many distant lands? Are you spies?"

Melchior involuntarily ducked his head at the jesting accusation. He knew the motion made him look guilty, and that knowledge made him flush and appear even more guilty.

Balthasar exchanged a glance with Melchior. The young astronomer knew they harbored a common thought: *How much news about the newborn King of the Jews should be shared with this servant of the king of the Jews until it was clear what Herod's response was?*

"Come now," Zamaris cajoled. "Surely after my hospitality—to say nothing of saving your lives—you owe me some explanation. Your companions hover over their strongboxes, scarcely leaving their rooms. They take turns even to come out to eat, as if they think I will steal from you. You must know that if I intended evil, I could kill you all and take everything. I am the law here. No one would dare try to stop me."

Melchior and Balthasar exchanged another glance. Remaining silent longer would only fuel Zamaris' suspicion and hostility.

Old Balthasar reached a decision. "Tell him, Melchior, what brings us here."

Zamaris studied Melchior with a condescending stare. "So he's a storyteller? Looking at his smooth skin, I knew he was no warrior or laborer. A scholar, perhaps? So, scholar, out with it! No, wait a moment."

Turning toward Esther, Zamaris said, "Bring us wine, eh, pretty one? Storytelling's thirsty work. Listening too, if the tale's a dry one."

When Esther returned with a wineskin, Zamaris steadied her wrist as she filled his goblet, favored her with a smile, and thanked her. "If you serve your husband as well as you attend your grandfather, what a fortunate man he'll be."

Melchior hated the attention Zamaris was showering on Esther. But he could think of no way to interrupt what was, on the surface, merely a polite pleasantry. Besides, he had no claim on Esther. Not really.

"So, storyteller, begin!" Zamaris commanded.

For the next hour Melchior recited the tales of the signs in the sky. He told of seeing Ma'Adim, The Adam of the wandering stars, touch the heart of The Virgin, called The Star of Atonement, some nine months previous. He recited the complex weaving circuit executed by The Righteous and The Lord of the Sabbath. He spoke of seeing the Holy Spirit moon eclipse Shabbatai and explained the connection between the people of Israel and the constellation of The Two Fish. His recital was broken only once when Zamaris called for more wine. Melchior concluded by referring to the miraculous star that had appeared ever so briefly at the end of Hanukkah.

"So all of you—Jew and Parthian, Ethiopian and Armenian—you're all stargazers? I put no stock in it myself, but they say Caesar has astrologers on call day and night. Charlatans, I expect."

Melchior's blood began to boil at the accusation. A barbed reply formed on his lips before Balthasar waved him to silence and spoke. "Have you not heard, Lord Zamaris: *'A star will come out of Jacob'*?[79] Astrologers say they can read the future in the stars. Nonsense or evil . . . take your choice. Either way, astrology is a tool of the Adversary to lead men from the truth. No. What we seek is confirmation of promises written in Torah. It is said the Almighty speaks his word in three places: in nature, in Torah, and in the life of Messiah. It is that Living Word we are seeking. We have seen his star in the east and are come to worship him."[80]

18

Zadok and Eliyahu were once again in Simeon's home. The weather had moderated some, and caravans were once more flowing in and out of the Holy City, both bringing news in and carrying news away to other lands.

The rumor went round that King Herod was preparing to return to his capital.

"Why would he come back now?" Eliyahu questioned. "It's too wintry and damp for him to be comfortable here. Better he goes to Cyprus . . . or even farther away."

"Amen to that," Zadok and Simeon both intoned.

Thoughtfully tugging the braid of his beard, Zadok continued, "Likely the Butcher King's heard about the babe, and that'll fetch him back like a bow shot! And how could he not hear it? Everyone here's a-gabbin' about it. When I brought the last flock t' Temple, a man I'd never met before—but he was cousin to Mordechai at the Beth-lehem caravansary—stops me in the street and says, 'You're Zadok. What's this about a miracle? Do angels speak to you, then?'"

"What did you say?" Simeon inquired, leaning forward over the scroll-laden table.

"I asked him if he thought it likely. After studying me a minute, he remarked, "'That's what I said! Mordechai was drunk as usual,' and he turned away!"

"Yes, but it cannot remain secret from Herod long," Eliyahu protested. "Once Talmai is here to organize Herod's spies and Hermes his cutthroats, no one's safe."

Simeon corrected, "We've been over this all before. Everything about this miracle is ordained by the Almighty. Each of us has been called to a role in it, and beyond that part, it is not ours to question."

Eliyahu nodded his acceptance of the point, but to Zadok, his brother-in-law's furrowed brow betrayed continued concern.

Simeon's pale blue and cloudy eyes nevertheless locked with the rabbi's and shepherd's gazes in turn before he also nodded. His face visibly brightened when he pushed aside other lambskin parchments, revealing the scroll of Bereshiyt, the Book of Beginnings. "Zadok, you have asked to better understand who this child is, eh? And the meaning? You and Eliyahu both wish to become my talmidim?" The elder laughed with a wheeze in his voice.

Zadok scratched behind his right ear, ignoring the joke. Shepherds did not become Torah scholars. "I don't question the miracle, y'understand, nor the angel's words. When I see the babe—and his mother—I know he is the Lord's Anointed. But I vow it's not what I expected! Not what any of us expected, eh?"

"Explain to us how it all works," Eliyahu encouraged.

"All? My life has about run its course, but do you each wish to study the rest of your life? Because that's what understanding it fully will mean. Everything means something, and *everything* takes a lifetime of study."

Eliyahu and Zadok both gave solemn assurances that such was indeed their intent.

"Then to begin," Simeon returned, his tone that of an elder of Israel.

Zadok recalled that Simeon was one whose life span reached back before King Herod to the time true sons of Israel last sat on the throne of the Jews.

Simeon drew Zadok's attention to the chosen text as his bony finger indicated a line of Hebrew script. "It begins with our very first father, Adam—created by the Almighty himself but still rebellious against him.[81] Here's what I want you to note. Every *beriyt*, every covenant, we speak of here concerns a man, deliverance, and a sacrifice."

Zadok nodded. God Himself had delivered the first man and first woman from immediate death when He performed the first ever sacrifice and wrapped them in animal skins.

"And the Almighty promised a Redeemer to finally win the battle against the serpent,"[82] Simeon continued. He was already rolling up the right-hand edge of the scroll and unrolling the left until a later passage of Bereshiyt was revealed. "Here again. Noah. God saved him and his family, and Noah sacrificed to the Almighty.[83]

"Father Adam and Mother Ishah were saved, and that allowed the rest of us to come to be, eh? Then later it was the same with Noah and his family. And creation was delivered from the threat of another flood."[84]

Again the simultaneous scrolling and uncovering took place. "The record of the third covenant is also in the Book of Beginnings," Simeon instructed. "Father Avraham. For him and the people promised to descend from him, the Almighty himself carried out a blood-covenant sacrifice and later spared Avraham from offering up his only son, Yitz'chak, by yet another sacrifice. And that only son was the one through whom the promised Deliverer would come."[85]

Eliyahu clasped and unclasped his hands as if expressing excited concurrence.

Zadok encouraged Simeon to continue, even if he did not fully comprehend. "So each covenant involves a promise to a man and a sacrifice to confirm it?"

"Just so. Now we must change scrolls, for the story of the fourth covenant is in the Book of Shemos . . . the story of the Exodus from slavery in Egypt. The Almighty had selected Avraham's descendants from Yitz'chak and then Ya'acov and then Ya'acov's twelve boys to found our nation. And in the desert, before the Mountain of the Covenant, Mosheh carried out the sacrifices ordered by the Almighty . . . the first time a whole nation was consecrated to Elohim."

"The fourth covenant," Zadok repeated, to prove he was following. "To the nation of Israel, but addressed first to a man, Mosheh the Lawgiver. Deliverance from bondage."

"Each new covenant mediated by one man, one could say," Simeon elaborated. "Adam talked directly to Elohim. Noah mediated between his family and the Almighty. Avraham between his tribe and Elohim. Mosheh between Elohim, the one who gave as his name I AM, and those he calls 'my people, Israel.'"

"Go on; go on!" Zadok urged. "Next comes David, eh?"

Simeon smiled at Zadok as one rewarded a determined but not overly bright pupil for dredging up a correct answer. "Deliverance from enemies all around. From idol worshippers. A kingdom—a whole kingdom—worshipping the One God. It had never happened before. King David brought the Ark into the Holy City. He sacrificed to the Almighty here.[86] Afterward his son caused the Temple to be built,[87] and the sacrifices continued from that day to this, except for the time of the Exile."

Eliyahu added, "And the Almighty said David would never lack an heir to sit upon his throne."

Simeon waved a cautionary hand. "So long as they kept the commandments. But he also promised that even if they failed, which they did, he would never completely reject David's house. This is the fifth, the Davidic covenant."[88]

"So now comes the time for the sixth covenant?" Zadok asked. "But deliverance from what? Herod and Rome? How?"

There was a knocking at the door. When Zadok looked a question at Simeon, the elder shrugged to say he was not expecting any other callers.

The rapping was replaced by the pounding of a fist, making the door panels jump. "Ho, in there," a gruff voice demanded. "Simeon the Elder, open by order of the captain of the Temple Guard."

Sweeping all the scrolls into a disorderly heap, Simeon silently indicated a pair of chairs in the adjoining room. Despite the insistent hammering, he waited until Zadok and Eliyahu were seated in the other chamber before answering the summons.

As soon as he pulled back the bolt, the door was flung open. A pair of guards garbed as Temple sentries entered. "Captain wants to see you," one of them ordered. "Now."

The other soldier noted Zadok and Eliyahu with narrowed eyes. "Names?" he demanded.

When both men from Beth-lehem had furnished names and occupations, the soldier barked, "Your business here?"

"We're friends and brother Levites . . . as are you," Eliyahu asserted calmly, stepping between Zadok and the guards. "But our visit was just about finished. We must be going."

"Beth-lehem, eh?" the first trooper repeated. "So, Master Simeon, we will escort you."

"A moment while I get my cloak," Simeon returned. Passing close to Zadok on his way to his clothing chest, he murmured, "Storeroom in the Court of Women. You know which one. Tell no one. Come when you can."

Seconds later only the room and its scrolls were left to bear mute testimony that the eyes of King Herod had started to turn toward a baby in a manger and the sixth covenant.

The day was almost warm. Yosef sat out in the weak sunlight as he carved toy boats for Zadok's boys and a matching one for little Dan.

"Shalom," a voice greeted him in a familiar Galilean accent.

Yosef, pleased to hear a voice from home, looked up at a round-faced, portly farmer and grinned. "Shalom, brother. You're far from home."

"As are you. I hear Nazareth in your words."

"And I hear the hill country in yours."

"Cana. Pretty good. I'm Reuven ben Zakai. I've come with a letter. Looking for Mary and Yosef of Nazareth. Said by the directions I was given to be dwelling in this house."

Yosef stood and stretched out his hand in greeting. "I am Yosef bar Jacob."

"Then this is for you."

The letter from Nazareth was a surprise. Addressed to Mary and Yosef bar Jacob at the home of Zadok, shepherd of the Temple flock, it was a single sheet of rolled parchment sealed in a clay jar.

"I'm headed home in three days. I'll be happy to carry some reply back to Nazareth. Your wife's mother, as you may read from the letter, is in bad condition. I met your wife's father in the marketplace at Nazareth. He and his daughter. They send this to you as a plea to come home soon . . . as you can read in the letter. Your wife's mother is very, very unwell. Fragile health. A mind overcome from the grief of your wife's youngest sister . . . as you will read in the letter. They asked me to tell you, in case the letter is not enough to convince you, that you should bring your wife and the new baby home to Nazareth . . . that is also what the letter says. Because perhaps the baby will cheer up your wife's mother and help her to have some hope. So says the letter."

Yosef did not open the letter from Nazareth. He carried it in to Mary and told her what it said.

Mary offered the traveler a meal and lodging, but he could stay only long enough for her to pen the return reply to her father. A two-shekel coin in his palm was all he wanted.

Honored Papa and Mama,

Greetings in the name of the Lord!

All is well. The Lord is with us! Yeshua flourishes and joy increases for all who draw near to see Him. The people of Beth-lehem have been very kind and would have us stay on with them forever. They are righteous people who live only to serve the Lord. Though we love them, our hearts long to see you and to be home again. If it is the Lord's will, we will come home to Nazareth soon after Yeshua is presented in the Temple for the Redemption of the Firstborn.

My dearest mother, your beautiful grandson, Yeshua, will be very happy to see you. Please be of good cheer and set aside your grief. Joy is coming to you! Yeshua is coming soon!

Yosef sends his greeting and love. May the grace and peace of the Lord preserve you each until that day!

Your obedient daughter,

Mary

Up all night studying the constellations. Thinking about Esther.

Notes and calculations. Thinking about Esther.

No sleep. Thinking about Esther.

An early start on the caravan route. Thinking about Esther.

All these things combined to hit Melchior like a series of hammer blows. His rough-gaited little donkey rattled his bones and jarred his brain until he could not stay awake. His head bobbed and his chin sank onto his chest.

"Esther! Esther!

"He's calling for you, Esther," young Prince Aretas said from what seemed like a great distance.

"Melchior! Are you all right?" Her voice penetrated his slumber. The bed seemed exceptionally hard.

The mocking words of Zamaris chimed in, "Is he drunk?"

Old Balthasar said, "He is an astronomer. He sleeps in the day."

Zamaris laughed. "But does he always sleep under the feet of a camel in the middle of the road?"

Melchior managed to open one eye. The mud-spattered belly of a camel was above him. On either side of the flat feet of the beast were Balthasar and Esther and Prince Aretas.

Zamaris, perched high on his prancing steed, grinned down at him. "Sweet dreams, astronomer?" Zamaris chuckled. "Come on. Wake up. Get back on your little donkey. We've got a long way to go."

Melchior flapped his arms to ward off the chill. Esther scooped coals from the brazier into a clay jar to warm her bed.

"It is especially brisk tonight," Melchior ventured.

"Yes." She seemed disinterested.

"But clear."

She glanced at the sky, obscured by the smoke. "You'll be observing again tonight?"

"Well, the moon . . . brighter than I'd wish. But I take what I can get. And . . ."

Esther averted her eyes as though his conversation irritated her. "Well then. Zamaris says the moon guides him as he travels far distances, patrolling the borderlands."

"I suppose. Yes. If a fellow was a fellow who needed to prowl at night, then the bright moon would be some . . . help."

"I didn't say he said *prowl*. I said *patrol*."

Melchior exhaled loudly. "There is a difference, I suppose, between *patrol* and *prowl*. One is attacking enemies when they're asleep and the other is when they are awake."

"You don't think much of Zamaris, do you?"

Melchior lied. "I don't think of him at all."

"Some might think you're ungrateful."

"Ungrateful? Me?"

"He saved our lives. All of us . . . me. *My* life."

Melchior had no reply to this. He hated Zamaris. He was jealous of Zamaris. But all that paled when he considered what might have happened to Esther if Zamaris had not charged in when he did.

"I am . . . grateful for that," Melchior conceded.

"Then it isn't true that you disapprove of him?"

"I can be grateful he knows how to slit throats without approving of him. Yes?"

Esther shrugged. "So. It's getting late. You'd better get on with what you seem to do best . . . observing, eh?"

Melchior nodded and rubbed his hand over the newly grown stubble on his cheek as she retreated into the tent. *Esther!*

19

It was a windswept late afternoon atop the Temple Mount. The business of vows and purifications was all but concluded for the day. The Court of Women was nearly empty of visitors, and what priests remained hustled about their duties, eager to return indoors.

Zadok, having helped deliver a flock of sheep to the Levite in charge of sacrificial lambs, had not turned about and gone home. Instead the shepherd had drawn his hooded cloak close around him, climbed several flights of stairs, and crossed the paved court north of the sanctuary. He passed the Soreg Wall with its signs warning Gentiles they could go no farther. Zadok thought of how he had always taken for granted the privilege of worshipping at the very footstool of the Almighty. Yet that right was reserved for the bar mitzvah, the sons of duty, the members of Yahweh's covenant family.

It was about covenants that Zadok hoped to learn more today.

Zadok had not seen Simeon since the Temple guards had come calling. There had been no rumors that the old man had been arrested, and after a few days, word was relayed that Simeon wanted to see him.

Despite the fact that there seemed to be no immediate danger,

Zadok took a roundabout route to the Temple courts. He timed his arrival to match a mostly deserted period.

On the far side of the terrace a brown robe moved. A hand emerging from a sleeve beckoned with a quick flutter, like one of the sacrificial white doves in their wicker cages.

Without even a greeting, Simeon drew Zadok inside one of the spice storerooms. Like the plaza, it also was deserted, but the fragrant air was much more pleasant than outside. "I knew you'd come when you could," Simeon said.

"Have you waited every day, then?"

A pair of dove-pale hands waved away the sympathy. "I have been here every day, but not on your account alone."

Zadok stared around at the sacks labeled *Cinnamon, Balsam, Myrrh*. "Here?"

The question brought a smile to Simeon's face. "You know this is the storage cupboard where Hannah the Prophetess keeps vigil."

"When she's not under—"

Simeon placed a cupped palm over Zadok's mouth. "Let us not speak of that here. Follow me."

The racks of the spice-storage shelves rose eight feet in height. They were staggered on either side of the center corridor and protruded slightly into the path so that a visitor had to weave around the ends to advance. Within three turns they were completely hidden from anyone peering in from outside.

"I am not being followed," Simeon volunteered, "but I cannot say for certain my home is not watched. Besides, one of my neighbors might succumb to Steward Talmai's bribes."

"Is Hannah here, then?"

"No, but we are going to meet her. I thought it unwise for someone to see you come to my house and then for neither of us to be found within if someone should call. It would raise too many questions."

Once before, by means of a secret passage hidden inside Simeon's home, Zadok and the elder had descended into passageways beneath the Temple Mount. There they had conferred with Hannah the Prophetess, a woman profoundly wise and full of the *Ruach HaKodesh*.

Zadok bit back the temptation to ask how they would meet Hannah if she was not here. The storeroom was tucked in a corner of the Court of Women, buttressed by walls on two sides, with a single means of entry.

The way forward was lit by flickering oil lamps blinking out from wall niches like watchful eyes. Though the corridor stretched on ahead, Simeon turned aside into one that smelled of karkom, or saffron, and the floor had a light golden sheen from the expensive powdered herb.

At the end of the passage was a dark corner containing a heap of broken pottery. So this was where the results of clumsy Levites ended their days, Zadok thought.

Simeon indicated a large, red-clay amphora, whose cracked form seemed to anchor the center of the pile. "Lift that," he instructed.

Hunching his shoulders, Zadok strained to shift the jar but could not. It had to weigh more than a half-dozen sheep, since Zadok could hoist that many easily. He raised a bushy, questioning eyebrow.

"Now watch," Simeon said. From near the bottom of the heap, on three sides of the rubbish, protruded a trio of amphora handles looking like they had all been broken from the same container. "It must be done in this order."

Going first to the back, then to the right, and then to the left, Simeon gave each fragment of pottery a sharp jerk outward. After he had completed this mystifying task, Simeon leaned one hand against the center amphora, and the mass slid sideways, revealing a square hole and a ladder leading downward.

"You first," he ordered. "I have to close it behind us."

Rufus Valens was a tall, patrician Roman statesman. His thick, brown-and-gray curls were oiled and perfumed and worn short on forehead and neck. He wore the praetexta, a toga with its distinctive broad purple stripe. Valens was entitled to this honor because he was appointed for life to be responsible for the books of the sibylline oracles. The other function of Valens' group of fifteen men involved overseeing the introduction of foreign gods into Rome.

His reserved dress and demeanor were in vivid contrast to Herod's ornate gilt-and-blue robes and the king's ponderously thick black wig. For this tour of the eastern empire Valens functioned as Caesar's eyes, ears, and, occasionally, mouth. He had already consulted with the Roman governor of Syria before heading south to confer with Herod.

Talmai knew Valens to be Caesar's trusted advisor, and the man had a reputation for honesty and integrity. He could not be bribed, nor was he easily influenced by rumor. If King Herod could avoid offending the man for the length of his stay while maintaining the appearance of calm, reasonable governance of his kingdom, Talmai was convinced all would be well.

So far, all had progressed smoothly. Valens reported that Herod's son Antipater made a good impression in Rome, so long as he refrained from gossiping about his surviving half brothers. Talmai winced. Antipater, not content with having destroyed his other siblings, was scheming against the ones that remained—Philip, Archelaus, and Antipas.

Herod and Valens were closeted in Herod's private study. They discussed the bandit situation in Trachonitis, the incursions of Nabateans into southern Judea, and a reported resurgence of Cilician pirates.

There was a tap at the door. This was a surprise, since Herod had left strict word that the conference was not to be disturbed.

Hermes, chief of Herod's bodyguard, peered into the chamber and summoned Talmai with a crooked finger. The king glared at the interruption but did not break his conversation with Valens.

With the door open only a crack, Talmai hissed, "What is this about? It better be important."

"The courier from Jerusalem. The king is to receive the report from there every day as soon as it arrives—without fail. He did not countermand that order even for today."

"What are you whispering about, Talmai? What is the meaning of this disturbance?" Herod demanded.

Talmai knew Herod noted the disrespect shown to his commands. The king would not want Valens to take the interruption as a sign of weakness.

"Merely the messenger from Jerusalem, sire," Talmai ventured. "I will instruct him to wait."

Valens spoke up. "By your leave, Your Highness, let's hear him. Because of the snow and this awkward weather and urgent business drawing me on to Alexandria, I will not be able to visit your capital on this trip. I hear it's a miraculous city." His Aramaic had a distinct accent and noticeably exact pronunciation, as if he found the taste of the words unpleasant. The Roman elite used Greek for literature and love, Latin for administration, and anything else with condescension.

Grudgingly, Herod called for the courier's admittance. "Speak and make it quick."

Bowing deeply and keeping his eyes fixed on the carpet, the soldier made his report. He was concise, mentioning how many caravans had arrived, where from, the amount of customs duties collected, and so on.

It was during a statement summarizing troop rotation into the Holy City from the desert fortresses that Talmai saw Herod's head recline and his eyes glaze over. Talmai knew the change in demeanor was not due to boredom.

Herod's conversational tone with Valens had been strong and clear for the aged monarch. Now it grew shrill. "And what about rebellion? Who has been arrested?"

Talmai saw Valens' gaze shift from the courier to the king. The Roman's expression took on a studied blankness. The steward's words tumbled over the soldier's as both men affirmed, "There's no rebellion, Majesty."

Then the courier made the mistake of adding with a shrug, "Wild rumor. Nothing more."

"What rumor?" Herod shrieked.

"Something about a miraculous child. An old Levite supposedly heard—"

Talmai was so relieved he blurted out, "Old news, Majesty! Is this gossip still circulating? This is from more than a year ago, and all our searching found not one shred of evidence. You remember: An elderly priest supposedly promised a son by an angel."

Herod's shoulders, which had hunched like those of a cat getting ready to pounce, sagged. He drew a shuddering breath, then said hoarsely, "Of course. Silly gossip. Enough of this, Ambassador. Let us adjourn to some wine and refreshments."

As Simeon and Zadok approached Hannah's underground chambers, the older man answered the shepherd's unspoken question. "I know Rabbi Eliyahu also seeks to understand, and you wonder why I have not invited him to join us?"

Zadok indicated that such were his thoughts.

"You know the saying 'Two may keep a secret if one is dead'? It is not safe for too many people to know what lies beneath the sacred mountain. All will come to light in time, but for the present its mysteries must belong to only a few. As I was chosen in my day, you have been selected for this privilege . . . but it is a burden as well."

Hannah greeted Zadok kindly, like an elderly grandmother welcoming a favored grandson. "Come in, come in, Zadok, shepherd of the Temple flocks."

Perhaps Hannah laid aside her role as thundering prophetess the way people took off their outer garments. By the warm yellow light she appeared stooped, ancient, and friendly—not at all imposing or eccentric.

"Simeon tells me you have explored the covenants," she remarked to Zadok as Simeon retired to a corner of the chamber.

"Each covenant involves deliverance, a mediator, a sacrifice, and a man," Zadok said, summarizing Simeon's earlier lesson.

Hannah smiled. "Then hear the word of the Lord as delivered by his prophet Ezekiel: *'I Myself will search for My sheep and look after them. As a shepherd looks after his scattered flock when he is with them, so will I look after My sheep. I will place over them one shepherd, My servant David, and he will tend them; he will tend them and be their shepherd. I the Lord will be their God, and My servant David will be prince among them. I the Lord have spoken. I will make a covenant of peace with them.'*[89] Tell me, shepherd: is the Almighty speaking of King David here? And if not, then whom?"

Zadok knew enough history to answer that question. "King David was dead four hundred years before Ezekiel wrote. So far as I hear, he's still dead. His tomb, y' know, remains in this city, even if Lord Herod would like to plunder it."

"So of whom is the prophet speaking?"

"Of Messiah, the promised Deliverer who will descend from the shepherd-king to be King-Shepherd of Israel."

Hannah beamed her approval. "*So agrees the prophet Malachi! 'Suddenly the Lord you are seeking will come to His Temple; the messenger of the covenant, whom you desire, will come,' says the Lord Almighty.*[90] As Avraham was to his tribe and Mosheh to the nation and David to the kingdom— each in turn embracing more of the world—so King Messiah's covenant must be the greatest of all."

"Meanin'?"

"Surely you know! Isaias writes: *'I, the Lord, have called you in righteousness; I will take hold of your hand. I will keep you and make you to be a covenant for the people and a light for the Gentiles. To open eyes that are blind, to free captives from prison and to release from the dungeon those who sit in darkness.*[91] The Lord himself will come to rule us. But if he came as the Power on High, who could endure his coming? No, he must come as a man. Then he will gather his sheep from Israel and from all the nations of Gentiles."

"So the sixth covenant has not merely a man as mediator but—"

"The Son of Man—the God-Man—who comes from within the Cloud of Unknowing. As the prophet Dani'el says: *'His dominion is an everlasting dominion that will not pass away, and His kingdom is one that will never be destroyed.'*[92] Could this ever be said of one who is merely a man?"

Zadok snorted. "Impossible!"

"Just so. Every other covenant involved a man. But men fail, so the covenant is incomplete. Avraham could not perfectly keep it. Mosheh could not. David could not. But King Messiah—the God-Man, born of the virgin—he will perfectly mediate the covenant between the Almighty and his children. He will deliver us, all who bow before him, from the power of evil . . . forever."

Zadok nodded slowly, drinking it all in. Savoring the sense of the rightness and completeness of the sixth covenant, as of a good vintage wine. Then he voiced the remaining question: "I see it clearly. But . . . a man, a covenant, a deliverance . . . and a sacrifice t' confirm the covenant? Where does that fit into the final covenant?"

Hannah's eyes showed pain, and her face registered sorrow. She seemed suddenly every bit of her eighty-odd years. "Have you not read? Is it not written? *'He was despised and rejected of men, a man of sorrows, and familiar with suffering. . . . Surely He took up our infirmities and carried our sorrows, yet we considered Him stricken by God, smitten by Him and afflicted. But He was pierced for our transgressions, He was crushed for our iniquities; the punishment that brought us peace was upon Him, and by His wounds we are healed. . . . The Lord has laid on Him the iniquity of us all.'*"[93]

Zadok felt a pain in his chest as if he had been stabbed with an icy blade. He saw again his brother Onias, crucified on the wall of his house by Herod's order. Then he saw also a tiny baby, completely innocent of wrongdoing, perfectly beautiful. . . .

It was all too horrible to think about. With a jerk Zadok yanked himself upright. "May it never be!" he vowed.

"Ah, well," Hannah offered with a sigh. "*'I will make an everlasting* covenant with you. For My thoughts are not your thoughts, neither are your ways My ways,' declares the Lord. This is what the Lord says: 'Maintain justice and do what is right for My salvation—My Yeshua—is close at hand and My righteousness will soon be revealed.'"[94]

$$20 \mid \text{CHAPTER}$$

elchior rubbed his patchy red beard and tried not to notice the way Zamaris observed Esther during the meal. A surge of resentment shot through him as Esther poured wine into the swarthy brigand's cup.

So, Zamaris was a Jew and had the thick black whiskers of a Jew. He rode his horse like an Arab raider and shot his arrows like a Parthian.

But none of that made him good enough for Esther!

Old Balthasar cleared his throat and inclined his head toward Esther and Zamaris. "He seems interested in my granddaughter, eh?"

Melchior's eyes narrowed. "He's probably got a harem in the desert. Seven wives. One for each night of the week."

"No." Balthasar shrugged. "Unmarried. A widower. Lost his wife in childbirth some months back."

"How do you know this?"

"Esther told me. I am assuming he must have mentioned it to her. Passing conversation."

Melchior felt his face redden beneath his beard. "There's only one reason for a fellow like that to tell a young woman like Esther such personal details."

Balthasar dipped pita bread in the hummus. "I agree. Only one reason."

"Will you warn her to stay away from him?"

"I? Warn her?"

"If she married such a desert rat . . . we would . . . lose . . . her."

"Exactly." Balthasar passed the bread to Melchior. "And so I offer a warning."

"You mean . . . to me?"

Old Balthasar smiled wryly. "Who is an old man like me to interfere with matters of the heart?"

It was too dark and cold now for the men to return to Beth-lehem. There were rocks and ravines, and it was unsafe to travel on a moon-less night. Rachel was certain Zadok, Eliyahu, and Yosef would stay out talking about politics, religion, and women until morning.

Perhaps they had wanted to remain out so they could freely talk of rebellion.

Rachel called out the back door for Mary to come and sit awhile by the fire. She went to fetch Havila. Grandmother was already in bed, so she did not come.

The three young mothers were good company for each other when their men were away.

Enoch, Samu'el, and Dan gathered round as Mary nursed Yeshua.

Enoch recited his line to Yeshua. "Enoch . . . walked . . . with the Lord."

Mary praised him. "Very good, Enoch! Someday maybe you'll grow up to be a rabbi, eh?"

Enoch answered solemnly, "We're going to fly away. Me. Samu'el. Dan. Obi. Everybody. To Yeshua's house to play."

"I hope you will come to our house to play." Mary raised her deep brown eyes to Rachel and Havila. "I hope you'll visit us in Nazareth. Bring the boys. Maybe in the spring? When Zadok and Eliyahu are away at other pastures? There are wildflowers everywhere in the Galil in the spring."

"We wish you and Yosef would stay in Beth-lehem with us forever. Raise the baby here. Live here among us," Rachel said.

Mary's brow furrowed. "Yosef says Herod will come back from the seacoast when the weather warms a bit. With the fortress of Herodium above Beth-lehem and Yerushalayim only a few miles away, it may not be safe."

"Herod has spies everywhere," Havila offered. "Even in Nazareth. But Eliyahu says no one can harm the Lord's Anointed."

Rachel added, "There's not been a single lamb miscarried this season since you came. Zadok says there's never been a lambing like this." Rachel held Obi on one hip as she kneaded bread in the dough trough.

Havila combined minced cooked lamb and lentils and rolled the mixture in grape leaves. "The babies all healthy and strong. Yes. Eliyahu hopes you and Yosef will stay with us." She touched her stomach. "And my baby must be a son as well. I wish you would stay on until he's born. Strong, he is! A runner!"

Rachel placed Obi on the rug and worked the dough. "Beth-lehem has no carpenter. The nearest lives in Ramah, six miles away."

Mary smiled wistfully. "I just received a letter from Papa. It's my mother. She's been asking after me. Since my youngest sister died in Yerushalayim during the Yom Kippur plague, Mama hasn't been well."

"Such a plague this year. It swept away the innocent with the guilty."

Mary explained, "Papa writes that Mama needs me to bring Yeshua. She needs to see the baby. A baby in her arms will give her hope. As soon as Yosef and I offer the Redemption of the Firstborn at the Temple, we must go home to Nazareth. Papa writes that he wants us to come home for Mama's sake. Bring the baby home to her."

Enoch, spokesman for the boys, agreed. "We're goin' . . . Yeshua's house."

Obi lay on his back and played with his toes. His face split with a contented grin. Four teeth gleamed beneath a ribbon of drool.

"Teething. But Obi hardly ever cries," Rachel commented.

Among the little ones of Beth-lehem, from the newest baby up to Enoch's age, there had been an almost supernatural contentedness, as if they knew they were in the presence of the Lord's Anointed. Neither had there been illness in the village since the birth of Mary's son.

Dan and Samu'el, so close to the same age, wobbled as they clung to Mary's chair. They gazed at Yeshua with undisguised fascination. It seemed so strange to Rachel that the boys were content to play quietly near Mary's baby for hours on end. Even if angels had not announced that Yeshua was an extraordinary child, it was evident by the calming effect of His presence on those around Him.

Surely, Rachel thought, if Yeshua could stay here in Beth-lehem, grow up in the place where David had grown up, the angels would keep Him safe from Herodian plots. His name was Salvation, after all. And if the infant King of Israel was safe, it made sense that all the children of Beth-lehem would be blessed as well.

"You are wanted here." Havila's voice trembled a bit. "We all like you . . . and the baby. You and Yosef. Such a nice couple, eh? You would fit very well. And you are happy here too. It's written plainly in your eyes."

Mary ruffled Enoch's hair. "In all my life I've never been happier than here in Beth-lehem. Such true friends. You, Rachel. Havila. And to tell the truth, Yosef is enjoying playing shepherd more than hanging doors or making tables. Perhaps for a while . . . if my mother could come to visit."

"Lots of room. Well then." Havila stretched and patted her tummy. "My baby thinks you should stay too. He's dancing again. You must stay long enough for him to be born."

Gerasa, one of the ten cities forming the Decapolis, was located in the hill country twenty miles east of the Jordan. Along with Damascus and Pella, Gerasa and five other towns were virtually self-governing, though under the ultimate authority of the Roman governor of Syria. The Decapolis cities of Hippos and Gadara had been given to Herod by Augustus. Herod coveted Gerasa as well. The olives grown in the region were especially valued for the quality of their oil, and olive oil was one of the most valuable trade goods in the Roman Empire.

The caravan route approached Gerasa from the northeast by way of a mountain pass connecting the Syrian desert with Judea. Gerasa was a pagan city, devoted to the worship of Artemis the Huntress, also called Diana, the virgin daughter of Jupiter.

There was a small Jewish population, but no affection between them and their pagan neighbors. Proof of this tension existed in the form of a herd of swine that was allowed to graze under the oak trees bordering the Jewish district. Only a low stone fence, much vandalized, separated the synagogue compound from the pigs.

So when Zamaris and a dozen of his troopers swept into Gerasa, along with Balthasar and the others, most of the pagan inhabitants appeared annoyed. The mood among the local Jews noticeably lightened at having Jewish travelers arrive, especially since the recent freezing, soggy weather had reduced news from elsewhere to nothing.

The leaders of the Jewish community welcomed Zamaris with enthusiasm, providing the entire group with free food and lodging. The community waited until the evening meal was completed; then the elders called an assembly in the synagogue to inquire what had brought the company to their city.

Esther looked pleased, Melchior thought, when Zamaris deferred the question to Balthasar. She beamed to hear her grandfather praised as "the wisest of the Jews of Ecbatana."

Before he spoke, Old Balthasar stared out the window at the torches outlining the Temple of Diana. "Your neighbors worship a virgin goddess. She is vindictive, possessive, and spiteful. You know the stories. I will not profane this place by retelling them here. But know that when the Adversary, the Great Serpent, creates counterfeits of truth, the very existence of an imitation points back to the truth of the Almighty."

"Speak plainly," one of the Gerasa elders complained. "You haven't come all the way from Parthia to tell us this."

"Give him a chance," Zamaris growled.

The complaining man instantly subsided.

Esther smiled at the rough-hewn Jewish trooper, and Melchior hated it.

Balthasar resumed. "To come to the point, then, it is this: According to the prophet Isaias, *Therefore the Lord Himself will give you a sign: The virgin will be with child and will give birth to a son, and will call Him Immanu'el.*'[95] Isaias suggests she will be the one who is the complete opposite of *possessive* and *vindictive*. She will show fullness of grace by her unquestioning obedience to God. She will be the woman whose seed will bruise the serpent's head, and by her faithful obedience, she will set in motion the removal of the curse that rests upon all mankind."

The Scripture lesson was a good one. Many of the elders nodded their approval.

Balthasar continued, "I and my colleagues—Melchior of Ecbatana and the others from all the wide world—have studied signs in the heavens that confirm this prophecy has come to pass. It has been fulfilled. Messiah has been born, and we go to Yerushalayim to seek him."

There was uproar in the synagogue. A babble of voices argued this conclusion, until Balthasar waved them to silence. He motioned for Melchior to stand and once again recite the celestial wonders of the previous year.

After an encouraging nod from Esther, Melchior did so.

When Melchior sat again amid a respectful silence, Balthasar added, "It is not only stars that lead us to this conclusion. Counting the years spoken of by the prophet Dani'el also leads us to this time, as does the fact that a non-Jew sits upon the throne of David. The Book of Beginnings teaches that *'the scepter will not depart from Judah, nor the ruler's staff from between his feet, until He comes to whom it belongs.'*[96] Clearly the scepter has departed from Judah when an Idumean king rules in Yerushalayim."

Several in the assembly voiced alarm at the treasonous ring of these words. Herod was not king of Gerasa, but he was too powerful a neighbor to offend.

Melchior was not interested in the reaction of the Gerasene Jews, but he was troubled to see Zamaris scowling.

"Search the Scriptures for yourselves," Balthasar suggested gently, as if unwilling to get into an argument. "So I will conclude with this: Other God-fearers, worshippers of the One True God, have also come to the same conclusion. The true King of the Jews has been born. That is why men from the East, the North and the South, journey with me toward the West. Now I have spoken. In no more time than it takes us to go to Yerushalayim and report back, we shall all know the truth."

Zadok was gruff with Rachel when she told him how she and Havila were trying to convince Mary to stay in Beth-lehem. "She wants to stay. She said she's never been so happy as she is here with us."

"Don't hold them here, Rachel. Not even by the bonds of our love."

Rachel put her hands on her hips in challenge. "But, Zadok, what can happen? If he is Messiah—"

Zadok exploded. "If he is? *If?*"

"Yes. If."

"Y' didn't hear the angels as I did, so I'll forgive y' such an ignorant thought."

"Ignorant! This is the truth, isn't it? No matter if Herod the Butcher King was to come in person to our door and demand we give up the baby—"

"Careful now, woman! It is not so far-fetched as y' may think! Herod is practically our neighbor. Or have y' forgot the fortress of Herodium that glowers down upon us all?"

Rachel waved away the threat. "If Yeshua is the Messiah, not even Herod can harm him!"

"Herod's a tool of darkness. The darkness is greater than the one who serves it. Rachel, the darkness is everywhere in the land, and it has proved murder suits the cause of evil very well."

She frowned in determination. "Even one candle is greater than the darkness."

"Y' talk nonsense, woman. The Almighty has put his Son in the hands of a man, Yosef, t' protect him. A bright fellow, Yosef is. If he has told Mary it's too dangerous t' stay here and live among us shepherds—right under the very nose of Herod—then somethin' greater than women's conversation is tellin' him what he must do."

"The Lord will watch over the baby." Rachel wavered in her conviction as Zadok reasoned with her.

"The Lord will use Yosef t' watch over the baby and Mary. Don't believe Herod will not seek him out once he hears the true King of the Jews, the Son of David, is born in Israel. He will seek him out and do all he can t' kill him."

Rachel grew silent and glum. "You're such a pessimist."

"I'm a shepherd. What sort of shepherd would I be if, when the wolf was near, I didn't draw my sword? So, Yosef and Mary must keep their eyes open. They're young and strong . . . and smart enough t' know what they're up against. Evil will seek t' devour this little one before Yeshua has a chance to accomplish for the world what he was sent here t' achieve."

Rachel clasped her hands. "But, Zadok, if they stayed . . . there's been no sickness among us. Seventy sons born in the last two and a half years. If that's not the blessing of heaven upon us . . ."

Zadok closed his eyes and murmured, "Seventy sons of Beth-lehem. As there are seventy in the Sanhedrin. A righteous Sanhedrin who will sit beneath the throne of Messiah and judge with him kings and empires. No others worthy in all of Eretz-Israel! Our lambs. Seventy innocent judges in Beth-lehem who will see into the hearts of men. Men who had it in their power t' resist evil . . . and did nothing at all."

A shudder passed through Rachel at his words. "Zadok?"

He did not reply but sat transfixed by some terrible vision that shut out all other thought. His skin grew very pale. "Seventy sons. Can it be?"

"Zadok? Please. You're scaring me."

At last he opened his eyes. They brimmed with fear and horror.

He turned quickly away from Rachel. "Y' can't imagine what Herod is capable of."

"I meant to say . . . Adonai is bigger than Herod."

"Aye. And the Lord uses people many times t' work his will. Anything else is a shepherd who invites the wolf t' come lay down among his master's sheep."

"I want to be wise."

"Then remember how Herod crucified my brother Onias on the wall of his house! Remember what Herod did t' his own sons. Remember what Caesar says about him: 'Better Herod's pig than his son.'"

Zadok tapped his finger on Rachel's temple. "Be smart, Rachel. If Yosef says they must leave this place where lambs are reared for sacrifice and led t' the slaughter, then let Mary and Yosef take the lad away! Let them hide him. Aye. Hide him far away from the Evil One. Satan no doubt has seen the stars in the sky. The Prince of Darkness knows the signs. He will turn his eyes in this direction. Here. T' Beth-lehem he will prowl in search of Mary's child."

He grasped Rachel's shoulders. "Woman, don't hold Mary and Yosef back with your love. Let them go! Aye, let them hide far away . . . *because* you love them!"

King Herod stood at the south-facing window of his bedchamber in the Caesarea palace. To ward off the chill, he had a fur-trimmed cape slung over his nightdress, but his feet were bare. He had been frozen in place in the alcove for some time after the evening's sleeping draught wore off, watching constellations spin into the west.

None of the seven lights commemorated by the Jewish menorah were visible. The waning moon would not rise for many hours yet.

It was Orion that first drew the king's attention. Standing upright, perfectly framed in the archway, the human figure called Coming Forth as Light marched across the sky. Herod stared in fascination. One foot of the hunter rested on a faint trail of stars some called The River.

Besides the club Orion was supposed to carry in his upraised hand, he was also depicted as wearing a sword on his jewel-encrusted belt. The stars forming the belt were sometimes called The Kings, but Herod did not know why.

But he knew the Egyptians had a story about Orion being the celestial representation of their god Osiris standing beside the river Nile. In their beliefs Osiris was murdered by a false claimant to his throne. The dead god was then somehow brought back to life. In the Egyptian explanation of life on earth, Osiris' death was connected with the way seeds are buried to bring forth new life. There were even cult rituals in which devotees ate bread and drank wine to participate in the god's death and rebirth.

The astrologer the king had consulted did not know of any Jewish legends connected with Orion. Nor could the sorcerer explain how the constellation came by its Jewish title, Coming Forth as Light. He suggested that perhaps the Hebrews had picked up some passing knowledge of Osiris during their slavery in Egypt. The diviner had not been able to account for how Orion appeared in the writings of Job, widely acknowledged to be much older than the gods of Egypt.

Herod shivered. The figure of Orion seemed to be in the act of stepping over the river. There was too much of approaching death in all the symbolism for an aging, ailing man, surrounded by death and potential betrayal, to make his view of the night sky enjoyable.

Still, Herod could not tear himself away.

An hour passed. Sirius—The Guardian, The Prince Who Will Come—peered in at Herod. At the far edge of the southern horizon loomed Canopus, second brightest star in the sky after Sirius. An almost perfect vertical line ran from Canopus to Sirius, as if splitting the sky into two parts.

Orion had already stepped across the dividing line. No longer waiting to make an entry, he came like a fearsome warrior. The border formed by Canopus and Sirius marked those who had been left conquered or slaughtered by his passage . . . from those who were next to be judged.

Herod's shiver became a tremor engulfing his entire body.

Beside the king's bed was a gong used to summon his servants. Moving to the bed, the king seized the mallet that hung by the gong and beat a frenzied rhythm to summon slaves and guards. "Send for the chief steward and my guard captain!" Herod ordered when the first attendants appeared.

The attendants scurried away to do the king's bidding.

Talmai arrived at the same time as Hermes.

"We go back to Yerushalayim tomorrow," Herod demanded. "As soon as it is light."

"Majesty?" Talmai inquired. "Has anything happened?"

"Yes," the king affirmed. "I have had a warning. I have stayed away too long. We leave for Yerushalayim tomorrow."

Melchior's excitement mounted as he realized the significance of their new location. Amathus would be, the Almighty willing, the last stop outside Eretz-Israel on their journey. The Jordan had been so high with the runoff from up-country that no one had crossed the river in many days, but the water level was falling noticeably. By tomorrow the fords near Jericho should be manageable.

As if in token of their changed fortunes, that evening presented the first clear view of the sky in a long time. Mars—The Adam—was setting in the west. Hovering in the southeast were Jupiter and Saturn, farther apart now but still visibly within the confines of The Two Fish as that figure's fainter stars appeared. Orion rose in the east, his upraised arm emerging from behind the mountains in a triumphant gesture.

Amathus was a fortress town north of the river Jabbok. For its resistance to the Maccabees during their successful conquests, it had been razed, then rebuilt within the last fifty years by the Roman proconsul Gabinius. It functioned as a customs collection point and stronghold at the northern end of Herod's territory called Perea, which was governed by Herod's brother Pherorus.

"Isn't it strange that no one we've met has heard of the birth of the child?" Esther remarked to Melchior as they strolled in the evening through a vineyard outside the city gates.

"I thought so too," Melchior commented. "But Zamaris reminded me that no one has been able to cross the river anywhere below the Galil. And if the country west of here has been half as soggy as I've been, maybe no one has heard anything, anywhere."

As if summoned by the use of his name, Zamaris appeared out of the darkness. His swaggering walk, hand resting lightly on sword hilt, his darkly handsome features, even the scars marking his face and hands, combined to give him a supremely confident air. He conveyed to Melchior the impression of a warrior prince or one of the ancient judges of Israel.

"Don't stay outside the gate too long," Zamaris cautioned. "It isn't safe. Unless you'd like me to stay and look after you."

Melchior hesitated.

"We're fine," Esther replied. "Thank you anyway."

Touching his fingers to his forehead, Zamaris gave a slight bow before sauntering away.

Melchior felt he needed to remove any hint that he was envious or intimidated, even though both were true. So he suggested, "Doesn't he strike you as a truly seasoned warrior? A David, perhaps, or at least a Joshua?"

"Grandfather says he's no more than a bandit chief, only with legal standing, because he's Herod's bandit chief."

This opinion was welcome news to Melchior, yet he dared not sound too eager to embrace it. "Well, he is courageous . . . like a David or a Joshua."

"And you? I saw you in the battle with the robbers. You fought bravely too."

"Yes, but I'm more of a Gideon, I think. A reluctant soldier at best . . . only without Gideon's successes."

Now the inferiority Melchior suffered was out in the open.

"Just because a man can make others fear him does not make him mighty," Esther retorted. "Nor does it give him the right to expect to get anything he wants. Melchior . . . teach me more of the night sky."

Scanning the heavens, Melchior selected a subject, then stood behind Esther and grasped her shoulders. Pointing her toward the southeast, he asked, "Do you see that bright star?"

"There?"

"Yes, right. That's Aldebaran. Now look up and to the right. See that glittering cluster?"

"The Pleiades?"

"You remember what the name means in Hebrew?"

"Teach me more," Esther urged. She did not pull away from Melchior's touch.

"In Hebrew, *Ki-Mah*. 'Who made?' Also spoken of as The Congregation of the Ruler. Job, ancient Job, wrote of them when he said about the Almighty: *'He is the maker of the Bear and Orion, Ki-Mah and the constellations of the south. He performs wonders that cannot be fathomed, miracles that cannot be counted.'*"[97]

"He is so big, isn't he?"

"Much bigger than we even imagine," Melchior replied, turning Esther to face him. "*Ki-Mah*. 'Who made it? Who caused it?'" Melchior let that sink in for a moment, then added, "Here's something your grandfather taught me. You know how much more powerful we are, say, than . . . than ants?"

Esther nodded.

"And we think of angels and archangels as much more powerful than us? Grander, wiser, stronger?"

Another nod.

"But when we see the stars and realize that the Almighty made them . . . and the angels . . . and us . . . and the ants . . . when we recognize that he made all there is, all that exists . . . then he is much, much bigger than even angels and archangels. Compared to The Lord of All the Angel Armies, even angels are as lowly as we, because even they, powerful as they are, were made, don't you see? And yet . . ." Melchior's thoughts grew tangled.

"Go on," Esther urged.

"It's . . . it's that I can't understand why he cares about us enough to send his Son to be born like one of us. What does it mean?"

Wrapping her arms around Melchior, Esther hugged him tightly. "Because the stars are too far away," she said. "Because even angels can't tell us. Perhaps to *show* us how much he loves us, it has to happen this way."

Melchior was too dumbfounded by the embrace to reply.

A long kiss later he managed to suggest hoarsely, "It's getting . . . late. We should go in before they close the gates."

Warm in their cottage, Yosef listened as midnight wind stirred the trees. Dry limbs chafed against one another, as if they were restless to fly away yet rooted forever in one patch of earth.

Like me, Yosef thought. *Blessed are you, O Lord, who has given us this refuge. I could stay . . . I could. Stay here forever. Live among these good people, grow old, and die here.*

Die?

Yosef rose and padded to the shuttered window. Leather curtains stretched over wooden shutters kept the winter out. Yosef moved the fringe a fraction and peered out. The wandering stars, the heavenly sign of Yeshua's birth, still remained near one another.

The upraised arms of barren trees flailed in the air as if to warn of danger ahead.

Die?

Mary's breath and the sounds of the suckling babe were clearly audible in the darkness. The constant day noise of the flocks was quiet at last. Below the village, sheep bunched together for warmth and safety.

Blessed are you, Adonai, who teaches me lessons from the flock.

Somehow these dumb animals knew there was safety in numbers. Safety and obscurity in staying close to the herd. Safety for the lambs by surrounding them in the very center of the group after nightfall.

Who will notice him among other children growing up here? Mary is so happy. So am I. These men are good men. They know the truth about us. About Mary. Your angels told them and they believe. Should we stay here among them? live in Beth-lehem of David?

The wind increased and whistled around the corner of the building. Skeletal trees scraped the cloudless belly of the sky. The gale urged Yosef's restless heart to move on, but the roots of the trees and the warmth of the flock urged him to take root. To grow old and die in this place.

He let the leather curtain fall back in place.

The embers glowed on the hearth. He tossed a stick of deadwood onto the fire and watched as it smoked, then ignited. Shadows danced against the whitewashed walls.

Blessed are you, O Adonai, who shows me wisdom in the flock. Safety in obscurity . . . and yet . . .

What was it about the wind? What warning in the frantic rattle of branches like dead men's bones? Even the trees, it seemed, wanted to leave this place.

PART III

After Jesus was born in Beth-lehem in Judea, during the time of King Herod, Magi from the east came to Jerusalem and asked, "Where is the One who has been born King of the Jews? We saw His star in the east and have come to worship Him."

When King Herod heard this he was disturbed, and all Jerusalem with him.

MATTHEW 2:1-3

The Holy City, Jerusalem, amazed Melchior. His reaction on first entering it was one of complete surprise at its magnificence. Ecbatana, his home, was a beautiful, ancient city, full of history and associated with empires going back hundreds of years. Ctesiphon, winter residence of Parthian royalty, was a magnificently constructed modern city of columns and arches.

But Jerusalem! Jerusalem! City of David. City of Solomon. Place where Father Abraham had, in his obedience, prepared to offer Isaac, his son. Already old when David took it from the Jebusites, Jerusalem had seen a thousand years pass since.

Captured, destroyed, besieged, polluted, and reclaimed, it had been, within the last forty years, newly reborn. The Holy City struck the first-time visitor, and many returning pilgrims, with awe.

Herod's palace, glimpsed from outside its gates, was a wonder of fountains and gardens. Amid the three hills accenting its high ridge, Jerusalem flaunted a theater, a hippodrome, and defensive bastions including looming towers. Numerous pools offered clear water brought by aqueducts from springs in the hills many miles away, Melchior was told.

Despite all the other wonders, it was the Temple Mount that caused Melchior to run completely out of superlatives. Stone columns formed double colonnades. Each individual pillar was hewn from a single, massive, white-marble block. The roofs were adorned with cedar highlighted with gold. Eight gates led into the Temple courts, rivaling each other in splendor and design.

The sanctuary proper adorned the highest hill like a sparkling diamond in the crown on the brow of Jerusalem—the place the Almighty said He would put His Name forever.

And all this Melchior observed by following the caravan route into the city from its northwestern entry.

Zamaris, evidently conscious that the arrival of his armed calvalcade and its odd assortment of passengers created a stir among the citizens, rode back along the caravan column. When he passed Melchior, he remarked, "Close your mouth, boy. You don't want all the locals to think you're *am ha aretz*, newly come from Nazareth or some other hayseed place like that."

Melchior shut his mouth abruptly.

Balthasar asked Zamaris to guide them to the Synagogue of the Babylonian Jews, where he expected to find his relatives. It was located in the Valley of the Cheesemakers near the center of the city. There, he assured the group, he could make arrangements for their lodging.

"But where are the banners announcing the newborn King?" Balthasar wondered aloud.

Perroz concurred. "Where are the trumpeters? Where are the heralds of his birth?"

Kagba muttered, "Where, indeed? The atmosphere here is not of celebration at all. It is subdued, almost fearful. What has happened?"

"Or not happened?" Gaspar suggested. "Could we have mistaken the signs after all? Perhaps he has not been born yet."

"Or is the answer something else?" Balthasar posed. "Let's go meet my cousins. Perhaps they can explain."

It was at this juncture that Zamaris interrupted. "I will take you to the synagogue as you requested, but there will be no time for explanations just now. I have escorted you this far because you are ambassadors of a sort and deserving of respect. But Lord Herod is my master, after all. I cannot give you leave to go wandering around the city until I report your presence to him . . . and he may want an immediate explanation. Balthasar, you will have to accompany me to the palace. Please select one of your comrades to go along. The rest of you will remain within the synagogue compound. That's an order, not a request."

Balthasar's relatives in the Synagogue of the Babylonian Jews had much to say about their cousin's arrival and his mission. And much of it was disturbing to Melchior and Esther.

"Ever since Hanukkah, the city has been full of rumors," an elder named Aaron ventured. "And Herod hates rumors!"

Another cousin, Tobias, added, "Some say this matter concerns Old Zachariah, a priest who saw an angel in the Temple, but that was well over a year ago. Some say a message was brought to Old Simeon at the Temple by shepherds, but no one puts much stock in that version. Shepherds! Not priests or scholars, are they? Why would they have news of Messiah?"

Aaron likewise dismissed that possibility. "More likely just repeating something they heard somewhere else. Mind you, there's been more gossip than you'd expect."

"Why do you say that?" Melchior inquired.

Tobias and Aaron exchanged a significant glance. "Because King Herod has been out of the city—off in Caearea—until recently. The stories will certainly stop now. Herod's return means gold in easy reach of informers' palms. No one wants to hazard a visit from Lord Talmai's secret police, or that murderer Hermes' cutthroats, or from the Temple Guards either. No, since Herod's return we thought we'd heard the last of Messiah . . . until you came!"

"What do you think will happen to my grandfather?" Esther worried.

Studying the looming giant Perroz and the lean, crafty features of Kagba, Aaron offered, "Nothing immediately. Too many nations are represented by your group. Herod does not care whom he kills . . . but Caesar cares. Herod's still anxious because the emperor disapproved when Herod killed his own sons. He'll not risk imperial disfavor until he knows more. Our cousin Balthasar is a wise man. He'll know how to proceed cautiously."

Chief Steward Talmai was harried. Once back in Jerusalem the king again alternated between rages about ingratitude and conspiracy, and fits of remorse. He wandered the palace halls calling for his lost wife and sons.

It was well Prince Antipater was in Rome. Doubtless the ambitious monarch-in-waiting would have tried something foolish and gotten himself killed . . . perhaps Talmai as well.

Behind the scenes there really was plotting going on. Herod's brother and sister were not above seeking to replace him. High Priest Boethus owed his position to Herod's favor, but Talmai guessed he was positioning himself favorably to support a successful rival candidate.

In the meantime much of the day-to-day affairs of the kingdom fell on Talmai. There were taxes to be collected. The new census to be tallied. Those who resisted the loyalty oath must be rounded up and punished. So it was with little patience that the steward agreed to an audience with a group of apparently ignorant foreigners seeking a meeting with the king.

They must be joking.

Of the three men who entered and stood before his desk, only one was known to Talmai: Zamaris, the mercenary cavalry officer hired to defend the Trachonitis border. Of the remaining two, one was short and brown-skinned. The other was elderly, Jewish by the cut of hair and beard but Parthian in the style of tunic and leggings he wore.

"Well, Zamaris, what is this about? What brings you so far from your duties?"

The soldier raised his chin. Talmai saw the glint in the man's eye . . . he knew his value and this man was not intimidated by Talmai despite his fancy title. "I suggest you listen to these men and then decide if it was important enough for me to escort them."

"So? Speak up! I don't have all day!"

The senior visitor replied, "I am Balthasar of Ecbatana and an elder of the Jews of Parthia. We—" here Balthasar indicated his Eastern companion with his hand—"this is Gaspar"—then swept it in a wider gesture.

Talmai frowned. He already knew there was a larger group of pilgrims.

"We have come seeking the answer to a question," Balthasar continued.

"Go on. Travel privileges? Trade concessions?"

Balthasar shook his shaggy head. "We have come to ask, where is he who is born King of the Jews?"[98]

Talmai was dumbfounded. What did the question even mean? Herod himself was not *born* king of the Jews. He was made so by Caesar. In fact, Caesar—and Caesar alone—could make someone king. Herod might nominate a successor, but the emperor had to agree before it was official.

"I don't know what you mean," Talmai replied, stalling for time. He prided himself that nothing happened in Judea without his knowledge. There was very little that was outside his control. "No one is born king. Prince, yes, we have several of those. Heir designate. Prince Antipater is that. But no one is *born* as king." Talmai glowered at Zamaris as if the trooper had brought a pair of madmen to his office.

Balthasar cleared his throat, then humbly but firmly stated, "Nevertheless, we believe the One who is the King of the Jews has already been born. We have seen his star in the east and are come to worship him."[99]

Talmai stared into Balthasar's eyes as if expecting to be let in on a joke he didn't comprehend. "To *worship* him?"

Gaspar nodded vigorously, and Balthasar affirmed the statement. "Worship is correct. For he who is born King of the Jews is the Messiah, the Holy One of Israel."

Talmai exploded, "So that's what this is about! The last of several so-called messiahs was a deluded servant, exploited by a group of Pharisees for their own purposes. He ended up dead! And so did they!"

Balthasar did not even flinch. He merely bowed and turned toward Gaspar, who remarked, "We come from many different nations—Parthia, Ethiopia, Armenia, east of the Indus—but all with the same objective. And we all agree. The signs of his coming are complete." With a hint of exasperation he suggested, "We have come many miles seeking him. Perhaps you should send for the high priest?"

"We'll send for no one. Sit down! I have to consult with the king!"

King Herod was agitated at Talmai's news about the visitors from the East and their quest for the one "born King of the Jews." Despite a drizzling rain, the monarch paced up and down in his garden. He held one hand pressed against his stomach while with the other he plucked at his hair and beard.

"You see, Talmai? You wanted me to stay longer in Caesarea, but I told you I was needed here in the capital. I was right, eh? Eh?"

The steward soothed, "Your instincts are always right, Majesty."

"It is another plot, this is! Like the servant fellow. And like that other bandit out in the desert who claimed to be the Messiah."

"No doubt Your Majesty is correct, and yet . . ."

"Speak up! What?"

"Every other messianic pretender started his campaign away from the city. Tried to gather the *am ha aretz* around him with promises and trickery. These men don't say they came in support of the new king. They say they're *looking* for him. They came straight to you first, expecting you to already know about this . . . claim. But we've heard no such rumors since . . ."

"Since what?"

"Since the burning of the genealogy records."

"I thought we killed them all! This is part of that conspiracy then?"

"Possibly . . . but . . ."

The king demanded, "Just arrest these fellows, torture them, round up their accomplices, and have done with it."

Talmai cleared his throat. "It's somewhat more complicated than that this time, Majesty. My spies confirm that none of these men are your subjects. They truly are from other nations. They've already been in communication with their fellow countrymen here in Jerusalem. One might conceivably disappear. Perhaps even two might meet with accidents. But there are many, and at least one is of royal blood. Caesar—"

"You do not have to finish," Herod concluded grudgingly. "Caesar would not allow such a diplomatic insult. But Caesar does not approve of a rebel claiming to be king either. I am the king of the Jews. No one else!"

"Then we must proceed carefully, Your Majesty. Let's keep the matter as quiet as possible. We'll confer with High Priest Boethus, the other chief priests, and the scholars, and present this claim to them."

Herod nodded, winced at a sudden pain, then instructed, "Meanwhile tell these emissaries to wait in their lodgings. Tell them I will send for them presently. But, Talmai . . . have them watched."

"Without fail, Majesty."

CHAPTER

23

It was morning on the Mountain of the House. Trumpet notes hung in the air like glistening drops of pure silver. The gates of the place where I AM said His Name would be forever honored swung open. The Levite singers, having offered their hymns of praise, retired to the warmth of their robing room. The sacred fire was alive on the hearth of heaven's antechamber.

The rituals for the new day were completed, exactly as they had been performed since Solomon's day, almost a thousand years earlier. The daily pause to reflect on the glory of the One God was accomplished.

Those who gathered around the altar felt their prayers ascend to the Almighty in concert with the incense erupting from inside the sanctuary and the smoke of the sacrifices outside it. Now the business of the Temple changed from public to private, from national spectacle to individual petition.

Mary, with Yosef carrying baby Yeshua enfolded in a blue-and-white-striped blanket, entered through the Eastern Gate into Solomon's Porch. Flanking them were Zadok and Rachel.

Between the colonnade and the gate called Beautiful were the tables of the money changers and the stalls of sacrificial animals. "Lambs for a denarius," a merchant noted.

"So much?" Yosef returned, frowning. The coins in his pocket amounted to enough for the redemption price of the firstborn and only a handful of coppers more. A denarius was a day's wages.

Mary's hand went to her throat. Reminded of Grandmother's gold coin and the admonition to save it for an emergency, she smiled and patted Yosef's arm. "Never mind," she said. "Two doves will do as well."

On this, the forty-first day since Yeshua's birth, two important *mitzvot*—duties—were to be performed. The first was the offering for Mary's purification, as commanded by the Law after the birth of a male child.[100] The second requirement was the *Pidyon HaBen*, the Redeeming of the Firstborn.

Yeshua was wide-awake and enjoying the colors and movement.

"The Lord you are seeking will come to His Temple."[101] Yosef murmured to Yeshua. "Welcome to Your Temple."

Zadok said, "We'll meet you back here when you're finished. The Almighty bless you."

Yosef selected two perfectly matched, pure white doves in a wicker cage. Handing over the pennies to the merchant, he passed the cage to Mary. He felt a pang in his heart when he saw how sadly she looked at the doves, knowing they would soon be dead . . . innocent sacrifices to fulfill the Law.

Once inside the Court of Women, just before the Nicanor Gate, a *cohen* met them. "Purification?" he inquired.

At Mary's concurrence the priest held the cage as she reached in and laid her hands on the cooing birds. She bowed her head in prayer. "My soul glorifies the Lord and my spirit rejoices in God, my Savior,"[102] she said, gazing tenderly at Yeshua.

"One for a sin offering, and one for the burnt offering," the priest said. "As required by the law of Mosheh."[103] The *cohen* whisked the cage away. The sacrifice was performed out of sight at the altar in the Court of Priests.

When he returned, his blood-spattered fingers were raised to show that the offering had been completed. "Your purification is complete. Your atonement is accomplished. Go in peace." Then, addressing himself to Yosef, the priest inquired, "Is it your desire to redeem the child at this time as well?"

Before Yosef could reply, a tall, stoop-shouldered, white-haired man detached himself from the steps of Nicanor Gate and approached the group. "If you will allow," the newcomer said, "I would like to act for this child."

"Of course, Simeon." Then to Yosef, "Quite an honor for you. This is Simeon the Elder. It is a special blessing for the child for him to perform the redemption."

Giving Yosef and Mary a smile, Simeon led the way to a sidewall of the court. There an opening shaped like the bell of a trumpet gave access to the offering box for the redemption money.

Simeon announced: "For 1,365 years the law of redeeming the first-born as instructed by the lawgiver Mosheh has been observed. As it is written: '*The Lord said to Mosheh: Consecrate to Me every firstborn male.*'[104] The price of each redemption is five shekels.[105] Is it your desire to do this?"

"To fulfill all righteousness," Yosef said firmly, exactly as he had rehearsed it.

Accepting the baby from Yosef, Simeon instructed Yosef to speak aloud the words of redemption.

"Lord, accept from my hand, this, the redemption price of The Firstborn Son." Then Yosef cast the silver into the trumpet.

Only Mary and Simeon overheard the substitution. Yosef had not said "*my* firstborn son" but "*The* Firstborn Son."

Yosef saw Simeon cradle Yeshua as one would hold his own dear child . . . as one receiving a loved one for whom the longing had lasted countless years.

"Sovereign Lord, as you have promised," Simeon said, tears spilling down his cheeks, "you now dismiss your servant in shalom! For my eyes have seen your YESHUA—Your Salvation—which you have prepared in the sight of all people, a light for revelation to the Gentiles and for glory to your people Israel."[106]

Yosef could not take it all in. So many lives, so many entire genera-tions, wrapped up in waiting for Messiah. Simeon seemed to be speak-ing for them all.

The old man did not return Yeshua to Yosef. Instead, stepping close to Mary, he placed the infant in her arms. Stretching out his hands over the family, he blessed them. Then with lowered voice and halting words he murmured in Mary's ear: "This child is destined to cause the falling and rising of many in Israel and to be a sign that will be spoken against, so that the thoughts of many hearts will be revealed. And . . ."

Yosef saw Simeon's cloudy eyes fill with sorrow as they beheld Mary's shining face. Then Simeon said, "And a sword will pierce your own heart too."[107]

Pierce her heart? Sweet Mary? Gentle, kind Mary? Why, O Lord? What does it mean?

Before Yosef could ask Simeon to explain, another person joined the group—a short, squat, elderly woman.

"Thanks be to the Almighty," the woman proclaimed, "who has let us live until this day and permitted us to see such wondrous sights! Today, in our presence, your covenant is fulfilled. And I, Hannah, have seen it with my own eyes!"

She spoke the blessing one offered for beholding a miracle of nature: a rainbow after a storm, a spectacular sunset, the blaze of a comet in the sky.

The mark of a covenant—a promise from God to man.

Then Hannah added: *"The Lord will be king over the whole earth. On that day there will be one Lord, and His Name—Yeshua—the only name."*[108]

ℚ

The cadre of a dozen Torah scholars and priests assembled in Herod's throne room represented the highest religious authorities and the brightest intellectuals in Judea. Every one of them owed his position to Herod's indulgence.

High Priest Boethus was not fully clad in his robe of office, but he did wear the priestly linen breeches and the seamless coat. His head was crowned with the miter, its blue ribbons holding on his forehead the golden plate called the Ziz, on which was engraved *Holiness to Yahweh*.

Despite the drafts of winter wind whistling through the corridors, a trickle of sweat emerged from beneath the high priest's turban. Boethus wiped it away with nervous fingers, smudging the Ziz as he did so.

Even though Talmai had ordered the foreign visitors to be sequestered, rumor and innuendo had flown about the streets of the Holy City. By the time the chief steward formally called the meeting to order, rapping his chamberlain's staff on the tiled floor, there was as much discussion of the matter outside the palace as within.

Addressing High Priest Boethus and the others on Herod's behalf, Talmai intoned, "You have heard of the message being spread abroad in the land: that there is one born who is King of the Jews . . . the so-called Messiah. Do any of you have any knowledge of this matter? Speak!"

Boethus flicked his glance left and right at the line of his companions. "None, sire. It's our opinion that this is another hoax or plot to stir up the *am ha aretz*."

Talmai continued the interrogation. "Have any of you knowledge about signs in the heavens or prophecies about such a birth?"

Up and down the row heads shook. No one knew of any such celestial signals. Every one of them knew that the book of the prophet Dani'el suggested something miraculous was due to happen, but none of them put any stock in tales of prophecy anyway.

"None, sire," Boethus concluded.

Growing tired of the formality of the exchange, Herod thundered, "But one *born* as king? A baby? Not me, nor any heir of mine, but an unknown child? How is it that foreigners know such stories? Where does your Scripture say this Messiah is supposed to be born?"

Boethus started to reply at once, but one of his assistants laid a hand on his arm and whispered, "My lord Herod is not a Jew. Don't answer too quickly or he may take it as criticism that he doesn't already know the answer!"

Boethus nodded his thanks.

Huddling with the group around him, the high priest carried on a pretended discussion of the question. This animated and wholly fictional debate, from which Boethus at last emerged, lasted several minutes.

"Well?" King Herod demanded. "Where?"

"In Beth-lehem in Judea, Scripture says . . . that is, it's our opinion . . . well, according to the prophet Micah . . ."

Here Boethus' assistant summoned a scribe bearing a scroll that he unrolled and held up as Boethus read: *"But you, Beth-lehem Ephrathah, are by no means least among the rulers of Judah, for out of you will come a ruler who will be shepherd of my people Israel.'"*[109]

"Beth-lehem?" Herod pondered aloud. "Muddy, smelly village south of here? Place where the sacrificial lambs are raised? And this *Anointed One* is to be called a . . . *shepherd*?"

"Like King David," one of the scribes blurted before Boethus waved him to silence.

"What about the Chief Shepherd? Does he have a son? Is he ambitious?" Talmai inquired.

High Priest Boethus, relieved at the question, smiled as he replied, "The present Chief Shepherd is seventy years old, childless, and past fathering a . . . child."

Herod, nearing age seventy himself, glowered at Boethus, who grew silent and lowered his eyes.

"Born, yes. But when? How old might he be already?" Herod muttered. Then more loudly, "Talmai, dismiss the assembly. But no one is to speak of this affair outside this room. Is that understood?"

After the religious officials had nodded and bowed their way out of the chamber, the king instructed Talmai, "Bring the foreigners to me by night. Let them come to my private entrance. Tell no one . . . but we must learn what else they know. How long this has been going on. You understand?"

"Perfectly, Majesty."

Little Obi pedaled his legs and grinned at Rachel as she washed him in a clay tub brimming with warm, sudsy water. Four new teeth gleamed in his mouth. A string of drool stretched downward.

"Show me your teeth." Rachel peered into the baby's mouth. "Lovely!" She felt the bumps on his gums. "More coming."

"That'll make it fun to nurse." Havila screwed up her face and rolled her eyes.

Obi giggled and kicked with pleasure.

"You do love your baths, don't you?" Rachel crooned.

Havila observed, "Perhaps his mother was from one of those tribes born near the water, eh? The sea on the coast of Ethiopia. They say the children swim like fish before they walk. Perhaps Obi's poor dear mother was stolen by slave traders as she played in the water."

"He is beautiful." Rachel could imagine sleek, ebony-skinned people slicing through the waves. She pictured Obi's mother, a little girl, being pursued and captured by the Arab slave traders who marketed human flesh harvested from the Horn of Africa.

Havila hummed. "Too bad about his arm. If he would only have been born with two hands . . ."

"Because he has only one, Herod's slave master did not really want him for the house of Herod—The Eternal be praised! The only thing he wanted was to be paid a ransom by us. No, the missing arm is a blessing. Even a terrible thing can be turned for good in the great plan of the Lord."

Obi's perfectly formed right arm was strong, compensating for the stump of his unformed left limb. He gripped the rim of the bath hard. Rachel was encouraged by Zadok's assessment that, in spite of his missing arm, Obi would grow up to be a fine, strong shepherd. One arm would work almost as well as two.

Rachel muttered, "I will always tell him as he grows that his left hand was lost so all of him could be saved."

"You tell him that. A good thing to tell him." Havila stitched baby clothes as Dan and Enoch played at her feet.

"A true thing." Rachel washed Obi's tight curls. "He won't miss what he never had. Zadok says so."

"That's the way of it." Havila did not look up. "Hardly miss what you don't know. But I think he may notice he isn't the same color as his brothers, eh?"

"We're all sheep in the same flock. Some white. Some black. Obi is a lovely black sheep."

Havila replied in her sweet, childlike treble. "The Lord is good to bring little Obi into the house of a shepherd to grow up. Eliyahu says so. He says you and Zadok have a way of putting the very best face on every unhappiness. I think it must be your influence on Zadok. I've known him all my life, and he was never such a pleasant fellow when he was only my brother. Before you married him."

Havila smiled. "Oh, the times we disagreed on this or that! The days I wished I could pick him up by his hair and toss him into the ravine! Father favored him because he was a boy. He could do no wrong. Good thing I am large like him. I could defend myself very well. I could make him turn and run! I matched my strength to his. I think you've made his heart tender like a little lamb, Rachel. I could crush him with one blow now." She made a fist. "I am the still, small voice that warns him to behave."

Rachel laughed. "He doesn't argue with me. I may be little, but I'm as strong-willed as he is."

"Stronger." Havila cut the thread with her teeth and folded her sewing on her lap. "A good thing. You have had a very good effect."

Rachel hefted Obi from the water and dried him on the table. The baby cooed. "Fed on the milk of a half-dozen mothers in Beth-lehem! He's getting so heavy!" Rachel exclaimed.

"Never a sweeter child. Everyone says so. Yes. Maybe his mother was a royal princess from Ethiopia. Obi's a prince from the seacoast. Pleasant people. Cheerful. Some Jews there. Descendants of old King Solomon, they say. He and the queen of Sheba maybe. Lots of Jews there with skin the color of obsidian, they say. Maybe Obi never was a Gentile. Maybe he was one of those who could trace their lineage all the way back to Solomon."

Rachel shrugged as she dressed him. "No matter. He's circumcised and will learn his alef-bet and Torah just like all our sons. Different color Jews but all the same flock. Zadok said so from the first."

She thought again of how tender Zadok was toward this little one though he was the illegitimate offspring of a slave girl. When demand for payment had been made by Herod's slave steward, Zadok and Rachel had tried to find some way to keep him. But the price had been too high—impossible for them to meet. Zadok had grieved with Rachel when they thought the child might be taken away. At the last instant the ransom of thirty silver shekels had been raised when every member of Eliyahu's congregation donated a small sum.

"Obi belongs to Beth-lehem." Havila examined her embroidery. "Everyone loves him."

"So many boys born this year and last." Rachel rested Obi on her hip and set to sweeping the floor. "I hope you have a girl, Havila."

"A girl. Imagine! I've almost forgotten little girls. Well, if she's a girl, she'll have her pick of husbands when she comes of age. How many boys in the last two years? Counting Mary's baby?"

"Seventy-one in all. Counting the ones born all the way south, in Ramah."

Rachel and Havila had delivered every one of them.

"Do you suppose it's our fault?" Havila laughed.

"The men are content to have more men."

"They're forgetting one small detail," Havila threw in.

"What's that?"

"It takes one of each gender to make more of the same. The population of Beth-lehem will decline in twenty years or so unless girls are born soon."

Rachel and Havila exchanged a look of mock concern.

"We'll have to go to Galilee to arrange for wives for all of them," Rachel said.

"We'd better hire the matchmaker now!"

The corridor outside King Herod's audience chamber was lined with guards, tall men who wore their blond hair in braids. As far as Melchior could tell, none had ever smiled in his life. Each was armed with a sword that reached from waist to floor. Each warlike visage was armored with a brushy mustache.

Melchior was glad that Perroz—bigger than any of these fierce-looking soldiers—accompanied Balthasar and him to this conference. Even so, Perroz was only one man, and ten sentries attended the king.

Getting into Herod's chambers was easy. Would getting back out also prove to be so? Melchior remembered all the stories about Herod's cruelty and was afraid.

Once inside the room, Melchior's worries subsided a little. Greeting them was Talmai, the king's steward, who said the king would join them shortly. The only other person in the room was a hard-looking soldier with a scarred face, who remained planted beside the chair of state as if rooted there.

The three emissaries were offered wine, which Balthasar declined for all.

Presently Herod entered through a door behind his throne. The portal was disguised to look like part of the paneled wall. One moment the space was empty . . . and the next, Herod was present. The lone guard assisted the king in mounting the dais, then took up a new station behind the visitors.

Balthasar and Perroz stepped forward. Melchior remained a pace behind but bowed as he saw them do.

"I am told you come from distant lands seeking one you say is born King of the Jews. Has he summoned you here? Did you come in response to his call?"

"Heaven's call, Majesty," Perroz explained. "Each of us has studied the stars. Each has reached his own conclusion. It so happens that all our conclusions agree."

"And what are these so-called signs? No one in my kingdom seems aware of them."

Balthasar spread his hands in a gesture of conciliation. "We cannot speak for others, Your Highness, only for ourselves. Our colleague, Melchior of Ecbatana, will explain."

So once again Melchior found himself designated to review the sky portents that had preceded and led the journey.

Herod expressed interest in the constellation of The Two Fish, in the triple conjunction, and in the eclipses of Shabbatai by the moon. He appeared to listen attentively.

Melchior kept his eyes on the marble floor while offering his recitation. Only once did he steal a glance at the king's face. The pupils of the king's eyes were distended, like those of a prowling, night-stalking beast. While Herod maintained a stiff, unemotional posture, Melchior saw that the king's complexion was mottled. Rather than unemotional, the king seemed to be controlling himself. Yellow, hollow cheeks were an ugly contrast to angry red spots on each cheekbone.

Melchior quickly dropped his gaze.

Herod listened until Melchior completed his report, then flicked a finger toward Talmai.

The steward queried, "It is said that someone, some figure of Jewish prophecy, will be born in Beth-lehem. Is this your understanding?"

Balthasar agreed.

Herod, leaning forward on his throne like a hawk eyeing its prey, asked, "Then why did you inquire of my steward where this *Anointed One* would be born?"

Melchior heard a rattle of metal and glanced over his shoulder. The bodyguard jerked the hilt of his sword, freeing it in its scabbard, but stopped short of drawing it. There was tension . . . danger in this moment.

Old Balthasar apologized for the misunderstanding. "Your pardon, Majesty. We did not inquire where the new King would be born but rather 'Where *is* he that is born King of the Jews?'"[110]

In his rolling bass, Perroz added, "Naturally we expected to find the young King here in the royal city, which is why we sought him here."

The king nodded, the clumps of his scraggly beard bobbing up and down like patches of moss on a dirty pond.

For the moment the tension relaxed.

Once more the king made a sign to Talmai, who asked, "Now this is most interesting. When did these signs first appear?"[111]

As the observer with an official capacity, it fell to Melchior to reply. "Considering the appearance of Mars in the sign of Virgo, it was the better part of a year ago, Your Highness."

Then the king did something Melchior had not expected. Gesturing with both gnarled hands, Herod summoned the trio to step closer. "I must take you into my confidence. There has been much civil unrest in my kingdom. This is a stiff-necked people. They love me, but they resent the presence of Rome . . . especially Roman taxes. Sometimes evil men—bandits and traitors, really—use stories about the Messiah for their own purposes. They deceive many and cause harm."

Leaning back in his chair rustled Herod's ornate robes. It was difficult for Melchior to avoid wrinkling his nose at the powerful aroma the motion released: costly, sickly sweet perfume that failed to mask the odor of death and decay.

Herod continued, "You understand that there would be danger to the child if such unscrupulous men found him. They might hurt him! For this reason I must be the first to officially welcome the newborn King. The Messiah! Think of it! The Anointed One has come in our lifetime! So, I must be the first to do him homage. It is only proper; it is also wise. Now go. Make a careful search for the child. As soon as you find him, report to me so that I, too, may go and worship him.[112] But tell no one else! For now it is imperative to keep this a state secret."

Melchior's thoughts flew like a meteor storm: *Herod wishes to protect the child? Others might do the baby harm?* Beth-lehem was said to be a small, unremarkable place. If the Messiah had been born there, only a handful of miles away, why wasn't His location already known and celebrated? And if His whereabouts were unknown, how could a collection of foreigners hope to find Him? It would be presumptuous to expect more celestial miracles than had already been displayed! After coming so far, could their mission still fail?

Melchior was embarrassed to find he had missed something the steward said, but he picked up the meaning midthread.

". . . in Beit Kodesh. The king commands that you be his honored guests. The House of the Spirit is where those who make the monthly report on the arrival of the New Moon are housed. You will be comfortable there, and the king thinks it most appropriate."

It was a royal command.

Balthasar thanked the king and the audience was over.

After more bowing, the three men exited Herod's presence, walking backwards.

Could all the stories about the king have been vicious lies?

The chief bodyguard's gaze bored into Melchior's face as they left. The man seemed to be memorizing every feature, as if to be able to identify Melchior in the future by a single freckle.

The Feast of Purim was fast approaching. There would be two days of celebration inspired by the story of Queen Esther, who had saved Israel from destruction.

Each year a pageant displaying the scriptural knowledge of Bethlehem's children was enacted. Beginning with the little ones called the Innocents, right through the ranks of boys preparing for bar mitzvah, each age-group would recite and perform some part of Torah's redemption story for the entire congregation.

This was to be Enoch's first Purim pageant. On the first night he would join other two- and three-year-old toddlers in a song about Esther the Queen and evil Haman, who plotted the slaughter of all Jews around the world. On the second night, stories from Genesis and Exodus would be performed.

"Now listen well to me, Enoch." Zadok held the boy on his right knee and Samu'el on his left.

Samu'el leaned back against Zadok with a dull, glassy-eyed expression. His eyes blinked and closed.

Zadok crooked his finger, summoning Rachel to determine if Samu'el was dismissed from class.

She agreed. "Samu'el's asleep. But Enoch is a big boy. Stay up with Papa and learn the lesson, eh?" Rachel took Samu'el from Zadok and put him to bed next to Obi.

Zadok resumed instruction. "Enoch, lad, y' have one half of one verse of Scripture to speak in the pageant. The verse is about Enoch."

"Me."

"Not yourself. Enoch. You're named after a great old man . . . a man of old. And old Enoch was this man's name. Just as young Enoch is your name. Do y' understand me, boy?"

Enoch's black curls bobbed as he nodded and tapped his chest. "That's me."

"Aye. You are named Enoch as well." Zadok glanced at Rachel for help. Was he being plain enough with the little one? Could Enoch understand him?

Rachel winked and resumed her work at the loom.

Zadok shifted in the chair. "Good. That's fine, then. I'm no teacher, but your uncle Eliyahu said I'll be thought an ignorant man if I can't teach my own son t' say his guardian promise for the Purim pageant from the Book of Beginnin's."

"Good, Papa. Story." Enoch stroked Zadok's beard and leaned his head against his father.

"Aye. A story. Your uncle Eliyahu, who is a man of learnin' and many words, has given me the very Scripture and the story that I am t' teach y' first. It is about Enoch. . . ."

"Me."

"Such a good and righteous fellow Enoch was that Adonai, the Lord, walked with him here on earth for a while. Then Adonai took Enoch away to heaven, out of this wicked world, so Enoch never died. Just flew away up to heaven." Zadok snapped his fingers.

"Me. Samu'el. Obi. Dan."

"So it's written: *'And Enoch walked with Adonai the Lord; then he was no more, for the Lord took him away.'*[113]

The boy brightened. "Enoch flew. Me too. I'm going to heaven."

Zadok sighed. "Tonight the lesson is not about you. You are Enoch the young, who must first learn this lesson, then live t' be a very old fellow and grow up t' be big like me."

Zadok showed the boy his muscle. "But tonight y' must recite the Scripture about the old Enoch . . . who lived long ago and flew to heaven and never died. The Enoch you are named for. He lived a very long time ago. Aye. Enoch, are y' sleepy, Son?"

Enoch responded with a negative shake of his head.

"All right, then. Here's the point. You are named for a very good old man. His name is also Enoch. And this fellow, we are told in the Book of Beginnin's, walked with Adonai, the Lord, as I said. We won't get into the part about Enoch bein' swept up t' heaven t' keep the Lord company away from this wicked world. We'll speak only the first part of the story. The part that took place right here on earth."

"At my house," Enoch piped authoritatively.

"Aye." Zadok scratched his beard. "In a way. So it goes . . . Adonai, the Lord, when he wanted to go on long walks and spend time with some pleasant human here on earth, he came down from heaven to Enoch's house, and Enoch walked with him."[114]

"That's me," the boy asserted.

"That's what it says about old Enoch in the Good Book. And that is what your guardian verse is and what y' will shout out when y' come before the congregation of Beth David on Purim with the rest of the lads. Y' will look right out at your mother and me and say loud and strong, 'Enoch walked with the Lord!'"

Rachel shushed him. "You'll wake the babies."

Zadok lowered his voice to a whisper. "Aye. Not so loud. We'll practice quietlike. On that night of Purim y' will shout it out! But not tonight, because your brothers are sleepin'. In front of the congregation at Purim when all the children give recitation you'll shout it very loud. 'Enoch walked with the Lord.' Can y' repeat that after Papa?"

The boy was silent.

Zadok urged him, "Enoch walked . . ."

"Enoch . . . walked . . ."

"with the Lord."

"with the Lord."

"Aye! Just like that! Well done, lad!"

The child beamed. "The Lord lives at Enoch's house."

"Close enough."

Rachel smiled and pretended she was not paying attention.

The phrase was whispered by father and son six times, until Enoch could say it on his own.

Zadok patted his back. "Well done, Enoch."

Rachel murmured, "You'll have to be certain he knows the meaning of it."

"What? Woman! The meanin'? He's no rabbi. Enoch walked with the Lord. And he was no more. Explain it? What's left to say about it? He's not meant to expound upon the verse. He's only meant t' shout it aloud at the Feast of Purim along with the other wee lads his age."

Enoch stuck out his lower lip. "Enoch . . . walked . . . with the Lord."

"Aye! There's a buddin' scholar! Well done, Enoch!" Zadok sat back, relieved that this first plunge into the waters of Torah had gone so well.

Enoch patted his father's cheek. "The Lord lives . . . at Enoch's house. Me and Samu'el . . . Obi. And Dan too. Going to his house to play."

Zadok laughed and lifted him high. "There's a good-hearted lad! An innocent heart! A better Enoch than the first Enoch. Not one of your playmates left out from the great journey when y' fly away, eh? You'll take all your wee friends and brothers with y' too!"

As soon as the foreigners departed, Herod beckoned for Talmai to approach. "The watchers will be in place around the Magi's lodgings?"

"Of course, sire," the steward acknowledged.

Herod scratched beneath his scraggly beard. "I want them followed . . . discreetly but constantly. If there is any truth to this tale, they will lead us to him."

"And if there is such a child?"

Herod shrugged. "Find him first. Then we will deal with him. As always, Talmai, we must learn who is in on the conspiracy. It is not enough to catch the small fish. We must cast the net wide and deep." There was a pause as the monarch's long nails dug red furrows in his pallid cheeks. He continued, "What if Nabatea is behind this plot? Or even Parthia? Watch them, but do not move too hastily."

"Shall I double the guard tonight, Majesty?"

Glancing about him at the gathering darkness and cocking his head to listen to the increasing howl of the wind, Herod disagreed. "It is going to be a bitter night . . . may even snow. No, they will not venture out before tomorrow. Do not give them any reason to grow suspicious. Just put your best man on it." The king flinched once as if struck by a pain but made no remark about it.

Calling the guard captain to his side, Talmai instructed, "Do you hear, Hermes? Constant vigilance, but do not alarm them."

"I know exactly what is required, Majesty," Hermes acknowledged. "Majesty?" he repeated when Herod gave no acknowledgment.

The king stared fixedly at a spot halfway up the tapestried wall. Absolute terror crossed his face, and even his jaundiced color drained from his features.

Unable to help himself, Talmai glanced that direction once, then twice. The steward's attention was drawn to a black shadow the size and shape of a dagger. Had it moved? But even if it had, surely a vagrant gust of air had disturbed the fabric . . . nothing more.

Still the king did not speak. Now his eyes were shut tight, his jaw muscles locked. Cords stood out in his neck and his back arched.

Uneasily Hermes said, "Shall I call his physician?"

"Wait!" Talmai hissed sharply. Lately the doctor's presence caused as many fits as it quieted.

A groan escaped Herod's throat, accompanied by what could only be described as a whimper. Herod's hands, which had been fidgeting at his waist, flew up to grasp his temples.

"Majesty?" Talmai queried. "Are you in pain?"

Herod's eyes snapped open wide as he sank to his knees. A muffled cry came from behind clenched teeth. Toppling onto his side, he lay there, panting and alternately clutching head and stomach.

Talmai bellowed for the servants. "Bring a litter. Get him to his bedchamber. Quickly!"

In the king's private rooms Talmai did in fact summon the physician. The doctor noted the rigidity in Herod's jaw and torso, clucked his tongue, then began calling out directions. He ordered a mixture of olive oil, balsam, and rose water heated to just above room temperature. The doctor would not permit the king to be moved to his elaborate bathhouse, so a porcelain tub with brass fittings was toted in.

As the preparations went forward, the doctor drew Talmai aside. "This will soothe him faster than any medicine," he promised. Without pointing, he nodded toward where the attendants undressed the king. "His skin . . . so scaly. Must itch abominably. And I can only imagine the condition of his liver. How can he govern in this state?"

"Limit your imaginings to your profession," Talmai warned.

When the bath was ready, Herod was lifted by six attendants, though his scrawny frame could have been hefted by Hermes alone.

As soon as the servants touched him, Herod babbled, "No! Hermes! Stop them. Do not let them kill me. Save me!"

Talmai's raised palm halted the guard's intervention. The steward indicated for the operation to proceed. With extraordinary care the king was lifted. Not a single jostle disturbed the arch that carried him from the floor, hoisted him over the tub, then lowered him gently into the warm oil.

The instant the liquid closed over his body Herod shrieked, "It burns! Burning my flesh! Burning me!" He clawed at the slaves and struggled to free himself.

The doctor stared, dumbfounded. All the servants backed away, except one unfortunate wretch whom Herod seized by the tunic, digging his nails into the man's arms.

Then, with a final tormented screech, King Herod fainted dead away.

"Have you killed him?" Talmai demanded. "What have you done?"

"I . . . I," stuttered the doctor. "Nothing, I assure you. See for yourself."

Moments later, wiped clean of the scented unguent, wrapped loosely in a fresh linen nightdress, the unconscious monarch was tucked into his bed.

Talmai and Hermes stared at each other in consternation.

$\mathcal{M}$elchior raised his head from writing in his journal when a throat was cleared behind him. It was Old Balthasar. "I'm sorry; I didn't hear you there," Melchior apologized. "Did you ask me something?"

Balthasar nodded gravely. "We—Gaspar, Perroz, Kagba, and myself—think we should go to Beth-lehem tonight. What do you think?"

Stepping to a west-facing window, Melchior drew aside the curtain. An icy breeze smacked him in the face. Snowflakes spiraled on the wind. Below, at ground level, a solitary figure detached himself from a shadowed doorway. Moving down the street, the lone man entered an inn, where the cheery glow from the doorway suggested a blazing fire within.

"It's a dreadful night. Even if we reach Beth-lehem, what then?" Melchior asked. He gazed into Balthasar's eyes.

The old man's face gleamed with excitement. "Melchior, he who has led us this far already will not abandon us now. Don't you feel it? It is now—tonight! We have Zamaris' horses. What do you say?"

Turning back toward the window, Melchior regarded an unexpected patch of pale sky in the southwest. The storm was fleeting, then.

Instead of another blast of winter, the frigid wind revealed the heavens for the first time in many days. Melchior saw the thinnest sliver of New Moon framed by the casement, and riding above the moon, Jupiter—The Righteous. They hung in the sky in the direction of the road to Beth-lehem.

It took Melchior a minute to realize what was wrong with the scene: Saturn was missing!

Realization dawning, Melchior thrust his left hand upward while gesturing excitedly for Balthasar to come and see. "The Sabbath! The Sabbath is again eclipsed by the moon, The Lord of the Sabbath wrapped in the Holy Spirit! But they will set in mere hours, and who can say when the weather will be clear again? You are right, Balthasar! We must go tonight! *Now!*"

Jerusalem's city gates were carefully guarded. The Herodian sentries were surprised to see a caravan setting out so late, but there had been no orders to prevent any such exodus, so they allowed Balthasar's caravan to have passage through.

Melchior rode at the point. Since it was he who had spotted the absence of Saturn from the sky, without any discussion he was awarded the place at the head of the column. His eyes fixed on the sliver of moon, Melchior pondered where this road would lead.

Beth-lehem lay no more than a half-dozen miles to the southwest. As they rode, the clouds rolled back from west to east like a scroll, clearing the heavens in front of the procession as they advanced cautiously.

Two hours later Mars—Ma-Adim, The Adam—sank toward the horizon. They had covered only half the distance to Beth-lehem.

Nudging his camel forward, Gaspar rode up alongside Melchior. "Do you see where Mars descends? Is it not directly above Beth-lehem?"

They were still too far away. If Mars was meant to be a sign, they had missed it, for it disappeared behind the Judean hills still separating the caravan from the City of David.

Urgency grew inside Melchior. What if the moon and Jupiter set without revealing anything? On such a dark night, could they go from house to house asking, "Where is he who is born King of the Jews?"

As the road wound south through the hills, orchards closed in on both sides. The olive trees barely glinted in the darkness of the lower slopes, but the higher reaches appeared snow covered from the early awakening almond blossoms. Here and there shepherds' watch fires dotted the folds of the canyons where they and their flocks huddled.

Long before they reached the village, one prominent landmark came well into view: King Herod's fortress called Herodium. Its parapets outlined by torchlight, Herodium brooded like an evil presence in the southeast.

Melchior shuddered within his cloak and was inexplicably grateful when the path turned away from Herodium to aim more westerly. The New Moon rode low, with Jupiter—The Righteous—merely a half degree behind it.

The Parthian prayed as he had never prayed before to the God he had chosen to serve. He had not been born a Jew, but he loved everything about Adonai Elohim—Yahweh—the One God, the Almighty.

But would Yahweh answer? Would the Son of the Most High be revealed to a seeker as humble as Melchior? What right had he to expect a reply?

The trail reached the bottom of one of the innumerable ravines dividing Jerusalem from Beth-lehem, then climbed the ridge on the far side. This was one of the twin heights forming the enclosure of the natural amphitheater around the village. All the country beyond sloped away, descending toward the sea.

From the summit Melchior saw faintly winking glows ahead. As they drew closer, he could see the light that escaped the windows and doorframes of the loaf-shaped homes of the city Beth-lehem, called The House of Bread.

And now what? The goal, but not the object of the quest, was in sight.

Esther grabbed Melchior's arm and gestured forward, pointing just over the rooftops. "Look!" she demanded breathlessly.

Beneath Jupiter, The Righteous, beneath the moon, the light of the Holy Spirit, a new inexplicable gleam appeared within the sign of The Two Fish. In the rapidly narrowing space between the moon and the horizon, a bulge appeared, swelled, grew, and detached itself from the moon till it was distinct and separate.

"What is it?" Esther murmured.

Melchior's heart pounded in his chest. "It's The Lord of the Sabbath!"

Saturn, emerging just before dipping out of sight in the west, appeared as a gleaming dot marking the rim of the world. Gently but clearly it anointed the roof of a house standing poised on the far ridge . . . marking it as plainly as if the watch fire of the Temple Mount rested on it.

And so, at the crucial moment, the star they had seen in the east went ahead of them until it stopped over the place where the child was.[115]

Zadok heard the footsteps running in the gravel up the trail toward his house. It was dark, three hours past sunset. The unknown sprinter might be seeking Rachel's help with a delivery, but who in the village was expecting? It was not time for Havila's baby yet. Surely there could not be another set of strangers searching for the midwife of Beth-lehem.

Or perhaps this was not about a baby still to come but about one who was already here?

Something about the nighttime commotion made Zadok uneasy.

At any rate, there was only one man approaching. Small threat in that, Zadok reminded himself.

Staff in his hand, Zadok said to Rachel, "Keep the little ones in the other room till I see what this is about."

It was Lem's boy Jesse. He panted with exertion. "Riders!" he said urgently. "Seem to be headin' here. Didn't stop in the village. Father saw them comin' this way. Sent me by the old quarry to tell you."

"Soldiers?"

Jesse, bent over his knees, drew a shaky breath. "Foreigners. At least, some of them. Not from Herodium either. Came down the Yerushalayim road."

Foreigners? Why would foreigners come to the house of Zadok the Shepherd?

"How many, lad?"

Jesse shook his head. "Too dark to count. At least half a dozen, Father thinks."

Too many to fight if they were a menace. And mounted, hard to outrun.

"Father is gatherin' men from the village. Said he'd come soon."

That news made all the difference. "Around the back with you, boy.

Tell Lem to send half the men by the regular path and the others up the quarry. Now go!"

Zadok went to fetch Yosef, Mary, and baby Yeshua. With a few quiet words he explained what was happening. "May be nothin' at all, but why take chances, eh? Best you three come into my house. Lem and the others will be along soon."

Horses whinnied in the darkness.

Near. Very near.

As Yosef strapped on his sword, Zadok clapped him on the back. While the carpenter from Nazareth appeared sensitive to the threat, Mary remained serene.

Melchior's heart raced as they neared the house directly beneath where the planet Shabbatai—The Lord of the Sabbath—emerged from behind the moon. One minute after they spotted the surprising signal, the edge of the moon seemed to push Saturn ahead of it into the west.

If they had looked up one minute later they would have missed the miraculous heavenly sign!

Even now Jupiter itself lay atop the roof of the house. In another brief interval it too would disappear.

But Melchior and the others had witnessed tonight's wonder as though it was meant for them—meant to mark the conclusion of their journey! It was as real as the star that had appeared before. And all the signs over the past year had combined to lead them here . . . to this place . . . to this night.

The glow from the cracks around windows and door increased as they neared the house. Could this humble stone building actually contain the end of their quest . . . the answer to all their hopes?

A night bird warbled in the reeds of the creek bed.

The Magi had moved across the face of the earth as though a mighty wind pushed them. Now they stopped, certain they had come to the right place, as though the voice of the Almighty and Eternal God had spoken aloud: **He is here!**

Melchior fixed his gaze on the descending stars. It was as though they declared to his heart the answer to his question: *Ki-Mah? Who made these?*

The child, the Son of the Living God . . . the baby you have come to worship . . . the stars are His! He made them all! He knows them each by name![116]

It was as though Melchior had reached up and gathered the heavenly jewels in his arms. The focal point of all the universe was now before them.

As he and Esther stood hand in hand, Melchior knew the end of his quest was within this humble home.

"We should approach on foot," Old Balthasar suggested, drawing rein and dismounting in a gulley. "There are willows here to tie the horses. In a remote place like this we might frighten them if we rode up to the door."

Perroz rumbled his agreement. "And we must be properly humble as well."

Esther's hand trembled in Melchior's fingers. "Can it really be? We've come so far."

Melchior could hardly find his voice. "I believe it," he managed at last.

Saddlebags were opened and gifts removed.

There was a rustling of silks in the darkness. To Melchior's surprise, Aretas and Gaspar threw back their cloaks to reveal finely woven robes underneath. Old Balthasar and Kagba, while still in common dress, appeared taller, grander in the starlight.

But the greatest surprise of all came from Perroz. Besides a cape of red and gold, he drew from his saddlebag a circlet of gold and placed it on his head. "This is how I would receive a visiting king in my own country. Shall I do less when I go to him?"

Perroz had not dressed this sumptuously when he appeared before Herod.

Each man carried something: pouch, chest, alabaster jar.

Only Melchior approached without an offering.

"Melchior? Where is your journal?" Esther asked. "What greater gift could you give the baby Messiah than the record of the heavenly signs of his coming?"

Melchior retrieved a leather pouch containing duplicate records from the past year of observations.

As the pilgrims emerged from the creek bed and approached the dwelling, the moon and star signs slid behind the western horizon.

Melchior spotted two men flanking the door. One was tall and lean, a fierce-looking fellow with a thick black beard. He wielded a shepherd's staff and a dog crouched at his feet. The other man was shorter and built more square, but his hand also rested on the hilt of a weapon.

The taller figure, dark eyes flashing, demanded, "You approach the home of Zadok, shepherd of Migdal Eder. What's your business? And who are you?"

It was for Old Balthasar to answer. The old man bowed deeply. "I am Balthasar, of Ecbatana in Parthia. Sir, we are travelers from many distant lands. We come seeking he who is born King of the Jews. We saw the first sign of his life in the constellation of The Virgin and after that, the declaration of his coming—the Anointed One—written month by month by the hand of the Almighty in the stars of The Two Fish of Israel. We—my companions and I—have come to worship the infant King of the Jews."

Both men who stood guard at the door sighed with relief and exchanged glances.

"I am Zadok. Before you is Yosef bar Jacob, descendant of David. Yosef is honored by The Eternal God of Israel to be husband and protector of Mary, the virgin who gave birth to the King of Israel." Zadok bowed slightly. "None may pass the threshold without Yosef's permission."

Melchior noted surprise on the face of Yosef as the whole company of travelers dropped to one knee before him.

"Shalom, Yosef son of Jacob, honored sir." Balthasar did not look up. "We have come thousands of miles to seek audience with the one true King whose birth was foretold by the prophets of old. The stars have guided us to this place. The hour is late, and we beg forgiveness for the intrusion. We will return in the morning if it is more convenient."

Esther leaned her cheek against Melchior's sleeve. Did she feel the same disappointment he felt? To come so far, to see the sign above the house. Then to be made to wait until morning!

Yosef stepped forward and helped Balthasar to his feet. He greeted the old man's gaze with a broad smile. "Shalom. Blessed be the Lord who has let us live to see this moment. You're welcome here. Since you've followed the stars and understood the meaning of what's written in the heavens, then the exact time of your arrival here in the town of David was ordained by the Lord from eternity. Your quest is at an end. You aren't late. Mary and baby Yeshua are inside. Stand up, please . . . no need to bow to me. Welcome and shalom! I'll let the baby's mother know you are here."

Men from many lands? Coming to worship here? Yosef could scarcely take it in. There had been no dream to prepare him for this, no angelic visitor to tell him how to react.

Like cold water to a thirsty traveler is good news from a distant land.[117]

So, the good news of Messiah's birth had reached the distant boundaries of the world. Yosef understood at last the quote from the prophet Isaias. He restated it now in a reverent whisper: *"Nations will come to Your light, and kings to the brightness of Your dawn.*[118] *I will make you to be a covenant for the people and a light for the Gentiles."*[119]

Yosef opened the door.

Mary appeared behind him, framed in the doorway. In her arms she held the bundled form of Yeshua.

At His appearing, the entire rank of visitors sighed with pleasure and once again dropped to their knees. This time Yosef did not prevent them from paying homage.

In turn each traveler announced name and land of origin.

"Balthasar of Parthia."

"Perroz of Ethiopia."

"Kagba of Armenia."

"Gaspar of India."

"Melchior of Parthia."

"Esther of Parthia."

"Aretas of Nabatea."

Yosef murmured, "Parthia. Ethiopia. Armenia. So many. They've come so far."

Addressing himself to the infant, Gaspar saluted and cried, "Hail, you whose name is Wonderful."

Kagba: "Hail, Yeshua! Divine Counselor."

Perroz: "Hail, Yeshua! Mighty God."

Old Balthasar: "Hail, Yeshua! Everlasting Father."

It was Melchior's turn, and he neither hesitated nor fumbled. Esther and Prince Aretas and the others joined him in chorusing, "Hail, Yeshua! Prince of Peace!"

"You've come so far. You must enter," Zadok urged. "Rest with us. Eat."

The little house was charged with the aromas of spices and perfumes as the scholars, kings, and princes entered. Mary, seated beside the warmth of the hearth, allowed each visitor to kiss the brow of Yeshua.

Rachel made mulled wine, and neighbors began to arrive with platters of food for the visitors. The atmosphere was one of reunion and celebration.

Perroz removed his crown and laid it before the feet of Yeshua. In turn each man advanced on his knees and placed his gift before Messiah.

Yosef inhaled the sweet pungency of frankincense, the dark musk of myrrh. A leather pouch jangled as Old Balthasar tossed it on the stones.

Overhead The Guardian shone due south. In the east The Lion of Judah was rising.

At last the red-bearded young man named Melchior came forward with Esther at his side.

Mary beamed as she looked into Esther's face. "You are betrothed?"

Melchior blurted, "Yes. My heart has sworn we are to be married at the end of our journey or I will never marry."

Esther's eyes widened with surprise and delight. Color rose to her cheeks as she smiled up at Melchior.

Mary laughed. "I thought so. You wear your vow in your eyes, Melchior. May the Lord bless you with long life and many children." She directed her attention to Esther. "Would you like to hold Yeshua?"

Esther nodded eagerly and took the baby into her arms. Instinctively she began to sway. Baby Yeshua sucked His fist.

"He's beautiful," Esther remarked. "Shalom! Shalom, little one. Oh, Melchior! Look at these dark curls."

"Esther." Mary repeated her name. "From Parthia, you say? Persia?"

"Yes. Ecbatana," Esther replied.

"Like Queen Esther of old, whose name means Star." Mary seemed pleased. "I'm glad you came."

Esther hummed softly. "It's only right since the stars themselves have come to Beth-lehem to pay homage to the Son of the Most High God."

At that Melchior stepped forward and extended a leather pouch to Mary. "Honored mother of the King, I have no gold or frankincense or myrrh to offer you. I am court astronomer to King Phraates. My gift is the gift of my studies. These are duplicates of my star journals. Observations of all the signs in the heavens from the first night when the sign of Ma'Adim—Mars—touched The Star of Atonement at the heart of The Virgin. The annunciation of this great event began that night. On that night the sign appeared within your constellation, honored lady."

Mary's hand stroked the worn leather containing the astronomer's records. "Thank you for your faithfulness. Someday I'll show him what you set down."

Melchior blushed beneath his beard and bowed awkwardly. "Honored lady, I believe he has always known how the stars would declare his glory to all of us who longed for his coming. My small record is only a confirmation of his greatness. The original account will be in the library of the King of Parthia."

26

It was several minutes before midnight when Melchior and Esther emerged from Zadok's house. Light and warmth, mingling with the rich aromas of dried herbs and incense, rolled out the open door as good-byes were said.

All the travelers seemed stunned by what they had experienced. They were unwilling to leave and almost unable to move.

Glancing at the clock of the sky, Perroz announced, "Too late to go all the way back to Yerushalayim tonight."

"We'll stay in the caravansary at Beth-lehem tonight and tomorrow return to Yerushalayim," Melchior suggested.

"By this time tomorrow, all the Holy City will ring with his praises," Kagba declared.

"And in a month the whole world will resonate with the news," Gaspar added.

Of all the worshippers, only Balthasar was subdued, even somber in his demeanor. Melchior asked the old man if he was feeling well. It had been a long day, a freezing night, and now there was the aftermath of great emotion. Was he ill?

The eldest of the Magi inclined his shaggy head in thought. Then, frowning, he replied, "All that is good, condensed into such a fragile container. All that light bound up in a single clay lamp. The hope of all mankind . . . in the body of an infant! We found him, but what if the eye of evil locates him as well? Was there ever a more dangerous time?"

Melchior was startled and unhappy at Balthasar's conclusion. Wasn't this night one of unreserved exultation? How could any evil intrude on such mysterious wonder?

"You're just tired," Melchior responded. "You'll feel better tomorrow."

Old Balthasar made no answer.

From Zadok's isolated home the caravan wound its way back to the center of Beth-lehem, stopping beside David's Well. All except Balthasar continued to express their wonder and amazement at the One they had seen and worshipped. What a different world the rising sun would dawn on tomorrow morning—the most glorious in history!

After helping Esther down from her mount and seeing her into the inn, Melchior assisted in watering and feeding their livestock. As he returned to the well on one of his trips, he chanced to glance into it. In its depths inky blackness surrounded a pinpoint of brilliant white light: a star reflected in the very center of the well.

The constellation of Aryeh, The Lion, stood directly overhead, and very near the zenith was Regulus, the star called The Little King. Glowing with silvery fire, it was Regulus that beamed down light into and back up again from the well of King David's longing.

And a star will come out of Jacob,[120] Melchior remembered with immense satisfaction. When the animals' needs were met, Melchior found himself a spot at the caravansary. Covering himself with his blanket, over which he heaped a pile of clean straw, he fell asleep almost instantly. His last waking thought was how silly it was for Old Balthasar to have any fear on a night such as this. With all the signs now complete, the quest fulfilled, and the child safe and about to be acclaimed by all the world, what danger could possibly threaten?

Guard Captain Hermes and High Priest Boethus met with Talmai in the chief steward's private office.

Located on the third floor of the administrative wing of Herod's

Jerusalem palace, its windows faced the Damascus Gate. Whenever Talmai wished, he could personally observe caravans laden with taxable goods arriving and leaving the Holy City's main portal. He often stood, as he did tonight, framed in the window, calculating how much he could extort from the latest shipment of spices or silks or dates. Every bit of frankincense or myrrh passing through Jerusalem yielded gold for Herod's coffers and Talmai's own pockets.

Despite standing in the place and posture that gave the steward much pleasure, tonight his thoughts traveled only as far as the opposite wing of the palace. Since succumbing to the convulsion in the oil bath, Talmai's master lay barely conscious, unspeaking, and hardly moving.

"What does the doctor say?" Boethus inquired nervously.

"That fool," Talmai snarled, his back to the other two men. "He talks and talks and says nothing! Spent an hour explaining to me the difference between *torpor* and *stupor* and *coma*, the last of which he says the king is not in, since he swallows broth and water and still feels pain." Talmai snorted a derisive laugh. "And since the good doctor is the one testing the king's reaction to pain, he'd better hope His Majesty is in a stupor or a torpor or whichever's the deeper!"

"But what's to be done?" Boethus fretted, wringing his hands.

Frowning as he spoke, Talmai instructed, "Whatever we discuss stays in this room; is that clear? Remember when the rumor of Herod's death caused those misguided Pharisees to take up arms? A hundred Judean hills lost their trees furnishing crosses to hang them on."

The high priest grew very pale. He involuntarily clenched his hands as if already feeling the nails. "Naturally! Nothing outside this room. Not even my wife shall know."

Hermes snorted, then spoke. "What about sending a courier to Rome? Shouldn't we let Lord Antipater know what's happening?"

"Yes," Boethus chimed in eagerly. "Let him know he has our full support."

Talmai whirled so sharply that Boethus backed up a pace. "That is what we must not do! Suppose when Lord Herod awakens, he hears that we could hardly wait to summon his son back from Rome to be king. The only remaining question would be whose head hits the floor first: Antipater's or yours."

"Oh!" Boethus muttered, his eyes wide and his mouth pinched as if to punish it for speaking wrongly.

Hermes still leaned nonchalantly in the corner. "So what is to be done?"

"For now? Nothing. We threaten the palace slaves with instant death if they breathe a word about the king's condition outside these grounds. Then we loose my men in the marketplace to say Herod is regaining his strength every day. Planning an expedition to . . . it doesn't matter where. Then we wait and watch, understand? That's all. To the king any planning we do right now would be regarded as plotting . . . and you both understand the difference? Now go and let me get on with my other work."

Boethus exited hurriedly, but Hermes paused at the door. "What about those . . . astrologers, were they? Magicians? The king seemed very concerned about them and their wild tales of some miraculous baby."

"Old men and fat men and easily recognized foreigners don't seem much of a threat to me. Do they to you, Hermes?"

The captain acknowledged that the group was unlikely to contain either rebels or spies.

Talmai continued, "Caught up in their own imaginings. They'll get disillusioned soon enough and show up back here asking for money to help them get to their homes. No, I think we can safely ignore that nonsense. Besides, if our good high priest has any more worries, he'll tremble himself to death! No, there's only one king of the Jews, even if he is unable to speak. For now that's as far as our concern should lie."

The straw under Melchior rustled as he turned in his sleep. The crackling noise roused him just enough to notice that the sky overheard had once again clouded over, obscuring the stars. Nestling farther into his blankets, Melchior composed himself for sleep.

The straw crunched again, almost like a footfall. Some animal wandering about, browsing in the middle of the night?

"The ox knows his master and the donkey his master's manger," says the Lord, *"but Israel does not know Me."*[121]

Melchior smiled drowsily. How soon that would change! Soon Israel would acclaim the heaven-sent king! Judea would ring with His praise. His Name would echo beyond the borders of the Jewish kingdom to the farthest corners of the world.

The crushing of dry stalks was unmistakable this time . . . but not made by horse or camel.

"Who? Who's there?" Melchior demanded.

Melchior.

A voice, low but not whispering, spoke his name. It was deeply resonant, like the roll of waves on the seashore.

"Who is it? What do you want?"

I have been sent with a message for you.

"For me? But who are you?"

Do not be afraid, Melchior. I am Gabriel, servant of the Most High, warrior of the Babe.

"This is a dream!"

Yes, but it is not for you alone. You sorrowed at not having a worthy gift for the King? This moment is your gift. You are called to serve Him.

A figure stood beside the heap of straw. In Melchior's dream the man towered above the palisade of the caravansary. His face was shadowed and indistinct, yet it glowed, as did his outstretched hands.

"This is one dream I'll certainly remember!"

Then listen: King Herod seeks to take the life of the child.

"I don't like this dream."

Nevertheless, it's a true one. Do not return to Herod. No one is to return through the gate by which he entered. Do not return home by the way you have come.[122] *Leave at once and do not stop until you are out of Israel. You must show them the way.*

"But shouldn't we take the baby with us?"

His safety is not up to you. Only remember all you have seen and heard here. Remember . . . remember . . .

"Melchior, wake up!"

Melchior bolted upright as a very real hand grasped his shoulder and shook it.

It was Esther. "Melchior, Grandfather's had a dream! An angel came to him, he says. We must flee from here, from Herod, he says. He's rousing the others. I'm afraid for him. For his mind!"

Melchior interrupted the tearful, frightened girl and seized both her hands in his. "No! It's the truth, Esther! I had the same dream. An angel, yes! We must go at once."

It was dark when the company of the Magi assembled again in the courtyard. All of the sky observers had experienced similar dreams. None of them argued with the message.

"But how will we escape?" Kagba mused. "We can't go back to Yerushalayim. The coast road either north or south is too long and well-known. They'd overtake us."

"East," Melchior said with surprising assurance. "We must go east."

"But Jericho is the best-patrolled section of highway," Perroz warned. "More troopers there than anywhere."

Melchior drew the youngest and quietest member of the group to the center. Aretas stood blinking in the torchlight. "Not east through Jericho, but first south around this side of the Dead Sea and *then* east ... into Nabatea! Prince Aretas, can we get safe passage through Nabatea?"

"Of course," the boy said. "It was my mother's home. We'll all be welcome there."

"And it is the least traveled of all the routes," Melchior concluded. "By the time they have searched the others, we'll already be over the border."

Yosef sat with sword in his right hand and his back against the door of the cottage. He had not felt at peace since he and Mary had returned to Beth-lehem from the Redemption of the Firstborn in Jerusalem.

Fear, thick and palpable, clung to Yosef like cobwebs in the darkness of a tomb. Simeon's warning to Mary replayed in Yosef's thoughts: *"And a sword will pierce your own heart too."*

Yosef had recognized the same awareness of danger for Mary and baby Yeshua reflected in Zadok's eyes.

Herod! By now he knows!

Surely Herod was the reason for Simeon's grim prophecy. Herod the Butcher King would seek out Mary, the virgin of Isaias' prophecy, and thrust a sword through her heart!

Yosef had not spoken of his fear to Mary over supper. She had searched his face to find the reason for his silence, but he did not meet her gaze.

In Zadok's eyes Yosef had seen the recognition of an approaching storm—encroaching thunderheads sweeping down from the north.

But Mary, sweet Mary, did not seem to notice as they broke bread together.

Yosef had witnessed the weight of evil pressing down on Zadok. And suddenly Yosef understood why the Messiah had been born in the lambing cave. Why the angels had announced His birth first to the shepherds of the Temple flock. Why Yosef and Mary and Yeshua had been nurtured and cared for by the families of Beth-lehem. It was within the power of the Almighty to call upon the earth to weave a canopy of protection so thick that no man could lay a hand on Mary or the baby named Salvation. But The Eternal God had instead chosen a few righteous families in Israel to help preserve and protect His great plan of deliverance and salvation!

Blessed are you, O Adonai, sovereign King, who brought us to this place and this moment. Blessed are the shepherd people of David's village who took us in and sheltered us, who never turned away from our need. Blessed are they who stand watch over your flocks generation after generation, who have watched over your Firstborn Lamb for this season. They are not poor; they are just without the riches of the world. Blessed are these unknown ones who stand watch quietly in the rain because you have called them to care for your own.

They will outlast the pomp and power of the false shepherds whose god is wealth and who sell your people to the wolves. Blessed are you, O Lord, who will cleanse your Temple! When the last Lamb of sacrifice, born in Beth-lehem, has bled out upon your altar, these shepherd families who cared for us will sit in honor by your throne. Bless them, O Lord. Bless these, your faithful servants in the field.

Yosef remained awake, vigilant and aching.

Mary's breath was deep and even.

And a sword will pierce your heart. . . .

Bells rang softly above the embers. A burst of wind exploded from the chimney, suffusing the room with smoke. Yosef stirred and opened his eyes to see a pinpoint of light glowing, growing on the hearth.

Yosef, son of Jacob, son of David . . .

"I am asleep," he whispered. "Dreaming."

I am Gabriel. Warrior of the Most High.

"Shalom."

Yosef. Guardian of the Son of the Most High. Protector of Mary, the chosen Virgin. Look upon me and tell me what you see.

The angel Gabriel, golden and shimmering with light, stood before

Yosef. Gabriel had a staff in his right hand and a sword in his left. His tunic was tied up in his belt for traveling and his feet were covered in mud.

"You hold your sword in your left hand. If you will fight for us, for the Messiah and his mother, why then do you carry the sword in your left hand?"

The angel held up the walking staff. *Herod, instrument of darkness, has awakened from his slumber. At last all his nightmares have come true. Yeshua, Son of David, Son of the Most High, lives!*

"He knows we're here then?"

As Pharaoh sought to kill Mosheh the Deliverer in days of old, so this evil man seeks the life of the Baby and His mother!

Yosef raised his sword. "Tell me what I must do. Give me strength to fight, and I'll die protecting them! So will all these good men in Beth-lehem die for him if they must!"

At Yosef's words, Gabriel's eyes reflected anguish. *You cannot stay with these shepherds of Israel another day. Remember the staff of Mosheh—how he stretched it forth and the sea opened before the people as they fled from Pharaoh?*[123] *And the coffin of Joseph the Dreamer that was carried into the bed of the sea before them? After that the people followed. So, Yosef, you must choose the staff rather than the sword.*

"We must leave this place? Where? Where shall I lead them?"

Yosef, like Joseph of old and the family of Jacob, you and Mary and Yeshua must go now into Egypt so the child Yeshua, Messiah, Son of David, Son of the Most High, will survive the terror that is soon to come upon this land. From Yeshua will come the salvation of Israel and of all in the world who call upon His Name![124]

"How will I know the way to escape?"

The shepherd Zadok has shown you the path. The shepherd has revealed the secret to you. Go now.

"Shall I wait until light?"

Take the Child and His mother . . . place them on the donkey of Zadok the Shepherd. Go now.

The jingle of bells upon the neck of a ram continued to ring as the glow of the angel faded. At last only the vision of the staff remained burning before Yosef's eyes.

"Mary," Yosef croaked as the bells jingled. "Mary! Wake up! Mary!"

"What?" her drowsy voice replied. "What is that sound? The bells? Yosef? Light the lamp."

Before dawn Mary and Yosef, Zadok and Rachel, Eliyahu and Havila embraced one another for the last time. Zadok's dun-colored donkey, loaded for the journey, munched fodder as the three couples and their children and Grandmother made their fare-wells.

"You know the way." Zadok's expression betrayed his fears as he instructed Yosef. "David's Pasture. My donkey is a sure-footed little beast. He'll carry Mary and the babe safely on the steepest path."

"We'll send word when we reach your brother in Alexandria." Yosef glanced nervously to where the first light of morning was beginning to lighten the sky.

Zadok placed a letter of introduction to Onias in Yosef's hand. "My brother Onias has suffered greatly at Herod's whim. He'll welcome you, take you in. He'll care for you as I wish we could . . . here in Beth-lehem. You've made a fine shepherd, Yosef, son of Jacob, son of David. And I'm certain you'll make a fine shepherd for as long as this wee lamb has need of your protection."

Mary brushed a tear from her cheek. "You have all cared for us with such kindness."

The four women and the little ones made a circle, kissing each other good-bye and weeping for one another.

"Oh, when will we see you again?" Havila enfolded Mary in her long arms.

Mary placed her hand on Havila's stomach. "May this baby within your womb be blessed and find great joy. May our children meet one day and remember . . . remember the bond that is between us forever."

"May The Eternal keep you and guide you on your way," Rachel added.

Yosef helped Mary onto the saddle. "We'll spend the first night with the shepherds in the hidden valley."

Grandmother instructed, "There's food enough for your journey. All the way to Egypt."

"Aye. Lem's in David's Valley now with his middle sons. Jesse and his mother, Sharona, are left here in Beth-lehem with the youngest babes. Lem'll be glad to see you. No need tellin' him . . . no need explainin' about your dream. He'll know why you're leavin'. Why you must." Zadok involuntarily cast a glance toward Herodium.

"How will we thank you?" Mary asked.

"Come back to us! When the Butcher King is dead . . . come back to your family here in Beth-lehem!" Rachel cried as Mary, Yosef, and Yeshua hurried away down the road.

Herod's shriek of outrage shattered the crisp Jerusalem morning like a falling icicle shatters on stone. Sentries froze in place like statues. Servants suddenly remembered duties at the far end of the palace.

Confronting both Talmai and Hermes in his private chambers, Herod demanded in a marginally quieter tone, "Where? Where are they?"

The soldier's pallor and lack of emotion in his report expressed his conviction that he was as good as executed already. "Gone, Majesty. This morning I send my servant to Beit Kodesh to check on them."

"And?" Herod's voice was now controlled, but one look at the king's eyes and Talmai knew anger lurked dangerously close to erupting.

"The house servants said they left. All of them . . . and all their baggage and animals. As there had been no order to prevent it, they were allowed to leave unhindered. But they must be sorcerers, Majesty, or evil spirits! I swear I saw no one go out of there!"

Averting his eyes from the groveling, dissembling guard, Talmai took up the tale. "The watch at the Gate of the Essenes reports such a caravan was seen heading out on the road toward Beth-lehem. A troop of cavalry will certainly overtake them there."

Hermes struck his chest with a clenched fist to show his eagerness to do his master's bidding. "Send me, Majesty. I'll bring them all back!"

Herod considered, apparently weighing the pleasure of removing Hermes' head against the need to keep the whole matter out of the public discussion. "Go! But remember: it is not them we want—not really! It is the child! The child. He is the one we are after."

Yosef, Mary, and the baby had been gone less than an hour when a plan was decided upon by Zadok and Eliyahu.

"Eliyahu, you go t' Yerushalayim today. Pick up whatever news may be flowin' in the gutter, eh?"

Eliyahu agreed. "Yerushalayim's a rumor mill these days. I can stand in one place and hear a hundred different stories about what Herod is up to. Some say he's dying. Not one story will match the next."

Rachel added, "Or maybe you'll hear nothing at all. Maybe we've been worried for nothing."

Havila's expression betrayed her fears. "You know how it is. A new storm every day. Maybe soon enough Herod will forget about the baby and begin nailing up foreigners as spies again."

"The Magi may not be safe either . . . at least until they're out of the land. Aye." Zadok patted Eliyahu on the back. "Eliyahu, keep your ears open and your mouth shut."

It was almost sunset when Yosef led the donkey down the steep slope into the hidden enclave of David's Pasture. In the distance he recognized the twin boulders that marked the secret track to the south.

"Tonight we'll sleep here," Yosef told Mary. "A chance for you and the baby to rest. The journey from here will be long and hard."

Mary did not reply for a time. She had been strangely silent on the journey through the pass. "I would have taken them all with us if I could."

Yosef understood her concern. "We'll come back," he promised. "One day when it's safe, we'll bring him back."

Lem and his two middle sons emerged from their tent and hailed the family's arrival.

Blessed are you, O Adonai, who has led us safely thus far, Yosef prayed. *And blessed are you who causes your Salvation to flourish.*

Hermes' attempt to overtake the Magi was unsuccessful.

Talmai heard part of the report as he and the soldier trudged up a flight of stairs leading toward the roof of the palace. Herod had left instructions that the two men were to join him there as soon as Hermes returned to Jerusalem.

The king was already on the platform waiting for them. Though two guards flanked him at a respectful distance on either side, Herod stood with his hands atop the balustrade at the south-facing parapet.

The king was without his usual black wig. His white hair was unbound and hung down his back. His shoulders were hunched together and he was bent forward—whether with pain, cold, or in thought, Talmai did not venture to guess.

As Talmai and Hermes stepped closer, they saw Herod's jaw muscles working, as if he were chewing on something, gnawing at something. Because the king did not turn at their approach, Talmai and Hermes hesitated to disturb him.

Without even seeing them, Herod sensed their arrival, for he spoke: "You did not find them, did you, Hermes? Them or the child?"

"Majesty, I . . . they must be magicians of great power! They vanished without a trace. Rumors of their being in the village everywhere . . . men dressed in rich robes of foreign style . . . but no one actually saw where they went! They have disappeared off the face of the earth."

Herod nodded, raising a crooked finger to point in the direction of Beth-lehem. "I knew it was another plot. Find a child . . . call him Messiah . . . crown him king. A traitorous plot! We must root him out!"

Talmai nodded, waiting.

"They think avoiding me protects him, you see? So we must do something they do not expect!" The king finally turned to face Hermes, his gaze boring into the soldier's. "This is your last chance, you understand? I dreamed it all last night, even before I knew they had tricked me. This is what I want you to do: Go back to Beth-lehem tonight. Take a troop—no, three troops—of men."

Hermes stood silent, waiting for an explanation.

"Majesty?" Talmai queried.

Herod continued his reverie. "Every boy baby in Beth-lehem—no, that is not enough—every *male child* within the circle of Migdal Eder. Yes, that is it . . . all their lambs, eh? And when did they say these signs first appeared? A year ago? But I will not settle for that either! Go, Hermes. Put a cordon around Beth-lehem. Kill every boy age two and under.[125] Do it tonight!"

28

The torch-bearing units of Herod's soldiers under Hermes' command were all Samaritans and Idumeans, together with one column of Syrian cavalry. Herod's recent executions had cleared the officer ranks of any who harbored disloyalty to his service, but for the present operation the king wanted no misplaced sympathy by the inclusion of Jewish troops.

These warriors, battle hardened in skirmishes with the Nabateans and bloodied during caravan duty against brigands, knew only three things: They despised Jews. They were hated by them in return. And loyalty was rewarded.

They would not shrink from whatever service was required.

In a fold of the hills between Jerusalem and Beth-lehem, Hermes and his force waited only for the cavalry to return from scouting the roads. "No sign of those foreigners anywhere," the captain of the horsemen reported. "Not on the road to the coast or toward Hebron. We encountered one caravan of Egyptians coming up from across Jordan by way of Machaerus, but they'd met no one."

"Given us the slip, then." Hermes grunted. "Never mind. We have other work this night. Captain, I want half a dozen of your men on each road out of Beth-lehem, in case any Jews slip by us in the dark. You know what we're after."

The cavalry officer saluted and began calling out his troop disposi-tions. Several columns galloped off in the darkness.

Hermes turned his attention to the infantry. Each man was clad in a cuirass of plate armor protecting from shoulders to below the waist. Each wore a conical bronze helmet and carried an oblong shield dis-playing Herod's crest of a sturdy, many-branched tree.

And each bore at his left side a long sword, recently sharpened and perfectly oiled.

"Right, the rest of you. No nonsense. Four to a house. Two out-side to watch for runners. Two go in." Hermes paused and added with an audible sneer, "All Jewish shepherds hereabouts, so you'll have no trouble. Most sleeping out in the fields even. And no exceptions, under-stand? Two years and under, and if there's any question . . ."

Half the force would surround Beth-lehem to the west and half to the east. Hermes led the western troops himself. "When we meet up, I'll blow a trumpet. That'll be the signal."

Two files of torches snaked away into the hills around Beth-lehem like a pair of fiery serpents encircling the town.

Dan sat in the tub of warm water and played with the toy boat as Havila scrubbed his hair. By lamplight, Grandmother embroidered a vine on the hem of Eliyahu's best cloak. He would wear it during the Purim pageant when he played the role of King Ahasuerus in the megillah of Esther.

"My eyes." The old woman leaned closer to the light. "It's all I can do to see a stitch in broad day. And at night?" She frowned. "I'm wear-ing out, Havila!"

Cup by cup, Havila rinsed the soap from Dan's head. He played, content in the warm bath. "You know, Dan is such a quiet baby." Havila felt the child within her womb dancing. "Now this new one . . . he'll be like Sharona's boys, I'm afraid. Hanging from the rafters."

"Ah, well. High spirits must climb high. As long as they're healthy, I always say. True? Of course true."

In the distance, dogs barked, followed by an eerie, high-pitched wail that hung suspended on the night.

The wind?

Havila cocked her head to listen. "What was that?"

"I said, high spirits—"

"No . . . outside. A sound like . . . like a woman . . . keening."

"The wind."

"There's no wind tonight."

Howling echoed in the distance.

"Someone drunk at the caravansary."

Then Havila heard it again. Louder. The shriek of a woman. Then another and another. "No! . . . No! Grandmother! Listen!"

"My ears are as bad as my eyes."

A chill coursed through Havila. "Someone weeping, I think . . . Grandmother. Something has happened. On the ridge. Someone has died." She lifted Dan from the tub and wrapped him in a blanket. Her heart pounded as she quickly dressed the little boy.

"Died?" Grandmother made the sign against the evil eye and laid aside her needlework. She stood.

Havila, frozen in terror, gaped at the door.

A chorus of women's voices joined in grief. The clamor swelled and grew as it moved down the slope toward the synagogue and the house.

Grandmother straightened with resolve. She hissed the warning, "Blow out the lamp!"

"But what—?"

"Havila! Do as I say! The lamp . . . out. Keep Dan inside. Stay here! I'll go!"

Havila extinguished the flame. The room was dark as pitch.

The old woman opened the door a crack. An unnatural glow illuminated the village. The tumult of some unexplained horror swept into the house from the outside. Grandmother slipped out.

Havila placed the carrying sling around her neck and put Dan and the toy boat into it. He clung to her and the toy boat and began to cry. "Ma . . . ma!"

"Shhhhh, Dan. It's all right. Mama's with you. It's all right." She nuzzled him beneath her chin. Surely he felt the hammering of her heart.

Long moments passed before Grandmother returned. The old woman's voice pierced the darkness. "Havila! Soldiers! Herod's men! Torches! Swarming over the upper village! Killing! Take Dan!"

The long shriek of a woman confirmed Grandmother's words.

Havila began to cry. "But *why*? *Why*?"

"Go now! Run! Hide!"

"Where?"

"I'll distract them! Go! Take Dan!"

"O Adonai! Where? Where will we hide?"

Grandmother grasped Havila forcefully by the arms and propelled her, barefoot and without her cloak, into the cold night. "Run, Havila! Run with Dan and don't look back!"

The garish light of a hundred torches illuminated the ruthless onslaught against women and children taking place in the upper village . . . moving ever nearer the center.

"*Not my baby! Oh! No! Not . . .*"

"*Please! Kill me instead! Not Zeke!*"

"*No! He's only a baby! Have mercy!*"

The terrified voices of little ones now mingled with the cries of their mothers.

The freezing night did not penetrate Havila's consciousness. She glanced at the synagogue, dark and brooding against the night sky.

It was the first place of refuge. The first place the Herodian guards would look!

Havila began to run, mindless and without direction. *Where? Away! Anywhere!* The stones of the road tore at her feet.

Havila did not look back as she dashed through the narrow streets. *Run where? Hide where?*

Away! Away from the encroaching flames!

The center of the village was deserted.

The onslaught advanced.

Havila tore blindly on. She stumbled and fell beside David's Well. *Where can I hide him? Help me, God! Help me!*

She leaned against the stone for a moment. Dan, wailing, clung to her.

The well! David's Well! Havila leapt to her feet and tested the rope that held the goatskin bucket. Quickly she tied it off to the wood post.

"Dan! Little Dan! Listen to Mama! Listen! You must not make a sound!"

The little boy somehow comprehended his mother's command. Suddenly silent, he pressed himself nearer as though he wanted to vanish into her flesh and climb into her dark womb with the baby.

"Dan. Can you help Mama? You must be very, very quiet, Dan. Please, baby. Please. Hold tight!"

Clinging to Dan with one arm, Havila grasped the rope and slipped over the lip of the well. The keening of Beth-lehem's mothers followed her as she descended into the darkness.

Silent night. The forlorn echo of a sheepdog's bark roused Rachel as she dozed by the fire.

She felt lonely now that the little cottage behind the house was empty. The hollow ache had not left her all day. She missed Mary and the baby already, and though she would not admit it to Zadok, she had hoped and prayed the couple would remain in Beth-lehem. The blessing of their presence, the sense of peace and joy at their nearness, had departed with them.

Rached sighed as she relived the events of the last several weeks. She wanted to seal the story in her mind. One day, when Yeshua was grown and sitting upon David's throne in Jerusalem, she would recount it to Enoch, Samu'el, and Obi. The birth in the lambing cave! The proclamation of angels! The joy and acclamation in Beth David Synagogue on the day of Messiah's *Bris*! The arrival of the kings and princes and great men from distant lands.

Rachel looked over her little brood, sleeping like a pile of puppies. They were too young to remember any of it. The honor of Rachel and Zadok being asked to serve as *Kvatterin* and *Kvatter*! Now it all seemed far away somehow. The glory had departed, and once again their lives had shrunk to small and insignificant.

Leaning back in her chair, Rachel gazed up at bunches of lavender hanging in the shadowed rafters. Mary's favorite scent. Rachel frowned and wished she had sent more with her dear friend.

How long would it be before she saw them again? Where could Mary and Yosef go to hide from the long arm of Herod the Butcher King?

The toys Yosef had carved for the boys were spread out all across the floor. Enoch's blocks with Hebrew letters. The toy boat that every two-year-old received as a gift from baby Yeshua after the *Bris*. All were reminders that the One they had come to love so much was gone, and none could speak of where He was going.

Yosef had said they must leave for the safety of the baby. And for the safety of Beth-lehem. Rachel admitted that the village of shepherds was too close to Herodium and too close to Jerusalem for anyone to feel entirely safe. But who would touch the Lord's Anointed? Isn't that what the Scripture said?[126] Why should they fear a dissipated madman like Herod when Messiah lived among them?

Rachel wished Zadok would come home, but he was out with the sheep. She longed for company when she felt so low.

Hearing a faint cry from outside, Rachel focused her attention on the children. She noted nothing but the contented snuffling noises of sleeping toddlers. Her boys were tucked beneath fleeces. She ascribed the far-off sound to someone else's fretful infant. Sharona's perhaps? Or was it only a memory or the fragment of a dream?

Rachel redoubled her efforts at putting her thoughts in order. Most of all she wanted to remember everything she could about the holy family who had lived with them. It would not be long before the recollection would fade for Enoch, while Samu'el and Obi would never recall it at all.

Rachel would not permit that to happen. She intended to retell the events so often and in such detail that all three boys would grow into manhood believing the memories to be their own.

When King Messiah came into His own, He would remember them. Of that fact she was certain.

The frantic barking of a dog interrupted her reverie.

Then a distant cry. Human? More like a wail. Or perhaps a screech? Maybe a wild animal was loose among the lambs of Migdal Eder. Rachel had heard lions before . . . wolves and jackals too. Sometimes even a band of striped hyenas from the Sinai drifted this far north. They could wreak havoc among the flocks.

Almost immediately the noise was repeated. Then the howls multiplied and increased in volume, rising and falling, raising the hair on the back of Rachel's neck. She glanced toward the door. It was unbolted.

Unbolted! Where is Zadok? Why doesn't Zadok come home?

Rachel leapt upright in inexplicable terror. Her feet tangled in the wool coverlet that had been over her lap. She lurched toward the bar that served as the only lock and slammed it home.

Enoch stirred. "Mama?"

Enoch! Samu'el! Obi! These three were her whole life! Why was she afraid? Was God not a merciful God? Had they not walked with Messiah? borne Him in their arms? rejoiced that He had come? What was this unexplained terror that squeezed her heart as though it would be crushed?

"Mama?"

Enoch's verse came to her mind with a new and terrible implication: *And Enoch walked with God . . . and he was no more.*

"Mama? I'm having bad dreams."

"Oh, Enoch!" She could not move. Somehow she knew what was on the other side of the door . . . why the dog barked. She breathed, "Oh, Eternal . . . God! Merciful . . . oh no!"

The frenzied barking increased. A sharp yip, a whine, and a mournful yowl marked the end of the dog.

Rachel stared at the door in terror. So little separated her and the boys from the evil that flowed down like filthy water over the bright village.

From three points of the compass wails and shouts of terror reverberated through the previously peaceful night. Human cries: anger and outrage mingled with panic. What could it mean?

In the corner by the fireplace was Zadok's old shepherd's staff. Rachel seized it awkwardly, held it across her body, planting herself between the bedchamber opening and the exterior door.

The cries continued. . . .

"Help me! Help us!"

"Murder! Help . . . my babies!"

And then footsteps slapped on dirt pathways, echoing throughout the vale of Migdal Eder. Exclamations of pain. Shrieks of agony and anguish, such as Rachel had never heard before.

She recognized the cacophony of terror from her childhood imagination. The cries that must have gone up from the Hebrews when Pharaoh had killed all the boy babies, nearly destroying the infant lawgiver.[127] And the way she had always envisioned the first Passover night sounded when the Angel of Death slew the firstborn of the Egyptians.[128]

The patter of desperately running feet came nearer and nearer, directly toward her home.

Then a frenzied pounding at the door. "Let me in! Oh, merciful God! Rachel! Rachel! Please, Rachel, open the door! They're killing them all . . . all the babies! Let me in!"

Sharona's voice!

With trembling hands Rachel threw back the bolt.

Sharona lunged into the room and fell to the floor. She held her youngest baby, Zhi, in her arms. He was dead. Sharona's teeth were broken. She was bleeding from the ear. Her feet were bare—torn and bleeding.

Behind her was young Jesse. He sobbed uncontrollably. His tunic was streaked with blood. He carried the limp form of his second youngest brother.

Beyond them the light of the torches told the horrific tale.

Sharona babbled, "They broke . . . down . . . the door . . . two years old . . . two . . . and younger . . . slit Zhi's throat. Crushed Tobias' head . . . against the wall."

Jesse wailed, "I fought them, Rachel! Tried to stop them! They beat me . . . killed . . . killed . . . my brothers! Mama said . . . we must warn . . ." The boy slumped into unconsciousness.

"Herod's men. They're coming!" Sharona shrieked. "Killing all the babies two and under! Your . . . three. Run! They're coming, Rachel! Take them . . . hide! Hide your sons! Before it's too late."

29

The shepherds of Migdal Eder were in the fields for the shift change. One night each week those who had performed only daytime duties traded duty watch with those who kept vigil in the dark. The two groups stayed together by the watch fires for an hour. Time enough to swap gossip. The herdsmen also passed on information about which lambs were ailing and which ewes needed their hooves treated with powdered copper mingled with vinegar.

Bear Dog's ears pricked upright.

"What is it y' hear, eh?" Zadok questioned.

The animal glanced up at his master, whined, then stretched out his neck as if straining to recapture a distant noise.

"Maybe it's the angels come again," one herdsman ventured with a hopeful chuckle.

Zadok opened a horn bottle stoppered with a whittled wooden peg: mustard oil for sheep stomach ailments. "Messiah's gone from us now. We'll not see the like again before he's a man grown. Had our bit of excitement, eh?"

Bear Dog jumped; all four legs stiffened at the scent of some approaching predator. The ruff of his neck rose, and a growl emerged from deep in his throat. He stared east, toward the king's fortress.

"Somethin's out there, right enough. Not angels," Zadok murmured. "Jackals, maybe?"

The distant broken spike of Herodium jutted against the sky like the shard of an upraised dagger. Normally dark and brooding, tonight it was ablaze with light.

Now the cries that had roused the sheepdog reached the ears of the shepherds as well.

They were human cries.

"Idumean raiders?" someone ventured. "Could be why Herod's men are on the alert."

Then the night's gloom was broken by scores of flickering lights, much nearer than Herodium . . . and in the direction of Beth-lehem.

"Torches! Torches in the village," Zadok said. "Whoever they are, they're near our homes." Then he issued an order: "Unmarried men, stay with the flocks! The rest of you, take up your staffs and follow me!"

The shepherds of Migdal Eder needed no urging. As one man, they sped toward whatever bandits had descended on their village.

Broomstick in her hands, Grandmother stood fiercely blocking the entrance to the empty house as though a dozen children were within.

She knew she could not fight and win. Tonight she would die, but she had a plan. Delay the jackals! Delay three murderers searching for nothing at all! Give the mothers of Beth-lehem and their babies time to run, time to hide.

Three drunken soldiers, bloodied swords drawn, eyed the old woman with amusement. "Move aside, old lady! We're here on the king's errand."

Grandmother spat. She would make the vipers believe a dozen babies lurked within. Babes in the rafters. Babies beneath the flagstones. Babies hiding in the cold oven. Babies escaping down a secret tunnel. After they killed her, they would search the house. Perhaps for hours. They would tear the place apart and find . . . nothing! No one.

Grandmother roared and threatened them with the broom. "You

devils! You brood of Satan. You will not pass by me while this old woman still breathes!" Over her shoulder she shouted instructions to the imaginary occupants of the house. "Hide, babies! Don't let them find you. Hide yourselves in the secret place old Grandmother showed you."

Then, shaking the stick at the villains, she spouted, "You snakes! You adders of Eden! By my own blood you shall not find or harm my children within. You will not enter the rabbi's house and harm all those women and children who have taken refuge under the roof and under the floor of a righteous man."

The oldest of the trio extended his bloodstained hand. "Please, old woman. We've work to do, and you're in the way."

Grandmother struck him with the broom handle. "Back! Get back!" Then she shouted into the house. "Run and hide, children! The secret tunnel. Beneath the stones. Close the trapdoor. Keep it closed tight, and they'll never find you unless they rip out the stones of the floor!"

The middle soldier, his face spattered with gore, crossed his arms and said to his captain, "We should just kill the old hag and be done with it. You see what she's doin? There's young ones within. You heard her shoutin' at them. Hidin' 'neath the pavements, they are. Creepin' themselves into a secret underground tunnel. Clever creatures, these Jews. Secret tunnels. I've heard of such a thing. Run all the way from here to Jerusalem, they say."

"Aye," concurred the man on the right. "Kill her."

"Aye," Grandmother snarled. "Kill me. Snakes! Kill me and the secret dies with me!"

"We'll be here all night pullin' up the flagstones."

The soldier in the center nodded in agreement.

He grasped the old woman's stick and jerked her toward him. Fragile bones shattered as she hit the ground. He kicked her, rolling her faceup. And in case she wasn't already dead, he ended any opposition with one final thrust of his short sword.

Torches! There were torches moving around Zadok's house. As he and Bear Dog sprinted toward home, the shepherd saw men going in and out of his door.

Rachel! His boys!

What was happening?

He ran faster, pelting over the stones.

He was alone, except for the dog. Zadok's house was too far outside the village. The other herdsmen, immersed in their own fears, had diverted along other paths.

Shepherds who defended their flocks against marauding bears or leopards seldom had time to call for help or wait for assistance or plan strategy before launching rescues. Nor was it in Zadok's character to do anything other than plunge headlong where his family's safety was concerned.

Nothing else mattered.

Zadok spied at least a quartet of marauders backlit by the light from his own open doorway. Perhaps there were even more inside the cottage that he could not see. The fact that Zadok was outnumbered by at least four to one did not matter in the least or make him hesitate even one step.

The flaring torches gleamed off shining metal helmets. Soldiers, then. The attackers were not desert raiders aiming for plunder or slaves.

Judging by the terrified screams erupting from the village, their mission was something far, far worse.

Why were no cries for help coming from Zadok's home?

When the shepherd swept out of the darkness there were only two men left beside the doorway, and both had their backs toward him. Wielding his staff with both hands, Zadok raised it high over his right shoulder as if swinging an axe to fell a tree.

The adversary on the left turned toward the onrushing footsteps. He was a Herodian trooper.

Zadok's blow, aimed at the man's head, missed that target when his opponent jerked aside. So the blow landed on the enemy's collarbone instead, smashing it.

The man screamed and staggered backward, dropping his sword and falling unconscious.

His companion lifted a sword to hack at Zadok's unprotected right shoulder. Bear Dog, arriving one second after his master's assault, sunk his teeth into the second opponent's sword arm, just above the wrist. The man with the torch cried out and danced in a circle, trying to shake the animal loose. Bear would not relinquish his hold, instead letting all his weight dangle from the wounded flesh. The soldier flailed at his own arm with the torch to try to free himself.

He managed to singe Bear's coat, but a second later the fire-hardened butt of Zadok's staff plunged into his midsection, knocking him to the ground and rupturing something inside him.

Two down.

Zadok arrived at his own doorway without a wound.

And was stunned by what he saw there.

A woman's body lay motionless on the floor. Beside her was a child.

Propped in a corner, his face streaked with blood, was Lem's boy Jesse. Across Jesse's lap was the gore-covered figure of another toddler.

Rachel! His boys! Dead or badly wounded! Could it be?

Zadok went berserk. He screamed and swung his staff in a flurry of blows.

The two warriors inside the house, warned by the commotion outside, were ready for him. One was armed with a lance, the other with a short sword.

Zadok lunged toward the lance bearer. He knocked aside a thrust of the weapon with the tip of his staff, then struck his opponent in the mouth. Blood and teeth erupted.

The other adversary slashed at Zadok's left arm. Zadok dropped his arm to avoid a direct blow, but the tip caught and made a gash from elbow to wrist.

The lance wielder aimed a jab toward Zadok's side. "Dirty Jew," the Samaritan cursed. "I'll stick you good."

Dashing under the thrust, snarling and teeth snapping, Bear plunged toward the enemy's groin. Suddenly the lance was purely defensive, being used to keep the animal away.

Zadok caught another downward hack of a sword on his staff. Blood running out of his sleeve dripped from his fingertips and made his grip uncertain. He felt the strength ebbing from his left hand.

With Bear still occupying the other enemy, Zadok used the greater length of his staff to parry blows from the sword. As long as Zadok received no more injuries to his hands or arms, he could jab at his opponent's face from a safe distance. Sooner or later the chance for a disabling strike would present itself. Zadok had felled jackals with blows to the head.

But he never heard the approach of the fifth trooper.

Bear Dog tried to warn him. The faithful animal jerked around and barked toward the door.

The lance man struck. The triangular spearhead stabbed Bear in the ribs.

Zadok, alerted to the new danger, swung about, but now the extra reach of the wooden pole was a disadvantage. The tip of his staff collided with the stonewall, slowing his turn.

The delay was only a fraction of a second . . . but it was too much.

His staff was out of position. The shepherd could not defend himself from a sword blow already aimed at his head. The edge of the iron blade sliced into forehead, eye, and cheekbone.

Zadok collapsed, and his senses fled.

The straw was clean, cut in the uplands of Judea last fall and bundled with twine. The shocks awaiting use, preserved from the damp, stood within the far recesses of the lambing cave. On mucking-out days bundles were cut and spilled into a big, fragrant heap to be forked into the stalls and pens. Yet none of the harvesters or shepherds could possibly have suspected the use to which the straw would be put this night.

Nestled under a pile of pale yellow stalks, lying on the stone floor, Rachel cradled Samu'el and Obi. Enoch lay snuggled alongside in an almost tangible darkness.

How tight was too tight to hold them? Would squeezing Samu'el make him cease fussing or cause him to cry out in protest?

"Dark," Enoch exclaimed.

Trying to keep her voice calm, Rachel whispered cheerfully, "It's called the quiet game, you see? We keep as still as mice. We don't talk, we don't move, and we stay here until it's . . . until your abba comes and finds us. Then we go home."

"Papa coming?"

"Papa will come. Show me how still and how quiet you can be. Right now, Enoch."

Rachel was certain her flight into the darkness had not been observed. She was equally certain that Herod's men would not leave this place unsearched.

Rachel had extinguished every lamp, hoping that the butchers would not remember the entrance to the lambing cave. Beyond that strategy, Rachel counted on the noises of ewes and lambs to cover any stray human baby sounds.

The goal was to exterminate baby Yeshua—Rachel was certain of that fact. Not knowing which boy child was the Messiah, Herod was taking no chances and was killing them all. How foolish she had been to try to persuade Mary and Yosef to stay in Beth-lehem! Oh! If only she had fled with them!

How much Herod must fear the power of Messiah if he would do this to the infants of Beth-lehem!

Obi sneezed. It was just an infant sneeze, but to Rachel's intensely tuned hearing it was as loud as an ocean wave breaking on the shore.

Samu'el was getting cranky too, tiring of the game. When he brushed a bit of straw out of his eyes, twice as much went down the collar of his tunic. Soon he wriggled with an irresistible itch.

"Be still! Not much longer, my lambs." She scratched Samu'el's itch with one hand, tickled Enoch's back and neck with the other. If only they would go to sleep! "Not much longer. Papa will come."

Rachel prayed silently that Zadok would come. Oh, if only she could hear his voice. Run to him! He would know what to do.

The tramp of marching feet approached the cave entrance.

"Papa?" Enoch tried to rise.

Rachel pulled him down. "Shhh. The game. Be very quiet now."

"You three! Search in there!" a gruff voice ordered.

In a barely audible tone, lips pressed first to Enoch's and then to Samu'el's ears, Rachel whispered, "Now! Most quiet of all! Not a word!"

Even beneath the mantle of straw the interior of the cave blazed with light. "Why don't we just put the torch to this whole place?" a Samaritan-accented voice said. "Roust out any as is hiding here and get us some nice roast mutton too."

Another laughed. "Why not? Stinking Jews anyway. Burn the whole village for all I care, starting here."

No! They cannot mean it! They must not! To be burned alive! O Adonai! Be merciful!

The crackling torches drew nearer and nearer. "There's a nice heap of straw. One good thrust in there and up she goes."

It was dark and cramped in the well. Havila's labored breathing was like a roaring fire in her ears, the pounding of her pulse like the ringing of hammer on stone.

Nothing shut out the noise of the harvest of death being reaped in the village. Children screamed and cried for their mothers to save them. Babies bleated like lambs at the slaughter, then fell silent.

"No, don't! Please, don't!"

"My baby!"

"Don't hurt him!"

"Oh, why? Why?"

When the terrified shrieks of Beth-lehem's children fell silent, the lament of mothers increased.

Hysterical, high-pitched wailing and guttural sobs mingled but never subsided altogether.

The clash of metal on metal was met with cries of pain as villagers fought back. What use were sticks and clubs against armored and well-trained soldiers? What could wooden shepherd's staffs do against iron and bronze?

Dan squirmed and fussed so much in the harness around Havila's neck that she feared he would fall into the water and be drowned. Clinging to the end of the cord used to draw the water, she braced her back against the damp stones and shifted her weight.

"Go to sleep, baby. Please!" she pleaded. "Mother needs you to go to sleep."

Improbably, the toddler obliged. His eyelids drooped, and his head bobbed forward on Havila's chest.

At the same moment the baby in Havila's belly awoke. It was only a month until her due date. What if all this exertion brought on her labor?

The muscles of Havila's arms and shoulders spasmed and knotted. Her hands were locked like claws on the rope. If she could not fall, neither could she climb out without help.

The killing went on.

Shouts just above her head made Havila drop her face lest she be seen. Swords crashed together as blows were exchanged. A blade clanged against the stones of the well, scattering sparks across the opening.

Havila closed her eyes as she heard a man call out with pain, then fall silent. A Herodian officer spoke above the well. Havila recognized the voices as belonging to Hermes, Herod's guard captain.

He praised his soldiers: "Good work! Off you go! Over that way. Run them down! Don't let any escape."

Fists thumped against bronze breastplates. Hobnailed boots crunched gravel underfoot. The warriors receded one pace . . . two . . . three.

Havila breathed more easily. Dan woke up with a start and a lurch, whimpering at the dark and the cold and the tension in his mother's body.

Havila stiffened. Surely no one could have heard that cry! So tiny! So thin! Less than a bleating newborn lamb!

"Just a moment!" Havila heard Hermes order. "Bring that torch here."

There was a tug on the rope, as if someone was testing it . . . feeling the extra weight.

Havila could not let go. Could not manage to free herself to drop into the water. Better to chance drowning, if only . . .

A torch was thrust over the lip of the well. Its flames reflected in the pool below and glistened on the moist stones.

"Ha!" someone snorted triumphantly.

Dan began to cry.

"One, two, three, heave!"

Havila wriggled, throwing herself from side to side. She had to wedge herself in a crevice. Make them come down after her. Help would come. It must!

A cubit at a time Havila was dragged out of the well. Rough hands laid hold of her arms, scraping her belly across the stones before throwing her to the ground.

"In the sling! Get him!"

Havila was rolled over. She clung so fiercely to Dan that when he was lifted she rose as well. Evil delight flared in the face of the Samaritan trooper. Clutching Dan left Havila no way to defend herself.

The trooper's hand slammed into her face, knocking her back to the ground. She hit her head on a stone. The last image in her conscious mind was Dan, held up by one leg like captured prey. The face of Hermes was jubilant as he smashed the head of the child against the rock rim of the watering trough, then tossed the body into the depths of David's Well.

They were leaving! By the bleating of lambs and the frantic bawling of bereaved ewes, Rachel could tell that Herod's men had turned from murder to plunder.

Another moment more and she and her babies would be safe.

Another moment more!

Obi cried out. He had absorbed the tension in Rachel's body until his own tiny soul was coiled as tightly as hers . . . and he burst into a full-throated, yelping wail.

"No! Shh, no!" Rachel urged . . . but it was too late.

"There's summat back there," one of the soldiers shouted. "That's no lamb, that ain't."

There was a heavy tread on the straw. A gate slammed open. Sheep bleated as they were cuffed out of the way.

How many were there? Could Rachel fight them? Could she escape by climbing over the pens and running into the darkness of the hillside?

But how could she carry all three?

"Well, what's here?"

Rachel heard a sinister chuckle.

"I know a way to find out," was the reply.

A lance head hissed through the straw like a hot stone dropped into water.

Rachel scooted toward the back of the enclosure, dragging Enoch and Obi after her.

Another thrust, nearer this time.

Obi squalled again. When Rachel clamped her hand over his mouth, it made him angry and he yelled louder.

Another jab of the spear missed Rachel's arm by inches.

She reached toward Samu'el to tug him toward her . . . and saw a spearhead plunge into his chest.

Blood fountained. His eyes looked into hers, then faded.

"Oh, ho!" one of the soldiers exulted. "Got one that time. Bet there's more."

Enoch under one arm and Obi under the other, Rachel erupted from the straw.

Throwing Enoch over one fence, Rachel shouted, "Run! Run and hide!" Then she attacked the nearest trooper. Though he laughed at her rising from the straw, the fury of her assault backed him into a gate. With one hand she grappled for control of his sword while she clung to Obi with the other.

When the soldier tried to club her, Rachel sank her teeth into his hand. When he knocked her sideways, she kicked at him and kept on kicking and biting while he yelled for help.

Instead someone seized Obi from behind and tugged at him.

"No!" Rachel screamed. "Please, no!"

"Look-et here! Only got one arm."

"Hack it off, then. Make him match."

The other soldiers laughed at Rachel's pleas.

"Oh no you don't," shouted one as he seized Enoch and tossed the boy in the air. "Here—you throw him for me. Betcha I can catch him on my lance tip on the first try."

The wounded soldier slammed his fist into Rachel's temple. She fell awkwardly against the wall. Her vision spinning, she still tried to get up, but another killer grabbed her arms from behind and pinned them through the fence.

They made her watch as they slaughtered first Obi and then Enoch.

And they laughed as they took the stolen sheep and left the cave.

It was pitch-black. Yosef lay awake in the tent. They were safe here for the time being. No one but a fool would follow them along the narrow mountain trail after dark. Yet some unreasonable apprehension gripped him.

Outside, the flocks began to stir. The frightened bleating of lambs was met with the barking of Lem's dog.

Mary asked, "Are you awake, Yosef?"

"Yes. Long time. I don't know what it is. Zadok told me once that jackals won't enter this valley. No predators."

"But there's something . . . something happening," Mary whispered urgently. "I feel it. I'm afraid."

Baby Yeshua awoke with a start and began to wail.

"What is it?" Mary crooned. "Oh! My love! My heart . . . what's wrong?"

Yosef sat up. Putting on his shoes, he stepped outside.

Lem was already up, patrolling the verge of the pasture as his dog ran ahead.

Yosef looked into the sky. The clouds parted briefly and the light of a baleful yellow moon glared through. A shadow drifted across its face.

What is it? What is it, O Eternal? You who made the stars, the heavens and the earth, and everything in them. What do you want me to hear?

In the far distance a high-pitched cry, a shriek like the voice of a woman in anguish, resounded against the stones, echoing a hundred times.

Across the field, Lem paused midstride and did not move again.

So he had heard it too.

"Yosef!" The shepherd was clearly disturbed. "What is it?"

Behind Yosef from the tent the infant's wail increased in volume and intensity. Mary called, "Yosef! Something terrible has happened. I am sure of it. The baby won't be comforted."

Lem cried, "Yosef? Was it an earthquake? Did you feel anything?"

"I don't know," Yosef returned. But the shaking of an ancient prophecy rumbled deep within his soul: *"A voice is heard in Ramah . . . the voice of Rachel crying for her children . . . for they are no more."*[129]

"It is done, my lord Herod. As you commanded," Hermes reported to the king.

"You are sure?" Herod said. "You killed him? No mistake?"

"No question," Hermes returned. "By my count, seventy boys in all. All age two or less. Some others too, but that's just because they got in the way. In a place as small as that mudhole of a village there can't be any more. We rooted them out of barns and even fished one out of a well. No, I'm sure of it. Whoever he was, he's dead now."

"Good. Good! And no one will dare protest! I will crucify anyone who even talks about this! Do you hear me, Talmai? I want that word to go out all over. Any repeating of this is treason—malicious treason—and punished by death. No one carries tales anywhere."

"Now that my Samaritans have their blood up, Majesty, they won't object to killing a few adult troublemakers too," Hermes offered.

"No need," Herod returned. "Now I can sleep well again. I—" A spasm jerked the king sideways and he clutched at his belly. Cold sweat broke out on his forehead and his breath came in gasps. Levering himself upright, the king waved away Talmai's offer of assistance. "It is nothing. A good . . . night's sleep. With such good news, I know that is all I need."

The route along the shoreline of the Dead Sea was treacherous. The air, thick with sulfur and the smell of the tar oozing from the ground, gave the night a hellish feel. The trail was terribly uneven, and there was always danger of breaking through salt-crusted patches into holes beneath. The pace was painfully slow.

Melchior wondered at the wisdom of suggesting they escape this way. When others voiced their concerns, he maintained a brave front, but inwardly he questioned why he had spoken so strongly, with so much assurance, about this choice.

Even as the creeping progress helped the riders avoid some dangers, it created others. If they were not safely over the border into Nabatea by the next daybreak they would have to find a canyon in which to hide. King Herod must know they were not returning to him as he had ordered; by now his patrols must be scouring the highways for them.

This time no diplomatic considerations would keep their shoulders connected to their heads.

They had almost rounded the far end of the inland sea when Melchior heard riders coming fast behind them.

The others heard it too.

"Shall we spur on?" Kagba asked. "Separate? Lose the pursuit in the dark?"

The group milled in confusion.

Once more Melchior surprised himself. "Not me," he said. "I won't leave Old Balthasar or Esther. If the rest of you wish to try it, go ahead."

"No," Perroz concluded firmly. "We have come this far together. We have seen the King . . . together. Whatever happens now, we will face it together as well."

There was not long to wait. Two dozen riders cantered into view, separating into columns that surrounded the Magi and cut off escape.

Then their black-robed captain arrived.

"So, scholar," Zamaris said, addressing Melchior. "I knew you'd take this route. I studied a map as you study the heavens and knew this would be your choice."

"And now you take us to Herod and collect your reward," Melchior remarked bitterly. "You could at least let Balthasar and Esther go."

"Without you? She never would!" Zamaris replied with a laugh. "My lord Talmai has ordered me back to Bathyra . . . but he left the choice of route up to me. Prince Aretas—" Zamaris addressed the young Nabatean—"you would not object to an escort as far as the border of your country . . . if your leader here, the scholar, agrees."

As they rode, Zamaris drew up next to Old Balthasar. "Tell me of the new King. I know you found him. I see it written plainly on your face. Tell me everything. When he comes into his own, he will make a better master than the Idumean dog. And since the scholar—and his wife, your granddaughter—will doubtless serve at the court of Anointed One, I must continue my education right now."

Epilogue

Written upon the 50th anniversary of our escape
from the Butcher King, Herod.
Final Journal Entry of Melchior, Chief Astronomer of Parthia
For my children and grandchildren

To sum up:

Little Enoch, son of Zadok and Rachel, walked with God . . . and he and his brothers were no more on this earth.

The flight of the holy family into Egypt, our escape from Herod and the terrible death of that evil king—all these things are a matter of historical record. The scientific data of the signs in the heavens is indisputable and exactly as I have recorded it.

On the 50th anniversary of our escape from Herod's vile power I write now to you, who are beloved offspring of myself and Esther, my wife of 50 years.

All my life I have tried to understand the mystery of the Almighty and Eternal God, who chose to be born among us to show His great love for us.

There is no written description of Yeshua the Messiah that the reality of His presence and His mighty works will not eclipse. His coming was as though we gathered all the stars of the heavens and held them for a moment in our arms.

The birth of Messiah in that small village is the hinge upon which the gates of the heavens and all history turn.

Because of His birth to save men from sin, the wrath of great evil was aroused. And so it was that the enemy of our souls heard a baby's cry from the manger and sought to put an end to God's plan for our salvation.

Roaring from the rim of his abyss, Satan turned and destroyed the innocent, the vulnerable, the kind, and the holy.

Though the story of Beth-lehem is legendary, it is no myth.

It was, in that dark hour, as it has always been when light threatens the darkness. It is written that when the people of Israel were slaves in Egypt, Pharaoh, like Herod, killed the two-year-old sons of the Jews.[130] Only Moses, the deliverer, escaped.[131] The children die first when Satan is aroused. Always. Countless little ones have been lost every day since evil first began to prowl the earth and seek out those easily devoured. Some die a quick death by violence or illness. Others perish inch by inch of neglect and the absence of love. These too are Beth-lehem's children.

The cry of Rachel resounds in the heart of every man and woman who love a child.

The cost of our salvation? Much more than the price of a single lamb sacrified on the altar of the Temple in Jerusalem.

The shepherds of Beth-lehem understood.

Yosef understood.

Mary understood. Much later, as Old Simeon prophesied, the sword of sorrow pierced her gentle heart as well.[132] She who protected His brow from a snowflake was destined to stand at the foot of the cross and watch Him suffer and die.[133]

For this purpose He was sent from heaven. Born of the virgin, He entered the world of fallen man to live a sinless life, to be crucified, to rise again from death to life—all for our redemption.

Yeshua, Firstborn Son of the Most High God, was born among the lambs set aside for sacrifice. He was cared for by those shepherds and their families who raised lambs whose innocent blood paid for the sins of men.

The battle between Light and Darkness began long before Messiah was born in Beth-lehem's lambing cave.

The cup of the New Covenant was sealed by the blood of Yeshua, the Lamb of God, who died on the cross.

Now the cries of Beth-lehem's lost generation resound in the whole earth as a shout of victory! The crucified son of Mary, Son of God, stepped from the tomb and is alive! So too those sons of Beth-lehem live eternally with Him in His heavenly kingdom. They, who were the pure and innocent children of Israel, will be raised from death to rule with Him in Jerusalem!

Many who are yet unborn in distant lands will call upon the name of Yeshua: "Lord, I seek your face! Cover my sin with the blood of your sacrifice! Save me! Heal me! Forgive me!"

Those who ask Him for mercy and salvation will never die.[134] All who call upon His wonderful name will joyfully stand upon the earth and see evil and sorrow conquered at last![135]

My children, the story of Beth-lehem must end here. The human mind has its limits, after all.

Who does not look up at the vast heavens with those of us who search the heavens for a sign? Who does not wonder how such glory came to be?

Who does not mourn with Zadok and Rachel and Eliyahu and Havila and the others who sit shiva beside Beth-lehem's graves? Who does not wonder why such sorrows continue upon the earth?

Who does not perceive evil in the world and ask, "How much longer until Messiah returns as Prince of Peace? When will the Righteous King sit on David's throne and reign over all the world?"

In the silence of Beth-lehem, Rachel, childless, asks,
"When, when, will the Lord call me to Him
and smile gently into my eyes
and wipe away my tears?"

Zadok holds her in his arms and sighs.
"All our tears he'll wipe away."

Carried on the wind a voice from heaven whispers,
Soon. Soon.

And all the congregation cry,
"Omaine!"

See, the Sovereign Lord comes with power,

and His arm rules for Him.

See, His reward is with Him,

and His recompense accompanies Him.

He tends His flock like a shepherd:

He gathers the lambs in His arms

and carries them close to His heart;

He gently leads those that have young.

ISAIAH 40:10-11

Digging Deeper into
SIXTH COVENANT

Dear Reader,

Imagine that you are a shepherd or a shepherd's wife, living in the humble little village of Beth-lehem. Your life is simple. Some would even call it meager, because you don't have, or expect, any of the finer things in life. You see, in Beth-lehem, there's not much more than small houses, fields of sheep, and lambing caves. But that doesn't matter because you are surrounded by what's most important to you—your beloved family members, complete with a flock of children to bring you joy, and villagers who are dear friends.

Six miles away is one of the wonders of the world—the ostentatious city of Jerusalem. Yet only the shepherds who drive the sacrificial lambs to the Temple go there routinely. You are happy just to live out your existence in Beth-lehem, away from the eyes of the evil Herod, king of the Jews. His very name makes you shudder and hold your loved ones closer. You've heard the stories of what happens to those he considers a threat to his throne.

At night you rock your babies to sleep and gaze up at the light of the stars. You ask one question of the heavens: "When, Lord, will you come to us?" Like all of your people, you long for the Messiah to descend to earth and make all wrongs right.

Then, after so many years of waiting, the Messiah does arrive. But not in Jerusalem, where you had expected! No, He arrives in your humble village, in the form of a tiny, frail baby, born in a lambing cave, surrounded by bleating sheep. Ah, the wonder of it! The fulfillment of all the prophecies of old—announced by the miraculous conjunction of the stars!

But can this be right? Can the long-awaited Son of God truly be "among you"? Have you read the signs in the heavens correctly? And, if so, why would the King of all kings choose to arrive as a baby, in a manger? And why in Beth-lehem, when He could have had His pick of anywhere in the world?

Your mind swirls with questions, stirs with hope. *Can it be true?*

Little do you know that, six miles away, the eye of Herod has turned toward your village. And that his mind, too, is swirling with questions. . . .

When you think of Yeshua, the baby in the manger, what questions come to your mind? Do you believe Him to be God, or is He just a good man, who helped others and performed tricks like a master magician? Is He truly the One who fulfills ancient prophecies—God come to earth—or are the "matches" to prophecy merely coincidences that just happened to fall neatly in line?

What you believe about the birth of Yeshua affects everything about your life now . . . and your eternity.

Following are six studies. You may wish to delve into them on your own or share them with a friend or a discussion group. They are designed to take you deeper into the answers to questions such as:

- Are there really messages in the stars?
- Was Yeshua just a baby—or God in human form?
- Is there a plan for the universe—and your life?
- What does it mean to truly "walk with God"?
- What are you waiting and hoping for?
- What is the greatest longing of your heart?

Through *Sixth Covenant*, may the promised Messiah come alive to you . . . in more brilliance than ever before.

REVEALED BY THE HEAVENS?

"I and my colleagues—Melchior of Ecbatana and the others from all the wide world—have studied signs in the heavens that confirm this prophecy has come to pass. It has been fulfilled. Messiah has been born, and we go to Yerushalayim to seek him."

There was uproar in the synagogue. A babble of voices argued this conclusion, until Balthasar waved them to silence. He motioned for Melchior to stand and once again recite the celestial wonders of the previous year.

—BALTHASAR (P. 176)

Do you believe that messages could be written in the heavens? that the stars themselves could reveal truth—things that Someone larger than us would want us to know? Why or why not?

_____

_____

_____

What is the difference between worshipping the heavens and worshipping the creator of the heavens? Explain.

_____

_____

_____

For nearly a year, Melchior, a court astronomer, and Balthasar, his mentor, had observed a series of heavenly events that had never before been recorded. Sign had followed sign until both were convinced that the long-awaited Messiah of prophecy had been born. But is it possible to prove such a thing in the movement of the stars?

READ

Nine months previously though, Mars—called by the Jews Ma'Adim, or The Adam—had nestled close to the heart of The Virgin, next to Porrima, The Star of Atonement.

It was a sign, Old Balthasar had said. It was a reminder that the One True God, Yahweh, had not forgotten His covenants with His people.

And that had been only the beginning of the wonders.

Since then Jupiter—which the Jews named Tzadik, The Righteous—had carried on a complex dance with Saturn—Shabbatai, The Lord of the Sabbath. The two planets had combined and recombined three times between May and December. What was more, those two bright lights spent all three seasons preceding this winter enmeshed in the sign of The Two Fish. The Two Fish, Old Balthasar instructed, was where events related to the Jews were written in the sky.

Nor was the triple conjunction of Jupiter and Saturn the sum of all the remarkable occurrences. Indeed, sign had followed sign, including an eclipse of The Lord of the Sabbath by the Holy Spirit, the moon.

To Old Balthasar, himself a Jew, and Melchior, a Gentile follower of Yahweh, God of the Jews, the parade of sights in the heavens foretold a momentous event. "A Messiah, a Deliverer, will be born to the Jews, and his coming will bless all the nations," Balthasar had taught his protégé. . . .

Old Balthasar had set out on a quest to meet the heaven-sent King.

They had already traversed the Zagros Mountains and the Plains of Mesopotamia. Then here, just before midnight, as The Righteous and The Lord of the Sabbath were setting, a miraculous vision, surpassing all previous ones, occurred. Low in the west a third evanescent star had appeared between the two planets—a star brighter than either, bright as a flame of fire. Old Balthasar likened the vision to the fire of Yahweh appearing between the cherubim atop the Ark of the Covenant.

"Messiah has been born. He's alive *now*," asserted the older man.

Their traveling companion, a magoi of the Zoroastrian faith from the Far East, Gaspar by name, concurred.

Melchior did not know enough Jewish Scripture to vouch for that claim himself, but he did not need to. The golden light in tonight's sky had been the culmination of the year's revelations. It must be true. The predictions of Mosheh the Lawgiver and those of the prophets Dani'el, Isaias, and others aligned with the signs in the heavens.

It had to be so!

—PP. 14–15

ASK

If you saw *one* of these signs with your own eyes, what would that say to you? If you saw *all* of these signs with your own eyes, what would they— combined—say to you?

_____

_____

_____

Would you believe these connections to be coincidence or the fulfillment of thousands of years of prophecies? Why?

_____

_____

_____

READ

"So, storyteller, begin!" Zamaris commanded.

For the next hour Melchior recited the tales of the signs in the sky. . . . Melchior concluded by referring to the miraculous star that had appeared ever so briefly at the end of Hanukkah.

"So all of you—Jew and Parthian, Ethiopian and Armenian—you're all stargazers? I put no stock in it myself, but they say Caesar has astrologers on call day and night. Charlatans, I expect."

Melchior's blood began to boil at the accusation. A barbed reply formed on his lips before Balthasar waved him to silence and spoke. "Have you not heard, Lord Zamaris: *'A star will come out of Jacob'*? Astrologers say they can read the future in the stars. Nonsense or evil . . . take your choice. Either way, astrology is a tool of the Adversary to lead men from the truth. No. What we seek is confirmation of promises written in Torah. It is said the Almighty speaks his word in three places: in nature, in Torah, and in the life of Messiah. It is that Living Word we are seeking. We have seen his star in the east and are come to worship him."

—PP. 152–153

Rachel lay down and gazed at the bunches of lavender in the rafters. She tried to sort out her questions.

Mary had not been surprised to hear that angels had sung about the birth of her child. What mystery did Mary comprehend that no one else grasped?

—P. 36

News that angels had appeared to Beth-lehem's shepherds was greeted by Mordechai, proprietor of the inn, with ridicule. He wiped his greasy hands on his apron and sneered at his thirteen-year-old daughter as she told him the rumor. "Angels, eh?"

"So they say. A huge host of angels! I heard all about it at the souk when I bought the cabbages."

"Huh! Dim-witted child that you are, you believe every word of it. Angels? Appeared to Zadok and Lem and the others? . . . Huh! Drunk. All of them. Last night of Hanukkah. They was in their cups a bit, I'd say! Heavenly visions of angels indeed!"

—P. 36

After Jesus was born in Beth-lehem in Judea, during the time of King Herod, Magi from the east came to Jerusalem and asked, "Where is the One who has been born King of the Jews? We saw His star in the east and have come to worship Him."

When King Herod heard this he was disturbed, and all Jerusalem with him.
—MATTHEW 2:1-3

ASK
Which of these people most closely resemble you in your views toward "heavenly things"? Explain.

- Zamaris
- Balthasar

- Rachel
- Mary
- Mordechai
- Herod

_____

_____

_____

What's the difference between astrology and what Balthasar claims to be seeking?

_____

_____

_____

How might the Almighty speak His word in nature? in the Bible? in the life of Messiah, Yeshua, the Living Word?

_____

_____

_____

READ

"Tonight he's just a baby. Tonight he's sleeping beside his mother."

It was a surprising thought. All along Melchior had studied the signs in the heavens in their grandeur and majesty. His thoughts had related to giving proper homage to a heavenly ruler, a figure of power and glory. But Esther was right. All those portents about the coming King pointed to . . . a child?

"A baby," Esther repeated, as if reading Melchior's thoughts. "Do you suppose those who are caring for him are looking at the stars, just as we are, and wondering what his future holds? . . . What can it all mean?"

—P. 17

The frigid wind revealed the heavens for the first time in many days. Melchior saw the thinnest sliver of New Moon framed by the casement, and riding above the moon, Jupiter—The Righteous. They hung in the sky in the direction of the road to Beth-lehem.

It took Melchior a minute to realize what was wrong with the scene: Saturn was missing!

Realization dawning, Melchior thrust his left hand upward while gesturing excitedly for Balthasar to come and see. "The Sabbath! The Sabbath is again eclipsed by the moon, The Lord of the Sabbath wrapped in the Holy Spirit! But they will set in mere hours, and who can say when the weather will be clear again? You are right, Balthasar! We must go tonight! *Now!*"

—PP. 213–214

As they drew closer, he could see the light that escaped the windows and doorframes of the loaf-shaped homes of the city Beth-lehem, called The House of Bread.

And now what? The goal, but not the object of the quest, was in sight.

Esther grabbed Melchior's arm and gestured forward, pointing just over the rooftops. "Look!" she demanded breathlessly.

Beneath Jupiter, The Righteous, beneath the moon, the light of the Holy Spirit, a new, inexplicable gleam appeared within the sign of The Two Fish. In the rapidly narrowing space between the moon and the horizon, a bulge appeared, swelled, grew, and detached itself from the moon till it was distinct and separate.

"What is it?" Esther murmured.

Melchior's heart pounded in his chest. "It's The Lord of the Sabbath!"

Saturn, emerging just before dipping out of sight in the west, appeared as a gleaming dot marking the rim of the world. Gently but clearly it anointed the roof of a house standing poised on the far ridge . . . marking it as plainly as if the watch fire of the Temple Mount rested on it.

And so, at the crucial moment, the star they had seen in the east went ahead of them until it stopped over the place where the child was.

—PP. 215–216

The Magi had moved across the face of the earth as though a mighty wind pushed them. Now they stopped, certain they had come to the right place, as though the voice of the Almighty and Eternal God had spoken aloud: *He is here!*

Melchior fixed his gaze on the descending stars. It was as though they declared to his heart the answer to his question: *Ki-Mah? Who made these?*

The child, the Son of the Living God . . . the baby you have come to worship . . . the stars are His! He made them all! He knows them each by name!

It was as though Melchior had reached up and gathered the heavenly jewels in his arms. The focal point of all the universe was now before them.

As he and Esther stood hand in hand, Melchior knew the end of his quest was within this humble home.

—PP. 217–218

ASK

If you were Melchior or Esther, following the signs in the heavens toward Beth-lehem, what thoughts would run through your mind? What emotions would you experience?

_____

_____

_____

What forces of nature combined to "push" the Magi to the place where the child was? Do you find this believable? Why or why not?

_____

_____

_____

If you had expected a Messiah who would descend to bring justice to a time of great evil, how would you respond to finding a baby in a manger?

_____

_____

_____

WONDER . . .

"I am told you come from distant lands seeking one you say is born King of the Jews. Has he summoned you here? Did you come in response to his call?"

"Heaven's call, Majesty," Perroz explained. "Each of us has studied the stars. Each has reached his own conclusion. It so happens that all our conclusions agree."

"And what are these so-called signs? No one in my kingdom seems aware of them."

Balthasar spread his hands in a gesture of conciliation. "We cannot speak for others, Your Highness, only for ourselves."

—P. 204

How will you speak for yourself in light of what's revealed in the stars? In what ways will that revelation make a difference in your life today—and every day?

_____

_____

_____

"Search the Scriptures for yourselves," Balthasar suggested gently. . . . "And . . . we shall all know the truth."

—P. 176

2 | OH, SO ORDINARY— OR OF GOD?

> "So . . . ordinary seeming," Eliyahu mused. "I mean the mother. Sixteen years old, I'd guess. And the father. A carpenter. Of the House of David. Here for the registration. It isn't at all the way I thought it would happen. If it wasn't for what we all saw . . ."
>
> —P. 7

If someone walking the earth today claimed, "I am the Messiah," what signs would prove to you—beyond all doubt—that claim was true?

_____

_____

_____

What would you expect the Messiah of the whole world—the person who will bring hope and peace and justice for now and all eternity—to look like? to act like?

_____

_____

_____

For centuries the Jewish nation had longed for the promised Messiah, the Son of God and heir of all creation, who would descend to earth to bring ultimate peace and right all wrongs. They were expecting a mighty warrior—someone who would destroy all their enemies with a vengeful flash of the sword. Someone who would establish a showy, obvious earthly kingdom. Someone who would roust cruel rulers like Herod and bring justice.

Instead, God chose to arrive gently and quietly, in a way that few would guess or understand. . . .

READ

The newborn was wide-eyed and quiet in the manger of the lambing cave. He raised His right arm, stretching tiny fingers toward the face of Yosef.

Such a calm, serious baby! The midwives marveled.

Mary, His mother, rested in fresh straw beside the makeshift crib. Yosef, earthly guardian of the Messiah, lovingly studied the infant's features.

Let us make man in our own image.

Nearby an ox and a donkey munched fodder. Lambs and ewes slept in pens, unperturbed by momentous events. The elapsed time since The Eternal Son of God first drew breath as a Son of Man on earth could be counted by a single hour and a handful of minutes. Yet His true age was beyond time—everlasting—and thus beyond human comprehension.

—P. 3

Could it really be true, the shepherds wondered, that the Lord Almighty chose to express His love for Israel through the birth of a baby? Upon reflection it was decided that the best stories in Torah almost always began with the birth of a long-awaited son.

Yet tonight everything had seemed so ordinary: A young woman in labor urgently seeking shelter in a village packed with travelers. A baby boy born in the warmth of Beth-lehem's lambing cave. It was hard to see the miracle in that.

Yet it was a miracle. The Son of God reached out to the world from the womb of a virgin as the prophets foretold. The first bleating cry of His voice was heard from the midst of firstborn male lambs destined for Temple sacrifice. Perhaps one day it would all make sense, but tonight the meaning remained a puzzle to the participants in the drama.

The brilliant transitory star that shone as first herald of the birth of the true King of Israel faded and vanished. The sign of two bright planets, which had been dancing within the constellation of Israel for months, was now concealed behind a layer of clouds that closed in over the territory of Ephratha. . . .

The rhythm of life in Beth-lehem resumed. There were things to do.

Tasks to accomplish. . . . The baby had simply been in need of washing, like all newborn babies.

Those shepherds who had seen and heard the angels from the pastures of Migdal Eder scanned the skies and hoped for more heavenly proclamations to resound from the hills of the terraced amphitheater of Beth-lehem.

Had anyone ever witnessed such glory before this night? What could it mean?

But instead of angel voices, the soft song of the infant's young mother drifted out to a dozen rough shepherds. "Hush, my babe, lie still and slumber. . . ."

—PP. 4–5

"Eliyahu says . . . such a night! What if angels come back and I sleep through it?"

"Angels have better sense than to go out a second time on such a night. So the baby is born. He looks like other babies. Eats like other babies. Needs washed and changed like other babies. I think heaven has said all it has to say about the wee King of Israel until he grows up."

—CONVERSATION BETWEEN HAVILA AND RACHEL (P. 9)

ASK

What about the baby's birth was ordinary, based on the text above?

_____

_____

_____

What about the baby's birth was unusual?

_____

_____

_____

If you came upon the young mother, the baby, and the blue-collar father in the lambing cave, what would your first reaction be? Why?

_____

_____

_____

READ

Eliyahu nodded and nodded again as he stared into the cave. His voice broke as he groped for words. "One day we'll be old, and they'll ask us to tell the story of this night. 'Where were you?' they'll ask. 'When did you see the angels? What did they look like?'"

Zadok's lower lip jutted out. "Have you ever seen such skin as angel faces? All aglow, like . . . like the luster of pearls on the crown of a prince!"

Eliyahu agreed. "And people will ask us what they said, word for word. What did we hear? Were we afraid?"

Zadok's eyes widened. "Afraid? Aye, I was afraid. We'll none of us forget where we stood or sat when they came. Or what we first thought when the light began to grow."

Lem added, "Or the sound of it."

Eliyahu glanced again at the entrance to the stable. "Angel voices. The rumble of earth and sky. And I! There by chance, standing watch with you in the fields because Noah was sick and asked me to stand his watch for him. Think what I might have missed!"

Zadok pulled his cloak close around his ears. "I'd sleep on the hard ground the rest of my life to see such a sight again! And hear their singin' again! Aye! Nothin' like it in all the earth. Not ever. It's not a moment any of us will forget!"

—p. 6

"A week gone since the world changed." Zadok turned his face to the heavens and closed his eyes. "Yet I see them still. Angels. Hear their voices singin' hope t' us poor fellows out in that field. Never expected it . . . not for me t' witness. We were there. Just there." He swept the tip of his staff toward a watch fire on the verge of the pasture. Sheep cropping the stubble resembled dirty heaps of snow.

"You. First witness," Yosef murmured. "So it is you and Rachel must stand with me and Mary at the circumcision."

Zadok's eyes opened wide, and he lifted his staff to point in the direction of Jerusalem. "And this is what I say t' the Fast of Nebuchadnezzar's Siege. Aye, if I were a learned man, which I am not, I'd say the day of his circumcision is the very day the siege of darkness against all of us is finally broken. All the world will remember his *Bris Milah* and celebrate our freedom!"

—P. 71

On the eighth day, when it was time to circumcise Him, He was named Yeshua, the name the angel had given Him before He had been conceived.
—LUKE 2:21

ASK

Imagine you are a shepherd, standing watch at night in a cold field. If an angel appeared to you, how would you respond? Would you be convinced of the angel's message—or dubious? Why?

_____

_____

_____

_____

Do you ever feel as though there is a "siege of darkness" against you? If so, when? And what would it take for you to celebrate your freedom?

_____

_____

_____

_____

How important is a name? Do you know what *your* name means? Why is it important that the baby was named Yeshua? How might the meaning of His name impact your life?

_____

_____

_____

READ

"Ah, Yosef. I'll make no lastin' mark upon this world. Poor shepherds are no more remembered than sheep." The staff rested on his shoulder, and he spread his broad palms as he spoke.

"Like me. Who'll remember the name of a carpenter from Nazareth? But, Zadok, like you, I've heard the voices of angels! They call me to carry him on my shoulders. I'll teach him how to make a beam level and smooth and how to drive a nail straight in with one blow. That's all I have to offer."

"Me! Stand as guardian at the *Bris Milah* of the Messiah. And my own Rachel support the mother of the King! He's King, though none know it yet. None but the righteous must know he's here. Herod would seek t' kill him. Think of it! Herod kill the One who commands the angel armies," Zadok reflected. "Till the end of my days I'll not forget his heavenly troops shinin' there above the field!"

"That's why you must stand with us at the circumcision. You and your Rachel. Rachel, whose gentle hands helped guide the Lord into this world from *olam haba*."

"Rachel. My own ewe lamb. Rachel. Aye. Now she's worthy t' stand as witness. She knows a mother's heart. She knows what it means t' bring forth life. Many's the child she's helped into this world. Seventy sons born in Beth-lehem over the last two years and my Rachel the midwife of them all. Seventy boys . . . may all grow up t' serve their King!"

"It came to me and Mary . . . yes! She said the vision of your faces was clear in her mind as we prayed. The two of you as honored witnesses. You two on the right and the left at the circumcision. The shepherd and the midwife as we speak aloud the name for the first time. His name. The name the angel commanded we must call him. And you, Zadok, by standing there with us, pledge you'll care for him if we should die? You'll take him in so he'll never be hungry or in want?"

They were questions, not commands. Yosef had pondered his own death many times. Suppose he died before the child was a man. Who would care for Him? This greathearted shepherd of God's Temple flocks seemed to be the only trustworthy man.

Zadok nodded. "Aye! I think often on the same thing. If I should perish, who would care for my widow and three children? 'Tis a worry when a man loves his family so much. Count on me, Yosef! That I can pledge to you. Me and Rachel . . . we'll embrace the honor of guardin' the wee lad with our very lives. Aye!"

Zadok patted his battered staff like a weapon. His eyes narrowed as he considered the glowering fortress of Herodium in the distance. "None of them dark hearts will harm one hair of his head or threaten his life while I breathe. Count on me, Yosef. Herod is a wolf. This babe is the Firstborn Lamb of The Eternal. Rest easy. I'll prepare and pray and wash and dress for his *Bris Milah*. And me and my Rachel will come with our family t' fetch you."

—PP. 72–73

ASK

If you were looking for someone to raise your child in the event of your death, would you choose people like Zadok and Rachel? Why or why not?

_____

_____

_____

Yosef, Zadok, and Rachel were ordinary people. Yet what special role did each play in the drama of the birth and early life of Yeshua?

- Yosef
- Zadok
- Rachel

_____

_____

_____

What role did the seventy sons of Beth-lehem play? Why do you think the children of Beth-lehem, in particular, were chosen?

_____

_____

_____

What do you think God's plan for your life is? In what area(s) can you uniquely influence the lives of others?

READ

The eldest of the Magi inclined his shaggy head in thought. Then, frowning, he replied, "All that is good, condensed into such a fragile container. All that light bound up in a single clay lamp. The hope of all mankind . . . in the body of an infant! We found him, but what if the eye of evil locates him as well? Was there ever a more dangerous time?"

Melchior was startled and unhappy at Balthasar's conclusion. Wasn't this night one of unreserved exultation? How could any evil intrude on such mysterious wonder? . . .

With all the signs now complete, the quest fulfilled, and the child safe and about to be acclaimed by all the world, what danger could possibly threaten?

—PP. 223–224

Rachel observed the tiny infant sleeping in His mother, Mary's, arms. Messiah! Light who shone in the heavens before the stars were created!

What message was contained in today's reading? Would heaven speak on this first Shabbat after the birth of Messiah? . . .

"*Vayigash!* Draw near to me!" . . .

Yosef raised his eyes to gaze above the heads of the men as though he could see Mary and the Holy Child behind the latticework. His voice boomed across the auditorium, filling the space.

As he spoke, Rachel felt certain that from the beginning of time this moment had been ordained. On this day, in this place, *Vayigash* was the Torah reading that would announce God's plan to redeem, deliver, and heal His broken relationship with man.

"Draw near to me!"

—PP 59–61

ASK

Do you think it's possible for the creator of the universe to be harmed by one of His creations? Why or why not?

_____

_____

_____

Why do you think God would choose to send a fragile infant to "redeem, deliver, and heal His broken relationship with man"?

_____

_____

_____

How can you draw near to God?

_____

_____

_____

WONDER . . .

Through thousands of years and countless generations, many men have claimed to be the Messiah. All of these claims, except one, have proved to be false. . . .

> _Here he is. Messiah. Son of David. Just a baby sleeping beside his mother in a little cottage. How can it be that The Eternal One is contained in a form that we can see with our eyes and hold in our arms? . . . He gazed to where the baby lay beside Mary . . . dark curls and perfect head against her breast._
>
> _There he is. Real and wonderful. But how does it work? That the Immortal One, who has existed since before time, can inhabit a mortal body? How can_

this baby, who will be called son of Yosef of Nazareth, also be named Wonderful, Counselor, Mighty God, Everlasting Father, and Prince of Peace?

With that question still unanswered, Yosef fell asleep.

—PP. 87–88

What does a tiny baby, born all those years ago, have to do with you, today? Was He ordinary—or truly the long-awaited Messiah?

What you believe about the baby in the manger is the most important decision you will make.

3 | THE GRAND PLAN

"Do you think the Almighty, blessed be he, left any of this to chance?
No, Zadok, no. In Beth-lehem the child was always to be born. And that
means Rachel—and you and me too—were seen and made part of his
plan from ages long past."
—ELIYAHU TO ZADOK (P. 27)

Is there a plan for everything that happens? Or do events occur by random
chance? Explain.

_____

_____

_____

Do you believe that *you*, individually, are part of a grand plan? that your part
could be played by no one but you? Why or why not?

_____

_____

_____

_____

How much does your personal choice have to do with what you accomplish in life?

_____

_____

_____

Mary was a young mother, from a poor village. Yosef was a simple carpenter, who made his living with his hands and didn't claim to understand "higher things." Zadok had lived his life as a shepherd, and Rachel her life as a shepherd's wife in an out-of-the-way village. Yet all four, because of their obedience to and humble acceptance of God's grand plan, played parts they would never have dreamed they might.

Ephesians 1:11 says, *"In Him we were also chosen, having been predestined according to the plan of Him who works out everything in conformity with the purpose of His will."* What might God have in mind for you?

READ
> But you, Bethlehem Ephrathah, though you are small among the clans of Judah, out of you will come for me one who will be ruler over Israel, whose origins are from of old, from ancient times.
> —MICAH 5:2

"Beth-lehem?" Herod pondered aloud. "Muddy, smelly village south of here? Place where the sacrificial lambs are raised? And this *Anointed One* is to be called a . . . *shepherd?*"

"Like King David," one of the scribes blurted before Boethus waved him to silence.
—P. 197

"Aye. And now there's a Prince and his mother in Beth-lehem! A Prince! Here! A once-in-a-lifetime event, if you ask me. Or less than once in a lifetime. Never again in my lifetime. A Prince of David comin' to stay. The honor of it! Though why a Prince would come here to stay, I can't say."
—GRANDMOTHER (P. 19)

"It's good you stay here awhile. No better folk than Zadok and Rachel. No place more filled with hope for the Son of David than David's hometown. Our folk will be careful with the news."
— ELIYAHU TO YOSEF (P. 107)

ASK

Why would God choose tiny, smelly Beth-lehem as the place where the Messiah would be born? List as many reasons as you can from the passages above . . . and add some of your own.

_____

_____

_____

David, the shepherd, was from Beth-lehem, the lowliest of villages. Yet he rose to become the king of all Israel. In light of this background, why would it be especially unnerving to Herod that a Messiah could be arriving in Beth-lehem?

_____

_____

_____

READ

"Do y' see this storm?" Zadok waved his staff overhead. "What if it had come before sunset, last evenin', eh? What would have happened t' the maid then? And the babe? I tell y', Eliyahu, this won't get over quickly. I know the feel. This is a big storm, this is. And a colder one I've never felt. It's a time for pregnant ewes and newborn lambs t' be in shelter, like in the lambin' cave. Came just in time, they did."
— P. 27

"Cold night, eh? You should write how cold it were, Eliyahu. The night Messiah was born? Standin' out here. Messiah picked the coldest, darkest night of the year to be born."

—LEM (P. 6)

Yosef considered how much the stories—the history of the people and the Lord and the land—all fit together seamlessly. All things in Eretz-Israel seemed to sing the name Yeshua!

Suddenly somber, Zadok confided, "Yosef, you're here for a purpose. It came t' me strong, when I heard the babe's name, that I must show you David's Valley. And that marker . . ."

The big man pointed to a heap of stones on the opposite side of the enclave. "That marks a trail south. An unknown path. Only a few have traveled it. . . . The Spirit said t' my heart, *Yosef must know of it.* Aye. And if there should ever be a need t' escape . . . as it is written, the Red Sea parted and they walked across on dry ground."

Yosef's eyes narrowed as he took in the implication of Zadok's revelation. A way of escape! But escape from what? from whom? He remembered Zadok's words: *"If there should ever be a need. . . ."*

—PP. 150–151

ASK

What was the weather like the night Yeshua was born? What purpose(s) might this have had in God's grand scheme?

_____

_____

_____

Why was the unknown path important? And why might God have sent Yosef with Zadok on such a journey over a treacherous road into the valley?

_____

_____

_____

READ

Zadok—honest, hearty, generous Zadok—knew he had a temper and other failings. Was it possible the Lord God Almighty had prepared Zadok, a rough-hewn man at best, to receive the child sent to be the Restoration of Israel and the Light of the World?

It was too much. The wonder of the angelic announcement and the fulfillment seen in the babe in the manger were already enough. Making himself part of that miracle felt wrong, almost blasphemous. Zadok was prepared to testify to what he had been privileged to witness . . . but to be prepared by Yahweh to play a role in the event?

—PP. 27–28

"Your Rachel delivered the baby. Think of it! My Havila came along to help."

"Our wives, Eliyahu. The long-desired babe not born in a palace. Not as we imagined Messiah would come. Our women washin' him in water drawn from David's Well and in Beth-lehem's wine. Just as our own sons were washed. Our women, rubbin' the royal Prince of God with salt . . . with their own hands. Anointin' the Messiah with olive oil from our scruffy olive trees. 'Tis an honor." . . .

Lem huffed, "And write about Mordechai at the inn. How he turned them away. Denied a room for the birth of the King. Sent them instead to a lambin' cave!"

—PP. 6–7

"His first Shabbat evening. Supper with friends. I'll keep this memory always. How you took us into your own home. Your kindness. A treasure in my heart. He mustn't miss attending his first Shabbat service on earth among his people! Tomorrow morning I'll be strong enough if you will help me. We'll walk together and bring the baby into Beth David, the House of David Synagogue. He'll attend his first Shabbat service in your synagogue, Rabbi Eliyahu. He'll worship the first time in Israel in the midst of your little sons. It was always meant to be. Right here in Beth-lehem!"

—MARY TO RACHEL (P. 49)

"They've opened their hearts to us, these people. Rachel. Zadok. Their boys. Havila and Eliyahu. All the rest. Is this why the baby was born here? why the angels spoke to the shepherds in the fields of Migdal Eder? So

we would stay and live without the gossip we faced in Nazareth? raise him around people who don't doubt the truth of our story?"
—MARY (P. 138)

ASK

If you were Zadok, would you believe God had chosen *you* to protect and house the Messiah? Why or why not?

_____

_____

_____

What roles did the women of Beth-lehem—including Rachel, Havila, and Grandmother—play in God's grand plan? Why was it important for Mary, Yosef, and baby Yeshua to stay in Beth-lehem among such simple folks?

_____

_____

If you were Mordechai and your inn was overflowing, would you give a woman about to give birth a room? Why or why not? Do you think Mordechai's refusal to give Mary and Yosef a place at the inn was part of God's plan? Explain.

_____

_____

_____

Joshua 24:15 says, *"Choose for yourselves this day whom you will serve. . . . But as for me and my household, we will serve the Lord."* Whom did Zadok, Rachel, Havila, Grandmother, and Eliyahu choose to serve? Whom did Mordechai choose to serve? What differences can you see in their lives as a result? Whom would you rather serve—and why?

_____

_____

_____

READ

You are Lord of All the Angel Armies from all eternity, Yosef thought, *yet you rest in the arms of your earthly mother! Look: a tiny face turned toward a mother's breast. From before time, you chose her to carry you; to bear you in suffering; to love, protect, and care for you. What am I to learn, O Lord, from your willingness to be vulnerable? What is the lesson, Sovereign Lord, that you trust us with the life of your Son before we have learned to trust you with our lives? What must the eyes of my heart see in this true vision by which you reveal your eternal attributes? What must I learn on your first morning living among us as a human child? . . .*

Yosef stammered, ". . . This is not what I intended. . . . I'm so sorry." He raised his arms and let them fall in a gesture of helplessness.

"It's as it should be." She smiled and tugged the swaddling cloth close around the baby's face. "Always meant to be." She motioned for Yosef to come close and grasped his hand, pulling him down beside her. "A fine stable. A night to remember! We'll laugh about it one day when we tell the story! . . . Yosef, don't you know? It's why he was born. Why he chose to live with us. He's here, like this, because you and I—everyone, I think—couldn't imagine what he was really like."

She kissed the baby's head. "You see it, don't you? . . . I've thought about it a lot. The why of it all. I knew the minute I saw his sweet face, looked in his eyes. He came to earth the same way we all have come. He came so you and I can see him and hear his voice and, yes, love him. He came to live in our family so we can learn how a family is meant to live. So we can care for his needs for a while and love him as our own child and let him love us—mother and father, aunts, uncles, and cousins—his family, you know? And I think he will show us how to forgive one another too. He came to us like this so we can rock him gently in our arms and sing to him. And you will carry him on your shoulders and never, never be afraid of him again."

—YOSEF AND MARY (PP. 21–22)

Yosef understood why the Messiah had been born in the lambing cave. Why the angels had announced His birth first to the shepherds of the Temple flock. Why Yosef and Mary and Yeshua had been nurtured and cared for by the families of Beth-lehem. It was within the power of the Almighty to call upon the earth to weave a canopy of protection so thick that no man could lay a hand on Mary or the baby named Salvation. But The Eternal God had instead chosen a few righteous families in Israel to help preserve and protect His great plan of deliverance and salvation!

Blessed are you, O Adonai, sovereign King, who brought us to this place and this moment. Blessed are the shepherd people of David's village who took us in and sheltered us, who never turned away from our need. Blessed are they who stand watch over your flocks generation after generation, who have watched over your Firstborn Lamb for this season. They are not poor; they are just without the riches of the world. Blessed are these unknown ones who stand watch quietly in the rain because you have called them to care for your own.

They will outlast the pomp and power of the false shepherds whose god is wealth and who sell your people to the wolves. Blessed are you, O Lord, who will cleanse your Temple! When the last Lamb of sacrifice, born in Beth-lehem, has bled out upon your altar, these shepherd families who cared for us will sit in honor by your throne. Bless them, O Lord. Bless these, your faithful servants in the field.

—P. 229

ASK
Why would God choose to send Yeshua, the Messiah, as a human baby?

_____

_____

_____

Why would Yeshua, the Son of God, choose to live among flawed human beings?

_____

_____

_____

If your life ended tonight, would you be remembered as one who stood watch quietly or one who lived for pomp and power? Explain.

_____

_____

_____

WONDER . . .

Many, O Lord my God,
are the wonders You have done.
The things You planned for us
no one can recount to You;
were I to speak and tell of them,
they would be too many to declare.
—PSALM 40:5

You sorrowed at not having a worthy gift for the King? This moment is your gift.
You are called to serve Him.
   —THE ANGEL GABRIEL TO MELCHIOR (P. 227)

Recount some of the things God has done for you. Then reflect on this question: What gift could you give Yeshua today?

4 | WALKING WITH GOD?!

"Adonai, the Lord, when he wanted to go on long walks and spend time with some pleasant human here on earth, he came down from heaven to Enoch's house, and Enoch walked with him."
—ZADOK (P. 208)

If you had the opportunity to take a walk with anyone, whom would you choose—and why?

_____

_____

_____

Do you spend time walking and talking with God regularly? Is God a part of your life

- every day?
- just on Saturdays, Sundays, or holidays?
- when you're in a crisis situation?
- not at all?

Explain.

_____

_____

_____

While Yeshua was on earth, He clearly loved children and treated them as special people. He said, *"Let the little children come to me, and do not hinder them, for the kingdom of God belongs to such as these. I tell you the truth, anyone who will not receive the kingdom of God like a little child will never enter it.' And He took the children in His arms, put His hands on them and blessed them"* (Mark 10:14-16).

Why were children so special to Yeshua? Perhaps because their hearts are pure, their prayers are heartfelt, their minds are trusting, and they have no greater joy than to walk hand in hand with those they love.

What does it mean to truly walk with God? There is so much we can learn from a child about simple, trusting faith.

READ

The night before the baby's circumcision ceremony was *Leil Shimurim*, which means "the night of protection." Mary and Yosef followed the custom that had existed for 1,365 years since the Exodus. The sages taught that the mitzvah of *Bris Milah* was so spiritually important that the powers of darkness wailed and gathered together to prevent the circumcision of a newborn child of the covenant.

Young children, souls pure and unblemished, were invited into the household. Prayers from innocent hearts, it was said, pierced the heavens and formed a spiritual protection that called down blessings on the baby, the household, and the family.

—P. 79

Rachel coached Enoch in his name verse: *"And Enoch . . ."*

The boy frowned down at the baby and recited. "I am Enoch. *And Enoch . . . walked . . . with Adonai . . . and was no more. . . .* That's ME. Baby! I'm Enoch!"

The baby Messiah wriggled in His mother's lap and opened His mouth with an *oh* of approval.

—P. 79

ASK

Do you believe "prayers from innocent hearts" reach the heavens? Explain.
Whom do you know who has an innocent heart?

_____

_____

_____

Can you see God opening His mouth in an *oh* of approval about you? Why
or why not?

_____

_____

_____

READ

Enoch did not yet understand the need for a Jew to be preserved by the
Lord in his goings and comings. She was glad the child had no sense of
danger in the world. . . .

Enoch's face lit up. His somber eyes locked on the newborn in Mary's
arms. He called out without hesitation, "Yeshua! The Lord shall . . ."

Rachel tried to coach him. ". . . preserve . . ."

Enoch seemed not to hear her. He touched his finger to his lips and
stretched out his hand to the baby as though touching the mezuzah. Enoch's
childish treble pronounced the words with surprising clarity. "Bless Yeshua
. . . bless! You! Going out . . . and bless you! Coming in, from for evermore."

Rachel knew that, in part, Enoch had recited the blessing spoken over
the mezuzah, but there was something else in Enoch's joyful cry when he
saw the face of his Messiah.

—PP. 123, 126

The Lord will watch over your coming and going both now and forevermore.
—PSALM 121:8

"You don't need gold to buy a place in the kingdom for your children and grandchildren. Your love for him is the only gift he will ever want."
—MARY TO GRANDMOTHER (P. 128)

ASK

If someone was to judge your character solely on what they saw on your face and in your actions, what kind of person would they assume you are?

_____

_____

_____

If you had nothing to give Yeshua except for your love, would you consider that enough? Why or why not?

_____

_____

_____

What difference would it make in your life if you asked God to "watch over your coming and going both now and forevermore"? Explain.

_____

_____

_____

READ

Enoch, Samu'el, and Dan gathered round as Mary nursed Yeshua.

Enoch recited his line to Yeshua. "Enoch . . . walked . . . with the Lord."

Mary praised him. "Very good, Enoch! Someday maybe you'll grow up to be a rabbi, eh?"

Enoch answered solemnly, "We're going to fly away. Me. Samu'el. Dan. Obi. Everybody. To Yeshua's house to play." . . .

Among the little ones of Beth-lehem, from the newest baby up to Enoch's age, there had been an almost supernatural contentedness, as if they knew they were in the presence of the Lord's Anointed. Neither had there been illness in the village since the birth of Mary's son.

Dan and Samu'el, so close to the same age, wobbled as they clung to Mary's chair. They gazed at Yeshua with undisguised fascination. It seemed so strange to Rachel that the boys were content to play quietly near Mary's baby for hours on end. Even if angels had not announced that Yeshua was an extraordinary child, it was evident by the calming effect of His presence on those around Him.

Surely, Rachel thought, if Yeshua could stay here in Beth-lehem, grow up in the place where David had grown up, the angels would keep Him safe from Herodian plots. His name was Salvation, after all. And if the infant King of Israel was safe, it made sense that all the children of Beth-lehem would be blessed as well.

—PP. 172–174

"Such a good and righteous fellow Enoch was that Adonai, the Lord, walked with him here on earth for a while. Then Adonai took Enoch away to heaven, out of this wicked world, so Enoch never died. Just flew away up to heaven." Zadok snapped his fingers.

"Me. Samu'el. Obi. Dan."

"So it's written: *'And Enoch walked with Adonai the Lord; then he was no more, for the Lord took him away.'*"

The boy brightened. "Enoch flew. Me too. I'm going to heaven." . . .

"'Enoch walked with the Lord.' Can y' repeat that after Papa?"

The boy was silent.

Zadok urged him, "Enoch walked . . ."

"Enoch . . . walked . . ."

"with the Lord."

"with the Lord."

"Aye! Just like that! Well done, lad!"

The child beamed. "The Lord lives at Enoch's house."

—PP. 207–208

ASK

In what ways did Enoch and the other little boys in Beth-lehem "walk with the Lord"? What qualities characterized their young lives?

_____

_____

_____

How was young Enoch like the Enoch of old?

_____

_____

_____

Is walking with God the same as the Lord living at your house? Explain.

_____

_____

_____

READ

Enoch patted his father's cheek. "The Lord lives . . . at Enoch's house. Me and Samu'el . . . Obi. And Dan too. Going to his house to play."

Zadok laughed and lifted him high. "There's a good-hearted lad! An innocent heart! A better Enoch than the first Enoch. Not one of your playmates left out from the great journey when y' fly away, eh? You'll take all your wee friends and brothers with y' too!"

—P. 209

"Every boy baby in Beth-lehem—no, that is not enough—every *male child* within the circle of Migdal Eder. Yes, that is it . . . all their lambs, eh? And when did they say these signs first appeared? A year ago? But I will not settle

for that either! Go, Hermes. Put a cordon around Beth-lehem. Kill every
boy age two and under. Do it tonight!"
  —HEROD (P. 235)

Enoch! Samu'el! Obi! These three were her whole life! Why was she afraid?
Was God not a merciful God? Had they not walked with Messiah? borne
Him in their arms? rejoiced that He had come? What was this unexplained
terror that squeezed her heart as though it would be crushed?
  "Mama?"
  Enoch's verse came to her mind with a new and terrible implication:
And Enoch walked with God . . . and he was no more.
  —P. 243

The Lord is my shepherd. . . . Even though I walk through the valley of the
shadow of death, I will fear no evil, for You are with me; Your rod and Your
staff, they comfort me.
  —PSALM 23:1, 4

ASK
What kind of heart did Enoch have? How did he look at death? How do *you*
look at death?

_____

_____

_____

If you were Rachel, how would you grapple with the reality that your three
boys—your only children and the joys of your heart—were part of what
seemed like senseless slaughter? Would your faith in a good God—or any
God at all—emerge stronger or weaker?

_____

_____

_____

Does walking with God mean that you and your loved ones will be protected from pain and death? Use an example from your own life, if possible, to explain why or why not. When bad things happen, how could walking with God each day affect your long-range perspective on suffering?

_____

_____

_____

WONDER . . .

Love the Lord your God with all your heart and with all your soul and with all your strength. These commandments that I give you today are to be upon your hearts. Impress then on your children. Talk about them when you sit at home and when you walk along the road, when you lie down and when you get up.
—DEUTERONOMY 6:5-7

At that time the disciples came to Jesus and asked, "Who is the greatest in the kingdom of heaven?"
He called a little child and had him stand among them. And He said: "I tell you the truth, unless you change and become like little children, you will never enter the kingdom of heaven. Therefore, whoever humbles himself like this child is the greatest in the kingdom of heaven. And whoever welcomes a little child like this in My name welcomes Me."
—MATTHEW 18:1-5

What does it truly mean to walk with God? How loving is your heart? How humble are you? How accepting of the little and lowly?

What needs to change in your heart and life so that, when your time to leave this earth comes, you will happily fly away to the Lord's house? And, like Enoch, see your friends there too?

5 | WAITING FOR FULFILLMENT

"All my life I've been waiting for this day. The Almighty promised . . .
and I've lived to see it come to pass."
—SIMEON (P. 29)

If only one remaining wish of yours could be fulfilled in your lifetime, what
would that wish be—and why?

_____

_____

_____

Has there ever been a time when you lost hope that something good would
happen? When? Tell the story.

_____

_____

_____

It has been said that hope is what makes the soul live on even under the
greatest of loads. If ever any people needed hope, the Jewish nation of the
first century A.D. did. They had been waiting so long and under such cruel
tyranny for the promised Messiah that many had forgotten how to hope.
Although they continued to pray to the Almighty, follow His commands,
and even make a yearly pilgrimage to Jerusalem, hope had dulled to a dim
memory. The Messiah had become, for many, a figure of their spiritual

history but had lost relevance for their daily lives. They no longer believed the ancient promises would be fulfilled.

In dark times in your life, you may have lost hope. You may have felt as if you were waiting for nothing—as if nothing good would ever come to you (or a loved one). Perhaps you're feeling that way now.

Simeon is an old man. "He is the last of the righteous generation," Eliyahu says. "Herod has murdered most of them. But Simeon has survived somehow. He expects Messiah's coming. He'll know much more than we" (p. 107). Simeon has waited a lifetime for a promise to be fulfilled. Could the arrival of this baby be the answer he—and all the world—has been waiting for?

READ

All the shepherds of Migdal Eder, the Tower of the Flock where the lambs for Temple sacrifice were raised, were brimming with the news. Well before sunup all the people of Beth-lehem had been roused and regaled with stories of astonishing sights, angelic announcements, and heavenly choirs.

And now Zadok and Eliyahu were the advance guard of those carrying the news to the Holy City.

"To Simeon the Elder," Zadok restated firmly. "First to him. That good, righteous old man. To him first, before any other. It's only right."

Simeon, an aged elder of Israel, was the keeper of many secrets having to do with the advent of Messiah. It was altogether fitting that he be the first outside Beth-lehem to hear the report.

—P. 28

"He's here! The child of promise! He was born last night in Beth-lehem. I've seen him! Eliyahu too. Many others! You were right, Simeon. This was the year!"

Simeon's frail, gnarled hands grasped both Zadok's brawny forearms. "Is he here, indeed?" he asked urgently. Without relinquishing his grip on the shepherd, Simeon looked at Eliyahu for confirmation.

The rabbi nodded vigorously.

Then the story tumbled out, alternating from the mouths of Zadok and Eliyahu. . . .

Simeon, eyes brimming with tears, sank onto a cushion on the floor. He rocked forward and back, apparently caught in the grip of emotion too powerful for words.

Zadok, concerned that the shock of the announcement had been too much for the old man, knelt beside him.

Tears flowed freely down creviced cheeks and into Simeon's snow-white beard as he patted Zadok's arm reassuringly. "Just . . . give me a moment. All my life I've been waiting for this day. The Almighty promised . . . and I've lived to see it come to pass."

—P. 29

ASK
Why did Zadok and Eliyahu go to Simeon the Elder first?

_____

_____

_____

What was Simeon's response to the news? Why?

_____

_____

_____

If you had waited a lifetime for a certain event (perhaps for the birth or adoption of a child, for someone to love, for a friend to share your faith) to happen, and it did, what would you feel? What would you think? How would you respond?

_____

_____

_____

READ

It had not happened in the way anyone had imagined it. Mary of Nazareth. Betrothed wife of Yosef of Nazareth. Not much more than a girl and so . . . ordinary. Yet the angels had declared that this was the birth of the Son of David! This baby boy was the fulfillment of every prophecy in Torah. The hope of all generations in Israel!

—P. 5

Israel had sought the Messiah like men search for gold in the heart of a great mountain. Stone by stone the earth was overturned, yet the Eternal Treasure remained locked away. So many generations had longed to see His face that now most suspected the Messiah was only a legend.

But on this last night of Hanukkah the final candle had been lit.

For unto us a son is given.

A single gold nugget, washed from the heavenly mountain by the will of God, glinted in the flickering light. Hope was reborn. Redemption, for which the suffering world longed, was fulfilled in the cry of a newborn. By design of Yahweh, The Eternal, this babe was the guarantee that Eternal Treasure awaited all who called upon His name!

—PP. 3–4

At the rising of the sun this very day, the rising prayers of every righteous Jew since Father Abraham had been answered!

The merciful God of Jacob has responded at last. True Salvation, Yeshua, is born to be King in Israel!

—P. 20

ASK

Why is it important that Yeshua was born on the last night of Hanukkah? What was reborn in the people—and why?

_____

_____

_____

_____

Why was this baby considered "a gold nugget" and an "Eternal Treasure"?

_____

_____

_____

Do you believe that "the rising prayers of every righteous Jew" were answered with the birth of Yeshua, meaning "Salvation"? Why or why not? If not, what signs would convince you?

_____

_____

_____

READ

"What exactly—*exactly*, mind you—did the angel say?"

Eliyahu's scholarly, trained memory stepped in. "His exact words were *'Do not be afraid. I bring you good news of great joy that will be for all the people. Today in the town of David a Savior has been born to you; He is Messiah the Lord.'*"

—CONVERSATION BETWEEN SIMEON AND ELIYAHU (P. 30)

"I hear he's come! All the scrolls of the prophets confirm this: Isaias, Micah, Mosheh the Lawgiver, the weeks of years in Dani'el's writing."

—SIMEON (P. 120)

"We know when our ancestors left Egypt, and because of that we know when the first redemption of the firstborn males occurred, true?" . . .

"Five shekels each!" Simeon exulted. "Five for each of 273 children! That's 1,365 shekels. The shekels are years, aren't they? One thousand three hundred and sixty-five years must pass until he comes who is the fulfillment of the redemption. It is the exact number to this year. It's true! He's come! He who is not a Levite will actually give his life in service to the Almighty. He is the Messiah, the Lord's Anointed."

—CONVERSATION BETWEEN HANNAH AND SIMEON (P. 121)

"'Good news,' the angel said, eh? *Shemuah tov. Shemuah*: an announcement, a report, tidings, yes. Sounds like the word for the heavens: *shamayim. Tov*: good news. So! A report so good as to be heavenly, true?"

Eliyahu nodded vigorously. "And where in Holy Scripture is such a phrase used except in—"

"Proverbs!" Simeon confirmed, gesturing at the scroll. "One place only! Listen: *Like cold water to a weary soul is good news*—shemuah tov—*from a distant land!* What a sense of humor has the Almighty, blessed be he! Heaven is indeed a 'distant land'!"

"And that relates to a newborn Messiah?" Zadok questioned calmly. He struggled to keep up but was unwilling for his brother-in-law to note his mental exertion.

"Exactly!" Simeon praised, as if Zadok had uttered something profound. "See here what Isaias says of Messiah." Simeon swept aside the Proverbs scroll to reveal one of the prophet Isaias. *"I will make you a covenant for the people, to restore the land. . . . He who has compassion on them will guide them and lead them beside springs of water!"*

"*Shemuah tov!* Good news from heaven, indeed," Eliyahu murmured. "Messiah refreshes our souls like a cool spring of water."

"And further it says, *I will also make you a light for the Gentiles, that you may bring My salvation to the ends of the earth.*"

—P. 40

ASK

What signs from the above passages point toward the baby being the long-awaited Messiah not only of Israel but all the earth?

_____

_____

_____

_____

What *shemuah tov*—good news from a distant land—do you wait for today? Have you considered the possibility that Yeshua, born all those years ago, *is* the good news you have been waiting for? Why or why not?

_____

_____

_____

READ

Yosef of Nazareth could not complete the reading! A tremendous roar of joy increased from the people of Beth-lehem. They leapt to their feet with clapping and cheering the good news. "*Vayigash!* Draw near to me! *Vayigash!*"

Had the angels not called out this very same thing? "Go, now! You will find him lying in a manger! Draw near to your Lord and Savior!" . . .

Vayigash! Draw near to me, declares the Lord. I love you so much I lay aside my awesome power and open my arms to embrace you as the brother you rejected.

The family rift between God and His beloved children, as foretold in Scripture, was about to be healed forever by the only Son of the Living God of Israel! . . .

In this reunion between God and man that first Shabbat morning, the Savior of Israel was embraced and adored by His family, the shepherds, and their families in Beth-lehem. Those who had given up hope that they would ever see Him face-to-face danced and sang as they drew near to Him.

It was, Rachel thought, as she whirled to the music with her boys and Zadok, something like a wedding celebration. Only this time the Bridegroom was only a few days old, and His bride was the nation of Israel.

And the reading was a promise to all who worshipped the newborn King that morning: *Vayigash!* Draw near to me and do not delay! And you will be near to me.

—PP. 63–64

ASK

What does *"Vayigash!"* mean to you personally? What message of love, forgiveness, and deliverance do you wait for?

_____

_____

_____

No matter where you have been or what you have done, God longs to open His arms and embrace you. Will you join His celebration?

WONDER . . .

Simeon believed it. "The *Ruach HaKodesh*, the Holy Spirit, promised me I would not die until I saw the Lord's Anointed, the Messiah."

—P. 120

Eliyahu believed it: "Oh! Blessed are you! Holy Child of the Most High God! We welcome you! Blessed are you, Son of David! Blessed are you, Messiah, who has arrived to dwell in our midst!"

—P. 97

Hannah believed it: "Thanks be to the Almighty," the woman proclaimed, "who has let us live until this day and permitted us to see such wondrous sights! Today, in our presence, your covenant is fulfilled. And I, Hannah, have seen it with my own eyes!"

—P. 196

What about you? Will you believe it? Will you wait no longer? Will you claim the promise fulfilled?

> *"Let us acknowledge the Lord;*
> *let us press on to acknowledge Him.*
> *As surely as the sun rises, He will appear;*
> *He will come to us."*
> HOSEA 6:3

6 | LONGING LOVE

Hope deferred makes the heart sick,
  but a longing fulfilled is a tree of life.
  —PROVERBS 13:12

For great is Your love, reaching to the heavens;
  Your faithfulness reaches to the skies.
  —PSALM 57:10

Do you remember the first time you fell in love? the giddy way you acted? how much you thought about the person you longed for . . . and agonized over whether he or she shared your feelings?

What happened to that first love? Did it fade away, or did it grow? Tell the story.

_____

_____

_____

If you could have the perfect love, what would it look like? What qualities would it have?

_____

_____

_____

All of us long for love. All of us have a void deep inside that desperately needs to be filled. We're convinced it's because of the age-old story—Adam and Eve choosing separation from the God who loved and created them in the garden—that we feel incomplete.

Let's be honest. We can *know* God loves us, but at times it's so difficult to *feel* the love of God. And we need that human touch—whether through a romantic love or the connection of family and friends—to remind us of the beauty of a loving relationship.

For over nine months, twenty-six-year-old court astronomer Melchior had been in the company of old Balthasar and his granddaughter, Esther. And he had grown to have feelings for Esther, but he wondered if she could possibly have feelings for him. . . .

READ

Melchior's heart began pounding again, but it was from fear of a different kind. For a long time he had watched Esther mature into young womanhood. But it was only within the last year that he had fallen deeply in love with the raven-haired beauty with the tawny skin.

But he—not a Jew by birth and pale of skin, hair, and eyes—had been afraid to ask her grandfather for her hand. And she . . . how did she feel about him? Was he still just a companion with whom she had grown up? . . . What hope did he have of being loved by such a woman as Esther?

—P. 16, 70

Esther leaned back against Melchior's chest. "And we are going to see him," she murmured.

They stood that way for a long time. Finally Melchior put his hands on her shoulders and turned her to face him. "Together," he said.

When Esther tilted her chin upward, the starlight sparkled in her eyes. Melchior felt her warmth against his cheek . . . inhaled the sweetness of frankincense in her hair. "I . . . ," he said. "We . . ."

Stretching up on tiptoe, Esther kissed him on the lips. Then, ducking under his arm, she darted back toward her grandfather's tent.

Melchior stood, unmoving, staring after her, thoughts and emotions all jumbled together. Finally entering his own shelter, he lay down.

But he did not go to sleep until the stars had fled from the sky.

—P. 17

"Lovin' you on earth is my one great joy. And the boys . . . our sons . . . the best gift from heaven."

"The best gift," Rachel reflected. "Our children."
—CONVERSATION BETWEEN ZADOK AND RACHEL (P. 51)

"Well then, a wife for each son t' one day love as I love you. That's my prayer. My heart can't contain what I feel for you when I see you here. When we sit together. You. Me. These three little ones."
—ZADOK (P. 110)

"He . . . will learn his alef-bet and Torah just like all our sons. Different color Jews but all the same flock. Zadok said so from the first."

She thought again of how tender Zadok was toward this little one though he was the illegitimate offspring of a slave girl.
—RACHEL (P. 200)

ASK

Why do you think Melchior was so afraid to tell Esther how he felt about her? What changed between the first and second passages above? Why?

_____

_____

_____

What was the most important thing in the world to Zadok? What is your "best gift from heaven?"

_____

_____

_____

_____

Whom do you consider family—and why?

_____

_____

_____

READ

"What is it you are searching for, Melchior? . . . We're all traveling so far. Grandfather's hope? I think I know what he is looking for at the end of the journey. The others we've met on the road from the East. But you, Melchior? You are a man of so few words, yet . . ."

He exhaled loudly and craned his neck to gaze at the heavens. He pointed at the cluster of stars that formed the constellation called The Pleiades by some. ". . . Your grandfather has taught me over the years to believe that someone . . . wonderful and mighty beyond our imagination . . . has created the stars."

"We Jews call the Pleiades *Ki-Mah*."

"Yes. It means 'who made?'" Melchior spread his hands. "And that is what—or rather, whom—I am searching for. The One who made the stars and ordered the heavens so that even the night speaks to men's hearts. It is written in the book of Job. I looked it up. *Can you bind the beautiful Pleiades? Can you loose the cords of Orion? Can you bring forth the constellations in their seasons?*"

—PP. 49–50

ASK

What is Melchior searching for? Why?

_____

_____

_____

_____

When you look at the heavens, what do you think of? *Whom* do you think of? Do the stars speak to your heart? If so, how?

READ

The lessons of the flock provided the truest parable of God's love for His people Israel. This legacy of learning was passed from father to son on lonely nights in the fields.

—P. 125

Yosef kept his eye riveted on the errant ewe who, even though she came back into line, was still searching for a blade of grass to claim as her own. "I never thought of them as having their own minds."

Zadok laughed. "Just like humankind, they are! No different at all. It's no mistake the Lord has called us his sheep. Stubborn, stupid, timid, foolish, careless, greedy. Prone t' follow wherever the flock goes . . . even over a cliff if others was runnin' that way. . . .

"There's a rule among us. It's written in here." Zadok tapped his chest. "There's lions and jackals in the desert pastures. A good shepherd'll lay down his life for the safety of the flock. That's the way it's always been with us. Since our father Avraham, the first shepherd of our people. Are there those who are in charge of sheep who don't care? Aye. When we reach the grazin' land, you'll see. There are hired men among the Arabs who'll turn tail at the first sign of danger. They let their master's sheep die and never think twice about it. But we men of Beth-lehem . . . we're hereditary shepherds of the Lord's own flocks. We walk the path David walked. Our shepherd-king. My boys will one day walk this path. . . .

"The Eternal has used these dumb, stubborn sheep—of all animals on earth—t' teach us how much he loves his people Israel. . . . Some sheep refuse my protection. Some will not be saved. Aye. There's Torah lessons a'plenty in the sheep."

—PP. 141–142

Blessed are you, beloved Lamb of God! Blessed are you, Good Shepherd who has come down from heaven to save your flock! "Though I walk in the valley of the shadow of death, I will fear no evil, for You are with me. Your rod and Your staff, they comfort me."
—P. 142

"Look there." Zadok pointed into the narrow finger of green that stretched between two steep mountains for about a quarter of a mile. "The tableland. Where the flock can graze in peace. All the best food and clean water sheep could need. Safe from the jackals. Those devils travel in packs. They won't come down this path. Mountains too steep. Sometimes at sunrise a man'll glimpse them evil eyes watchin' the flocks from the crags above. Oh, they may wish for a taste of mutton, but they can't touch the lambs. Can't enter this valley."
—P. 148

> *The Lord is my shepherd, I shall not be in want.*
> *He makes me lie down in green pastures,*
> *He leads me besides quiet waters,*
> *He restores my soul.*
> —PSALM 23:1-3

ASK

What is the role of a shepherd? What's the difference between the shepherds of Beth-lehem and for-hire shepherds?

_____

_____

_____

How are people like sheep?

_____

_____

_____

In what ways do you act like a sheep? Do you accept or refuse the Shepherd's protection? Do you allow yourself to enter God's lush, green valley of protection? Why or why not?

_____

_____

_____

READ

Simeon drew Zadok's attention to the chosen text as his bony finger indicated a line of Hebrew script. "It begins with our very first father, Adam—created by the Almighty himself but still rebellious against him. Here's what I want you to note. Every *beriyt*, every covenant, we speak of here concerns a man, deliverance, and a sacrifice."

—PP. 156–157

"'*I, the Lord, have called you in righteousness; I will take hold of your hand. I will keep you and make you to be a covenant for the people and a light for the Gentiles. To open eyes that are blind, to free captives from prison and to release from the dungeon those who sit in darkness.*' . . .

"Every other covenant involved a man. But men fail, so the covenant is incomplete. Avraham could not perfectly keep it. Mosheh could not. David could not. But King Messiah—the God-Man, born of the virgin—he will perfectly mediate the covenant between the Almighty and his children. He will deliver us, all who bow before him, from the power of evil . . . forever. . . . Ah, well," Hannah offered with a sigh. "'*I will make an everlasting covenant with you. For My thoughts are not your thoughts, neither are your ways My ways,*' declares the Lord. *This is what the Lord says: 'Maintain justice and do what is right for My salvation—My Yeshua—is close at hand and My righteousness will soon be revealed.*'"

—PP. 168–170

ASK

How did these events, recorded in the Bible, "concern a man, deliverance, and a sacrifice"? (See pp. 156–158.)

- First covenant: Adam and Eve
- Second covenant: Noah and his family
- Third covenant: Avraham and his only son, Yitz'chak
- Fourth covenant: The nation of Israel (the Exodus from Egypt, led by Mosheh)
- Fifth covenant: David (who led the nation against enemies, fought idol worshippers, and united a whole kingdom in worshipping the One God)
- Sixth covenant: The God-Man, born of the virgin

How can you "maintain justice and do what is right"?

READ

The first snowflake of winter spiraled downward, landing on the baby's brow as He nestled in the crook of Mary's arm. At the sensation of cold, tiny lashes fluttered. Mary brushed away the crystal with her thumb, pulled Him closer, and spread her fingers to shield His face beneath the palm of her hand.

He who dwells in the shelter of the Most High will rest in the shadow of the Almighty.

O Lord! How effortlessly she protects him even from the snowflake. Is this the way you protect us?

He will cover you with His feathers, and under His wings you will find refuge. His faithfulness will be your shield and rampart. You will not fear.

Yosef silently recited the morning prayers. His heart rejoiced as comprehension of God's message unfolded like successive waves against a desolate shore. *In every gesture of her love for this little one . . . this One . . . your beloved Son . . . O Lord! Through a mother's heart, you reveal how much you love your children!*

—P. 24

"*He is the maker of the Bear and Orion, Ki-Mah and the constellations of the south. He performs wonders that cannot be fathomed, miracles that cannot be counted.*'"

"He is so big, isn't he?"

"Much bigger than we even imagine," Melchior replied, turning Esther to face him. "*Ki-Mah.* 'Who made it? Who caused it?'" Melchior let that sink in for a moment, then added, "Here's something your grandfather taught me. You know how much more powerful we are, say, than . . . than ants?"

Esther nodded.

"And we think of angels and archangels as much more powerful than us? Grander, wiser, stronger?"

Another nod.

"But when we see the stars and realize that the Almighty made them . . . and the angels . . . and us . . . and the ants . . . when we recognize that he made all there is, all that exists . . . then he is much, much bigger than even angels and archangels. Compared to The Lord of All the Angel Armies, even angels are as lowly as we, because even they, powerful as they are, were made, don't you see? And yet . . ." Melchior's thoughts grew tangled. . . . "It's . . . it's that I can't understand why he cares about us enough to send his Son to be born like one of us. What does it mean?"

Wrapping her arms around Melchior, Esther hugged him tightly. "Because the stars are too far away," she said. "Because even angels can't tell us. Perhaps to *show* us how much he loves us, it has to happen this way."

—PP. 182–183

ASK

How does a mother's love for her child reveal God's love for us?

In what way(s) does Melchior and Esther's conversation affect the way you think of God—and especially how much He loves you?

_____

_____

_____

WONDER . . .

The Parthian prayed as he had never prayed before to the God he had chosen to serve. He had not been born a Jew, but he loved everything about Adonai Elohim—Yahweh—the One God, the Almighty.

But would Yahweh answer? Would the Son of the Most High be revealed to a seeker as humble as Melchior? What right had he to expect a reply?

—P. 215

Is your heart humble and seeking, like Melchior's? Do you long to feel the depth and height and breadth of God's love?

God promises that if you call upon His name, He will declare to your heart the answer to your question: *"Ki-Mah? Who made?"* And you will know, beyond all doubt, who the baby in the manger is: the Son of the Living God, who made the stars, who made each of us, and who knows and calls you by name.

> *"And everyone who calls*
> *on the name of the Lord will be saved."*
> —ACTS 2:21

Dear Reader,
You are so important to us. We have prayed for you as we wrote this book and also as we receive your letters and hear your soul cries. We hope that *Sixth Covenant* has encouraged you to go deeper. To get to know Yeshua better. To fill your soul hunger by examining Scripture's truths for yourself.

We are convinced that if you do so, you will find this promise true: *"If you seek Him, He will be found by you."*
—1 CHRONICLES 28:9

Bodie & Brock Thoene

Scripture References

1 Gen. 1:26
2 Isa. 9:6
3 Matt. 1:23
4 Num. 24:17
5 Isa. 7:14
6 Exod. 25:10-15
7 Num. 6:24
8 Num. 6:25
9 Ps. 91:1
10 Ps. 91:4-5
11 Micah 5:2
12 Luke 2:8-16
13 Luke 2:25-35
14 Luke 2:10-11
15 Luke 2:12
16 Prov. 25:25
17 Isa. 49:8-10
18 Isa. 49:6
19 Matt. 1:1-16; Luke 3:23-38
20 Ps. 98:1-7
21 Deut. 6:4
22 Phil. 2:10-11
23 Job 38:31-32
24 Song of Songs 2:14
25 Song of Songs 2:15
26 Song of Songs 2:16-17
27 Song of Songs 2:17
28 Gen. 35:16-20
29 Gen. 44:18, 30-34
30 Gen. 45:1-3
31 Gen. 45:4
32 Gen. 45:3-4

33 Gen. 45:4-7
34 Gen. 45:8, 14-15
35 Luke 2:11-12
36 Ezek. 37:21-24
37 Ezek. 37:24-28
38 Ezek. 37:24-25
39 Ezek. 37:27-28
40 Deut. 6:4-6
41 Isa. 9:6-7
42 Luke 1:31-32
43 Judg. 13:2-5
44 Judg. 13:6-7
45 Judg. 13:8
46 Judg. 13:15-18
47 Judg. 13:22
48 Ps. 86:5-6
49 Ps. 44:26
50 Num. 25:12
51 Prov. 23:25
52 Ezek. 16:6
53 Ps. 105: 8-10
54 Gen. 21:4
55 Ps. 106:1
56 Num. 6:22-27
57 Hos. 6:1-3
58 Hos. 6:4, 7
59 Hos. 8:1, 3-4
60 Luke 2:25-26
61 Num. 3:39-51
62 Deut. 3:11
63 Ps. 121:8
64 Isa. 30:20

65 Ps. 23:1
66 Ps. 23:2
67 Ps. 23:2
68 Micah 5:2
69 Ps. 23:4
70 Ps. 23:4
71 Ps. 23:5
72 Ps. 23:2-3
73 Ps. 61:2
74 Ps. 23
75 Ps. 91:1
76 Ps. 91:2-7
77 Ps. 91:16
78 Exod. 14:21-22
79 Num. 24:17
80 Matt. 2:2
81 Gen. 1:26-28; 3:1-24
82 Gen. 3:15
83 Gen. 8:20
84 Gen. 9:11
85 Gen. 22:1-18
86 2 Sam. 6
87 1 Kings 6
88 2 Sam. 7:16
89 Ezek 34:11-12, 23-25
90 Mal. 3:1
91 Isa. 42:6-7
92 Dan. 7:14
93 Isa. 53:3-6
94 Isa. 55:3, 8; 56:1
95 Isa. 7:14
96 Gen. 49:10

97 Job 9:9-10
98 Matt. 2:2
99 Matt. 2:2
100 Lev. 12:1-5
101 Mal. 3:1; Luke 2:22
102 Luke 1:46-47
103 Lev. 12:6-8
104 Exod. 13:1-2
105 Num. 18:15-16
106 Luke 2:29-32
107 Luke 2:34-35
108 Zech. 14:9
109 Micah 5:2; Matt. 2:6
110 Matt. 2:2

111 Matt. 2:7
112 Matt. 2:8
113 Gen. 5:24
114 Gen. 5:21-24
115 Matt. 2:9
116 Ps. 147:4
117 Prov. 25:25
118 Isa. 60:3
119 Isa. 42:6
120 Num. 24:17
121 Isa. 1:3
122 Matt. 2:12
123 Exod. 14:21-22
124 Acts 2:21

125 Matt. 2:16
126 Ps. 105:15
127 Exod. 1:22
128 Exod. 11:4-8
129 Jer. 31:15
130 Exod. 1:15-16
131 Exod. 2:1-22
132 Luke 2:25-35
133 Matt. 27: 55-56;
    John 19:25-27
134 John 11:25
135 Isa. 51:11

Authors' Note

The following sources have been helpful in our research for this book.

- *The Complete Jewish Bible.* Translated by David H. Stern. Baltimore, MD: Jewish New Testament Publications, Inc., 1998.

- *iLumina*, a digitally animated Bible and encyclopedia suite. Carol Stream, IL: Tyndale House Publishers, 2002.

- *The International Standard Bible Encyclopaedia.* George Bromiley, ed. 5 vols. Grand Rapids, MI: Eerdmans, 1979.

- *The Life and Times of Jesus the Messiah.* Alfred Edersheim. Peabody, MA: Hendrickson Publishers, Inc., 1995.

- Starry Night™ Enthusiast Version 5.0, published by Imaginova™ Corp.

Our grateful thanks to Dr. Albert E. Cramer for his keen theological eye, knowledge of the Scriptures, and fastidious checking of biblical references on the A.D. Chronicles series. His credits in academia are many: a BA in history and a BS in education; master's degrees in colonial U.S. history, Old Testament, New Testament, and theology; a ThD in Old Testament; PhD studies in modern European history, and over forty years of college and graduate-school teaching and administration. A World War II combat veteran, Dr. Cramer's avocation is rural sociology.

About the Authors

BODIE AND BROCK THOENE (pronounced *Tay-nee*) have written over 45 works of historical fiction. That these best sellers have sold more than 10 million copies and won eight ECPA Gold Medallion Awards affirms what millions of readers have already discovered—the Thoenes are not only master stylists but experts at capturing readers' minds and hearts.

In their timeless classic series about Israel (The Zion Chronicles, The Zion Covenant, and The Zion Legacy), the Thoenes' love for both story and research shines.

With The Shiloh Legacy and *Shiloh Autumn* (poignant portrayals of the American Depression), The Galway Chronicles (dramatic stories of the 1840s famine in Ireland), and the Legends of the West (gripping tales of adventure and danger in a land without law), the Thoenes have made their mark in modern history.

In the A.D. Chronicles they step seamlessly into the world of Jerusalem and Rome, in the days when Yeshua walked the earth and transformed lives with His touch.

Bodie began her writing career as a teen journalist for her local newspaper. Eventually her byline appeared in prestigious periodicals such as *U.S. News and World Report*, *The American West*, and *The Saturday Evening Post*. She also worked for John Wayne's Batjac Productions (she's best known as author of *The Fall Guy*) and ABC Circle Films as a writer and researcher. John Wayne described her as "a writer with talent that captures the people and the times!" She has degrees in journalism and communications.

Brock has often been described by Bodie as "an essential half of this writing team." With degrees in both history and education, Brock has, in his role as researcher and story-line consultant, added the vital dimension of historical accuracy. Due to such careful research, the Zion Covenant and Zion Chronicles series are recognized by the American Library Association, as well as Zionist libraries around the world, as classic historical novels and are used to teach history in college classrooms.

Bodie and Brock have four grown children—Rachel, Jake, Luke, and Ellie—and six grandchildren. Their children are carrying on the Thoene family talent as the next generation of writers, and Luke produces the Thoene audiobooks. Bodie and Brock divide their time between London and Nevada.

For more information visit:
www.thoenebooks.com
www.familyaudiolibrary.com

THOENE FAMILY CLASSICS™

✪ ✪ ✪

THOENE FAMILY CLASSIC HISTORICALS
by Bodie and Brock Thoene
*Gold Medallion Winners**

THE ZION COVENANT
*Vienna Prelude**
Prague Counterpoint
Munich Signature
Jerusalem Interlude
Danzig Passage
*Warsaw Requiem**
London Refrain
Paris Encore
Dunkirk Crescendo

THE ZION CHRONICLES
*The Gates of Zion**
A Daughter of Zion
The Return to Zion
A Light in Zion
*The Key to Zion**

THE SHILOH LEGACY
*In My Father's House**
A Thousand Shall Fall
Say to This Mountain

SHILOH AUTUMN

THE GALWAY CHRONICLES
*Only the River Runs Free**
Of Men and of Angels
*Ashes of Remembrance**
All Rivers to the Sea

THE ZION LEGACY
Jerusalem Vigil
Thunder from Jerusalem
Jerusalem's Heart
Jerusalem Scrolls
Stones of Jerusalem
Jerusalem's Hope

A.D. CHRONICLES
First Light
Second Touch
Third Watch
Fourth Dawn
Fifth Seal
Sixth Covenant
Seventh Day
and more to come!

CP0064

THOENE FAMILY CLASSICS™

✪ ✪ ✪

THOENE FAMILY CLASSIC AMERICAN LEGENDS

LEGENDS OF THE WEST
by Bodie and Brock Thoene

Legends of the West, Volume One
Sequoia Scout
The Year of the Grizzly
Shooting Star
Legends of the West, Volume Two
Gold Rush Prodigal
Delta Passage
Hangtown Lawman
Legends of the West, Volume Three
Hope Valley War
The Legend of Storey County
Cumberland Crossing
Legends of the West, Volume Four
The Man from Shadow Ridge
Cannons of the Comstock
Riders of the Silver Rim

LEGENDS OF VALOR
by Luke Thoene

Sons of Valor
Brothers of Valor
Fathers of Valor

✪ ✪ ✪

THOENE CLASSIC NONFICTION
by Bodie and Brock Thoene

Writer-to-Writer

THOENE FAMILY CLASSIC SUSPENSE
by Jake Thoene

CHAPTER 16 SERIES
Shaiton's Fire
Firefly Blue
Fuel the Fire

✪ ✪ ✪

THOENE FAMILY CLASSICS FOR KIDS

BAKER STREET DETECTIVES
by Jake and Luke Thoene

The Mystery of the Yellow Hands
The Giant Rat of Sumatra
The Jeweled Peacock of Persia
The Thundering Underground

LAST CHANCE DETECTIVES
by Jake and Luke Thoene
Mystery Lights of Navajo Mesa
Legend of the Desert Bigfoot

THE VASE OF MANY COLORS
by Rachel Thoene (Illustrations by Christian Cinder)

✪ ✪ ✪

THOENE FAMILY CLASSIC AUDIOBOOKS

Available from
www.thoenebooks.com or
www.familyaudiolibrary.com

CP0064